NO TIME TO LOSE

A Novel by

Matt Baak

1

ISBN-13:

978-0-9961228-1-8

for Tracy…

5

Chapter One

The Riddle

He used his computer on Sunday.

He drove two miles.

He stayed twenty-four hours.

He returned to the place where he began.

All on the same Sunday.

Chapter Two

Los Angeles, California

December – Saturday – 2:15 a.m.

The silence was only broken by the whisper quiet sound of the air conditioning. It hummed and droned on uninterrupted, circulating air at a comfortable seventy degrees Fahrenheit. Not unlike the sound made in a subway, it mimicked the first faint rumblings of the far off city train traveling through the darkened tunnel. Regular subway patrons strained to listen for the sound, knowing that when it could be heard the train would soon follow. The low hum came before the tracks clattered or before the burst of air rushed forward out of the tunnel, propelled by the train's momentum. Touching two senses, both announced the train's imminent arrival.

But this noise, on this night, in this place, only gave the first inklings of what may yet come. No clatter of tracks or feeling of warm air on faces would follow. The train would not arrive. It was only the air conditioner that distantly whirred on.

Into the silence, four mysterious shapes slipped out of recessed shadows and began their work, planned down to the last detail. They were in no hurry but instead worked slowly and methodically. It was more about getting it right the first time. They had donned the usual nefarious garb, gloves, hooded masks, Tyvek jumpsuits, all in your basic black. They wore booties over the soles of their combat boots to avoid track marks or scuffs that would brand the polished marble floors. No trace left behind. They worked downstairs and in the back of the building in total darkness, therefore night vision goggles were necessary. When not wearing NVG's they wore reflective sunglasses to mask every part of their appearance. No one involved gave away a clue as to their identities, and each carried a very large sack. Guided by schematic designs and with the benefit of conducting trial run after trial run in mocked up stages, ensuring all contingencies were covered, they carried out their assigned tasks for the first half of the mission. Now it was time to rest.

Chapter Three

Laguna Beach, California

December – Sunday - 4:58 a.m.

He opened his eyes and rolled out of bed awake and alert. It had always been that way. As he padded across the room and headed for the bathroom, the sky outside had yet to surrender the darkness to the waiting dawn. The warmth of his mattress would soon grow cold as he moved on with making plans for a new day. Rising early every morning came naturally. Lying in bed and making love to his pillow did not.

On this morning just before dawn's fresh canvas arrived, he would begin a light workout, a warm-up. He would bike five or so miles. He enjoyed exercising every day if possible; in unexplainable ways, he felt compelled to do it. It kept the juices flowing, fresh thoughts ticking over in his mind. The blackness outshone the twinkling stars and that was enough to allow the light sensor to illuminate the bathroom as he entered and moved towards one of two sinks and vanity mirrors. Turning on the cold water he looked up and stared at his reflection.

He saw a man who was thirty-six but looked younger. His flaxen blond hair was ruffled, mainly due to its unusually longer length. His eyes were sharp, clear, and cobalt blue, with the suggestion of a smile at the corners that disarmed most people. For onlookers, an act of nature gave him innocent pleasing eyes with a dash of charm to boot, while from his perspective, they were trained observant tools. He had the good fortune to swim in a vibrant ancestral gene pool that rewarded his family members with good health and good looks. With the physique of an Olympic swimmer and well-measured height, back in the day he was one who almost always came up for consideration on college basketball teams. There remained an echo of a tan that came easily and lingered long into winter. He was one lucky guy.

He brushed and cleaned his teeth before taking a shower. After toweling off, finger-combing his hair but neglecting to shave, he exited to begin another day. The bathroom lights faded to black behind him.

His name was Kip Keplar.

Chapter Four

Los Angeles, California

December – Sunday - 7:57 a.m.

Four figures came together and stared at a vault door. With the seconds slowly ticking away, one of them checked his watch. Waiting for a slow elevator, that's what it felt like. You just knew once you pressed the call button it would arrive, eventually. But on certain occasions, always when you're in a hurry, the elevator would take its sweet time, and the urge to push the button again … and again, would in no way speed up the process. But the overwhelming urge was to just do it. It felt like the right thing to do. It was human nature. So it was with a hint of urgency the man checked his watch again. During the wait, sideways glances were exchanged and feet were shuffled. It would happen soon enough.

But what if it didn't open?

Knowledge was the key. With knowledge and information came the ability to plan and think things through and escape without being caught. Any street thug could walk into a bank during trading hours and hold it up. They may even walk out with some cash. But witnesses and cameras were always a problem. Getting away with the crime and having the freedom to spend what you stole was just as important as the heist itself.

The planners lived guarded lives, out of the limelight and away from attention. Their method was to hire third party agents to do their bidding and to find qualified professionals to complete their assignments. The further away from the action, the more difficult it was to prove a conspiracy. So they provided the cash and information to make it happen, and then stayed away.

All information about the security systems was available to be discreetly bought, or if need be, compromised. And it was. The technology and secrets on the cameras, motion detectors, alarm systems and any and all security measures were obtained and studied. It was painstakingly laborious, but it would pay off exponentially.

The security company's information was the easiest to obtain and dissect. The motion detectors were simple enough to evade. They switched them off. No one monitors the monitors. A false relay signal sent back to the control panel indicated they were still functioning normally. No complaints.

The cameras had taken more time to disable, but the end result showed empty hallways replacing actual felonies being committed in real time. The relay feed displayed an "all is as it should be" scenario to the guards monitoring the screens, and no one suspected a thing.

There remained the obstacle of the vault itself, always a problem for people who wanted unauthorized access but are denied. The impenetrable envelope was innovative and unique. The latest designs and technology. Surrounded on all sides, above and below, the vault was constructed of molded, high impact, hardened concrete panels. Even the vault door itself had custom-made molded panels sandwiched between multiple layers of inches thick stainless steel. The concrete was poured in place and contained a specially formulated hardening agent that was marketed as "invulnerable." Breakthroughs in advanced engineering allowed for the reduction in wall thickness surrounding the vault. It superseded construction methods that were industry standards for over a century. So the revolutionary concept actually increased structural integrity while shrinking wall thicknesses by half. A boastful six inch reduction, this eases concerns for installing the new vault, particularly in existing banks. Technology makes security easier and much more affordable.

Banks liked that.

The concrete panels were interlaced with stainless steel rods, ensuring maximum fortification. Beyond the added strength of the vault enclosure, embedded motion detectors, heat sensors and seismic indicators were placed within the walls and beyond. The disturbance sensitive seismic indicators were installed so the bank, and security company, could differentiate between earthquake tremors and other disruptions such as vibrations from drilling. There was a need to eliminate as many false alarms as possible. In all, the protective measures put in place created a security cage around the vault, which was theft-proof. Anybody attempting to break-in through a "back door," or by blowing a hole in the wall, or by taking the door out would instantly alert authorities. Half the L.A. police department would bear down on them within minutes. The vault was an impenetrable fortress.

And then there was the vault door. *Where do you start?* On inspection, there was no standard dial combination lock, no keyhole latch, no alphanumerical access panel, no voice recognition system, no fingerprint pad or any retina identification.

There was nothing. It was a polished sleek, blank, stainless steel slate, set flush with the walls.

Dial combinations could be cracked, always have, always will. The same applied to keys that could be forged; nineteenth century technology. Numerical access panels presented a potential security breach similar to voice, fingerprint and retina defenses. In the middle of the night, an intruder could enter the home of the bank manager and drive him to the bank itself, in his pajamas, gun held to his head; wife and kids ransomed at home and tell him to open the safe. What are his options? Is the bank's money worth his life or that of his family? Nine out of ten times …. No!

Voices could be digitally recorded, fingers could be severed; even an eyeball can be scooped out. The bank's selection was simple when confronted with these scenarios. The alternatives were disregarded. They chose new technology, and it was ironclad.

What was required was a system, whereby those with authority and direct access to open the vault were taken out of the equation.

The answer?

The one thing that could keep the vault safe and secure night after night was a time lock.

The process was simple. In synchronization with an atomic clock, at exactly eight o'clock every business trading day morning, the vault door would silently open and display its contents to the world. Bearing witness to this would be the bank president, or his representative, and three armed guards. At night, the routine varied slightly. The bank had certain obligations to "select" members of the public. The ones who could afford to have valuables, cash and other discretionary items held within; this meant that if someone wished to linger a little longer to conduct business, well then, so be it. Time is not always money, and if it is, well … then, that is why fees were invented.

When the vault was finally emptied of all persons it was closed and sealed for the day, and a computerized trigger took control of the safe. It was a constantly altering twenty-three digit alphanumeric code. The code was always entered into the system from a distant secured location hours before. The code would initiate the time lock countdown and could not be reopened before the designated eight o'clock hour on the next business day – no exceptions.

The designers thought of everything. Just having the code was of no use to would-be thieves. It did not open the safe. During the day the place was a regular Fort Knox. Banks had learnt a trick or two from the security measures of Las Vegas casinos, which were capable of dealing with volumes of people and mountains of cash mingling together. If you managed to enter the bank at night to attempt a burglary, there was no alphanumeric keypad into which to enter the code. There was nothing. There was no way past the vault door. Or was there?

Chapter Five

New York City, New York

December - Friday – 1:46 p.m. - Two days before

The volume was low on the phone that rang on his buffed blonde wood- grained desk. He allowed it to ring once, then a second time as he finished off some blue colored liquid from a wide-necked energy drink bottle. He was also coming to the end of a sentence of the memo he was reading. The memo was of little importance and he was only a "cc" on it anyway. It was a slow Friday afternoon. The week was winding down, the weekend in his thoughts.

"Cam Walker," he spoke into the receiver, while still reading the memo on his computer screen. Chew gum and walk at the same time – right!

"Get your cellphone and open the message your wife just sent!" said the mysterious voice. Cam was no expert, but it was quite clear that this voice was digitally altered and he sensed the trouble. Cam sat bolt upright and was instantly alert.

"Who is this?" Cam asked, questioning the anonymous voice that made no introduction.

Cam Walker, senior vice president of American Trust, a twenty-one year veteran employee. Fresh out of college he landed a junior position at the bank and served his time working through the ranks that was the system. No bright shining star slotted on the fast track to success here. Not Cam. Just methodical, no mistakes. With a risk averse strategy he inched his way up as other more aggressive players around him either moved to higher positions more rapidly, different employees due to the success or failure of their actions or were thrown to the wolves in corporate restructures. He kept his head down, endured the work and served his time. That was his ticket to upper middle management and perhaps no greater height.

Cam was a forty-four-year-old banker with tightly curled hair that was ebony black and eyes to match. As his face revealed above his shirt collar and tie, youth was escaping his grasp due to the consequences of the lifestyle choices he enjoyed. The job came with its perks of corporate lunches and after hours wining and dining. While the sporadic visits to the gym for a workout helped, they were not enough to prevent an adjustment of the prong on his belt buckle from time to time slipping over a notch or two. He reached just over five feet ten and appeared to be average in almost every way.

The office he occupied in downtown Manhattan was located in a stately 1920s fifty-three story classic. Not noted as one of the tallest buildings, it nonetheless was a pride-filled majestic one. On the few occasions its ownership changed hands, the lobby would be the target of transformation as a sign to the public and tenants alike that operations would be different under new management. It was public space and could be played around with, and so it was. It was currently adorned with polished brass accents, noticeable faux plated gold, shining metal and architectural glass finishes everywhere.

Enormous in size, the lobby featured a glass encased atrium that towered all of five stories and contained enough clear space for a perpetually busy open air café and an impressive array of select haute couture stores. Smooth music piped in from somewhere and swirled in the background, giving pedestrians their piece of serenity for the day. As it was, the music flittered away mostly unnoticed due to the noise from the talking and clicking of shoes on the tiled floor. The atrium allowed natural light to pour into the area which aided in lifting the spirits of the working men and women as they passed through on their way to eight-plus hours of work a day.

The designers went even further. In an effort to alleviate the glare that streamed in from the reflections of adjacent glass buildings and the direct sunlight bouncing off all the polished metal in the lobby, a waterfall was installed that cascaded down from … somewhere high above. The water fell from an opening five stories above but its entrance was obscured by bulbous cloud puffs and wisps of mist. These accent pieces helped disperse some of the intense light while simultaneously providing a serene setting. The falling water splashed into a clear pool, which made a surprising clap of noise. Between the sounds of the water, the music, the cacophony of people's voices and the footsteps in that glass chamber, no pin drop would be heard at this location.

The building held serious money and conducted serious business; one of the bastions of New York City that generated continued success. Cam was a part of that continued success and worked out of his corner office forty- seven floors above the din in the lobby. A perk of the corner office was the sweeping panoramic view of the city, albeit interrupted by taller buildings' interference of the vista. Architects and interior designers stopped by every five years to update the work environment with fresh new wallpapers, paints, carpets and canvasses for the walls. He was currently surrounded by the latest sterile European *chic* look. Blonde everything. Décor, he was assured, that would comfort the soul, but he felt nothing except blandness about the makeover.

The caller spoke. "Do…you…see…it?" he protracted the words, saying them deliberately, like talking sternly to a child and waiting impatiently for the reply.

"I need to get my phone." Cam scanned the top of his desk, found and grabbed his smartphone. His was preloaded with the same apps as his wife's. He pushed a button and it came out of sleep mode then he then returned to the caller. "I'm switching it on now, give me a second."

They both waited.

"Yes … yes I see it."

"Open it!"

He did as he was told and it took a long second for him to contemplate what he was seeing. He felt his heart pound in his chest as his mouth went dry.

"What the -" is all he could manage to say. He felt clammy and ill.

The caller repeated the question once more, in the same tone, the digital voice demanding. "Do…you…see…it?"

Surprise and fear make for a powerful emotional cocktail. It rocks your world, throws you off your game, especially for the untrained. Sure, Cam could handle a crisis situation within his sphere of expertise but this quite frankly was way, way above his pay grade. This was a sucker punch to the gut. Reaction times slow, judgments become clouded and it renders you motionless, frozen. Time ticks slowly, it allows, and even invites panic to enter. It can get you into trouble. Your caught helpless, off-guard, even as brain activity is heightened. Adrenaline increases and is pumped into your system like high octane fuel poured into a formula one car on race day after pulling into the pits. There's too much information for the body to handle. All these inner body functions delivering many, many messages simultaneously, each calling out to be heard, all screaming out that they are the right choice for the situation at hand. You just need one clear signal to grab onto.

But nothing wins. Nothing happens. You cannot make that decision.

"Well, do you see it?" the voice asked again, firm and in control.

"Please don't hurt her," was his pleading reply.

He was staring at his wife, Lynette Walker, via the video stream, in the living room of their home. Hands and feet bound, duct tape covering her mouth and eyes as she struggled against the gun that was pressed against her temple. A gunman's outstretched shirtsleeve was all he could see of her captor. Although her eyes were covered, he could sense her entire body was wracked with fear. He could feel the inner pleading that was trapped within her.

Oh, God please help me! Cam! Help me!

The camera panned away from Lynette and the gunman and showed other parts of his home, so Cam understood where they were and that they were in control. A bouquet of fresh flowers rested in a vase that was placed on a side table sitting in the small window of their living room came into view; he himself had sent them to her just yesterday. It was the abduction of his wife taking place before his eyes. It was all crystal clear. Then the streaming ended and he surrendered to their will.

"We want the code!" demanded the voice, jolting him back to the nightmare playing out before him.

"The what?"

"The code!" he barked. "We want the code to the L.A. branch bank time lock or she dies. Now!"

"But I don't have it!" Cam bleated out, knowing this had no chance of appeasing him. Hoping beyond hope that perhaps the voice would say; *you don't? Well, OK, we'll just let little Miss Muffin go then. Sorry to call.*

It was an awful response. The man on the line knew better.

"You will, in ten minutes. Here's what you are going to do. Right now, a package is being dropped off for you at the reception desk. Go get it! It's a single use phone with a pre-programmed phone number listed. Go through your regular routine with dispatching the code to LA. Memorize the code. I say again, memorize the code. When you have completed your task, talk to no one; we will know, we will be watching. Go to the fire escape stairs at the west end of the building and push the send button on the phone. Wait for it to be answered. Wait two seconds, and slowly and clearly recite the code numbers. Pause, wait five more seconds and slowly and clearly repeat the numbers again. Dispose of the phone outside of your building somewhere, and then get on home. If you don't carry out these instructions to the letter, your wife is dead. If we suspect something is wrong, your wife is dead. You talk to anyone more than you should your wife is dead. If you try to write something down or hint to anyone something is happening, your wife is dead. You'll never see her body again. Then we're coming after you."

"Having the code won't do you any good. Please don't do this!"

"You have a job to do. Pull yourself together. Focus. Do as you're told and you will see your wife on Monday. It goes without saying, no cops."

The line went dead.

Cam placed his curly head in his hands. He wanted to sob like a baby. He could not do this; if he did, he was going to kill his wife.

He had to do it. He straightened up. He took a few deep breaths. He felt wobbly, so he put his hand out and placed it on the table in an effort to brace himself. He tried to remain calm by breathing slowly. He drained the last of the blue liquid in the bottle although his mouth remained dry. He left his office and went to the reception area.

At the reception desk the young attractive woman behind the counter looked up and smiled at the Vice President, handed him the package and said, "That was quick, it just arrived."

He went back to his office and closed the door. He looked at the front of the envelope, just a computer printed address label. Typed on it was his company name and marked to his attention - URGENT, was in bold red print. He tore open the padded envelope and reached in for the phone. There it was, sleek in design, a color pattern in one of today's fashionable choices. Cool today, outdated tomorrow. Tomorrow will find a new color. That's marketing at its best. Give them what you want to give them.

He slipped the phone into his pants' pocket, took a few more minutes to compose himself and then checked his watch. God, his mouth was dry. He raised the empty bottle that was still on his desk and examined it but there was nothing left to drink. His heart was pounding; he wasn't going to make it. He redid the top button of his shirt, cinched his tie, reset his tiepin, threw on and adjusted his coat, left his office and walked down the corridor.

The room he entered was stacked with electronics, the likes of which he had no idea how they worked. It was a computerized clean room and inside waiting for him were two junior associates.

Not too junior for the assignment, but there as part of the ritual. The procedure and protocol required three present at all times to commence operations.

Cam just gave them both a curt nod having already seen them during the day and no more courtesies needed to be extended.

With his head down he said, "O.K., let's get on with it."

All three men had been through the routine many times. Three present at the receiving of the day's code as the computer delivered to the display console the randomly picked twenty-two alphanumeric digital code numbers. The operation was set up so that the security was divided between the head office and bank branches. No writing tools of any kind were permitted in this "clean" room and the display of the code was only visible for as long as it took to download and transfer it to the secure line at the bank.

Being a ritual procedure that was repeated over and over, naturally it became commonplace. The first one hundred times it was carried out, everybody was all business and very serious. But as time wore on and nothing of consequence ever happened because the system functioned flawlessly, the pretense of it all slowly ebbed away. Everyone was more relaxed. The job was still carried out to the letter, just not quite as intently. Cam stood directly in front of the display, slightly obscuring the entire code display from the other two. Because of his nerves and the pressure upon him, he fidgeted and fumbled for a few more seconds than normal. No one noticed. Or if they did, they did not say so.

A secure computer produced the code for the day, and then management took control to transfer the security code for the time lock initiation to another secured portal that sent it to the bank's lock systems. If there was a problem, someone could be held accountable.

Three of the bank's branches were equipped with this particular time lock safe and all required the code input. A different code for a different bank and then it was done.

He turned to the two others with a forced smile on his face. "We're all done here, guys." He brushed past his two colleagues and was out the door.

Jeff called after him, "We're going to the bar after work, want to join us?"

"No," said Cam without looking back, and kept on walking to his office. He closed the door, sat down and once again laid his head in his hands. "What am I doing?" he said to no one.

He sat there for a long minute then raised himself out of the chair and began to pace up and down the carpet behind his desk, his hand rubbing his forehead, trying to make a decision that would solve his dilemma. Slowly he drew the phone out of his pocket, held it in the palm of his hand and stared down at it. Finally, sliding open the top right hand desk drawer a narrow six inches, he placed the phone inside. He closed the drawer, locked it and walked out of his office. He closed and locked that door as well, and left the building.

Chapter Six

Paxton – New York

December - Friday – 9:43 a.m. - Earlier the same day

The day was pale and dreary and the air held a chilled dampness that would persist all morning. Lynette Walker was reading at her kitchen counter. Standing, not sitting, with her hands braced on either side of the magazine that lay open in front of her and her feet spread apart, she read an article about Bed and Breakfast retreats in New England. It had arrived in the mail yesterday and she was ready to dismiss it as junk and toss it into the recycling pile, but a last second change of mind had her flipping and scanning the pages. There she came upon a praising article of B&B's, two of which she and Cam had visited. Once, to stay by the sea in Maine, at a wonderful cottage that indulged them in lobster tail and fine wines. They hardly saw the town. The other time was in New Hampshire. It was in the fall. The colors were right; the place they stayed, exquisite. They were tourists and proud of it, spending dollars to help the local economy. Although the weather was cool, they behaved like whimsical teenagers, putting the top down on the car and driving through the country roads with the wind in their hair, loving every shivering minute of it. Later, they would return to the quaint country inn, soak in the hot tub, eat mouth-watering foods, more than sample great cabernets, and enjoy each other's company immensely. She smiled to herself at the stroll down memory lane. *Yes, let's do it again,* she thought. *I'll talk to Cam and we'll make arrangements soon.*

They could afford these soirees, on a moment's notice if they liked. Both in time and money. It was a second marriage for each of them, over eight years of wedding bliss. They had no children from any of their marriages; both deciding it wasn't what they wanted. He spent long hours at the office or wining and dining customers, and she had her own social activities to keep well lubricated. She never nurtured the maternal instinct - it was not her calling. So it was that they enjoyed a lot of free time together without the worries of children's needs, wants or schedules.

She dog-eared the page in the magazine and flipped further through the pages. Within the next thirty minutes she would skip out of the house to run some errands. Nothing too dramatic - a simple grocery run, Cam's pants at the tailor's, grab some lunch. No rhyme or reason, just a run-around sort of day. It was one of those rare occasions when the calendar was not full.

At forty-two, Lynette was five feet six with a slim physique and fine brown hair she kept short. She wore stylized glasses as much for a fashion statement as anything. Today she was dressed in black, all black; it was after all, December. Bracelets jingled on her left wrist when she moved her arm and if she noticed it did not seem to bother her; her professionally polished and manicured nails turned a page. A white, thick ceramic coffee mug, with ruby red lipstick partially smudging a section of the rim, was placed to one side of the magazine. She would drain its contents that were made up of rich Sumatra beans in three or four more sips.

The doorbell rang.

She was not expecting anyone but when the bell tolls, you take a peek. They lived on a generous piece of land with exquisitely landscaped lawns manicured by contracted services to make sure it was maintained that way. The home was set well back from the country lane; it was further masked by heavy woods; many great trees of maple, oak and sycamore that even without leaves in December still shrouded the residence with privacy, keeping it distant from neighbors or anyone traveling on the quiet road. Progress lights lined both sides of their long curving driveway that lead to the home. The exterior of the comfortable mansion stated that "yes, indeed, money lives here." It possessed all the hallmarks of seclusion and anonymity.

She saw the semblance of a man through the etched glass that was inserted either side of their double-leaf front entry doors. The doors were shaped from solid Bolivian rosewood, dipped deep in warm brown tones. He was facing away from her and wearing white coveralls with a white hooded sweatshirt on top of that. He had the hood pulled over his head; his hands were shoved in the front pockets of the sweatshirt, probably due to the cold. In the partial view beyond him she could vaguely make out one of those service vans that contractors drive. It too was white. She did not recall a scheduled appointment with anyone today, more than likely a misunderstanding or perhaps the wrong house? *This won't take long* she thought. She would clear it up it up in a jiffy and be on her way.

After opening one of the two leafed doors, Lynette framed herself confidently in the center and with accustomed authority in situations dealing with service personnel simply demanded, "Yes?"

In an instant, the man spun around and with great force shoved her with both hands in the chest, sending her sprawling back into the house. She wind-milled her arms desperately trying to maintain a lost balance but backpedalled into the foyer and finally fell hard, causing the back of her head to slam into the marble floor, which may have left her with a serious concussion. She lay spread-eagled on the floor and dazed. Her glasses flew off her face at impact with the marble and skidded across the floor. Using his momentum of thrusting Lynette into the house, the man made his way inside closely followed by two other assailants who had hidden themselves just out of Lynette's view. The last man through the door quickly closed it behind them and although shaken by the incident, Lynette was able to look bewilderingly at three men all dressed in white and wearing haunting skeleton masks. She screamed!

One of the skeletons reached down and slapped her hard and man- handled her roughly while covering her mouth with duct tape. At the same time one of the other men who clearly knew where to go, raced down the stairs to the garage and opened up two of the three stall doors. The first bay opened to reveal Lynette's latest model black BMW X5 SUV sitting idly. The second door showed a vacant space where Cam's silver Mercedes SL550 Roadster called home if not for the fact he had taken it to work. The third stall was always left vacant, to be used by guests if they stayed over. As the two garage doors opened the man raced over to the white service van, hopped behind the wheel and drove it into the garage stall closest to the house. He closed that door behind him and went after the other vehicle. It was a dark blue Buick Park Avenue. It was nondescript amongst the vehicles on the road and for added privacy tinted windows had been installed. It, too, went into the garage, and now both doors were down.

As Lynette's assailant finished gagging her securely and while the burning of her cheek still stung viciously, she felt the pinprick of a syringe needle break her skin and it made her wince. Unable to yell for help, she asked herself, *what the hell is happening?* She wanted to scream again or cry or kick someone or something and fight for her life, but she couldn't. A warm sensation ran through her body but at the same time she shivered; now her head was swimming and between the concussion and the drug she was fading. One, two, three ... lights out.

While Lynette was in a comatose state, two skeleton masks prepared her limp body while the third crew member rummaged through her purse and found what he was looking for. There was always some difficulty handling smartphones with anything other than bare hands, but he was adept at working in latex gloves and so it did not slow him down. He easily sailed by her password-protected screen and scrolled through the menu to find the app he wanted. The app came pre-loaded on her cellphone; it was one of the many new toys now available to all. It was a program that could send text, data, photos, even video to a recipient and within seconds of the images being viewed, just like that- they were gone. Never to be retrieved. The sender also had the ability to disengage the receiver's choice of saving a screenshot, which in this case, he did. The app was perfect for this situation.

The drug had Lynette out for an hour or so. She needed to be conscious to taste terror, they wanted the fear factor. Terror and fear of the unknown and of what could happen in her vulnerable state and at her captors' will. With her hands and feet bound, mouth and eyes taped shut; from her wriggling body they would show him her fear. An unconscious victim would not send as powerful a message. Also, Cam may question if she was even still alive and their threats of her survival would weaken their demands. From her they needed the struggle and a will to live. She was coming to.

It went according to plan and then another needle was jabbed in the arm, this time something more powerful. Two of the men grabbed her limp arms and legs and carried her to the van, tossed her in the back then jumped in the front. The van reversed out of the garage and the third man closed the door once more. The remaining assailant waited in his car for 1:46 p.m.

At 1:46 p.m. he hit the send key, tossed the smartphone on the epoxy floor, opened the garage door, started the Buick, reversed out, went back and pressed the button inside the garage to close the overhead garage door for the last time, then slowly and carefully drove out of Paxton.

Chapter Seven

Lynette was groggy from the chemically induced coma when she woke. With a dry-bone mouth and a head that truly felt as if it would crack open any second due to the unbelievably intense throbbing pain pulsating inside her skull, she ached for water. The duct tape had been removed from her eyes and mouth; as she instinctively touched her eyes searching for the tape, in doing so she realized also gone were her glasses, along with her bracelets. Peering down, she saw no shoes on her feet. Tentatively, she reached to touch the back of her head at the location of a dull pain. She had recalled it was hurting from the impact of a shove that had her hitting the tiled floor. As she lightly pressed, hot shards of jagged, razor sharp pain raced through her head and neck. On reflex her hand pulled away and she hushed a scream. Almost hysterical now, she searched around her new strange environment and asked herself obvious questions - *Where am I? Why? Why me?*

Just a vanilla white wall, that's all she could see. She raised herself up. She was lying on a thin dirty mattress placed on the floor. She sat up, ooh ... *a little too fast,* she knew it, and that hurt her head even more. She squeezed her eyes shut for a moment to try and make the pain stop. She opened them again and noticed again she was missing her glasses, but she could get by without them. Again she looked around the room slowly, and quickly realized there was nothing interesting to see. A square room, ceiling seven feet above the floor; no windows, and a solitary metal door with ... no handle. It looked like a storage room, very cold and very empty. A faint odor could be detected, a lingering smell of paint applied to the walls no more than two months ago. Although she was backed up close to a wall, Lynette felt a presence behind her and turned around and gazed up to see a fifty inch flat screen monitor – black and mounted in the center of the wall. Lynette could not detect it but the monitor had a small camera lens inserted in the casing.

Still unsure of her condition or her fate, Lynette decided to move towards the door. As she approached she called out in a raspy voice, "HEY! …HEY! … IS ANYBODY THERE?"

She called out again while banging a fist on the door and then with her head up against it, feeling the coolness and shallow relief of it on her burning forehead, she waited.

There was no response.

She pounded and screamed some more, "LET ME OUT OF HERE!!" More raps on the door with her fist.

Nothing.

She started again for a third time, "WHY AM I HER-"

An ear-splitting shriek interrupted her plea. It came from the monitor.

She slowly slid down the door and closed her eyes tightly while attempting to plug her ears and twisted around to face the source of the screeching. Her head was in intense pain and she cried out a silent scream. The pain in her skull was overwhelming and she just wanted her head to explode so it would all end. The desperate plea on her face begged the monitor to stop. *Please … just stop!* As she surrendered to it all, the alarm went silent.

She dropped her arms, opened her bleary eyes and stared at the screen. Words in red had appeared.

say nothing no one hears you

at the sound of the alarm lay on the mattress turn and face the wall

shut your eyes

don't move
you will have 5 seconds to do so
failure to follow these instructions means you will die
open your eyes at the sound of the second alarm

Once again, giving her no chance to react, the alarm broke the silence. She froze with fright for a second, then a survival instinct told her to obey; she did what the words on the monitor told her to do. She lay on the mattress, turned to face the wall and closed her eyes tight, hoping to God they did not just come into the room and shoot her. Lynette quietly laid there, facing the wall in the fetal position.

They had her in a state of total and complete submission.

The alarm stopped, the door opened. She heard quiet padded footsteps walk across the room.

Oh no, this is it, she could feel it. Within, she managed to complete a very quick prayer. Fear and panic were rising up in her once more. The seconds ticked away. She dared not move, certainly not open her eyes; she could feel herself go pale. Whoever had entered the room may at this very moment be stretched all the way over her body to make certain she was complying. *I am, I am!* But she could not sense anybody that close to her. No sound, no breathing, no body heat. What she did sense was someone standing a few feet away and just watching. Standing perfectly still and watching.

She heard a quick tap on something, more like a ... *tink* ... like glass kissing concrete. The footsteps then moved away, she heard the door close and the alarm began its high-pitched scream once more. In five seconds it was over.

Then it came. The fear she had felt was melting away. The shock was wearing off. The adrenalin that had been coursing through her veins had exhausted itself and emptied out. First, it was the quivering lip. Then the watery tears that welled up, forming large pools in her eyes. It soon became deep gushing sobs, and she had no way of stopping it now. It poured out of her. It was such a relief to let it happen. She did not know why she was here, who had taken her, where she was, or if she was going to live or die. But at this very moment, crying rivers of salty tears felt like the best thing in the world, next to sharing all this with her closest girlfriends.

She continued crying and sobbing and sucking in halted gasps for what seemed like hours. Finally she was able to battle the tears. With the tips of her professionally polished and manicured fingers she was able to avoid stabbing herself in an eyeball and flicking away what she always thought were the last of her tears. But the tears kept coming until she was able to calm down enough, which took quite a while, and the scene was forced to play itself out.

Finally, finally, it was over and she stopped all the sniffling and used her sleeve to wipe away the running mascara from her face. There was a trail that had streaked down and onto the mattress at the place where had laid her head but she couldn't care less about that. Lynette found the courage to turn around and face and look towards the door, at the place from where the sound, the … *tink* … came from.

A glass of water! A glass of water, a peeled orange and several gel caps of what appeared to be ibuprofen had been left on the floor. Hot tears rushed forward again and Lynette just let them flow.

Chapter Eight

Los Angeles, California

December - Sunday – 8:00 a.m.

With no announcement the vault door opened. It popped out of its recessed cove and silently slid back and passed the little gathering. Right on cue and right on time … as if by magic! When the door cleared the entrance to the vault it came to a dead stop. Four men who acted like this was an everyday occurrence walked in and began part two of their plan. For them, this was the best part of the job, where the fringe benefits lay. No one spoke, they had their assignments, and they needed to get on with it. They had two hours.

Chapter Nine

Los Angeles, California

December - Sunday – 9:54 a.m.

People were lining up everywhere. Limbs were being shaken out and loosened. People were bent over in uncompromising positions and stretched every limb in their generally thin bodies. A lot of talking, laughing, and generally a good time being had by all.

It was another great southern California winter's day. The sun was out, the sky was a royal blue, and the temperature rose to a slightly chilled but comfortable fifty-eight degrees and rising at almost ten o'clock that morning.

Palm trees swayed in the gentle breeze - it was going to be picture perfect for the annual 'Santa Claus Is Running Thru Town' Fun Run. It was an oddball 15k race that attracted a lot of local, national and some international attention amongst the competitors. Most everyone in some form or another was decked out in Santa attire. People wore red, people wore caps, sported long white beards; it was all part of the fun of being at the event. Still they did have their Grinches. There were those that were there strictly to run. They wore the most threadbare amount of jolliness they could get away with. Besides, just one look at most of these run junkies clearly told you they had no hope of winning the audition at the local mall to sit on Santa's throne. No child would dare go near their gauntness.

Estimates for the first time had participation in the race exceeding 70,000 this year and everyone was contributing to making this an enjoyable day. There were mothers and fathers who brought along the entire family. The children were outfitted in an assortment of costumes from tiny elves, to reindeers, little Santas, you name it; if it had anything to do with Christmas, they wore it. Grandmothers, grandfathers, uncles, aunts, cousins and newborns; friends, work colleagues and people traveling in groups raising money for charities were all there. There were Santa puppies, dogs pulling sleds, cats being carried. One novel young guy was pulling a block of ice. Assigned runners to keep to a certain pace time floated reindeer or Rudolph with the big red nose or sleighs, or Frosty the Snowman above them to tell those interested follow the beacon. But it was primarily a race for Santas. The color red could be seen everywhere. Musical bands from all over were striking up choruses, playing marching tunes, Christmas songs and Latin tunes. It had everyone in the right frame of mind.

Kip Keplar was there too with his family. Kip was caught somewhere between wanting to be the die-hard runner or just sharing the fun and good times with the family, and his outfit displayed his mixed sentiments. He was wearing a red t-shirt, red running shorts, a Santa cap and a white beard. He figured somewhere beyond the first bend, away from eye contact with his wife, he could somehow, "I don't know how it happened", accidentally lose the beard and head apparel. It was a nice thought, but in keeping with the spirit, he would keep it all on. Others in the family were in full red regalia and enjoying the festivities to the fullest, and they just knew they would see him at the finish line in a couple of hours.

Everybody lined up and shuffled forward and the starter moved into position. The clock counted down to ten o'clock, a puff of white smoke was seen, followed by a loud bang and they were off.

At that exact time, over at the bank, the gang of four was finishing up. The raid was a success and more. Each man gave the thumbs up, good-to-go signal, picked up their belongings and vacated the vault. The impenetrable door was guided back to the closed position. Once again the vault was sealed up nice and tight. Before they could leave, however, there was one last thing to do.

Chapter Ten

Los Angeles, California

December - Sunday – 10:17 a.m.

"Four Santas walk into a bar …."

Actually, they walked out of a bank. Usually, dressing up as Santa Claus at mid-morning gets you at least a second glance but today … well, today was different.

The bank lacked underground parking so in order to leave the premises, they had to exit in plain sight and take great risk at being noticed. Cameras from almost anywhere could pick them up. They would not leave a van on the street for three days - that would invite suspicion. No telltale signs of their presence, absolutely no clues. In disguise, cameras would identify four white-bearded Santa Clauses. They came out of the employee's entrance door that led to a side alley that ran along the bank's west wall. The front façade, built one hundred years ago from smooth grey granite, traveled beyond the bank's true west wall and created a small wing wall.

The building was constructed, as are most commercial properties in the wealthier downtown areas of larger cities, with money spent on projecting an image where perception was everything. The result was a lasting impression of security and trust in a bank that can stand the test of time. The message was clear, "we are here to stay and so is your money." So, in order to justify the additional costs used to convey the message, the owners had to offset costs elsewhere. Somewhere out of sight and out of mind. The wing wall helped resolve part of the problem. It leaned out far enough that most passersby never caught sight of the west wall, which was constructed of grey masonry block papered over with a thin brick veneer. The wall had turned dark and gritty from over a century's use of service vehicles trucking up and down the narrow alley with their gas and diesel engines. The men halted behind the winged wall, and it was indeed the best place to wait. Already bands of runners with great strides went sailing by. Small groups came and rushed on by; it was almost their time. Larger groups started to appear, their pace slower, waving to crowds lined along parts of the route. The men in waiting peeled off one at a time with their red sacks, full to almost overflowing, thrown over their shoulders as they joined in.

They timed their departures at sixty seconds intervals. Into full crowds of runners and or walkers they melted. If anyone did notice them joining in (but nobody seemed to) it may appear like a badly timed emergency bathroom break. Clothed in all of Santa's regalia, they were covered from head to toe. Complete with full white beards, red coned caps with white pompoms, black gloves, black calf length boots and dark wrap-around sunglasses for the California sun. The flocks of people they joined went at a pace that was no more than a simple stroll. They waved at the crowds and were carried onward, bathed in a sea of red.

Transportation was located five blocks away in a parking garage. As they neared their destination, each one simply stopped playing the part. The idea was to look around like they needed to stop for a break or wait for a friend then simply walk away from the procession. It all went unnoticed. Upon entering the vehicle with its tinted windows, the men shed their clothing and were once

again in civilian clothing. Once all the men were in the black
utility van, they carefully drove away.

Chapter Eleven

Los Angeles, California

December - Sunday – 10:56 a.m.

Kip rounded the corner and was clearly troubled by the man who was tracking him. He occasionally glanced over his shoulder. Still there!

He quickened his pace but he could not shake him. Kip was now breathing hard and this was tougher than he wanted it to be. He managed to pull out something extra, he was almost home. His pursuer now drew along- side. Kip refused to let this happen. He emptied his tank and gave it everything; with his head pointed to the sky and his arms flailing, he crossed the line inches ahead of his fellow athlete.

He was spent. Exhausted. Doubled over and unable to find the energy to lift his weighted-down head, he gave a half-hearted pump of his fist into the air. He straightened, walked over to his pursuer and congratulated him, then looked around for the results board. He found them, while removing the funny red cap and the uncomfortable wispy white beard. He was having some difficulty separating the clawing cotton beard from the stubble on his chin. Strands of white fluff clung to whiskers, strands that lengthened and refused to leave his face. He also contended with the spittle-laced remnants of irritating fibers surrounding his mouth. Runner #3516 had a time and position that were now posted. He dropped to a crouch and blew out a deep breath. He placed in at twenty-third.

With a half-eaten bagel in one hand, his second in three minutes, and a bottle of orange juice in the other, he sat with his knees drawn towards his chest on the grassy slope. He watched as the runners drizzled through his field of vision to cross the finishing line. It continued to be a bright and sunny day and he was enjoying every minute of it. By now the determined sprints to the finish had almost petered out. People were laughing as they crossed, personal accomplishments achieved, pairs of women doing the slow jog or fast walk came in together, mostly just talking to one another. *What do you talk about for nearly ten miles?*

He saw younger teenagers sweating or red-faced as they came to the finish line giving it everything they had. He could tell, for a lot of those kids, this was one of the first of many marathons to come. He enjoyed watching the father/son or mother/daughter team, or mixed combinations of the two that finished together. The father would typically clasp the boy around the shoulder and pull him in tight, smiling with pride or give him the high five, or for the younger dad, it was the fist-pump. The mother/daughter combination always finished with an embracing hug. These common displays of affection for their accomplishments were also shared by the father/daughter or mother/son match up. He paused for a second and felt a pang of guilt for not sharing this special time with his family.

These runs, when performed to prove your self-worth, could be a very selfish indulgence, and he did have occasions to regret his actions. His kids were growing up before his eyes and he often had to remind himself that you can't get times like these back. Soon enough, but hopefully only for a brief period in their lives, you are the last person on earth they want to be with. He enjoyed a solid relationship with them, all of them, but even the best of things can sour if neglected. He had to constantly watch against this. *Next time, I'm with them,* he thought to himself.

Kip saw them approach the finish line - Raef, now twelve, Trek, eleven and Annika who just had her tenth birthday were with their mother. The two boys were tall and sporting the straw blond hair, blue eyes and looks of their father, while Annika possessed the fine golden hair, green eyes and remarkable features of her mother. Their children were everything to them.

The family was waltzing down the last two hundred yards. Giggling, his daughter Annika was cute as ever in her miniature Santa outfit. A cherry red cotton shirt, matching red skirt finished with white trim, a black belt, a cute red cape and topped off with a red cap and a white pompom. Her braids of blonde hair flowed out behind her as she happily skipped towards the finish line. Ah, yes, no time like the present to start tomorrow's plans. He got up, stretched, then went down to greet them and catch up on what he had missed.

Chapter Twelve

Long Beach, California

December - Sunday – 12:22 p.m.

The crew traveled on their uneventful journey to the port at Long Beach. They had made several trial runs, so getting to where they needed to go was no problem. It was Sunday, and the place was all but deserted. They arrived at the rundown wood-framed, paint-peeled warehouse and the driver pulled out the remote, aimed it at the large hangar door and pressed the button. They sat idling for the next ten or so seconds as the door slid along a rutted track pulling its sagging weight sideways to allow them to pass through. After the door rattled, creaked and squeaked to a stop, they drove the van inside and the driver made sure the door closed behind them.

As was the case elsewhere on the premises, the inside was deserted. The driver killed the engine and all four men exited the van. There was weak light filtering in from the grime covered clerestory windows above. The warehouse they found themselves in was enormous. Its primary purpose had not changed for over a hundred years, that of being a storage facility for incoming and outgoing containers from the port.

It was destined to be demolished in the not too distant future, replaced by an ultra-modern climate controlled, with all the latest bells and whistles, superstructure. It was now empty and therefore the perfect place to wait it out. For now.

The sunlight, however humble, was profitable for the crew as switching on lights may attract unwanted attention to the vacated building. Ink blotches from oil stains pooled in scattered areas on the floor, and where the light struck it at certain times of the day the liquid reflected muted colors of a rainbow. Concrete dust floated on by undisturbed, the captured particles found in sunbeams that highlighted the uninterrupted stillness within the building. Any briny taste of the sea that was found just outside the doors was missing in this stale, dank environment; only the smell of over a hundred years of sweat, toil and the metallic smear of scarred containers remained in these walls.

After the long and exhaustive days that just passed, these men with their rough and tough exteriors welcomed the break from silence. Not a word had been spoken in days; it was considered a safety measure in the event someone's voice may have been inadvertently picked up on a recording. You just never knew what could trip you up. The men whooped and hollered, shouted, laughed and cleared their dry throats. They had done it. Even Tony joined in and that was unusual. This was the ultimate heist; they knew it and they released their built-up tension by slapping each other on the back and doing some man shoving. But there was still much to do.

The group leader of this band of thieves was Enrique. Enrique Alvaro. He called himself Ricky.

"OK, OK guys, time to clean the van out." He pointed away to his right. "We need the sacks on those carts over there." He turned back to Tony, "Help the boys with the stuff, Tony."

Tony paused to give Ricky his usual leering stare but did as he was told all the same. Tony was not one accustomed to taking orders from the likes of …. of these guys. There was still little in the way of talking even though the need for silence had passed but they were after all, only men.

As the guys were grabbing sacks, a crack of light appeared and spread across the warehouse floor, and the light stopped his momentum. All the other men also froze. The man door had swung open and the cut of a lone figure stood in the frame. The men relaxed for although the silhouette's face was in shadow, they recognized their boss. This guy blew a cloud of blue smoke into the air and walked through the opening.

Their boss, Mogul had in recent years tangled with smuggling illegal goods, drugs, human traffic, whatever made money, across the US-Mexican border. For him, it was a living. A tax-free lifestyle! In his circle he was known by many and was gaining a strong reputation as a winner-take-all player. But he was no fool and he knew his place; there were other kids in the playground that had more authority, more power and had gained more respect than him. He wanted what they had.
But how to get it? That's what he constantly asked himself.

"Swans don't swim in the sewer, son!"

"What are you talking about?" he had asked.

"We need your help in busting up this network. It will go well for you with the D.A's office. We can make a deal."

It was way back when and Mogul was caught in the net along with some other petty, small time street thugs; hauled in for questioning and possible arrest for racketeering and drug running.

Mogul went on to tell her, "Go to hell!! Put one of your own on the inside. Let them get killed!" It wasn't going to be him doing their dirty work. He knew the legal system and all its threats, it was like third grade detention compared to what would happen to him if he were found out to be a snitch.

And so, he remembered the words of the agent, "Swans don't swim in the sewer." She repeated those words. "We can't use one of our people, it takes the likes of you." She looked him up and down. "The way you act, the way you talk, the way you smell," she wrinkled her nose in disgust, "One of our own would be made much too quickly. We're not like you."

That's right, Mogul thought to himself, *I'm no swan.*

Years after this incident occurred, he gave himself the gift of the name Mogul; he thought it had potential. He liked the way it sounded and what it stood for. Everyone respects a self-made Mogul.

He went on to grind it out in the trenches and sometimes savored the sweet taste of success, but would also feel the bitter cost of failure. He experienced the price to be paid for incompetence. In one memorable instance, they ripped off the small toes from both feet. Unceremoniously, with a haphazard hard tug from some aging pliers, all the while being held down and forced to watch the handiwork being carried out while a razor sharp knife scratched at his throat. It left a bloody mess he needed to clean up himself. He never visited a hospital.

An underground tunnel had collapsed and two reasons caused the loss of his toes. Three men had died. There was no grief or punishment at their loss, but the tunnel had been discovered, which meant it was now a closed route. It was 4,500 feet long, with a fork in the tunnel that led to two entry points into the United States. One finished inside a warehouse and came up through a broken unused toilet that could be slid to the side to reveal the opening to the tunnel. Anonymous closed cabin trucks and vans would back up to the loading docks and haul away whatever came out.

The other tunnel opening was even more ingenious and fortuitous. It snaked through to a cemetery and eventually found its way to a mausoleum. Through a shell company, the gang owned the mausoleum and through threats, intimidation and bribes, also owned the proprietors of the cemetery's silence. Once inside the mausoleum and respectfully leaving it undisturbed, they would bring out and send through the tunnel whatever they wanted to, day or night. Hearses with darkened windows transported the goods to and from the location undetected. The business was a two-way traffic bonanza. It was literally a gold mine.

The tunnels were equipped with everything, lighted passageways, ventilation systems, conveyor belts, and cameras. Like the ancient Pharaohs, the owners even created false corridors to elude authorities in the event of a chase through the tunnels. *Which way did they go?* This would be the question from the confused trackers. Only the experienced knew. It was beautiful, it was perfect. And now they were gone.

Four times it had been extended. It had been handed to Mogul to supervise and lengthen for the last two occasions. Bring the merchandise in, send the guns and money out. It worked for the longest time; however, he was not thorough enough. He did not pay enough attention to the details to make sure the tunnel was sustainable. He was the good soldier and made absolutely sure the new additions were sound and secure and that these were workable tunnel systems. But what he failed to do was inspect the work that had gone on before he arrived. The previous "manager" had skimmed, made shortcuts and pocketed the savings. The back end of the tunnel was not sustainable. The tunnel had collapsed in

Mexico and the authorities came along to view what was inside the hole. No amount of bribes was going to make this one go away.

The second infraction for this reprisal was that drugs were lost to US authorities.

The gang would have easily slain the guy who created the mess but he was long dead. Killed in a rival gangland shootout. But Mogul was still around and although not entirely at fault, they felt he should have checked and maintained the entire tunnel, not just the addition he was responsible for creating. What surely saved him was his idea of using the cemetery as an entry point, but it was not enough to avoid total retribution. He needed to be held up as an example to others and what happens in the light of failure; and so he lost his toes.

Long term it had taught him a valuable lesson. Know and understand everything you are undertaking. Plan carefully and no shortcuts. You only get one chance to make it right the first time.

The lesson had been learnt, no mistakes. He continued to have ghost feelings for where the toes once were, and he would often feel the wiggling of flesh and bone that no longer existed.

From that day forward he became a clever man. He limited his exposure. He stayed off rap sheets. He sent others to do his dirty work. When in charge – delegate. He mercilessly punished failure and was one to be afraid of. He lived in an unknown world and was an unknown name for everyday law abiding citizens. For this reason he drew the attention of the guys out east. They called on him and made introductions.

He listened respectfully to their opportunity, what other choice did he have? His mind raced as he heard about the content, the size and the scope of the operation. He was in. Mogul had hit pay dirt.

Mogul made one more plan. Five months before the operation was to begin, he knew it would take time to put together, so he left town. He let the rumors float that he had moved on to … somewhere, maybe South America? He cashed in his chips and was retiring or went to hook up with the cartels. No one knew for sure. They just knew he was no longer around. This would be his alibi when the time came and if anyone asked, he was nowhere in sight, had not been for some time, and no one knows where he is, where he went or why.

Mogul wore nondescript dark blue jeans, a plain black t-shirt under a lightweight black jacket and cowboy boots. He wore a red roped band on his right wrist that was just now covered by the sleeve of his jacket. He was anonymous. He hid in plain sight in many ways, height, weight, and hair color, all just average. His hair was gelled and sunglasses hid those eyes that never seemed to care.

He would kill indiscriminately and on occasions for the slightest provocation. A double tap to the head and then a body would turn up anywhere. A carcass lying in a shallow grave in the desert, decaying floating bodies in the sea, or a burnt shell in what was left of a smoldering gasoline fed fire. Most were left to waste in the deserts across the border in Mexico, for as he knew, these men were vermin to law enforcement and had little to no chance of justice finding them. Mogul stuck to his tactics, he was simply just plain ruthless.

He slowly surveyed the entire area and with squinting eyes inhaled hard as he sucked on the cigarette and exhaled smoke once more. "So ….. Any problems?" he said as though this was a run-of-the-mill, everyday event. There was also a suggestive tone of, *there better not be*!

Ricky answered with enthusiasm "It was great, boss. No glitches, no problems, no sweat. Like clockwork. We took what we could carry."

"Any chatter?"

"Not a word, Mogul."

They had taken all known security measures but Mogul was not about to take any chances. Hooded masks, gloves and sunglasses on at all times; pills were popped for hydration and hunger pains, other pills were taken to prevent them from the need to use body functions for three days, and no one was to utter a word. All the precautions were taken because, even with the best-made plans, there could still be a camera they did not know about that was active. They were not about to leave behind any traces of prints or DNA. Not after all this planning. And in the odd event there was a voice activated detection device, no one was to speak. All communications were carried out through hand gestures.

"Just like I planned it," said Mogul, shaking his head in a self-satisfied way as he looked at Ricky with a sly grin. He continued to grin and stare at Ricky. "I haven't seen you guys since you all got your makeovers, you look …pretty."

"Hey, screw you, boss!" came Ricky's retort too quickly, but then he threw a smile on his face to cover up. He hoped he could slide it by after what they had just gone through.

Mogul just chuckled and let it go, then turned to view the others.

The men, all four thieves, had bodies that were completely devoid of hair and their bald heads showed it.

Part of the beautiful plan. From head to toe, they were completely waxed and shaven so as not to leave as much as one hair follicle behind at the scene of the crime. They looked a pretty picture now, even missing their eyebrows. But they were looking to stay out of sight for some time to come and carrying with them what they had, it was a small price to pay. Besides, the hair would grow back. Well, at least for some of them it would.

Every man selected for this mission was involved for a reason and that was why the job went so well.

Ricky, considered to be Mogul's right hand man was an ex-marine and had served multiple tours in Afghanistan. He had witnessed his share of death and destruction but while most found it abhorrent, Ricky relished its darkness. Once out of the military he pursued professions with this entertainment value attached. He floated into Mogul's life and became a key asset who handled his dirty work. He had a sergeant's discipline to keep these guys in line and carry out their mission. It's why Mogul put him in charge.

Then there was Tony. Tony wasn't one of theirs. When he joined the unit they asked, "What do we call you?" He thought for a moment or two, and then smiled and said, "You can call me Tony."

No one had any illusions regarding the fact that Tony was not his name, but what did they care? Most people in this racket went by an alias or two. Tony was an import. Through a third party he was given to the gang. Tony did not even know who his real masters were. He just knew he was there to protect an interest. Tony did not like being told what to do by the likes of these West Coast two-bit thugs, but he understood it was only temporary and he made it very clear with his cold dark eyes that you could only order him around so much and so far. It was a warning even Mogul understood.

Ray, the tall lanky one, handled the alarms. Carried out hundreds of burglaries, never caught. It was why Mogul selected him for the job. Recruited from Florida after spending some time in Vegas. There was no way he could be traced back to Mogul. Ray was also ex-military and sported several blue-colored tattoos along both arms. Besides his deft ability with alarms, he could handle explosives, and Mogul also knew him to be a crack shot with a rifle.

Bo. "Bo the Beautiful," they called him. From an early age, the guy with the mischievous good looks knew how to draw in girls like a magnet. He had that bad boy charm. His parents were lost about coming up with ways of dealing with his behavior, and so were the courts. His escape route was to enlist him in the Air Force, where they hoped the excitement of being around expensive toys would quench his thirst for trouble. What he found was a way to enhance his expertise and natural talent for electronics and computers. Finally drummed out of the Air Force, his resume could say, *He enjoyed playing military action video games against pathetic online competitors when not breaking into secure corporate and government computer networks.* He was their boy wonder hacker. Bo also enjoyed the results of pumping iron that aided in sculpturing his body, so together with his looks he easily had no problem attracting all the women he wanted.

Mogul knew his weaknesses and that he could be a loose cannon but Mogul chanced it due to his talents, and Bo was warned.

"Did you grab the notes we needed?" Mogul asked Bo, who was removing the vest he was wearing under his clothing. All the men who came out of the bank wore one. The vests were additional "suitcases" on their bodies used for carrying out of the vault more than the sacks could handle. It also worked well as extra stuffing for their Santa attire.

He took a handful of notes from the vest and waved them at Mogul. "We took what we could find."

"Then get going and start transferring."

"Right. Should take me a couple of hours."

"Your problem, not mine." Mogul walked off. "Just get it done."

Mogul left the warehouse but returned moments later in a well-worn six-year-old Minivan. An inconspicuous car meant he would not stand out. He stepped to the back of the vehicle, raised the rear door and began tossing onto the floor buckets of fried chicken and cans of pop. The men not only saw the food but also could smell it; their salivating mouths could almost taste it. They dropped everything and hurried towards him. Hunger had invaded their thoughts ever since leaving the bank. They had eaten nothing in three days. The appetite suppressants had worked, but had worn off some time ago. The same went for the need to use the bathroom for three days.

"Throw everything back in the bags when you're done," were Mogul's last words before driving off in the minivan to a public storage facility he had rented for a year, paid for in advance. Ricky would fetch him shortly in the van to join them on their journey.

They waited for the cover of darkness to board. The ship was scheduled to leave at 8:30 p.m. The sky reflected a tinge of the purplish-blue hue that remained when the five left the safety of the warehouse and made their way along the wharf to the cargo tanker. They briefly stopped at the gangplank and were met by their contact. With some effort they pushed the carts up the ramp and prepared to settle in.

They were all tired and getting wearier by the minute, but the anticipation of inspecting their bounty was keeping them all awake.

The men and carts were lowered by a hydraulic platform down into the cargo hull where they would not be disturbed. Strict instructions were disseminated to all crewmembers from the captain of the ship to this effect. The penalty for anyone disobeying this order would be harsh and violent. The crew kept their distance.

The van involved in the heist was lifted by crane into the hull and sealed into a sea container. The men made use of and gathered into a cargo container that was painted red, but had dulled over time from its years of use. The container was eight feet wide and forty feet long with a height of eight feet. Mogul led the way and all the men followed pushing the carts with their prized treasures. It was prearranged that the container be fitted with overhead lights and a long table placed in the center. Mogul looked at the rickety table with its warped legs and buckled top and shook his head from side to side. He hoped to hell it would not collapse under the weight of what it was about to receive.

There was no rhyme or reason in how they were going to do this.

Mogul spread his arms out wide and said, "Go ahead and dump it on there."

One by one the men grabbed their heavy sacks and spread the contents on the table then threw their vest on top. The table groaned a couple of times and swayed slightly, but it held. As they went about emptying their lot they looked at each other with toothy grins and boyish anticipation for what they were about to receive.

When it was laid out before them, like a pirate, Mogul bent over and spread his arms out, reaching through it all in search of something in particular. Inside a felt-covered bag he found what he was looking for.

"Everybody out!" he ordered.

Everyone stared at him in amazement.

"But we've only just started!" protested Bo.

"You'll have your chance to look this over. Now get out and leave me alone."

No one moved.

"Go to your quarters and rest up. We'll start this again tomorrow."

He left them with a warning. "And nobody come down here without me. Remember, I have the key to the lock but don't any of you pickpockets try anything dumb," he tapped the handgun slung under his jacket, "because I'll know and I'll do something about it."

They filed out in confused but stony silence.

Chapter Thirteen

Laguna Beach, California

December - Monday – 6:33 a.m.

Kip concentrated on his breathing. Slow and steady, in and out. Nothing stressful, he spent that energy yesterday. How he loved to be out here doing this; at this pace he could go on for miles. A seabird kept him company and glided next to him. It flapped its wings briefly then floated on air. Every now and then it would rise above him, caught in a small thermal lift and then drift back down. Then, just as suddenly as it appeared, the bird abandoned its companion and peeled out over the ocean, sailing away and squawking as it did.

  Kip kept moving, occasionally stamping down and squelching the thin layers of water that had just rolled in from a spent wave. The ocean waters reached out like fingers to touch as far as they could the edges of the shoreline. Leaving foot-size temporary memories on the squeaky compacted sand, Kip recalled how, many years ago when he began to run along this very beach, soft wet sand would grind under his bare feet and between his toes and rub his skin raw. But he soldiered on and over time it no longer affected him as it once had, and he made better choices by maneuvering closer to the shoreline. The well-watered sand sets quickly like semi-hardened wet cement once the water had drained away, and the runway left behind created an excellent running surface. The sand compressed softly under his weight to absorb the pounding and it felt more desirable than a run along the asphalt roads.

These days there always seemed to be an early morning beach crowd. He passed fellow joggers who gave the obligatory head nods to most of the regulars. Walkers, with or without dogs, in ones or twos also used the pedestrian strip along the shoreline. Often the singles were off in their own world listening to whatever was fed into their brain from gangly wires connected to hand-held or arm attached devices. Whatever carried them along - high-energy rhythms, favorite songs of the past decades, audio books or so on, it kept them apart and solitary. Elderly couples that could be relied upon to patrol the beach from 5:00 a.m. onwards, kept in touch with each other by gently holding hands as they shuffled along. They sheltered in windbreakers, elastic waist pants and large hats. But there they were, every morning, making a go of it.

The surfers were scarce this morning. The sea was calm and flat and there seemed to be only a handful of diehards, or a couple of the younger ones who had to taste surfing everyday come what may. Too early as well for skim boarders, although the conditions at the shoreline were ripe for an excellent ride.

Kip noticed a guy in the distance in a yellow sea kayak making his way from one rock outcrop across an expanse of open water to another. He was cutting across the horizon. He had a good tempo and was making excellent time. It had Kip pulling on memories of his kayak days with the kids and how much fun they had with it. Always a thrill when you can catch that wave into shore.

He glanced east towards the mountains and witnessed the pale dawn sky, telling him that the sun's first rays would be slow in coming that morning. There was cloud cover hanging above the hilltops, keeping the day at bay and holding onto a grey early morning.

He ran on, having saltwater splash him every now and then as a rogue wave came roaring in. In time, he was joined by a few more gulls hoping against hope that a few morsels of anything would be thrown their way. Home in fifteen minutes, then off to a busy day.

He had no idea.

Chapter Fourteen

Los Angeles, California

December - Monday – 8:00 a.m.

Reginald G. Parrington, never Reggie, could be characterized as a nervous man, a company man, and a precise man. Perhaps in that very order. Just the right profile for his position as bank president, Los Angeles branch, for American Trust. He had held the title for twelve years and he cherished every minute of the day he was in "his" office. With military-like precision, he kept the cogs greased and turning effectively and efficiently while the squeaks in the wheels were almost inaudible. At least to a level that would not be heard all the way across the country. He did not like squeaks. He wanted only to present crisp, sanguine reports to his superiors out East affirming that everything was "shipshape." He fretted over the tiniest details; he honestly believed they knew his every move, and maybe even his thoughts? It is the reason why he poured one hundred and ten percent of himself into his duties.

Reginald was built for the role he played. With the sharp side-part of his jet-black short hair, heavy black-framed fashionable eyewear and the (never any other color) dark blue suit. He looked the picture of everything banking. He rounded out his attire with a pressed white shirt, dark blue tie with grey striping, and highly polished black leather shoes.

The man was a serious and diligent custodian who stayed away from trouble but today, something had begun to cause Reginald to be anxious. Not a good start to the day and it had happened within seconds. Then the seconds started ticking away and he could feel a bead of sweat start to break out on his brow. He reached into his pants' pocket for a kerchief to wipe at his forehead. This was not right.

The problem lay in the fact that the clock had given up the hour. Eight in the morning to be precise. The vault door, reliable as ever, did not open. He understood the protocol if this continued and he dreaded it. A call to New York had to be made to alert them of the problem. He needed the door to open!

Prayers were answered. The delay lasted an entire minute. He would have that looked into, but the vault door was quietly sliding to one side and Reginald could rest easy.

Reginald G. Parrington looked over at the three guards that stood by him and gave one of those rare smiles that silently said, *all is well again*. All three returned the grin as they, too, sensed the relief. Then, with wide unbelieving eyes, Reginald G Parrington stared inside the vault but the staring was only fleeting, for two reasons. Firstly, it did not require hours of studying the situation to realize what had happened. And secondly, he fainted.

The three guards left Reggie lying on his back as they rushed into the vault to find many opened safety deposit boxes and no intruders. The collapsed figure showed the first signs of body fluid leaking out from his tailored pants, which began to encircle him, and now there were two messes to clean up.

Chapter Fifteen

Laguna Beach, California

December - Monday – 10:39 a.m.

Kip was attending a ceremony for a charitable organization he ran. It was his favorite. They chose to call it the "Room for Improvement" scholarship fund. Kip and his wife had started it up several years before. He had observed through the years of attending like-minded functions that many such organizations were out there, and very good ones, indeed, that predominantly catered to the upper and lower spectrums of academic achievements.

Several of these groups searched far and wide for poor and disadvantaged children who especially needed help. This was a true and worthy cause, to bring these children out of poverty and give them the chance in life afforded by their peers who were more fortunate. This was a crowded field of genuine people looking to help.

So too were the scholarships and funds dedicated to cherry-picking the high achievers who were already well and truly noticed. The kids were easy to find and conditioned to succeed. It was just a matter of sending them off to the best schools, and there was certainly no shortage of great schools that raised their hands to enroll these mostly trouble-free kids. Then it was just the matter of tracking their progress that generally flourished within the benefits of their surroundings.

Later, when these talented and more often than not, well-to-do students accomplished their lot in life, the university was back with cap in hand requesting large alumni donations. After all, was it not they who made those kids what they are today? The money flowed back to the spring.

No, these were not the children Kip pursued. His work was more complicated and his people had to dig a little deeper. He searched for the children who primarily came from working class parents, who neither had the time nor the knowledge of scholarships and what they could do for the future of their kids. So the "Room for Improvement" fund was chartered to find them. But it was never easy.

His people were the preying lion staring at a herd of zebra. For so long as the zebra stood together as a collective, it presented the lion with his challenge of pinpointing the target while viewing the entire striped landscape before him. One giant black and white wall, nothing stood out. The children they attempted to reach were the same. Rarely did they volunteer their talent. They ran with the pack and were inclusive in the wall, and so blended in. These gifted underachievers scored fair to good grades and performed just well enough to stay out of trouble, but sidestepped the need to exceed. It meant they could deal with the tangible issues in their lives and not be burdened with distractions like extra-curricular activities from school and other social pressures.

A typical scenario that played out usually had both parents, if they had two parents, working hard for meager wages and often never home in the afternoon, meaning the child would return home after school and needed to fend for them self. They were expected to complete household chores, supervise the younger ones if necessary, and prepare meals. They grew up too fast - generally a child with the responsibility of adulthood thrust upon them so that they missed out on their youth. The question of, "When can I leave school so I can become less of a burden to the family?" was always one that was never too far away. So in light of circumstances like these, although the children usually had a "gift" it was not nurtured and often neglected due to the more pressing needs of family life. There were never any childhood dreams here as reality crushed these kids under its very weight of circumstances.

So when report cards arrived they often stated the frequently touted line by teachers who had little insight into the situation, saying, "*Your child shows potential, but is lazy, or bored, or distracted or ....*" fill in the blank. But with a greater effort at home there is always "Room for Improvement."

Perpetual poverty is the ultimate and lifelong punishment for these children. Following the long family line of missed potential they know of no other way to endure.

The lack of awareness for opportunities or stubborn pride to never ask for the perceived "handout" meant no one ever did. So a large collection of potentially useful minds went unnoticed and instead of making great contributions to society, they would move on to low paying jobs and in turn perpetuate the cycle.

So Kip's foundation's mission was to seek out as many of these kids as possible, give them the tools, help and funding so that they have the space in their lives, or for lack of a better phrase, the "*room for improvement*" to compete on a level playing field as much as possible. This can be accomplished through grants and mentoring programs and old-fashioned encouragement.

Kip had just finished giving this very speech to rounds of applause. Before question time could commence, a concierge from the hotel where the event was taking place handed him a note that asked him to use the hotel phone. It was an emergency. Kip nodded, said thank you and curiously took the call.

"This is Kip."

"Kip its John. You're a hard man to track down."

Kip made hand gestures to the other guests on stage that in turn gave him puzzled looks, but he indicated that they should cover for him and so they did.

"I'm at a fund raiser and giving a speech and … answering questions."

"Sorry, Kip," John responded hastily and with a tone that quite clearly brushed aside Kip's agenda's importance. "I need you to come in immediately. We have a matter of urgency we need to discuss."

"Can it wait? Can you tell me what it is?"

"No, not over the phone. Please, it's a delicate situation. Could you come on up to the Bureau right now?"

"I'll leave now but I'm down the coast, more than an hour away."

"As quick as you can. See you when you get here." John ended the call.

Kip walked over to his wife and said, "I'm sorry, it's an emergency, can you finish without me?"

She nodded and asked, "Is everything alright?"

"I don't know," he replied. "I'll catch up with you later at home. Can you get a ride?"

"Yes. I'll be fine."

With that, he kissed her goodbye and headed for his car.

The black A8 Audi's interior retained the warmth from the morning sun. He buckled in, slipped on his sunglasses, touched the ignition switch, slotted the vehicle into drive and pulled out of the hotel parking lot, heading for CA-73 N that would take him north.

This would link up with the 405 N, and that carried him all the way to Wilshire Boulevard, FBI headquarters in Los Angeles. He was hoping the traffic gods were with him.

Chapter Sixteen

Los Angeles, California

December - Monday – 12:07 p.m.

Kip was seated in the guest lobby on the sixteenth floor of the FBI Headquarters Building waiting for the Assistant Director. The Assistant Director was temporarily detained and Kip was asked if he could wait. Well, what were his other options?

He could have picked up one of the tired old magazines piled up on the side tables, but he didn't feel like rehashing old news. Instead he had sunken down into the recently acquired chocolate colored leather couch, one of a matching set. Two couches mirrored each other across a glass and steel coffee table. The couch retained its new smell and annoying squeaks. He surveyed the room while looking for nothing in particular and as there was no one else about he could not strike up a conversation. A conversation about what? An exchange of minor secrets, perhaps? Finally for some unknown reason he settled his gaze on an unassuming clock. It hung on the fabric-covered wall across from him; there was nothing significant about the clock. It was round, with a thin metallic rim and a white background supporting basic black numbers. The hour and minute hands were also black, but the second hand was red. It was practical and served a purpose and that was all.

But the red second hand tirelessly swung around the clock. Kip watched it intently and without knowing it, began to be mesmerized. He was having odd, deep thoughts. Here he was, in a waiting room, no different from countless times before in his life.

Everybody did it.

Just waiting around. Killing time.

Waiting for someone else to take his life off of hold. Kick start him back into gear once more. But the bigger picture was this. As he stared at the second hand circling the clock, two insights were revealed to him.

One, it obviously told him the time of day, but the notion that time had not always been measured suddenly occurred to him. It was an invention of man to manage life and place his needs in order, give them a sense of priority. And two, he was literally watching his life tick away. Those were the precious seconds that turned into minutes, and then hours counting up the days of his life that were just draining away. Waiting. Doing nothing.

Tick … tock … tick … tock. He just sat there, waiting, and that clock, pushing time forward, it kept on going, the timekeeper of our lives; all the time we take for granted, the instrument we check multiple times every day, taking away our lives. It kept on ticking away right before his eyes.

He shrugged the thought off and chuckled at how morbid he had just made himself. Time was a void to be filled productively and life was to be enjoyed not spent sitting around moping and philosophizing on strange sentiments.

These thoughts finished as the Assistant Director strode in. With a welcoming hand fully extended and a genuine smile, John Brozski shook Kip's hand vigorously as he said, "Kip, glad you could make it."

"Well, you did say it was urgent, so how could I refuse?"

"Please, this way," John replied and slipped a hand in the small of Kips back to gently urge him on down the corridor to his office.

John Brozski, Assistant Director of the Los Angeles office of the Federal Bureau of Investigation. Dressed in a well-tailored suit, crisp white Oxford button-down and a serious dark blue tie. The clothes were a cut above the rest, just in case anyone had any doubts about who was in charge. At six two, he was athletic, lean and had authority figure written all over him. His hair had retreated to form a crown around his baldness; what was left had matured to steel grey with only a sprinkle of his original dark hair remaining. The grey and his height conveyed his authority that allowed him to discharge his duties with conviction.

They entered his office and Kip sat in a visitor's chair opposite the expansive desk as John closed the door then returned to his executive chair. His office was located on the sixteenth floor overlooking Wilshire Boulevard. Beyond the boulevard was the Los Angeles National Cemetery, operated by the Department of Veterans Affairs. John's office was spacious and appropriately decorated. He had three windowpanes installed between the white-grey concrete of the building's exterior. The windows were vertically hung, rectangular panels allowing in the morning and midday sun.

"Here's the situation," John started out. "American Trust was hit sometime after the close of business day Friday."

"Are you serious? I ran right by that bank on Sunday morning," Kip told him.

"Really?" John asked, "See anything suspicious?" He needed a lead.

"Sorry, I was concentrating on the race. There were thousands of people out there that day. They must have broken in and left the bank well before then. Too many people around on Sunday to I.D. them."

"Well, we won't know that until we study the surveillance footage." John stated.

"So it wasn't an armed robbery then? How did they do it?"

"That's the thing, Kip…it's still too early to tell, but right now we have absolutely no idea how they did it! That's why I called you in."

John walked him through the bank's newest security system and talked extensively about the time lock operation. How it was set up, how it operates, how it is foolproof and how it is impossible to break into according to the bank's people.

John continued, "It gets more complicated. There are other …." he searched for the right word to say, "complications going on here as well. A woman has been kidnapped in Connecticut. She is the wife of a Senior Vice President of the Bank who is headquartered in New York."

"I don't understand, John. What has that got to do with the robbery?" Kip asked.

"Well, as I just went through with you, the banks time lock code is a random code entered into the system in New York. In their head office. That was part of the genius of the system, or so they say. Her husband was one of the men who received and entered the code. It looks like they took her to get to him and to the code."

"When did this happen?"

"She was taken on Friday."

"Friday? Then you must have known this was going down on Friday."

"No, we didn't. You see, Kip, this is all part of the mystery. Her husband received a call at work and was told about the abduction on Friday, at which time they demanded the code. But he neither gave them the code or told the authorities about the abduction."

"That doesn't make any sense," said Kip, thinking out loud.

"Right," John agreed. "No sense at all. They have him at FBI headquarters in New York. He came clean about the abduction today. There is still no trace of his wife."

John leaned forward and asked Kip, "I'm sorry - can I get you anything, water, coffee?"

"Water would be great," Kip replied.

John touched a button on his desk phone and asked for water and coffee. Then he continued, "It's been a helluva morning around here, I can tell you. The phones have not stopped ringing, and there are a lot of influential people who had one thing or another stuffed in that bank vault. For the most part we don't have a handle on what was in there or who we are looking for."

Just then John looked up as his administrative assistant entered the room with a tray and their refreshments. "Oh, thanks, Anita. You can just leave them on the table," he instructed.

Anita smiled, put down the tray and quietly left the room.

John passed a bottle of water to Kip who twisted off the top and tasted the cool water. John placed the mug with black coffee in it on his desk in front of him. Then he returned his attention to Kip and said, "I'm going to need you to go to New York and find out what you can from this V.P. He's our only lead."

"Is that an order or a request?" Kip asked.

"I'm sorry, Kip. It's certainly a request. We would welcome your assistance in this investigation."

"Let me talk to Mette and I'll let you know."

"I'll need a quick answer I want you flying out of here tonight."

"You're not fooling around here, John, are you?"

"You don't know the half of it. Let me tell you what I now know about what Hollywood had in there."

"Hollywood?" Kip inquired.

"A group or consortium if you will, from most of the biggest studios in town. There were some exceptions, but the rest of them banded together a few years ago. You see, they were amassing huge losses due to competition and a collective run of flops and profits were declining, or at the very least, they were taking bigger risks and budgeting more money for movies they were not even sure were going to come up aces. They felt they had to keep throwing movies out there, good or bad, to satisfy the public's thirst for more entertainment. Their problem was not enough good scripts floating around. And when one came along that was a hit, they'd rushed right out and create the sequels, or ..." John threw an open hand gesture towards Kip,
"Well, you know, you've seen it done, split up one good movie and make into parts one and two and release them a year apart. It was either that or remakes of old classics, and you can only do so many of those."

"What about the sales from rentals and online streaming?" Kip wanted to know.

"Well, yes, that's a good source of revenue downstream, but even there they are attacked by piracy, digital sharing and all sorts of ways people have come up with to siphon the movies from the internet and then the studios surrender profits. We've got our hands full dealing with that mess ourselves. It's through the studios' pressure and influence you see our name first on anything you rent. Remember what was happening to the record industry a few years ago? Well they sensed it was starting to happen to them."

John paused, took a couple of sips of the coffee then sat way back in his chair. He formed a temple with his fingers and placed them just below his lips, recalling where to pick up again on the narrative.

"So what they feared like any business was limited access to funds; the budgets to produce a movie were skyrocketing, and the return on the investment is not guaranteed. It made the banks nervous. The banks had their share of money-losing ventures in the last few years. The Hollywood guys wanted to head off their troubles and direct, so to speak, their own destinies. They got together and hatched a scheme and after a lot of wrangling, an agreement was struck between studios that included transferable bearer bonds. They would pool their highly liquid funds and borrow amongst themselves. I'm sure with the occupations within this group, no one was shy on dramatic quotations. Someone surely reminded them of that old saying by Benjamin Franklin, *We must all hang together, or assuredly, we shall all hang separately.* He paused to take a sip of coffee.

"So, they went ahead with it, but you're not talking about a bunch of neophytes here when it comes to money. These were Hollywood moguls after all, and everyone had their own favorite bank for one reason or another. Trust is one reason that comes to mind. So they spread it around. Our guess is about fifteen to twenty billion dollars was floating around out there. No one knows for sure, or if they do, they're not saying, and exactly how much was sitting over at American Trust is a mystery. What we do know is some, if not all of it was taken in the heist. Conservative estimates have the figure at around one billion."

"But surely they are not transferable to be used as cash?" Kip asked.

"Oh, yes, they are," said John. "That was the value of the notes. At the request of one of the studios, anytime, anywhere, these bonds could be whisked anywhere to help fund projects when they required cash fast. Money on demand, when they needed it."

"But how would they stop themselves bleeding the funds dry? Pigs feeding at the trough. I would think the money would be syphoned off by someone at the first opportunity. Integrity's not exactly a great asset with a lot of these guys," Kip observed.

"There were limitations. Movie plots were reviewed by everyone and actually through collaboration, movies had more potential. They all shared a collective interest for this to succeed, for now it was their money on the line. And when all was said and done, audits were performed to make sure the movies did indeed make money and the funds went back in the coffers for another try. And no one could slip a fast one past anybody; they all knew the same tricks. Why? Because they had all pulled them on unsuspecting investors in the past themselves. It was an even playing field and it seemed to be working."

"So the money is essentially cash?" asked Kip.

"Well, yes, with limitations," John repeated. "We have naturally put a freeze on any transactions being performed here in the United States, and we have asked friendly countries around the world to do the same thing. But..."

"But?" Kip prodded.

"But we don't control the entire world banking market, never have, and even less these days. Many more players are standing up to our threats, and some ignore us completely. These bonds could be converted to cash in Eastern Europe, China, or Venezuela for all we know. The Swiss, for crying out loud, may see no problem with it. We only have the power to do things within our jurisdiction and with help from our allies."

"How much?" Kip asked.

"We don't know. Hollywood is being tight-lipped about it."

"I can see how the people in Hollywood could apply pressure on you for results. They know people, your bosses, I'm sure, and they no doubt want quick action and a return of what's theirs," Kip remarked.

"It's always different when it's yours. Skin in the game, so they say," John stated. He glanced at his watch. "Listen, Kip, I've got two more meetings to attend after this. You can stay if you like to listen in on my next one. It's a woman; her name is …err," he reviewed the screen of his computer's calendar, "Yes, here it is, a Jessica Eggins. Apparently had something in the bank she needs to discuss with me." He shrugged his shoulders in ignorance. "Urgently."

"O.K. I can stay for a bit, but then I should get going," Kip said.

John kept reading from his calendar. "Yes, and after that a meeting with the Navy." He raised his eyes to look at Kip. "Best to keep you out of that."

They sipped and drank their coffee and water, talking for a few more minutes and then Brozski's intercom buzzed.

"Your next appointment is here sir."

"Thanks, Anita, send her through."

A diminutive woman of about forty-five walked through the door. She looked at both men and then announced in a hushed whispered voice,

"Jessica Eggins – Smithsonian Institute."

Ms. Eggins was short in stature, about five feet even, dark hair pulled back in a tight bun, dark eyes, and pale skin. She was wearing a white trench coat, not a lab coat, over a cream colored dress and matching shoes. Short in size, but she, too, commanded authority. And as she talked in that quiet whisper, it drew you in closer to hear what she had to say. It was always going to be something you did not want to miss.

"Jessica, nice to meet you." John started out. "I'm Director Brozski and this is Kip Keplar."

"They have Yurushi," she said matter-of-factly.

"You mean it's real, not a myth?" Kip piped in.

"Who is Yoroshy?" John asked as he mispronounced it.

Kip and Jessica kept the conversation going between them without responding to John.

"Oh, yes, quite real! It was discovered about two weeks ago," Jessica said. "It was on its way to the Smithsonian."

"Who is Yuroishy?" John tried again.

"Who found it?" Kip asked.

"A quasi archaeologist, slash treasure hunter, slash scientist named Bigelow," answered Jessica.

"I just can't believe it," Kip said once more, shaking his head.

"Believe that we had it and now it's gone," Jessica sighed, shaking her head.

"WHO THE HELL IS YURISHY?" John Brozski finally demanded, raising his voice to be heard.

He got their attention.

"*What* is Yurushi," Jessica calmly corrected as she turned to face John. "Well, then," she smiled wistfully, "Let me tell what I know of the story of Yurushi," Jessica's intense whispered tone had their undivided attention.

Chapter Seventeen

THE LEGEND OF NEI QIANG

Kublai Khan's heavy frame rode steady on his dark horse, a dark horse the color of night. His fleshy wide round face sternly inspected his troops, ready to severely discipline anyone who failed to meet the standards. But his men were more than ready.

His long white tunic rippled softly in the restless wind, Imperial robes easily recognized by his subjects. Those who were not troops standing stiff at attention in their ranks, eyes dead ahead, were officials who bent low at the waist, heads bowed, to honor their great Emperor as he passed by.

He, The Great Khan of the Mongol Dynasty, looked out over all his men, as far the eye could see and he was pleased with what he saw. Battle hardened men who would fight to the death and willing to do his bidding. He turned to his right and surveyed the ships in port and throughout the harbor, these vessels that would be used for the journey across the sea. The time was at hand.

The year was 1274 AD. His men were preparing for battle. A battle that would give them a great victory over the obstinate island people that lay to the east. The people of Japan. He was tired of their arrogant refusal to capitulate to his power. An affront to the ruler of half the known world. Many emissaries had journeyed across the sea to prepare the way for his dominion over their lands, their ways, and to pay their tribute. But these people would not submit. What's more, they ignored him at every offering. Most often the replies were in the form of a headless corpse. This infuriated the Great Emperor. He would not be refused by inferior peoples on tiny islands. These people were nothingness compared to the great lands and skilled warriors already subdued and under his control. All those under his sphere of influence both bowed before him and paid tribute. He had had enough. These people from the islands of Japan would bend to his ways.

Kublai Khan had at his disposal 24,000 Mongol and Chinese fighting soldiers and 10,000 Korean soldiers. Aiding them was an army again of supply staff. No army walks and fights on an empty stomach. The Korean contingent were assembled from the Goryeo Dynasty, a land Khan swept through and conquered years before. Three hundred and seventy-five large troop-carrying ships and a contingent of five hundred smaller vessels bringing forward supplies, horses, gunpowder and weaponry were ready to sail. He would destroy these people with overwhelming force and the technological advances in weaponry that his armies had at their disposal. They would know firsthand his mighty strength and power.

So in October of that year his troops were launched towards Japan. On the voyage across the straits they encountered and pummeled the native Japanese people on the small islands of Tsushima and Iki who stood in their way. Small victories, of course, but a taste of what was to come. It boosted the men's morale. They landed on the island of Kyushu at Imazu and Kakata on November 19th, 1274 and met the inexperienced Japanese forces who had not met foreign enemies in battle for over fifty years. The Japanese lacked the know-how to successfully engage large onrushing armies on the battlefield as their tradition was accustomed to one-on-one duels settling the matter. Those Samurai who stepped into the middle of the field alone to request a duel were overwhelmed by Khan's troops and cut to pieces.

On the first day after easy fighting and many victories because of their superior weaponry and fighting formations, the Mongol armies retired to their camps at the onset of dusk. But they were conscious of a major storm developing and the advice they were given was to retreat to the ships for protection. The sea captains feared that if the boats were damaged and had to flee, the army would be marooned on shore and unable to escape. The storm was larger and fiercer than any had imagined. It was a typhoon, and many of the Mongols' fleet was lost, sunk by the power of the storm. The next day, those left standing and not ravaged by the previous night's menace, were chased down by the Japanese boats, which were more maneuverable in these waters, and to top it off, their sailors had the firsthand knowledge of the currents and challenges. Onto the Mongol ships the Japanese Samurai warriors came. The fighters were experts in close quarter hand-to-hand combat and many Imperial army soldiers were cut down. Those who survived fled back to Mainland China, humiliated in defeat.

Kublai Khan would not forget what took place in 1274 AD. He vowed to avenge it. In April, spring of 1281, he assembled an awesome fighting force that dwarfed his earlier legions of warriors by a multiple of five. He scheduled an attack for a different time of year to avoid the mistakes previously made due to weather conditions. The seas were still, the weather clear and his fleet sailed across the straits once more. A combined Korean, Chinese and Mongolian force, some 50,000 strong sailed out from Happo, Korea in nine hundred ships. Happo was chosen due to its close proximity to Japan across the Korea straits. Additionally, a second fighting contingent of over 100,000 troops scheduled to set sail from southern China would not be denied.

Unfortunately for Kublai Khan, his invasion army sailing from southern China was delayed, and the initial coordinated attack was abandoned. When finally joined by his additional 100,000 warriors, the force landed at locations near the site of the first invasion seven years earlier. Despite the overwhelming numbers against them, the defenders of Japan fought ferociously and repulsed the invaders who would retreat to their ships only to regroup and attack again and again. For months, Kublai Khan's men attempted to break through, but Japan's people were prepared for war and determined as ever. Still, Khan had the advantage of manpower and how long could these outnumbered Japanese last?

The virtual stalemate pushed the encounter deep into summer. What began on August 15, 1281, as history repeated, was the intervention of a raging storm, which evolved into an enormous typhoon. It churned the sea and barraged the shore where the Mongol army lay. It continued for two days and nights. Kublai Khan's forces were decimated. For a second time the Japanese people acknowledged the "Divine Intervention" that played such a significant role in securing their victory against the invaders. Not only was it timely and just, it was primarily confined to the sea and shoreline around Khan's army, which were destroyed in large numbers. The Japanese forevermore paid homage to *Kamikaze*, the "Divine Wind."

With Kublai Khan's acceptance that he could not capture and control the islands of Japan, he magnanimously sent gifts to Japan's ruler. It may have been Kublai Khan's attempt to appease the gods for having twice failed, but this gesture of good will signaled that he no longer desired to conquer the land to the east, and that at last he accepted it.

Chapter Eighteen

THE GIFT

Among other treasures, Kublai Khan presented a gift that was nothing short of extraordinary. This most precious of all gifts was crafted from a practice that prevailed for only a very short time, and no one understands how or why it vanished.

Jade, or "Yu" in China, is a sacred gem. The privilege of royalty allowed them to possess the very best. It was from the finest jade that could be found, painstakingly carved into the symbol of a dragon. The dragon signified potent powers, with control over - *water and rain.*
But what put this beyond measure, what made this a masterpiece in its own right; the magnificence of its extraordinary casing. Through a distinctively clear, highly polished and pure solid rock of diamond the jade symbol could be admired.

The jade dragon was set within the diamond and once joined, the two objects belonged to each other, working together in harmony as one. The diamond was over twelve inches in circumference, and with the dragon, weighed over six pounds. With flawless clarity the gem sparkled brilliantly and the 4,000 carats had no equal. Its cut, a fashion that reflected light to the pinnacle of its potential, was beauty personified.

It was pure. It was one of a kind.

Diamond is the hardest mineral source known to man. What twisted form of alchemy did they possess that enabled them to perform such a trade? No one knows - the answer, as the art, was lost to history. Lost, as is the knowledge of how the Great Pyramids of Egypt were built. So-called experts can only surmise about these true engineering feats, but in reality it is all still a mystery.

Kublai Khan called this treasure "Nei Qiang," which means "strength within," acknowledging the resolve the people of Japan had to preserve their culture and way of life, and to never surrender their cherished land. The gifts were gracefully accepted but the Japanese chose their own meaning for what the dragon in the diamond represented. They named it *Yurushi*.

Chapter Nineteen

The ships lay anchored in the harbor early that morning of that 8th day of July 1853. A mist rose from the water masking the city that should have appeared before them. The squadron nestled at Uraga Harbor, Edo, Japan. Commodore Matthew Calbraith Perry of the United States Navy had embarked on this epic journey the year before. He left Norfolk, Virginia in 1852 with his ships and a letter of introduction from President Millard Fillmore. His mission: to open up trade by means of a signed treaty, by force if necessary, with the closed country of Japan. And with force he came, for he was aboard a steam-powered frigate, the *Mississippi,* and had by way of escorts another three warships. The frigate *Susquehanna* and two sloops-of-war, *Plymouth* and *Saratoga.* The ships had on board firepower by means of canons that the Japanese had never before witnessed.

Perry had intensively studied the Japanese culture, their customs and their ways of dealing with foreign traders. As a consequence, he refused to sail onto Nagasaki as instructed by representatives of the Tokogawa Shogunate. The Japanese were impressed by his boldness that was backed up by force and an iron will. In order to put a stamp on his authority, Perry ordered several canon bursts using the Paixhan exploding shell as a show of strength. The cannon fire scattered the Japanese wooden boats floating about his ships. On July 14th, 1853 he sent four hundred seamen and marines ashore. They were the advance guard for his regal arrival.

Commodore Perry presented his letter of introduction from his President and stated he would be back to receive their answer. Three days later he sailed out of the harbor.

As promised, Perry returned once more, in February 1854. Always one step ahead of the Japanese, who had fortified areas around the harbor anticipating his arrival, he brought a force consisting of twice as many ships. Having no answers for ridding themselves of this belligerent American fleet embedded in their waters, with vessels that had the ability to fire at will on anything within range, the leaders of Japan during this era, unlike those who fought the Mongols almost six hundred years prior, decided to welcome him and open negotiations.

Therefore on March 31st, 1854 Commodore Matthew Calbraith Perry achieved what no other representative of any other nation had before him. He signed the Treaty of Kanagawa to initiate the commencement of full and open trade between their two countries.

In good faith, Perry presented the Imperial Emperor with gifts from the United States of America. Things that go *BANG!* usually impress, and for the Imperial Emperor, this was no exception. He was given a canon and the exploding shells that went along with it. Up until now the Japanese were using wooden or bronze canons with straight shot cannon balls. These relics were not up to the task of competing against the modern age technology.

To complement this gesture, Perry ceremoniously handed the Emperor an allotment of Sharps rifles. These new rifles were both highly accurate and excellent at long range, and as Perry pointed out, could fire eight to ten rounds per minute based entirely on the competency of the rifleman. The Emperor was duly impressed and accepted his new gifts with good grace.

That night, an Imperial messenger with an attachment of Imperial guards was dispatched to meet with Commodore Perry and request that the good Commodore should once more be available for the Imperial Emperor. A rare honor indeed.

The next morning Commodore Perry appeared at the palace unsure of the circumstances for his honorable presence. Perry noticed a great number of dignitaries on hand to witness something he knew nothing about.

The Emperor approached him in full traditional attire and everyone bowed. It was ceremonial, it was lavish, and it was beautifully staged. After a chorus line of Geisha danced around, Shinto priests performed ritualistic incantations and Samurai warriors displayed shows of courage and strength, the Emperor moved a few steps forward and Perry was asked to do the same. They stood opposite one another four feet apart. The Emperor removed a veil that was covering the object being presented. Perry looked at it for a moment and nearly staggered backward at its sight, its beauty, its awe. He recovered quickly, bowed graciously and received the object.

He asked, "By what name is this magnificent gem called?"

Yurushi – was the reply.

"My president, my country, and I myself honor you for this remarkable gift, Your Imperial Highness."

The words were translated to the Emperor who looked into the Commodore's eyes, smiled then turned and walked away.

In his quarters onboard his ship later that day, he stood around discussing this wondrous marvel with his officers, when the question was asked more than once, "why would they give such a glorious gift?"

Naturally, Perry had inquired about *Yurushi* and was enlightened about its history. The final assumption was that the

Royal Japanese family had held this regrettably prized gift for almost six hundred years. They did not consider this the winner's spoils of hard won wars. But rather, as a back- handed compliment disguised as a trinket from Kublai Khan, who was offering up a token of his power. They believed it to be a constant reminder that defeat was close at hand, twice, and they decided to finally remove it from their shores. Remove this yoke from around their neck, and pass it onto others who regarded it in a completely different light. It gave the Royal family a sense of relief.

Commodore Perry's mission in the Far East was not complete. He was sailing onto the island of Formosa to assess if the United States of America could lay claim to this far away territory. But he did not want his prized possession, *Yurushi* to lay idle with him on his ship. He needed it sent back to Washington immediately, so President Fillmore would know that great progress had been made with the Japanese. It would also be a stunning preamble to his return.

He sent for Commander Abraham Lloyd, Master in Command of the sloop-of-war *Andronicus,* which had arrived to join the contingent of vessels the day before. He would dispatch Lloyd and *Andronicus,* post haste to the United States. The quickest route was directly east across the waters to San Francisco, where it could then travel overland to Washington.

It was pressed upon Lloyd the great importance of his mission and to keep safe *Yurushi*, even if it took the last breath of his life to do it. Lloyd understood and made plans to sail the next day for San Francisco.

At an informal handoff, so as not to attract attention, Perry gave all the gifts received to Lloyd, who locked them away in his cabin. All hands on deck witnessed the event, but Lloyd simply nodded to his second to commence proceedings and get her underway. The second duly shouted orders and soon afterwards they were under steam and heading out to open waters. It was a clear day, the seas were calm and Lloyd saw no problems. His cargo would be safely delivered; Commodore Perry could bank on it.

On the third day of the voyage, the winds shifted, dark broiling clouds rapidly rolled in, the air was heavy with humid vapor. The crew saw it, they sensed it but they had seen this predicament many times before. The order to batten down the hatches went out. Above them, storm clouds broke open with a downpour of rain but a gesture courtesy of Mother Nature, at the very same moment, created a twisted ending for the day. The last rays of light from the distant horizon's sun were peeking through a crack in the clouds and touched the boat; it was a majestic sunset, but all on board missed the irony.

It rained hard in heavy sheets, unending, never giving quarter. The night sky often flashed blue with streaks of lightning so fierce and so near that most crew members could not recall being so close and within reach of such bolts in all their sailing days. The seas rumbled, they tossed and bucked at what was now a tiny speck on the great ocean. The crew's training was excellent, they were professional sailors and they held the ship steady, they maintained control of the situation to the point when a lightning strike made a direct hit. The strike coincided with a huge rogue wave that swamped the boat and tipped her on its side.

From a crew of one hundred and sixty-seven souls, only four washed up onto the cay. Broken, wrecked and exhausted they lay on the sand that was as hard as coral. The small group comprised the Commander, a marine and two seamen. It took several hours that morning for all of them to fully come around, check their injuries and make sense of what had taken place the night before. All that three of them could claim as property were the clothes on their backs, but the Commander had the good sense to collect a thing or two before giving orders to abandon ship. He strapped on his sword and securely threaded the strings of the pouch that held the gem to the hilt of his sword above the handle guard.

The strip of land was not much to inspect. It ran about two hundred paces long and thirty paces wide. The only living things on it worth mentioning were half a dozen palm trees. The sand was coarse and there was no fresh water. After collecting some coconuts they were able to open them with the help of the sword, drink the coconut water and eat the white fleshy meat. The men then scooped out the shells for collecting any rainwater that may come their way. But they were all aware of their fate and knew they could not survive like this for very long. Late in the afternoon Commander Lloyd spied the two seamen talking conspiratorially by a tree and glancing at him every now and then. *This could not lead to anything good*, he thought.

It's a strange thing what greed does to a man. These men were hopelessly marooned. It was in everyone's best interest to stick together and maybe come up with a plan to get off this tiny piece of land they found themselves on. But men are men, and greed is second nature. It was not long in coming. They made their move that night. They were each armed with a coconut and that was part of their mistake. The coconuts they held were not small round ones that fit neatly in the palm of the hand. Rather, in their raw and natural form straight from a tree, the coconut is a hard shell within a larger hard-shelled green brown pod. Being so big, they needed to be weighted evenly in two hands to serve the current purpose of murder.

The Marine knew nothing of them coming, showed no signs of waking up. The coconut came crashing down and crushed his skull with one mighty and powerful blow. For a brief moment it was two against one but Commander Lloyd had luck on his side that night. He had the conspiring whispers of the two seamen weighing heavily on his mind, and so in only a light sleep, he easily awoke to the heavy footsteps from crunching sand as the men drew near. It was enough to alert him to the approaching danger. Armed with this information, the small window of time gave him the opportunity to prepare. The additional luck of a moonless night with an overcast sky meant that the night remained pitch black.

A Commander in charge takes charge, and as he was doing the bidding of Commodore Perry, his service to duty and country were clear - resist the attack and protect the treasure. It was dark, so his attackers made guesses as to where his head might be. They struck but missed their target by three inches. Lloyd was also already rolling to his left. When the blow came he could feel the rush of air go by. He was quickly on his feet and in one motion drew his sword and swung it. The seaman that attempted to end the Commander's life seconds before had used all his weight and strength to deliver his offensive blow. Therefore having missed, he found himself bent over at the waist with both hands still placed firmly on the coconut that was now buried in the heavy sand. Lloyd's sword found its mark and came in contact with the seamen's back slicing through flesh and organs. The once bent over seaman now pitched forward and lay dead on the sand.

The second crewmember knew better than to tangle with a sword, unlike his dead fellow pirate. His tactic was to seize it. He was close enough, so he lunged for the sword. There was a struggle for control. Both men held onto the hilt, knowing losing this battle would be fatal. Then the seaman introduced an old tavern brawling trick. He reversed his pulling strength into a push and with the aid of Lloyd's unwitting help, the sword's hilt butted Lloyd in the mouth. Two teeth busted loose and his lip was badly split. The Commander tasted coppery blood. Quickly, the seaman swung the sword down sharply and Lloyd's left hip suffered a deep wound.

He cried out at the searing pain, but from this he drew desperate strength. He spun them both around one hundred and eighty degrees; the rotation kept the seaman off- balance in the heavy sand. Lloyd then summoned his withering strength to collapse flat on his back and flip the seaman above and over him. The man released his grip and landed on his back also in the sand; a mirror image of Lloyd with their heads almost touching. Simultaneously, the Commander drew his knees towards his chest, arched his back, and with continued momentum plunged the sword over his head and drove it home through the man's throat.

He then passed out from agony and exhaustion.

He was done for. He knew it. He could do nothing the next day but lay under the shade of a tree. He did not bury the bodies; he neither had the will nor the strength. The only thing he could think of was his failure to complete his mission and the shame it would bring his family.

All he could do now for his own peace of mind was save the treasure in the event someone came looking for them. But he was sure they were blown miles off course, and so that was a wishful dream. He collected one of the coconuts that had been hollowed out. In it he placed *Yurushi* and a piece of gold that he had pried loose from the hilt of his sword. He lashed it together tightly with palm frond strips he made and buried the coconut as deep as he could in the crusty sand with the aid of his sword.

With the intense heat from the tropical sun bearing down on him, he drank what coconut water he could from what he considered his *farm-supplied bounty* in the trees above him. If he were lucky, a tender young coconut would drop nearby; these had the sweetest taste of all. He would continue to devour the fleshy white meat that the coconuts also provided. Lloyd could only collect a scant amount of rainwater from the hulled out shells.

Except for the storm that put him where he was, there had been little rain and it was not enough. The deep wound in his hip, which inhibited his movements, would not allow him to climb the trees for more coconuts or to search for a passing ship. He was limited in his harvest to only those that fell to the ground. So it was, from an unquenchable thirst, a festering wound that was badly infected and smelled woefully bad and the affliction of his failures on his conscience, he lacked the will to live. Commander Lloyd, who sat slumped against the trunk of a palm tree and under thinning shade, grimly holding onto life, finally slipped sideways and died face down in the sand eighteen days later.

Over the years, due to the cay's shallow rise above sea level, ensuing high seas easily washed over it, and together with storms and seabirds all traces of the men's existence on that land were swept away.

When Commodore Perry arrived back in Washington he asked merrily about his prizes. With blank looks from everyone, all shook their collective heads and told him in no uncertain terms they had no idea what he was talking about! There was suspicion though about the whereabouts of the USS Andronicus. Mutiny? Lost to pirates? No one would ever know. Perry tried in vain to impress upon them the magnitude of the masterpiece now gone missing. The men of Washington saw this as seamen's tall tale and gallant boasting on Perry's part. With his good record and accomplishments, however, he was able to have an entry listed in the records of gifts received by foreign countries.

It was noted as "Lost in Transit."

Perry vowed he would not rest until *Yurushi* was once again found and returned to its rightful owner, The United States of America. He died a few short years later in 1858 and the matter of *Yurushi* died with him.

Chapter Twenty

LOST AND FOUND

To anyone else he was mad. He was way off course. Anybody with an ounce of deductive reasoning knew he was way, way too far north and too far west. The International Group for Historic Aviation Recovery (TIGHAR) had told him so on more than one occasion.

But Dr. Lawrence Bigelow persisted. He knew better. A research professor, on sabbatical, he was obsessed with his hobby and he was going to find the missing remains of Amelia Earhart.

Instead, he found something completely different.

His assumption was that she could not be where conventional wisdom had placed her because the islands of that area had been picked over by others, the miniscule pieces of evidence found being lab tested and the results proven to be "inconclusive." People like Bigelow always discount the fact that Earhart may have simply gone down in the water and that was that. So it was with his personal theory and his blind ambition to find her remains that he came across the tiny cay with no name. It was so small. It had eroded since Perry's time and measured no more than one hundred and forty paces by twenty paces.

He searched for three hours and found nothing. Head down and working in the hot sun, he was exhausted. He stopped and removed his Panama hat to mop his brow and wiped his neck free of the sweat. It was then that he caught sight of something almost entirely buried in the sand. It would surely amount to nothing, after all he was looking for man-made articles, bits of metal from the plane; the remnants of leather headgear or glass from goggles, perhaps, but this was maybe just a coconut. He slipped his hands underneath it and swore as his hands were cut by the sharp coral edges of what was making up the sand. As he cradled it in his now bloody hands, he could see for the first time that it was indeed a coconut but it was more than that. It had been intentionally wrapped in what appeared to be seaweed or twine of some sort, and this was definitely not a natural phenomenon. He eventually pulled out a coconut, tightly bound. This was not done by nature. He curiously but slowly unwrapped it and then realized he could pull it apart where it had obviously been cracked open. His heart was pounding, he was right and his critics would eat their words.

It was Amelia's final contact with the outside world, well concealed.

"And so," Jessica said as she rounded out the story, "he made contact with our Institute to see if we knew anything about it. You see, the piece of gold he found in the coconut, along with the diamond, was an eagle's head, and Bigelow knew enough US armament history to recognize it. It belonged to the hilt of an old military officer's sword of The United States Navy. No one knew for sure what it might be, we had all heard the vague rumors about *Yurushi* for years, but it was a legend!

Then one of our researchers caught wind of the whispers swirling around our offices. She was researching some old documents from Perry's travels. These documents recently became available due to construction beginning on the front entry steps of the Capitol Building. Repairs were called for as the steps were crumbling and becoming dangerous. Workmen had uncovered boxes of old archive documents stored beneath the steps in a large crawl space. Musty but in reasonable condition, these documents revealed significant insights into events of the era and Perry's personal voyage logs were among them. We have yet to complete the work on these papers, but she knew enough and Perry was adamant in his writings about the existence of *Yurushi* and described the beauty of it at great length. We were naturally extremely excited to see it.

It was another week of back and forth horse-trading with the nutty professor, negotiating his terms and conditions before agreeing to hand it over. We had it whisked back to the States and it was to be briefly kept in that vault until we could securely ship it east to The Smithsonian. It was only there three days!"

"Why did you wait?" John asked, astonished at the fascinating tale.

"We wanted to first verify the diamond was real and not a fake. And we wanted tight security for transportation. Gone are the days, Mr. Brozski, when you can mail a diamond like that via the United States Postal Service the way Mr. Harry Winston sent The Hope Diamond to the Smithsonian."

"And was it … a fake?" John asked.

"Absolutely not," Jessica replied. "It was – excuse me – it is, one hundred percent genuine."

"Why did he hand it over to you?" Kip asked.

"He's a scholar. They live by the motto, "publish or perish." The diamond and its heritage is now his "new favorite" hobby. All he wanted was compensation expenses for his wanderings in the Pacific, the authorized rights to publish a book about his find, with our ringing endorsement of course, and the Wing into which it would be ultimately placed, named after him. How could we refuse?" She paused, taking a moment to reflect upon it all.

"Oh, and one more thing, gentlemen," Jessica continued, "The State Department has a vested interest in this, too. Although Bigelow found it, it technically belongs to The United States government. The government accepted his "donation" to avoid any unnecessary disputes and mess over the incident, call it a finder's fee, if you will. This was however originally a gift from one government to another and their claim in the case is significant. They do not want to lose this treasure a second time. Therefore, the State Department will want to be kept fully abreast of your attempts to recover what is theirs." She stood up and extended her hand to be shaken.

After making their goodbyes to Jessica, Kip left the office and John walked out with him to meet his next scheduled appointment. As Kip strode out through the lobby, all he heard the Admiral from the Navy say was, "We've been waiting for twenty-five minutes; your secretary has been paging you ..."

Well, they're off to a good start, Kip thought as he made his way to the elevator and descended all sixteen floors.

Chapter Twenty-One

As Kip was learning more about *Yurushi*, Mogul was making his way up a ship's ladder looking for Bo. He found him relieving himself off the side of the ship. Mogul thought how lucky he was that the ship's ladder was not located downwind from Bo.

"Wha's up man?" Bo asked, not even breaking his rhythm.

"Need you downstairs in the container - now. Put that monster away and join the rest of us." Mogul left the way he came.

They settled in to review what they had hauled away and to make an assessment.

Mogul turned to Ricky, "So, what's the final score?"

"Looks like we came up with about two million in cash, give or take a few dollars, hundreds only. Jewelry, value to be determined, a guess would put that figure at about five to seven million, some junk and the Hollywood bonds at…" he paused a beat, "four hundred and fifty-two million, man."

The men around the table whooped at hearing the numbers, well whoops emitted from three of the other guys at the table, anyway; not a peep from Tony or Mogul.

Mogul shot out of his chair and then with one motion grabbed the chair and flung it across the confined space, not seeing it crash hard against the steel wall. He took a swipe at the air with a right cross aimed at nothing in particular. He cursed then said, "Is that all? Are you sure?" He jabbed a finger at Ricky, "because if you're holding back…"

Ricky cut in, "I swear, boss, that's all of it. Isn't that enough?" he asked, exasperated.

"Man," Mogul ran his hands through his hair and locked his fingers together at the back of his head. "There should have been close to a billion in that damned vault in Hollywood bonds. How many deposit boxes did you crack open, anyway?" he asked.

"We hit about sixty, forty-five percent of the boxes in there. You only gave us two hours, boss!" Ricky said, a little perplexed.

"And you started where you were told?"

"Exactly, where we were told. Isn't that right, boys?" Ricky looked around the room for backup from the others.

They all nodded their heads in agreement.

Mogul looked at Tony. He slowly nodded his head in agreement, too.

Mogul turned away from the table cursing, running his hands through his hair once more. He knew there was more in there. He was expected to get more.

With Mogul's back to the men, Ricky added, "We found these in a briefcase; the only reason we brought it along was Bo and Ray said the initials on the side of the briefcase said D.O.D. and it could be something."

Mogul turned slowly back around, not really paying attention to what Ricky had just said. He was going to have to explain his shortfall to people who did not accept excuses. They wanted results.

"Huh … what?" Mogul said trying to refocus.

"These." Ricky thrust ten or so flash drives at Mogul.

Mogul took a few of them, staring at them for a few seconds. "Well, what the hell are these?"

"Could be something," Bo cut in. "If it's The Department of Defense, and it's in that vault, it may be worth checking out? It took a lot of work just to crack the case open. I tried to look at the contents but as you would expect, it's heavily encrypted. I would need more resources to find out what it is."

"Y e a h ...," Mogul drew the word out slowly, thinking. "OK, I'll look into it for you," he said sarcastically, still concerned about his future. "Anything you say, Bo. It's probably going to tell us who shot JFK." He pulled the pouch out of his pocket and showed it to the men, "Meanwhile we've got this baby to think about!"

The huge diamond with a jade dragon at its center caught everyone's eye immediately; even in the meager light it sparkled.

The men around the table all stood up and leaned in closer to towards Mogul. They could not believe it. They were all speechless for a moment.

"How much is that worth?" asked Ricky while pointing at it.

"More than you clowns could grab in bond notes from that bank, that's for sure," Mogul responded. "Now you all know the deal," he continued, "we get a cut of the total value of everything collected. Tony here makes certain everything we hauled out goes to his boss." He looked at his three men and continued, "No holding back. We are to meet with the party who is going to take this merchandise off our hands. We lay low for a year or so. Then you get your share. We're talking millions for each one of ya."

Plenty of *yeahs* and *alrights* were voiced, and then everyone quieted down.

Mogul looked at them all. "Now go get some sun on those bald scalps of yours, the light reflecting off them is blinding me."

He eased *Yurushi* back into his pocket; it took some effort and could barely fit, but it stayed with him. Then he collected the flash drives and snagged Tony and they both headed upstairs to make a call.

Chapter Twenty-Two

East Coast

December - Monday – 3:27 p.m.

Once again she was groggy, with a dry mouth and the nagging headache that remained, but its intensity had subsided. That was not the worst of it. She was cold, she was very cold. She opened her eyes to see a grey sky that was showing signs of darkening. She was outside!

She lifted herself up, slowly, and looked around gingerly. No one was in sight. She was in a wooded area, still without her shoes. Trees stood empty of leaves, and she could just make out a black ribbon of road winding away in the distance. She ran towards it, feeling the hard cold ground beneath, the pain on the soles of her feet was agonizing as she raced over sticks and stones.

It was not snowing yet, but it was threatening. When she made it to the road she had no idea which way to go, and so instinctively she turned right, running along the road desperate to find someone.

Lynette ran and walked for about fifteen minutes; her feet were ice cold, but she did not care - she needed to find someone. She froze, blinded by the oncoming headlights of an approaching car. She stood in the middle of the road, waved her arms frantically, and once again started to cry. The car stopped several yards away. An elderly couple remained inside the vehicle as the car stood still and idled. The husband, who was driving, timidly scrolled the window down several inches. He eyed the woman who ran up to the side of the vehicle; she was clearly showing signs of hysteria. They spoke quickly and then the elderly man unlocked the car doors. She climbed into the back and the car drove away, headed for the nearest hospital.

Chapter Twenty-Three

East Coast

December – Monday – 3:42 p.m.

"Could you please bring me some coffee?" Sam asked slowly, in a croaky old man's voice. Sam Cirrelli was never worried. Sure, he'd had his trials and tribulations over the years, and had seen it all. Been to hell and back. They call it "experience." A family business will do that to you. Sam Cirrelli, or "Little Sammy" as everyone affectionately knew him, was the son of a father who was a Sammy also. He sat at his desk, waiting for the call. His sleepy appearing eyes panned over his desk and rested on a picture taken of him and his father sixty years earlier. His father, gone now these past seventeen years, then too, his brother and a beloved son, snatched away and out of his life.

Little Sammy was not a book to be judged by his cover. The physical looks were not foreboding. He was five feet nine, but was showing signs of frailty by leaning forward and hunching his shoulders as he shuffled along. He did retain a healthy head of dark hair, but his head was oversized and out of proportion with his slim shoulders and the rest of his slight frame. Physically there was nothing to him, the smallest runt in a street gang could take him out, but mentally he was as tough as they come. It was to anybody's detriment that they underestimated the secretive Little Sammy.

They say there are only two things in life that are certain – death and taxes. Well, in Little Sammy's world the entire motto did not apply. Sure, they more than likely doubled downed on the

first word but for those wheeling and dealing in this profession, that's the gamble worth taking. The irony about this line of work was, it was just like a real job! You rise and shine every day like everybody else. The *executives* usually wore a suit and maybe a tie. On this day Little Sammy was wearing a well-tailored Italian charcoal grey suit, blue shirt and a very expensive yellow silk tie. The difference was the countless nights and weekends physically involved in running the business. More so than your average 9 to 5 schmuck. Day in and day out they had to grapple with the same petty issues that every business deals with.

You get the call from one disgruntled employee and told that Frankie didn't show up for work again last night, so at the depot, he had to load the cigarette cartons into the truck … alone! *Where the hell was Frankie, anyway, huh?*

Meanwhile Frankie was having his own bad day of too much drugs and booze, so work for him was not the priority. He was also fighting with the live-in girlfriend once more, who was giving him a hard time. He heard the same old complaint about staying out too late with the boys again, and so he decided to go get drunk and smoke something instead of listening to that garbage.

It never changes.

The business had, "public relations" to attend to, and accountants to keep track of the expenditures, profits and some form of payroll. So in many ways, they ran their little organizations like any other private enterprise. So like every business it has its ups, and it has its downs. Current economic conditions did not affect business cash flow but something else did - the competition.

Lately, the heat was coming from the Russians, these guys who had strong backing from people within their own government. That was a laugh, they get help from their government, while Sammy's government jeopardized every move he made. And then there were the Mexican cartels. The more they were squeezed south of the border, the more they looked for fresh areas to move into, and they announced their arrival very violently. Not a major concern; others had tried before. It simply took more resources, time and money to fend them off.

And so the plan was concocted. It would be big and bold, just the sort of scheme to inject money and respect back into his organization. And so here he was at the office, just waiting. He looked out the window and noticed the onset of a soft snowfall. He smiled to himself. An added bonus, he would take it. The call came and Little Sammy calmly picked up the receiver. The phone whose number only one person knew. As a cut-out man, the man on the other end of the line had no idea who he was talking to or what he was saying. He was simply told to relay a message, then to forget the conversation and the number. Warning received.

Sammy just sat and listened.

The voice on the other end of the line said, "I have news."

Little Sammy said nothing. The other man continued.

"At the beach they found the *pebble* and collected newspapers but left some litter behind. Need you to check something. Initials *D.O.D.* and the name *Hammerhead*. Now heading to *Aunt Carroll's*."

Little Sammy hung up the phone.

He put on his reading glasses, wrote the words down, then picked up another phone as his coffee was placed on the desk and he made a call.

Chapter Twenty-Four

FBI Headquarters - Los Angeles, California

December - Monday

Admiral Everett Sheppard Alcott stood tall at six feet seven inches, and cut an extremely refined figure in his uniform, considering his sixty-four years. He had white hair cut short and neat; bright blue eyes and a distinguished thin moustache that suited his persona. He was a career Navy man. He was proportionately built, not overweight, not lean but trim, and he carried himself like the Southern gentleman he seemed to be. There was no hint of a Southern drawl that would be associated with his hometown of Savannah, Georgia. The Navy life drummed it out of him, but all his mannerisms were slow and thought-provoking, which was a masterful thing to control in these trying times. Even his slight outburst upon meeting John Brozski was not one of panic, but a literal observation. He was however, accompanied by a man unlike himself.

His name was Jock Madsen. A former military man, he had retired after twenty years of active service. He spent the last few of those years at the Pentagon rubbing shoulders with the decision makers. But he wanted other things. He left the Navy wearing his uniform but stepped back onto the playing field within two short months, through the same revolving door many others before him had used. He returned to his old stomping ground wearing expensive suits, polished smiles and deep tans. Cosmetic surgery was certainly involved. Clearly a man driven by new goals, the sweet sound of the cash register ringing appealed to him greatly. By his current track record, Jock showed he excelled at his second career in life. He was far better at it than he was at serving his country. The Admiral knew this, but unfortunately, this man represented the product and he was stuck with him.

When they were situated in John Brozski's conference room Admiral Alcott began. "We are all very busy men Mr. Brozski, so I will come straight to the point."

John was curious. He had no idea why the man from the Navy wanted this meeting, but he sensed something big coming.

"You are one of many scheduled appointments for the day. We have met with the intelligence organizations within our own department and those of the other military branches. We have also met with the CIA. We come to officially inform you of "material" we are seeking, and because your office is heading the investigation into the bank robbery that took place at American Trust."

"I guess I don't follow you, Admiral. Did the Navy have something in the bank?" John asked.

"Not officially," the Admiral said after a brief pause. But he had already swallowed this bitter pill many times today and he went on.

"Let me tell you about our circumstances. The fact of the matter is, Naval property, which should not have been in that bank, has now been lost, and the Navy, moreover your country, Mr. Brozski, requires it back."

"Can you give me some background information, Admiral?" asked John, now becoming frustrated at these cryptic clues. John thought, *If it was private property belonging to this other guy's company* (he was now looking at Jock) *and he was sending in the Navy in to grease the wheels, well, then, they were*

at the bottom of the list, and they were also now just wasting his time.

"Certainly, Mr. Brozski, we owe you that much for your cooperation," the Admiral said. "I should like to make formal introductions at this time. I have brought with me today, Mr. Jock Madsen, representative of a military contractor we engage in business. Mr. Madsen is with a company called EP.M.VI."

"Pleased to meet you," Jock said in a strong confident voice with a smile that was just a little too wide to be genuine. As he extended his hand, John felt for certain, even now, this man was trying to sell something. He accepted a very firm handshake and John returned the firm grip in kind. Beneath the veneer Jock winced just a little. John smiled.

The admiral went on, "Mr. Madsen's company developed a new class of submarine for the Navy, and their timing is fortuitous. It is beyond the development stage and is in production. At the time of awarding the contract several years ago, there was no clear directive as to what we could do with this submarine. The Navy was already producing the Virginia class subs, but we had money left in our budget, Mr. Brozski, and as you know, you don't give money back. You never know when you will see it again, not to mention a reduced budget for the following year. Apparently, as the thinking goes with government, if you can't spend it, you don't need it." His mouth felt parched and he stopped talking to take a drink of water from the glass that was on the table in front of him. He drew on it slowly.

He continued, "Then a new party was elected into office. A change in direction of public policy. It happens all the time. Sometimes we are halfway through research and development of projects and new directives shelve certain projects, some good and showing potential, and some not so good… wasting our time, to be honest. They bleed our budgets dry and just waste taxpayers' money. All these are scrubbed, and we get to start all over again with the newest flavor of the month. In this particular instance, the government was closing down the Eastern European defensive missile shield against Russia and shifting focus to the implied threats from the Middle East - Iran, quite frankly. The shield in Eastern Europe did not involve the United States Navy, Mr. Brozski, but the new positioning of missiles against future threats places us squarely in the middle of the action." At this time Admiral Alcott turned to Madsen and indicated he should continue the oral dissertation.

"The timing could not have been more perfect for *Hammerhead* to play the role for which it was designed."

John had the awful feeling he was about to hear a well-rehearsed sales pitch about this guy's sardine can.

Madsen enthusiastically continued, "You see, John, *Hammerhead* is the name of our boat. Our concept was developed based on the research that clearly shows the limitations of human endurance and the high levels of fatigue that men and women display while spending prolonged periods underwater." Madsen clearly enjoyed the spotlight, despite the situation. John had no time for this guy.

Madsen went on, "*Hammerhead* closely mimics the Predator unmanned drones that were successful operating over Iraq, Afghanistan, Pakistan, and other areas of interest. We have designed a submarine, smaller in size than conventional subs, at a fraction of the cost, and they roam the seas, undetected of course, for extended periods of time. The *Hammerhead* is capable of firing on targets in the water as well as having nuclear attack capabilities. It is operated remotely from bases anywhere in the world."

"So why *Hammerhead*?" John asked.

"Some key features of the *Hammerhead*," Madsen continued, "well, firstly, its offensive fire power lends to its name. Secondly, the tip of its bow flares out due to multiple cameras embedded on either side. It is designed this way to allow for unobstructed views, and so it closely resembles the look of its namesake. It also has cameras mounted in its stern. The same design. With full rotation, the cameras can capture unobstructed views of everything around it. And third, uniquely it can literally be cradled in the underbelly of our ships. Existing ships can be retrofitted, and new ships are being designed with a bay door that acts as a cargo hold for the *Hammerhead*. They can be launched and retrieved from any place, at anytime, anywhere. This meshes well for the current purposes of our government concerning …. combative states of interest. "

"Well, that sounds interesting," John said, trying vainly to show concern, but his thoughts continually strayed to his problems with the bank heist. "So, how can I help you gentlemen?"

"*Hammerhead*, Mr. Brozski, has been stolen. *Hammerhead* was in that bank vault." Admiral Alcott said with conviction.

"I'm sorry," John said, "what part of the sub was in the bank, admiral?"

Alcott answered, "All of it, sir! Turn-key plans including schematics, construction designs, electronics, weapons systems, lists of names of global suppliers, everything down to the size and grade of bolts used to build and launch this vessel, including its potential flaws that we are working on, these were on flash drives held inside that bank vault at American Trust. This vessel can be built and set loose against us from the information contained in documents taken from that bank."

"Why would it be there?" John asked incredulously.

"Why, I take full responsibility," Admiral Alcott said. John noticed as the admiral made this statement Madsen had looked away. No partnering of blame was to be volunteered from over there.

"We were conducting sea trials and everything went extremely well. This vessel will be a fine asset to the Navy's fleet. Unfortunately we ran out of time on Friday to perform all her tasks. I have a sister living here in Los Angeles, Mr. Brozski, and I proposed that we continue with the demonstrations and conduct further meetings at EP.M.VI's offices here in Los Angeles on Monday. That gave me the opportunity to stay the weekend and visit. Mr. Madsen here offered his company's protection in what we all assumed would be the very best of secure premises. We were, however, mistaken."

"Surely the flash drives contain encrypted data?" John asked.

"Yes, but when the best computer hackers in the world come from outside the United States…" Admiral Alcott paused. "Well, you can imagine, I'm sure, that we have very grave concerns. I am here mostly as a matter of courtesy to you and your Department, Mr. Brozski, given that you are leading the robbery investigation. The official paperwork is coming through the appropriate channels. But you need to know, this incident has National Security implications and you will be reporting all your fact-finding information to the CIA. This is a directive from the White House as you will soon see."

"What am I supposed to do when we catch the people who took this?" John asked, now feeling his authority slipping away.

"If, and we pray that changes to a *when* you catch up with the professionals who have stolen this information from our country, your orders are to retrieve the flash drives at all costs, and failing in your attempts to do that, the information regarding *Hammerhead* must be destroyed." This statement was delivered categorically from the Admiral.

"Can you help me out with who you think could have done this?" John asked.

"There are lots of choices, Mr. Brozski," said the Admiral. "Russia is of course is a prime suspect, then there are the North Koreans. They would be jubilant to have this, to both embarrass the United States, and to demonstrate with sheer terror their newfound ability to roam the seas undetected. Honestly, Mr. Brozski, it is quite a long list."

Madsen interjected, "The thing is, John, we don't think we were the target of the heist. This raid had to be planned well in advance. We made an eleventh hour decision to place the flash drives in the vault. It's possible that whoever has this does not even know what they possess."

Smartest thing he said all day, John thought.

"OK, then," John said, standing up to conclude this meeting, *(what a helluva day!)* "The Navy's property becomes the focus of our concerns."

"That's encouraging to hear," said the Admiral as he gave John a polite smile and shook his hand warmly.

John sincerely asked the Admiral, "But what of you in all of this, sir?"

"My situation is untenable, and I can say with the thoughts of my country first, my longstanding career in the Navy, which I truly love, is perishable, Mr. Brozski. Once we see our way clear beyond this incident, I shall be resigning my commission. As I said earlier, the data was entrusted to my care; my responsibility, my blame. Good day to you, sir, and the very best of luck."

Chapter Twenty-Five

Laguna Beach, California.

December - Monday - 3:54 p.m.

Kip swung his car into the driveway and eased into the garage. He wouldn't stay long, only long enough to explain to Mette he was needed in New York, pack a few things in an overnight and then catch his flight.

Kip's family home faced westward overlooking the beach and endless ocean views. The design was contemporary with European touches; a home that underscored modest flair and yet was not pretentious, just the way Mette loved it. The house sat on two generous parcels of land, and all 8,000 square feet were washed in white to keep it cool in the summer, comfortable within the other seasons. Numerous windows allowed natural light to filter in and although it was a maintenance feat to keep clear panes of glass sea mist free, it was a small price to pay for the returns. The entire property was open and inviting and they would not dare live anywhere else.

Kip's accumulated wealth was earned the old fashion way, he inherited it. Previous generations honed natural talents and practiced savvy business skills in banking, investing and insurance. The vast fortunes were always looked upon as a beneficent burden and never taken for granted. The counter-weight to this enormously gifted lifestyle was a strong calling for courage in the face of danger, a clawing sense of responsibility that kept knocking on the collective consciousness of the clan throughout the generations. An unexplained trait inherited, just like the blood coursing through their collective veins, showed itself in the form of dedicated service to their country. Security and protection, never politics. The latter ideal having a self-interest that they tended to avoid; the belief was and still is, politicians have blurred vision for the way forward, with the initial right thing to do lost amongst the way it had to travel to be accomplished. The swimming hole was too murky to tread water in. Their way was straight and true, the intent clear, and the objective always the same. It also took a strong dose of personal willingness and sacrifice. Something people in politics had in short supply; there were never enough politicians in the front lines taking the fight to the fight, but rather conducting the orchestra from the safety of the rear.

Their charitable involvement was large and generous as well; funds established early in the pioneering days had the family helping the less fortunate. Not unlike other families in the nineteenth century who through their endowments are still funding projects today. Even Benjamin Franklin had the foresight to leave two trust funds in two different cities, Boston and Philadelphia, each with two hundred year curfews. At the end of their durations, while providing numerous donations by way of grants and loans, the funds had accumulated millions of dollars two hundred years after they were founded. So Kip, with the help of his banking brother, navigated the family resources wisely and avoided the usual pitfalls of trying to make a fast buck, but rather stuck to sound trusted principles. It worked extremely well.

He entered the house and found his wife Mette peeking through the plantation blinds that dressed the window. He was profiling her, wearing a slim fit white t-shirt, dark blue cut-off denims and polished toes as she wore no shoes. He watched as wisps of hair broke loose from behind her ear that she tried to contain, but her long blonde strands were having none of it. Shafts of late afternoon light bathed her in a golden glow and as he stood still and enjoyed the moment he understood again, not for the first time, from her unassuming pose and chiseled features he was held gazing upon her poetic symmetry. Mette had that rare balance of strength and beauty. She was poised between … athletic agility and grace. Yes, he smiled to himself, that's my girl.

Mette. They had found each other more than thirteen years ago in Washington D.C. He was attending a function at the Swedish Embassy. Being a newly fledged member of the FBI it was an after-hours and off-duty business function he was attending. Dragged along by his brother, rumor had it that there was some Swedish ancestry in the family, or someone had visited Sweden once. Whatever the pretense he moseyed along, and besides, he did note a few people he would know at the function. Kip was engaged in small talk, very small talk that is, for ten minutes or so with the crowd when he noticed her. She was tall and noticeable at six feet. Blonde hair cascaded down her back and continued to tumble over a stunning black cocktail dress. It was appointed and elegant. She turned his way and he was staring into eyes as green and tranquil as the calm waters surrounding a tropical paradise. They were warm and inviting, bathed in a gentleness that kept away the cursing storms and welcomed you in.

A smile always danced within those eyes and it was hard to look away. There was more to Mette, but her eyes kept his attention. Then she smiled at him and raised her glass and he returned the honor. That was his cue and so he crossed the distance between them through the throng of guests and they each made introductions.

Her name, Mette Eymunsson. She was working at the Embassy as an assistant to the Cultural Attaché Counselor. Her background was in Fine Arts and she had been at the Embassy for only three weeks.

When asked by family, friends and colleagues about her name in the days, weeks and months to come, he would smile and answer this way, "I called my girlfriend up and *Met-her* for a drink!"

They spent way too much time together that first night. She was quietly reprimanded by her superior and told to mingle with more than just one handsome American man, and he had to be pulled away by his brother. He left under protest but managed to successfully obtain a cell phone number. Both had trouble sleeping that night.

As soon as it was possible for her to take an extended leave, they spent even more time together, then again and again and again. Five months after first laying eyes on each other they were married. Three children later, they had no regrets. The only sad note came in their desire to have a rabbit warren full of children. With the news of her fourth pregnancy they were thrilled, but Mette suffered complications after seven months. She developed what she thought were severe stomach cramps, but somehow knew there was more to the problem and the baby … the baby was in trouble. And so with the pain came the blood and she was rushed to the hospital.

After suffering in surgery for fourteen agonizing hours and cresting in critical condition, she lost their baby and felt terribly alone. She would later reflect on the memories many times over and mourn silently as to the painfully short period of time spent with her newborn son. The pain was accentuated by the fact that Kip was on assignment on the other side of the world and unable to make it her bedside when she most needed him for comfort and support. Mette was weak, the trauma was great. She underwent a number of surgeries and recovery would take time.

With Kip by her side and Mette, as they could best determine, being within an acceptable state of stable health and of sound mind, they were sat down and told, that for her, the birth of a child was no longer possible. It was a painful reminder of how fragile life was. The event had taken its toll on Mette. The appointed room for the newest member of their family and the smell of newly purchased baby clothes suffocated her in that room. She wept openly into Kip's shoulder. Attending the funeral only added to her sorrow. The day was cold and everything was wet. All Mette could remember were muddy footprints that surrounded the tiny grave as the baby boy was laid to rest. She could not bring herself to look up, instead just staring at the ground. The day's events still remained hazy for her, and all she could recall were the adult size shoe prints left in the mud, and forever knowing that her child would never fill those shoes. She held those thoughts privately.

Mette suffered through post-partum depression. Kip would be there to help, but like anyone not entirely feeling the pain, there was only so much he could do. It would take all of eleven months of mourning and reassuring counseling to help her recover from the loss. Until then the child's bedroom had been left exactly how it was. It became more like a shrine than a bedroom. The support groups helped but with Kip's demanding work schedule Mette often felt alone; this added weight and pressure to her day-to-day life and raising three still small children, a lot of the time on her own. It kept the pain in place.

And then, it just happened. Early one morning, Mette rose from her bed, a smile across her face; she almost skipped along and out her bedroom. She went to each of her children's rooms and woke them with a kiss on the cheek. Then she walked into the empty bedroom and over to the large windows, flinging aside the curtains to allow the light to shine in. The windows were opened so that fresh ocean-scented air and fragrant aromas could waft in and fill the room; the same air that had been held at bay all these months. She busied herself giving the room a blank slate and starting again. Her pain was by no means gone, but she had turned a corner and now she wanted to be there for her entire family.

Kip saw the change, encouraged her along, but it would be almost another two years before he would come to his decision to leave the CIA.

Now some men who have the *gift* of getting woman, find that upon the victory of conquest, they are already looking towards the next challenge. Kip knew these men and they were, if truly honest with themselves, unhappy and empty in the lives they led more times than not, despite all the notches in their belt. Turning out the lights alone at night is not all it's cracked up to be. He was lucky. They kissed often and it still felt as good as it had the very first time. Fresh, sweet, warm, loving. There was no one else for him. When he already had the best, why search for anything else? He was completely happy with his lot in life and he had no problem with that at all.

Mette now sensed Kip in the room. She turned towards him, the afternoon light catching the color in her eyes; they sparkled and she smiled.

"Anything wrong?" he asked as he walked across to her and kissed her gently on the lips.

"Oh … no," she seemed to half-sing in her accent, "Just looking at the children down on the beach." She enjoyed the kiss and kissed him back.

"John has asked me to join his team on assignment for an important and perplexing case. I told him we need to talk it over first."

"Any details you can tell me about?"

"A few. American Trust in Los Angeles was robbed sometime after closing on Friday. There's little to go on but what I do know is a great number of important people are anxious to have it solved and their belongings returned."

"Ja," she said slipping into Swedish affirmative. "I heard of it on the radio today."

"John wants me to fly to New York, tonight," Kip told her. "It's got a lot of people worried. I've been asked to assist in gathering some background information from victims out there, see if it's helpful. That's apparently where this all started."

Mette listened with interest. Kip wasn't sure if she was convinced whether he should be working on this or not, but he needed her full support to be comfortable with leaving. He placed his hands on her shoulders. "Look, if all goes well and there is absolutely no reason why it shouldn't, I will be back tomorrow night." He softly touched her forehead with his own. "It will be OK. I need your blessing on this."

Mette shook her head in the affirmative and blinked a few times. "OK," she said softly.

Kip lovingly squeezed her shoulders and smiled, then reached for a fresh red apple in the fruit bowl, tossed it in the air, caught it, and took a bite. He started down the hall to their bedroom.

"Why does John want you involved?" Mette asked, following him while occasionally peeking out a passing window to check on the children playing on the sand.

"Not really sure," Kip answered truthfully. "Perhaps a different perspective, ideas outside the box, maybe? In any case, it's very interesting. I would be happy to lend a hand and help in any way." He was rifling through his drawers and closets, grabbing things and throwing them into an overnight bag.

Mette placed a gentle hand on his arm. "Why don't you go down and say goodbye to the children and I will finish packing for you."

Kip looked at her sideways. "Right," he said. "Thanks for your understanding," and he kissed her again. "I'll make this up to you when I get back."

"I know you will," she said as she wryly smiled at him while placing underwear in the bag.

He smiled back. He got the message. He went down to kiss his kids goodbye.

Chapter Twenty-Six

Los Angeles International Airport, California

December - Monday – 8:22 p.m.

It is big and busy, an airport with flights coming and going from all over the world. Parked over in a discreet section of the airport, far away and hidden from the public and prying eyes, the FBI hangars support a fleet of fixed and rotary-wing aircraft that are at their disposal 24/7. There is a simple enough reason why the FBI is stationed there - Los Angeles is a mess to get around. Simple. Los Angeles International Airport, or LAX as it is known to all, is close by the FBI Headquarters on Wilshire Boulevard. Their guise is maintained under the security blanket of the U.S. Coast Guard Air Station, located west of the Tom Bradley International Terminal.

The military work hard at keeping the FBI out of their limited space at Los Alamitos Joint Forces Training Base in Orange County. This base is just to the south of LAX and closer to FBI headquarters than Edwards AFB, but they give no ground to outsiders in keeping what is theirs, and the FBI is not on the invitation list. Santa Monica Municipal Airport is a smaller, auxiliary airfield but closer still. Unfortunately for the FBI, with restricted flight times and curfews, due to imposing noise on the surrounding civilian population, it is ruled out.

So for safety's sake, Kip buckled into the comfortable leather- wrapped oversized chair, onboard the G-V Gulfstream Company jet at LAX. While traveling on business for the FBI, he had exchanged one suit for another. This one's color was black. He wore his suit with a pinpoint fine white cotton Oxford shirt and a pale blue silk tie. The plane received permission for clearance from the tower and after takeoff they quickly navigated a course of east by northeast and settled into their cruising altitude. Kip was perusing the notes on his tablet screen and bringing himself up to speed on the entire case. Included were the up-to-the-minute reports coming in that told him Lynette Walker had reappeared.

More information on this was to follow. John Brozski had also sent him the minutes on the conversation he had with Admiral Alcott and a file on *Hammerhead*, stating its new priority in this mission. The stakes kept getting raised. Was there anything else that could be thrown into the mix? A lot of information was swirling around but very little of it was useful enough to provide solid leads. A lot of theories were extrapolated, but again, with little to go on, the experts were throwing darts at a board while the lights were turned off. They had a kidnapped wife whose distraught banker husband had not given up the information the extortionists were looking for, a perfect entry into a theft- proof vault, and a vault only half-looted. That last mystery was one to ponder.

Why did they only ransack half the safety deposit boxes?

Was it the fact they knew what they were after and where it would be?

Was it they could only carry so much?

Or was it they ran out of time in what they were doing?

He noticed something else in the report that was curious. He entered his thoughts into his notes and made a mental note to follow up later.

He rubbed his straining eyes and stretched long and hard. His tie had been loosened long ago. He had been poring over documents for well over three hours. Inside, the cabin hummed with a constant whir, the sound emanating from the cylindrical vessel's vents allowing stable cabin pressure and the even airflow moving within. He peered out the window at the night sky.

Dark. Silent. Cold. Endless.

It was the deepest midnight blue sprinkled with thousands of tiny twinkles seen clearly from the luxury of an uninterrupted view at 30,000 feet. A rich dark-colored parachute canopy opened to its full arc, covering everything. He had a flashback and it brought a smile to his face. He and his family were enjoying Chinese food just the week before, and he snapped open a fortune cookie as did everyone and they each shared their fortunes. He's claimed, *you will soon be on top of the world!* Well, he couldn't argue with that!

The plane landed in New York four hours and sixteen minutes after takeoff. The Bureau had a car waiting, motor running, on the tarmac beside the plane. He went through the exit hatch and momentarily stood at the top of the stairs to draw in a breath of cold December night air. He nestled deeper into his thick wool coat as the soft snow swirled all around, floating down lighter than a feather to land in his hair and on his clothes. He had forgotten how cold New York could be in the winter, but with the aid of the chilled wind he quickly remembered. It was still snowing, not letting up for even a minute since late that afternoon. He carefully made his way down to the tarmac.

Waiting for him with the standard dark shaded car were two agents. Special Agent Sameer Chowdhury greeted Kip outside the vehicle, while Special Agent Bob Gannich remained behind the wheel of the vehicle. Both men climbed in and they drove away leaving Kip alone in the back seat. Kip studied the men in front of him. Gannich was clearly the lead agent and doing most of the talking. He was over forty, closer to fifty, Kip thought; a man who the agency showed leniency towards by generously allowing quite a few extra pounds to hang around. He was over two hundred pounds and by no means was all of it muscle; his thick hair was ashen grey at the temples and his fattened fingers gripped the steering wheel as if preventing someone from taking it away from him. It seemed to Kip a bad driving technique in these slippery conditions. His many comments also acknowledged he was not shy about coming forward with his opinions.

His partner Sameer was under thirty, Kip guessed about twenty-eight. His complexion was silky and rich tanned leather, which hinted towards his heritage. Both his first and surname were clearly Indian. Kip measured him up at five foot nine, and easily deduced that Sameer was a more polished FBI agent than his senior partner. His academy training was evident; Kip noticed he was observing, not just seeing; listening, not just hearing. He was a credit to the organization and someone keen on doing his duty to the best of his abilities.

"So, Sameer …" Kip started…

"Call him Sam!" Gannich interjected, staring at Kip through the rear view mirror.

"Yeah, Sam's good," Sameer said, half-turning in his seat. "Sam is fine with me."

"So, Sam," Kip went on, "are you from the Midwest?"

"Indianapolis, Indiana. I'm third generation American," he responded proudly.

Kip wasn't sure if this was said to reassure everyone in the car that he was indeed "American" enough, but it seemed to Kip that both his accent and disposition represented three generations of the Midwest.

"My father is a chemical engineer back home, and my mother is an oncologist. But I wanted action and to serve my country. I always have," Sam said matter-of-factly.

"I love the way I can use my badge to get to the front of any line," Bob chimed in.

Kip looked to steer the conversation back to the task at hand.

"I understand Mrs. Walker has been found ... alive?"

"That's right. Flagged down a motorist on a country road about fifteen miles from her house," Gannich said. He continued, "She is suffering from shock, some dehydration, hypothermia and exhaustion; also a small contusion to the back of her head, but overall she is going to be fine. She also said she had been drugged. The doctors are running tests to establish what she was given and if we can make anything out of it. I've made arrangements with the hospital to see her early tomorrow morning to see if we can learn anything from her directly."

"What about the place where she was found?" asked Kip.

"We have a few of problems there," said Gannich, still leading the conversation. "First, she moved from the site where she was dumped so we don't have a proper fix on that exact location. So scouring the area for clues will be difficult. We don't know where to start! Second, these guys were either very clever or lucky; it started snowing just after she was found. By the time the authorities were contacted, the entire area was blanketed with snow and it's still snowing, as you can see. And from what little we've gathered so far, they dropped her near the side of a sealed road, probably carried her in as far as they needed to. So the likelihood of finding fresh tire tracks in the dirt is slim. These guys were smart; they knew the ground was firm because of the cold; so more than likely no shoe prints either. That's if we even know where to look, and we don't. So we're coming up with zip."

Bob changed subjects and continued, "I've nearly got you at your hotel. We'll pick you up in the morning at -"

"No, let's head to the office, I need to keep working on this puzzle," Kip said.

"What?" Gannich exclaimed. "So why are you involved anyway?" He said bluntly, "I mean, you're not even official!"

"Well," Kip said cautiously, trying not to upset the locals, "I am official, as you put it, I'm just not an FBI agent anymore. I'm involved in cases from time to time to perhaps offer a different perspective."

It was true. He provided input into a number of cases after leaving the service. He spent five years with the Bureau before sliding across to the CIA because they wanted him. Understanding there was no love lost between the two agencies in these constant tug-of-war of assets, it was also a request of Kip's. His request helped maintain peace between the two factions in this instance. He spent five fruitful years with the CIA, successfully closing two dozen or so critical assignments. But ultimately, the time away from his family proved to be too much and he headed for the door. On hearing of his departure, both the FBI and CIA wanted the right to call on him if they required his assistance. That was their way of extending an open invitation to Kip, so he stipulated that it would be conditional on his acceptance of acting as a consultant on a case-by-case basis. It was agreed.

Kip had a good read on the type of agent Bob Gannich was. A career man with the Bureau, just not a soaring career. A tenured agent who had become accustomed to acting as the opinionated driver and chief tour guide for others.

Gannich exhaled loudly and with a, "Huh … whatever." He indifferently turned the next corner and made his way back to the Bureau office.

Chapter Twenty-Seven

Paxton – New York

December - Tuesday – 8:45 a.m.

Paxton, New York is located in the northeast corner of the state pressed up hard against Connecticut. Cam didn't make quite enough to take on one of the estates over the border, but he came close. So for him, close enough was good enough. He commuted to and from work on the express trains most days.

It was 8:45 a.m. the next morning when the two Special Agents and Kip arrived outside Lynette Walker's hospital door. This was as early as the doctors would allow them to see her. Her rest was paramount, the doctors had told them. A uniformed officer from the local police force was on guard at the door and he checked their credentials. A prolonged inspection of their identifications told him what he needed to know; he then looked up and nodded his approval with the confidence that his newly empowered authority brought him over everyone entering the room. He turned and tapped the door with a few short raps of his knuckles. The room had that typical hospital welcome. Sterile and overwhelming antiseptic smells hit their nostrils from the all too familiar environment. The room had only one wide rectangular window, with a heavy navy blue curtain drawn across it to keep out the dull morning sun. The dreary light still managed to slip beyond the curtain's corners and spill into the room. A sheet rocked half-wall ran continuous below the window; it had a wide ledge that was well suited for the placement of flower vases, candy boxes or coffee cups - the convenient *lay your stuff somewhere*

spot for visiting friends and relatives. The air conditioning grill
also made use of the wall, whirring and breathing temperate air
into the room. The room itself was painted in the unforgivable
expression, hospital white, with flowing waved lines of aqua green
and blue on all four walls, clearly designed to cheer the place up.
But the décor did not strike the right chord in the cold wintery
setting, hence another paid for idea gone wrong.

Outside large, heavy snowflakes that had fallen from the
sky continuously for over sixteen hours were now tapering off.
Waiting for them beside the bed of his resting wife was Cam
Walker. Cam did not look good. In fact, his wife, with all she had
been through, looked in better shape at that particular moment. He
obviously had suffered through much anguish and distress, and he
was not taking it all that well. The disheveled business clothes on
his back appeared to Kip to be last Friday's attire, still in use. His
shirt hung down over his pants and it was deeply wrinkled, the
sleeves rolled up haphazardly to the elbows. He was not wearing a
tie and his top two buttons were loosened. Lynette Walker was still
dozing and they quietly made introductions. Badges were flashed
and condolences given.

"So, Mr. Walker," Bob asked happily, "You got a brother
named Johnnie?"

Everyone awake in the room turned incredulously to Bob.
Cam's stare was ruthless.

"Sorry," Bob murmured sheepishly, "I was trying to break
the tension."

At that moment Lynette started to rouse. They waited for a
few moments longer while she fully wakened. Cam poured her tea,
and she felt embarrassed at having three strangers in her room
while just her hospital gown, sheet and blanket were all that was

between them. Once again she felt vulnerable, so she raised the bed covers and pressed them up under her chin. They spent about thirty minutes with Lynette, trying to slowly go over what had taken place. She could offer very little information. No faces. No voices. No destination. Maybe there were three of them, could have been more. She could not even guess as to heights, weights, hair color, etcetera.

Lynette was tiring from all the questions. She reached out with an extended arm and gestured for Cam to hold it. He solemnly received it with both hands then leaned over and kissed her hand, then her forehead. She gazed at her husband, a pleading request in her eyes to end this session and remove these men from the room. This was the third time recounting the terrible events; it was getting to be too much. They thanked her and asked if they could borrow her husband for a few minutes more out in the hall in order to allow her to rest some more. The nurse stepped in and read her vital signs as the men left the room.

Once outside Cam appeared a little more composed. They asked him to go over the events of Friday afternoon once more and walk them through everything, in his own words. He did so slowly, methodically, leaving nothing out, mentioning that all conversations on his office phone as well as everything on his computers were copied and recorded, company policy, and they could review the transcripts. More questions were asked, but he could not add much to the mystery.

Kip asked, "So why didn't you give them the code, Mr. Walker?"

"I've been over this already," he said with a degree of frustration.

"Just once more, please."

"OK," Cam blew out a breath. "I was thinking of my wife the whole time, you understand."

The three men nodded their heads almost simultaneously.

He went on, "But I just couldn't bring myself to betray the bank. I just couldn't do it."

"Weren't you afraid for your wife's safety if you didn't go through with their demands?" Kip asked, thinking about his own wife.

"Of course I did!" he almost spat out the words. "Look at me, I'm a wreck; but the bank is all I've known, it's my livelihood. I just couldn't. I just couldn't," he repeated the words over and over again as they trailed off into a murmur. He had already despondently dropped his head as he was saying the words.

Cam looked up quickly, "Please don't tell my wife this!" he pleaded.

Bob patted Cam on the shoulder. "Your secret is safe with us." He stated it in a way that clearly said, *yeah, it's good for now but don't give us a reason to tell your wife.*

"Another question," Kip went on, "Where have you been since Friday? I mean, you walked out of your office Friday afternoon and it was only yesterday that you contacted the police about your wife."

"I went home, I poured myself plenty of strong drinks; I paced up and down my living room floor for a couple of days. I had a stranglehold on the phone, hoping they would call, I dialed 9..1.. a thousand times, but couldn't bring myself to complete the call. I have not eaten and I've had about two hours' sleep in the last three days."

It was a run-on collection of statements. It seemed like he really wanted to blurt it out and get it off his chest. He was spent.

"You may return to your wife now, Mr. Walker," Kip quietly told him.

Cam turned and was about to push the door open when Kip caught him with a final question. "Oh, one last thing Cam."

Cam stopped and turned to face Kip.

"Could we get your office and home numbers in case we need anything else?"

"Ah, yeah … sure." Cam paused for a moment or two, rubbing his left eye with the joint of his index finger before saying, "I'll just have my secretary send those to you."

Kip smiled and said, "That would be great." as he let his hands drop to his sides. His right hand with the pen that was poised to write down the numbers and the small notepad ready to receive the information in the other were left wonting.

Kip turned to the two agents, "I don't think there is anything more here."

Bob said, "Great! I could do with a drink!"

"Coffee would be great," Kip said.

"I was thinking of something stronger?" Bob suggested.

"It's 9:30 in the morning!" Sam told him.

Bob just shrugged his shoulders and responded, "It's beer o'clock somewhere!"

His colleagues had nothing to say.

"No…? OK, then, let's grab that coffee," Bob said and started walking towards the exit.

They entered one of those ubiquitous coffee houses, the ones with the latest contemporary music playing like *Muzak* in the background. The music that will become *Muzak* in a few short years. Kip took in the pungent, heady aromas of the coffee beans and it was a pleasant substitution for his olfactory sense after the hospital visit. The sense of smell is a powerful thing - out of the five senses humans possess, it is the one with the greatest recall of memory. More's the pity for those who work in such environments as hospitals, coffee shops or florists every day and eventually lose the ability to continue enjoying the smells and aromas as they once did. This was actually a common complaint from people who work with roses.

They stood at the end of the long line of people waiting to order. Kip took the moment to survey the establishment. Yep, it seemed to be populated with the standard fare of customers. Sets of two chatty women at a table, both young and old, huddled close together in rapid-fire conversations. A collection of the younger, loner crowd, spread throughout in well-placed locations by themselves, but not alone. They usually managed to grab the select few lounge chairs. Hooked into all sorts of the latest gadgets, wires in ears, cell phones against the side of a head, texting wildly with their thumbs to persons unknown, tapping keyboards filling in empty spaces on their laptop screens. He noticed not so many of the very elderly visited these places as often. They would be comfortably seated, with their ninety- nine cent cups of coffee with bottomless refills, at the place they had been visiting for most of their lives - if the place still existed, that is. It was also the place where they would find most of their friends and talk to them – face to face.

He continued searching until he spotted the person he knew would be there, he or she always was. And so he was. What was he this time? Insurance recruiter? Maybe the financial planner? A pyramid scheme enterprise representative? Get the latest recruit in on the next big thing. Always a possibility.

He could imagine the introduction line: *Thanks for coming down, let me buy you that cup of coffee, you like the house blend, don't you? Let me tell you how I can make you wealthy beyond your dreams with a couple of easy steps in a just few short years!*

It didn't matter who it was. But there always seemed to be one of them here, welcoming a new recruit. Swank coffee houses appeared to be their new satellite offices.

They crept along and came to the place where orders are taken and with both hands firmly placed in the pockets of his pants, Bob announced he needed a triple espresso, large, or however you say it. Kip ordered a strong Colombian brew and Sam ordered herbal tea. Bob walked away to the other end of the counter to collect his coffee. Sam and Kip looked at each other, Kip said, "I've got this one."

He also ordered some bakery items, handed over the cash including the tip to a perky assistant and joined Bob and Sam at the other end.

"Thanks for picking this up," Sam said. He said this within earshot of Bob, who clearly heard it but chose to ignore the comment.

They grabbed their paper cups with steaming hot liquids inside, placed cardboard protective holders around them, distributed the pastries amongst themselves and moved on.

On the sidewalk making their way back to the car and sipping coffee, Kip said, "Let's get back to the office, I understand we have a major meeting with the station chief to try and make some sense of what we have and where we go from here."

Bob grunted and wrestled in behind the wheel with the other two sliding into the backseat. They made their way down I-95 and eventually into the thick of the traffic. Slowly they weaved through the downtown Manhattan gridlock to Twenty Six Federal Plaza, New York City. The FBI field office headquarters in New York is located between Duane and Worth just south of Canal Street. They were headed for the twenty-fourth floor.

Chapter Twenty-Eight

New York City, New York

December - Tuesday - Noon

Twenty-eight ergonomically designed basic black Herman Miller Aeron chairs were gathered around an enormous rectangular conference table, absorbing the collective weight of bodies ready for a tense session. The table itself was so large, so solid and heavy it was custom-built onsite. Its light textured desert ironwood surface was inlayed with three bands of boxwood along its edges. More chairs and people populated areas beyond the main table, and more people yet again managed standing room only. It was a lively place, with lots of heavy hitters involved. The count came to seventy- six important men and women in a room that was close to the size of a small banquet hall. The room was finished in neutral pale grey tones. The textured fabric wallpaper was a few shades lighter than the grey tone patterned carpet. It was all meant to be subdued and provide the least amount of distraction possible. This was, after all, the exclusive meeting center for the New York Office of the FBI. Without exception, everyone in the room wore slightly varying shades of dark colored suits, blouses and skirts.

Kip had been in and out of the Bureau so many times after leaving his post and he had met with so many people; usually names and faces he could recall instantly. But at this gathering he recognized very few faces. People come, people go and reshuffles are common in the halls of power.

"Can I have everyone's attention, please," a voice boomed, and broke through the separate conversations going on in the room.

This was effective enough to quiet down everyone very quickly. "To bring this meeting to order we need to go around the room and have everyone identify them-selves."

The voice was deep, firm, confident and in control. It came from Acting Director of the FBI Jasper Liggot. Jasper wore wire-rim glasses in front of hazel brown eyes. The glasses were a more conservative look, not tracking with the latest fashion frames of the day, which supported a thicker, heavier design. Fashion was the least of his concerns. His dark fine hair that was fading to grey was trimmed short and neat. He always wore an expressionless face. More than likely it came with the job and the responsibilities, but one could assume he wore this look long before he landed his current position and duties. He peaked just under six feet and maintained a healthy physique. In fact, most people in the room did. It was an unspoken rule - leadership demanded a healthy body and a healthy mind. Stay strong.

Around the room they went, identifying the cast of characters and their roles. Here they were, made up from many of the sixteen members of the United States Intelligence Community (IC). The key players and their territory included:

The Director of National Intelligence (DNI) – given the role of overseeing all those involved with intelligence gathering, and the one person responsible for reporting directly to the President. He was here not so much to talk, but to listen.

Ken Maylon, Kip knew him well, Deputy Head of the Central Intelligence Agency (CIA).

The Secretary of the Navy, Jim Carmichael. Carmichael did not look happy. With him was the Head of the Office of Naval Intelligence (ONI).

The list went on to include the Deputy Secretary of Defense and the Defense Intelligence Agency (DIA)

Department of Homeland Security – Office of Intelligence and Analysis (I&A)

Department of State – Bureau of Intelligence and Research (INR)

National Security Agency (NSA)

Department of Treasury – Office of Terrorism and Financial Intelligence (TFI)

Other concerned parties at the meeting were as follows:

The Chief of Naval Operations (CNO), representing the Joint Chiefs of Staff

The Undersecretary of Defense for Intelligence (USD)(I)

The Under Secretary for Acquisition, Technology and Logistics
(USD-AT&L)

At their request, Navy was the only Military Service organization represented, with the exception of DIA. The Navy wanted to avoid the embarrassment of this incident so as not to be preyed upon by the other military branches. The Navy knew the other branches would get their shots in, so to speak, until somebody dropped the next ball; then the glaring stares barely masking the perception of incompetence would be passed to them. Right now, the Navy had no time for the snide comments and insinuations. As was standard protocol, the other intelligence organizations of the Armed Services would receive reports of the meeting at a later date. But as they all well knew, a failure would be recognized for what it was, and another strike would be chalked up against the Navy's record. No matter what the stakes, egg on your rival's face was something to be shared with everyone.

Members of the Air Force community still had a bad taste in their mouths from several incidents, including when nuclear bombers went flying off across the country with *live bombs* aboard, and yet another when fighter jets went unaccounted for days on end and nobody knew where to find them. Two high-ranking Generals with longstanding careers and large pay scales had been unceremoniously dismissed. When the gravity of the situation had settled down, the Air Force got quite the shellacking from the other services. No love lost, and there wouldn't be any this time, either.

There was also an assortment of senior level advisors, aides and meeting minute-takers and tag-alongs. The FBI itself had seven people in the room including another Special Agent from the Los Angeles Office, Ted Atherton.

Kip took a place off to the side, and with no real official capacity, he stood through the entire meeting simply taking his own notes.

There was much to debate and the going over of already trampled old ground that had been covered extensively up to this point. The reasons for this were twofold - both for bringing everyone up to speed and on the same page, and because nothing new was breaking through. There were many hypotheticals and much conjecture thrown out to consider, but no new evidence or leads; nothing of note to pursue.

Twenty minutes after introductions were made, Al Reznic from the Department of Energy - Office of Intelligence and Counterintelligence (OIC), entered the room with an aide by his side. They apologized for being late, several delays here and there were offered up, and of course New York traffic was thrown into the mix for the recipe of disasters as to why they did not appear on time. A seat was found for the leader somewhere near the main table; the aide was left standing and had to fend for himself. The interruption was out of the way and they moved on.

Acting Deputy Liggot asked for more thorough investigating from his people and to lean harder on local law enforcement for more assistance. He had trouble believing he was handling two investigations, one on each coast, and he had nothing to go on from anyone.

Questions were raised such as, *what the hell was the Admiral doing carrying around a briefcase full of classified information, anyway?*

It was answered that he and the contractor were bouncing around to multiple sites, changes in data were made and he was given updated versions for his use. He asked for, and was given security clearance for his actions before he left; it did not seem to be a breach of current security protocol. It was further pointed out that this unfortunately seemed to be a recurring problem for people who held onto classified information. There had been several instances of government employees leaving laptop computers on the front seats of locked and unlocked cars. Instances had been reported whereby laptops, containing U.S. citizen's social security numbers and credit card information, stored in the memory of the stolen laptop computer, were taken out of high security offices without a thought to security protocol and its breaches. It was situations like these that had the people in the room shaking their heads in wonder.

Then there was the embarrassing occasion that they all clearly remembered. When a Scotland Yard officer in England held classified documents under his arm while walking along Downing Street in London. He was heading for a meeting with members of the Intelligence community to discuss an up-and-coming raid to arrest suspected al-Qaeda terrorists throughout England. Unfortunately for him, information on the paperwork he carried was visible for everyone to see and could be clearly photographed by reporters – and it was - almost jeopardizing a major operation. More than one person resigned over this incident.

So it happens. Along with a few smiles from people thinking, *huh, glad it wasn't us,* many pens were picked up writing frantically and keyboards were tapped at a furious pace. All were notes and memos to expeditiously amend current procedures at all levels and by all departments.

"Has the admiral since been vetted to see if he himself was the cause of the breach?" someone asked. *Vetted,* not really being the appropriate term.

Answers from several sources all supported the fact that his record was beyond reproach. Also financial records were scoured, deeper background checks were made, and they all came back negative. From all reports he, too, was a random victim of this crime.

It was recorded that there was negligible intelligence chatter on the airwaves or through other sources that *Hammerhead* plans had been stolen. And so everyone held out for the best that in fact the robbery's target had been the money in the bank, and therefore some chance of retrieving the disks before their actual value was discovered still existed.

After hours of dialogue and everyone getting a chance to voice his or her agency's concerns, Jasper Liggot asked if anyone else had anything to add. Finally, Kip was given an opportunity to speak as he had a few questions of his own that never seemed to be addressed.

He began to speak, to no one in particular. "My name is Kip Keplar, I am attached to the FBI and working under their jurisdiction. Are we any closer to knowing when the break-in occurred?"

"What difference does it make when it happened?" boomed a voice from the other side of the room. "We need to think about getting it back first and foremost!"

"I believe it has some bearing, sir." Kip looked directly at the responder. "It can tell us how much time is between us and the perpetrators for one thing," Kip answered.

"We still do not have an answer on that, Mr. Keplar," another voice answered.

"Do we have any answers or speculations as to why only about half the vault was raided?" Kip went on.
"Again, that is time wasting with background noise and history." The same man who berated him before spoke again. "What we need are concrete leads as to where they are now. We need to apply all our energies in that direction and to zero in on that first and foremost. Let's not waste precious resources on asking how and why. Save that for the newspapers and historians if they ever get a hold of this thing."

Jasper Liggot looked over at the speaker and then tried to have a calmer voice prevail. The meeting was dragging on and nerves were beginning to fray. "Thank you, Jim, for crystallizing our path. I agree with Secretary of the Navy Carmichael about staying the course on this investigation. We can ask the "hows" and "whys" at some other time. Do you have anything else to add, Mr. Keplar?"

"Yes, sir, I do. Once again, I think knowing what they were after might point us in the right direction. They either found what they wanted or got spooked, or ran out of time for some reason. I think these are important facts to know."

Jasper Liggot wanted to finish this line of questioning and move on. "Your questions are duly noted and we shall investigate them at a later time."

Liggot started to look away and was preparing to make for another topic when Kip cut in quickly.

"I would like to know more about this vault and its security features?"

Liggot returned his attention back to Kip. He hesitated for a second with a look in his eyes as if to say, *are you still talking?* But he knew they were all on the same side here and it was a good question; everyone should know something about the vault.

Liggot looked around for one of his aides. He found him and said,
"Yes, well, I believe Mr. Riedell can best answer that question."

He gave the man a curt head nod and Riedell pushed his chair back and slid his glasses up his nose before scrolling through to the correct page on his computer screen. Then he began reading matter-of-factly, "The modern time lock vault concept became a joint venture called Hausen-Tervo between two European companies. Hausen, a German manufacturer of world class safes and vaults established in 1882. They partnered with a Finnish company, Tervo, who specializes in computer technology and software. Together they created the means of replacing manual combination and key locks on vaults, and to eliminate the chance of burglary after hours by making an impregnable entry into the vault. The time lock was conceived, developed, tested and its claims proven to be true. It has been in use in Europe in major banks for two years. Not one break-in has been reported since the first vault door was installed. The concept was to guard the safe by all possible means by day when it was open and vulnerable, and protecting it at night – when it was alone and vulnerable. The time lock meant the security risk was out of the hands of personnel at the bank and given over to anonymous parties in an anonymous location. Once the door was closed for the day the time lock was activated and it would not open until the designated time the following business day. The vault door would be locked using a newly selected, random computer-chosen, twenty-three digit alphanumeric code. Access to the vault before the designated time of opening was denied. However, and to no one's satisfaction, at the time of the break-in, the method of entering the alpha-numeric code was performed manually."

Carmichael interjected, "Why the hell would they implement such an archaic way to enter the transfer of the code from one computer to another? Isn't there a better way? This is the twenty-first century, for crying out loud!"

The aide continued without looking at his notes. He did have some research of his own to add without the need to verify what he was about to say. "Internally, Hausen-Tervo was experiencing software errors. They could not successfully complete the coded system without issues arising and hampering their progress. They told no one of the obstacles they encountered. Embarrassment, security concerns, that sort of thing, so they say. But with the current track record of no break-ins and American Trust's enthusiasm to install the system, they saw this as a temporary small risk that would be resolved in the near future. As it turns out, with our government agencies seizing their computers, it has since been discovered that a worm virus infected their systems, which directly contributed to prohibiting them from creating the software to implement the auto-code transfer. The worm bore similarities to the one the Israelis used against Iran for their nuclear program. Completely undetectable and similar strands of that worm are now being used by other rogue governments and criminal elements."

"The small risk came back to bite them, didn't it?" Carmichael mused.

The aide returned to his seat. Liggot took over the proceedings once more by adding, "Yes, I think you will find more extensive information on these companies in your briefs." From there he moved on to other matters.

The meeting wrapped up forty-five minutes later and Kip realized there was nothing left to do in New York. He was going back to Los Angeles. On the way out he was caught by the arm by Ken Maylon, CIA Deputy Head.

"Nice to have you on board, Kip. Wish we could have met under more pleasant circumstances, but I guess in our profession, there seldom are better ones ... right," Ken said.

Kip tried once more to glean more information about the vault out of someone. Kip had a healthy relationship with Ken from his CIA days, so in searching for clear answers he asked him about American Trust and its decision to choose this vault and its manufacturer.

"You know how it is," Ken said. "the latest and the greatest. There's always going to be somebody who wants to be the first kid on the block to get his hands on the newest technology. They want to impress the relatives and the neighbors, I suppose. Include it in their marketing blurbs. First it was the black and white TV. Then the color one. Then someone had to be number one to buy the big screen plasma TV. They fork over a premium for it while the rest of us wait a year or two. The bugs get ironed out and they let the prices drop. In this case, American Trust, wanted to tout the latest security system on the market. They were the first in North America to install it." As an afterthought he added, "More than likely now, the last."

Kip nodded.

"Listen, Kip," Ken said to him and lowered his voice as he did so. "So far this case has nothing to hang its hat on. We have one kidnapped woman who can't identify anyone or tell us where she was taken. We have no fingerprints, no DNA or even a voice to go by. All we have from her is maybe three men, dressed in white, a white utility van, a mask, a monitor and a white room. We have the husband of the kidnapped woman who is threatened with the life of his wife and is asked for the code but doesn't give it up, but the vault door opens anyway. And the guys who performed this caper, they take out all the security systems and there is no trace of when they did it or who they are! I mean, come on! Not much to play with here. If you uncover anything of interest in this case, I would personally appreciate it if you would contact me …OK? You always performed outstanding work for the CIA." He clasped Kip on his upper arm and gave him an encouraging nod.

"I'll do what I can," was all Kip would say.

Ken smiled, "That's all I can ask for."

Chapter Twenty-Nine

Only Sam Chowdhury drove Kip back to the plane that would send him home to California. Bob Gannich decided to quit being nice and went home for the day. But Kip had a passenger. It was Ted Atherton. Kip had not met Ted before today, but they got to talking about the case and both found it intriguing. Ted was wearing the standard FBI colors, in the usual attire. He was shorter than Kip by a few inches, maybe two or three years older, and presented that clean-cut persona that the FBI is known for. Light brown hair sat above blue eyes shrouded by heavy brown eyebrows, his face ending in a square jaw. Kip noticed a pink scar on his right hand that was lost as it entered his shirtsleeve. *Pink, not white, so it must not be an ancient scar*, he mused.

They arrived at the plane. Not the G-V Gulfstream. That was made available for a trip back to Washington D.C. for animals higher up the food chain. The two men thanked Sam for his time, and Kip asked him in turn to thank Bob Gannich. He said he would and waited while they boarded.

The two men entered the modified version of the BBJ, Boeing Business Jet, which itself is configured from the Boeing 737. It was a U.S. government chartered flight for employees of the U.S. government. A small perk for the hours of service provided by all the men and women aboard. Both men grabbed a prepackaged meal and a bottle of water for the journey. They were both particularly interested in the water. Nothing like getting a high altitude head pounder - they were nasty; especially for Kip since he had been up so long. Drinking the water would go a long way to help prevent the pain.

Kip had chosen the turkey wrap with mayo and lettuce. The selections were limited. It tasted as bland as it looked, but it was something. The water was refreshing, though. The men continued talking for some time after takeoff, but Kip was now feeling the absence of sleep since rising very early on Monday morning - it was now late Tuesday afternoon. The hums and drones of the plane and its turbulent-free journey through space caused him to drift off into sleep.

He felt a jolt and awoke with a start. He looked around to see several other people in the plane, and no one paying him any attention. He knew he had felt turbulence, and he could see now looking out of the plane's window they were on their descent, and what he felt were the typical bumps coming down through the cotton ball clouds. Then a strange thing happened; something he was not accustomed to onboard government transportation and as he was still sleepy-eyed, he heard it all more in a dream-like state, not business astute at all. As if on a commercial flight, the captain used the intercom to announce their approach into Los Angeles airspace. His voice was rich, deep and soothing. A smooth bass range. He spoke slowly and methodically. He could have been a classical music station radio announcer in another life. Maybe he was practicing for an upcoming interview with a commercial airline? Kip could clearly make out what he was saying over the intercom. He heard him better and clearer than the pilot's announcements on commercial flights that would speak too quickly through airwaves of static, or spoke in mumbled, hushed tones. Occasionally, it seemed to Kip, that when the captain of a commercial airliner did not wish to speak to the passengers, he, or she, would shove the announcement card in front of the junior co-pilot and say, "Here … your turn to do this thing." And with that, the co-pilot would start in with a nervous tremor in the voice, and stumble through the speech. Never convincing at all about the 'pleasant' news they were delivering, it certainly did not provide comfort for those already frenzied passengers to hear the inexperienced and not so sure of them self-pilot's squeaky voice.

This particular pilot, however, was enjoying a monologue and went on to give them the tidbits of information given by all the commercial pilots, and more! He included their descent into L.A., the weather, how much longer before they touched down, what sights they could possibly take in if they were just here visiting lovely L.A. and so on. He was good at it, with a gregarious whist to his speech. Kip looked around and noticed almost everyone had stopped what they were doing to enjoy hearing the colorful and unexpected words. It was different. It was unexpected. Kip looked directly at a woman across the aisle. She looked important - older, serious, but she looked at him, too, and then they smiled together at the captain's ramblings. They shared a moment. The captain finished his little announcement by saying, "Have a good day in L.A., folks."

Chapter Thirty

December - Wednesday – 5:41 a.m.

Laguna Beach – California

Kip was involved in a serious workout. He was in his fitness room, lifting weights, straining, sweating, and feeling the stress and tension fall out of his body. His muscles were burning and responding to the commands of the repetitive motions he was demanding of himself. He had not worked out for two days and he could feel it. Like a junkie needs a fix, this was his addiction. It fueled his fire and made him more alert. The juices needed to flow. He felt he was missing something in this case, something that was right there in front of him. Several times he felt the sense of a theory formulating in his brain, or perhaps a vital tidbit of information coming forward in his thoughts, but then ... the thread was gone. The bells were not ringing loud enough yet. But he knew, if he kept digging, something would be overturned. There are not many perfect crimes out there, fewer in more recent history. Technology was making it harder. Mistakes are made, the littlest items are overlooked, and possibilities of error, or chance circumstances you just cannot account for in a hundred trial runs. Things just ... happen the way they happen.

    Kip had arrived home the night before and taken a long, hot shower. He really needed that shower. His worn clothes were to go to the drycleaners; they were sorely wrinkled and soiled. Refreshed somewhat, he attacked his hair with the towel, then replaced tired old clothes for laundered new ones, pulled from his drawers and extracted from his shelves. He stepped into a favorite pair of well-worn faded blue denims and a familiar orange polo shirt. The shirt he left hanging out over his jeans. Then off he went to join his family for a meal of fish tacos and a tossed salad that consisted of crisp butter lettuce, ripe plump tomatoes, baby carrots, tiny and delicious sweet cucumbers and locally grown avocado. Finally it was drizzled with a balsamic vinaigrette dressing. They washed it all down with tangy lemonade. It was a treat enjoyed by all his kids.

Although, this meal was placed in the ranks of "acceptable meals" for the Keplar family, that was not always the case. Their children did not always willingly go along with the diet requirements that Mette and he had laid out for the family. They rebelled occasionally, and sometimes Kip would side with children to let Mette know, *if you can't beat them, join them.*

They carried on a lively conversation about the last two days' events while he was gone. Their stories of people and activities at school, especially young Annika, who also reminded everyone she had an upcoming parent's day, and that *Dad* would be reading to the class this Friday. He winked at her and said *he wouldn't miss it for the world.* She in turn gave him one of those brilliant smiles that said *I'm so glad you're my Dad, and I can't wait for you to come to school so I can tell everybody.* Yes, she was still at that tender age when parents are infallible against wrongdoing or any form of embarrassment for their children.

He lay in bed that night holding his wife close. He told her the small details that he could about the situation, but it was very little. Both because he couldn't, due to the sensitive and confidential information involved, as well as the fact that unfortunately, there was simply not that much to tell.

Kip was drawing to a close with his workout routine when Mette walked into the room. She had just finished her yoga and stretching session and was ready to go with her own workout routine with the free weights. She was thankful there was a fan going in the corner of the room and that they had installed a ventilation system with an air extractor. It was needed to take away the stale smells and odors of sweat. The kids would be up in about twenty minutes or so, and it was Kip that would see to their morning routine needs and help get them off to school.

He showered quickly and raced to the kitchen. It was a morning for fresh fruit. A mixture of juicy pineapple and mixed berries. He stopped midway through pulling the fruits out of the refrigerator and changed his mind. He grabbed for the yogurt and milk. He returned the blueberries and raspberries to the fridge but kept the strawberries out.

Let's turn it into a smoothie, he thought to himself.

He then twirled around and grabbed a promising mango and a slightly blackened banana. He cut up the ingredients, guessed at measurements required for the yogurt and milk and poured everything into a blender. Then he added scoops of coconut Sorbet.

The mixture looked just right. The children must have agreed. He called them to the kitchen table and in no time at all the entire contents of the glass container was empty.

Yum!

They finished off breakfast with various choices of cereal accompanied by strawberry chunks and then it was time to leave for school. It was to be another big day.

He left Mette to finish getting dressed. Her long blonde hair was fashionably bundled on her head. She was wearing business professional attire. It was red. Red topcoat and a red short skirt with matching red shoes. She decided to do without red nail polish. Instead they were clear coated. She was meeting with a benefactor to discuss an upcoming art exhibit. She may have left the Swedish Embassy as a cultural attaché, but the desires and needs to be deeply involved in the art world were still strongly entrenched. Laguna Beach was a thriving art community and it was a passion of hers to be involved in it and provide her expertise. Kip told Mette he would call her later. They kissed goodbye. They both wished each other good luck and lots of love.

Kip would head back to Los Angeles and the FBI Offices to report in with what he knew and to sit in on another meeting and obtain further updates from the West Coast boys.

Chapter Thirty-One

Los Angeles, California

December - Wednesday – 9:48 a.m.

The drive up to Los Angeles was slow and torturous; it always was this time of the day. He took it in stride, but occasionally when the gridlock never looked like unfurling itself, he would quickly glance at his car's clock to see if time was still on his side. Planning ahead because of experience, which naturally came from getting it wrong more than once, had allowed him plenty of time. He walked into the building twelve minutes before ten o'clock for a meeting that was taking place on the hour. But they were already waiting for him. He exited the elevator in his dark grey suit, dark blue shirt, black stripes lapped over a sky blue tie and black leather dress shoes. He stopped as he saw Ted Atherton standing close to the elevator, waiting for him.

"Good morning Ted. Any news?"

"The meeting has already started," Atherton announced. "We have a breakthrough." He then led Kip into the command room. They entered the room where John Brozski, among others, was viewing video footage that seemed to come from a traffic camera. The images were at a steep angle, taken high up and looking down onto a street. The clarity of the images was not poor, but it certainly was not high definition either. But then again, the intent was never to produce motion picture quality.

These traffic cameras were popping up in ever increasing numbers on the nation's busiest highways, by-ways, main roads, tunnels and bridges and perhaps coming to a street near you Kip thought. But the intended purpose was sound. The community needed to know where the traffic flowed well, and where it did not, so such things as the revised timing of traffic signals could help to ease congestion. As if that was ever possible in Los Angeles. The information from the cameras was also relayed to the TV and radio stations and broadcast in real time, offering up information to those on the road, or those who were about to get underway in order to help motorists make better informed decisions as to which route to take. It could also identify where crashes had taken place and to advise fire, rescue and law enforcement officers of precise locations, maybe saving lives in the process. All good, in this modern age of the up-to-the second quest to know everything as it happens. And unfortunately, in a society like ours, having information instantly is a privilege that has its drawbacks. You cannot get the information as soon as you want it without having the cameras installed that provide it, and that infringes on our personal liberties.

Cost versus Benefit.

Kip joined John and asked, "What have you got, John?" John craned his ahead around while still sitting in front of the monitor, and said, "Oh, I'm glad you're here. Listen we have something; well, at least the start of something. Sit down, I want to show you this."

Kip sat next to Brozski as instructed. John went to the frame of footage he was looking for and continued his conversation.

"We have been concentrating our efforts on finding any evidence within the bank and inside the vault. We have combed every inch of that thing – twice, maybe more by now. We keep going over the same ground – hoping to find something. We have no fingerprints,

footprints, fiber samples, hair follicles, no DNA of any kind. No
tire tracks outside the building, nothing that leads to anything
conclusive. How is that possible?" John asked of no one in
particular.

He continued as Kip became intrigued, thinking, *this was
going somewhere, please move it along.*

"We ran the images from the cameras inside the bank to
find suspects – nothing. They somehow produced images that
deceived the security company. A bank vacant of people."

He shook his head in quiet wonder at this caper. "We had
hopes of finding something, but nothing came of our
investigations. Chasing ghosts is not part of my job description."
Again he talked to no one. Private thoughts spoken out loud.

John continued, "Then we switched to reviewing any
outside cameras. Sounded good, next logical step in the process.
The bank has several attached to the building. One in the alley
aimed at the fire door exit, another for the employee entrance, two
viewing the front door from different angles and two on the roof.
They all came up negative. The same as inside the bank. All
systems controlled by the bank were compromised. As an
afterthought, we asked Caltran if they had any cameras monitoring
the main street. "*No,*" for a permanent installation in the vicinity,
but they were running a trial camera on Pernell Drive in front of
the bank about three hundred yards to the north. We ran the
footage, everything since Friday afternoon after the bank closed.
The nighttime footage was lousy. If something registered then, we
were surely out of luck – again. The guys have been busy viewing
the images, running it more than 24 frames per second, just to
speed things along. Not fast enough to miss anything, but we need
to find something, fast. As it happens they spotted the strangest

thing. A person had walked out from that alley on the south side of the bank and joined the race a little after 10:00 a.m. on Sunday. The camera never picked him up going into the alley, say for a toilet break – which is a disgusting thought in itself, as there were plenty of dedicated facilities to stop at along the route. But a man dressed from head to toe in Santa apparel came out and joined the race. What's more he was carrying an extremely large red sack and it was full. We played it back several times. He never went in, he only came out, we are sure of it."

"Were you able to form a description?" Kip asked.

"No, I'm afraid not. The camera is too far away, the picture quality is poor and grainy," he answered. "But keep watching. This guy, we'll call him Santa Number One, joins in with the runners and walkers and heads in the same direction. He is gone. Now keep watching. We timed it out at one minute later. Kris Kringle Number Two emerges from the very same place, south wall of the bank, out of the alley and joins the crowd. Same dress, same *M.O.* Walks into the throng of people, blends in, and he is gone."

John turned to face Kip sitting next to him. "If you keep watching, which we won't, we're running out of time here - we counted four of them."

John rose from his chair and beckoned Kip and the others standing around to join him at the main conference table. He hit a button and the lights dimmed while curtains were drawn across the windows. John gave it about fifteen seconds. The room went dark, and then it went silent.

He continued, "After we discovered this possible lead, we contacted the media and asked for their cooperation with sending us copies of their coverage of the race. Any file footage, including all the unedited material, still photos from the print media and so on. We have come up with more leads."

John tapped a key on the computer keypad and an image appeared on the screen at the front of the room. An illuminated image of Santa Claus. Number One, Two, Three or Four, nobody would know, but there he was, literally holding the bag. This was John's show and he would repeat this presentation and display these images half a dozen times in the next few days, and it would always be conducted with vibrancy and enthusiasm. He was breaking in this narrative over "his" people's heads. Any faults in the show-and-tell and he would correct and amend them for the audiences that followed. This was serious and important work they were involved with, but after all, let's be honest, his role was to function in part as a would-be politician.

"We have a snapshot, ladies and gentlemen." And it was there on the screen for everyone to see.

The photograph in question was snapped by a local print media photographer, taken to accompany the female journalist's story that covered the event. But this particular photograph was rejected in lieu of another, as the image selected deserved its recognition. The winning picture froze in time a sea of Santa's rushing toward the camera. Likely a single stand pod held the camera steady, and a slow shutter speed together with a high aperture setting rewarded the photographer with the intended outcome. By instant gratification, compliments of the digital camera age, the field photographer would have been pleased with the result. The camera screen displayed a crowd of Santas, taken as the starter's pistol had fired and the race had begun. A tightly packed group of runners worked their arms and legs furiously. Faces already showing contorted features were there, while others were smiling. As the people's momentum drove them forward, the photo captured elongated forms that bled color trailing behind them, red being the most prominent color of all. It was an effect not unlike a technique seen in sci-fi movies when a craft streaks into *warp speed*. It was an excellent shot. But the photograph the officials in the room were studying that day was yet trapped in stasis inside the digital camera.

After pausing several seconds for effect, and to allow the image on the screen to soak in for the audience, John continued with his narration. "As you can see, the unidentified male in the picture is carrying the red sack in question, but he worked the disguise well as his entire body is fully cloaked by using such items as black gloves, calf length black boots over red pants, a red coat, cinched by the wide black buckled belt, and a very long white beard. He accessorized with a red cap beaded with fake fur-lined white trim, a wig of white hair falling out from under the cap and covering up yet more of the face. The costume was complete with a modern day twist - very large dark wrap-around sunglasses to cover up what remained of his exposed face. The finishing touch as you can see," he moved his laser pointer across the image to indicate what he was referencing, "are heavy bushy white eyebrows. *Why?* He has the bulging sack thrown over his shoulder and gripped tightly. We cannot at this time, identify this person of interest, even though we have a clear picture of him. But we feel confident we finally have something to go on."

The man dressed as Santa was standing alone, feet slightly apart. It was mid-morning and the sun was in his face; it brightened his already gleaming suit, made it look even crisper. He was facing the camera but his head was turned ninety degrees and looking north, causing him to give up his profile. It appeared he had stopped walking or running and was looking back down the path from where the runners came. Almost like he was waiting for someone to catch up.

The photographer's keen eye spotted the man, and seeing a non-moving target posing as a fine Santa specimen to boot, he snapped the photo. The photographer chose to blur the background, which helped to accentuate the central figure. It worked. The result was a well-framed man, in crystal clear focus, with no distractions beyond. And the only physical part of the man exposed, giving any hint of description, was his nose. A Caucasian nose.

John continued, "Now we cannot identify the man, though we are certain he is a male. As you can see, he is wearing a number on his chest; one was assigned to every runner. It is number 8372. We did a cross check with the registration of all the runners in the event. Number 8372 was registered to a Ms. Genna Clermont. This man who remains unidentifiable, with a sack full of ... something." John used the laser and pointed at it. "He has to be one of our guys."

"Now, on this basis we are attempting to track this man throughout the race, to see where he made his exit, so to speak, because I'm confident he didn't make it to the finish line."

The meeting broke up then and there, and everyone began screening still photos and television footage to locate this, the only lead. He was to be known as, Santa Suspect Number One.

Kip was sitting down pouring over stills, trying to catch a glimmer of something, when John came over to him, laid a hand on his left shoulder while leaning down to talk into his ear.

"How you doing, Kip? Have you been able to come up with any alternative scenarios we can explore?"

Kip shook his head slowly, "Sorry, John. Right now this case is just too fragmented." He pointed down to the photographs. "This appears to be as good as it gets at the moment. If we can pull this piece of thread and stretch it, maybe it can lead us to another clue. I'll keep looking through all these prints like everyone else for now. It may trigger something."

John smiled. A coach's smile. The coach of a team being whacked by fifty points, and it is only half-time. There are no words of encouragement; what do you tell the team at this point? You just want the bleeding to stop. He had nothing for Kip, and Kip had nothing for him. The smile remained, but the tone of his words said it all.

"OK. Well if you come up with anything, let me know." He lifted his hand from Kip's shoulder, straightened, and walked away to a waiting assistant who handed him a file as they padded down the carpeted corridor together.

Kip's sinking feeling of failure weighed on him. In previous cases, he was the one guy who could see through the fog and the mist, and grab the right answer. This time – nothing.

Was he rusty? Not enough skin in the game? Not feeling the drive? He was very interested in the case all right, but was it that maybe the fire in the gut for this work was beginning to die down? He didn't think so. He truly did not think so, but he needed to show he could be of more help than just looking through photos. For now, however, that was his assignment, and he wanted to make a contribution, any contribution. There would be time for self-analysis later.

Sandwiches, pizza, hot coffee and cold drinks were brought in several hours later so the team could work continuously. It was tedious stuff. Besides the red sack, they were looking at all kinds of Santas to try and find one in particular. The only constant? The color red. Candy red, or poppy red. That is what they gazed at. Soon enough they all came to despise the color red.

The breakthrough happened at around 2:30 that afternoon. Colleen Herrera-Dore was viewing television footage. She had passed over this section three times now. Although, this was the first time she noticed it. It was there! There. Just as the file footage began. If you blinked, you missed it. Leaving the frame just as the film rolled, she saw the very end of the red sack exiting the screen. She reversed the footage, then ran it again, and ran it again. She was almost sure, but she backed it up and ran it again once more. She repeated the process four more times to be certain before calling over her team leader. They looked at it again several more times together before they would announce that they had a possible breakthrough.

It was confirmed that a red sack had moved down field another three blocks. They were making progress. Less ground to cover when they went searching. The hours dragged on and Kip finally made the call to Mette that he was going to be late again, and to not wait up, again, as another all-nighter was not out of the question.

Chapter Thirty-Two

Los Angeles, California

Meanwhile, so as not to leave any stone unturned, the Bureau, in tandem with local law enforcement, was working all angles of the case. They had to. They were expected to. But the inclusion of more people on a "need to know" basis invited yet more possibilities for gossip and leaks. The particulars of the items in the bank remained confidential, but everybody had their suspicions. From tidbits of information from "sources within" the rumors were rife and plenty. The most prominent one circulating around the water coolers consisted of carefully wrapped packages of heroin for some Hollywood well-to-dos, right through to Hollywood big wigs caught on film in compromising positions; hence the sustained harassment coming from the studios. There was talk of priceless precious jewels nabbed, and so someone with a wild imagination spread the rumor that the actual Crown Jewels of England were on the stolen items list. *Well, wasn't it true that everyone knew the jewels on display in the Tower of London were fakes? Didn't they?*

A constant flow of official personnel streamed in and out of L.A.P.D. offices all over the county. Clean cut types in tidy blue suits, crisp white shirts and serious looks on their faces visited all too frequently. Local detectives were leaned on hard to push the local network of gangsters, thugs, pimps and all types of two-bit thieves to get the smallest sniff of who was possibly behind this. They dragged in known snitches and tried to bribe new ones. Threats of jail time were metered out indiscriminately while others received the threat of not spending time in jail with the aim of spreading the idea around town that they gave up priceless information. Let them walk the streets with that out there.

Veiled threats and often just outright threats pure and simple were made, but still nobody talked, nobody knew anything! Lame leads were chased down and every conceivable idea on how to recover the contents from the vault was pursued. But nothing came of it. The thieves came and went with the wind.

Absolutely no headway. It was just not possible. Or so they thought. It was slowly emerging as the theory of the week that no local people, gangs or masterminds were involved in this case. They would continue the search for minions, the small-fry, but it was just a sea of mystery out there. It was the local professional opinion that the FBI should look elsewhere for the criminal guru.

The trail ran cold after the red sack was spotted in the film footage three blocks south from where the posing photo of Old Saint Nick was taken. No more sightings of the mystery men were caught digitally or otherwise.

People were tired, and the enthusiasm and energy was draining out of everyone. They were told to keep trying for thirty minutes more and then wrap it up at 5:00 a.m.

There were numerous participants passing by as the photo was taken, but none were of the Santas they were looking for, and it was not the runners that the agent was concentrating on. It was the background. Not blurred by aperture selection, but not as sharp as he would like either. He was studying a vehicle well beyond the runners. A tiny blob, almost indiscernible.

Questions he asked himself included, *how many vehicles were in the vicinity on a Sunday at that time of the day while a large race was in progress? How many of them were service vans?*

Not the entire vehicle was in the shot, only from the front bumper to just beyond the front cab. It was about to turn onto the main road away from the race.

The agent studied the photo and thought, *the van was coming out of .... somewhere. But where? Apartment parking space? A parking ramp?*

Once again a supervisor was called over for a second opinion. The photo was date stamped and they compared it to "Exhibit A", the photograph of Santa Claus. They were thirty-one minutes apart. They had no idea which Santa was caught in the frame, but drawing on some conclusions, they estimated all four suspects could be in the van and clothing swapped out within that time frame. It was assumed they exchanged Santa suits for something more in keeping with casual Sunday driving wear so as not to draw attention to themselves. While police and officials close to the scene of the race would not take a second look, by driving further afield from the event our thieves would make for more unforgettable figures, particularly seeing someone driving along the open road dressed as Santa.

After examining its distinctive features, it was established that the vehicle in question was a Ford Econoline cargo van. An older model and very non-descript from what they could ascertain. It would be lost amongst a plethora of similar vehicles in the area. Although unseen in the photo, this particular model typically had no side windows and was also offered without window panels in the back, either. It made for great concealment. But they had no way of telling with certainty if this was the one to go after.

Specialists were already checking for recently stolen vehicles that matched the description. As for the driver, well, the technology was not available that could pull the background in close enough to reveal anything beyond a grainy blur. Just too far away. The extraordinary feat of tracking a vehicle with that little to go on are reserved for the television shows only that can also wrap everything up in one hour (commercials included). Just to make things interesting, the van they chose to drive was basic black.

As far as everyone in the office was concerned at this point in time in the investigation, this late at night, or early in the morning as the case may be, possibly this one van, leaving the scene of the crime five blocks away, with absolutely no way of tracking its license plate or its owner, was far and away their greatest lead.

Chapter Thirty-Three

East Coast

December - Thursday – 6:54 a.m.

He was lost in a thousand thoughts, absent-mindedly turning the pinky ring on his right finger around and around and around. His was satisfied that he could still turn it. Why, he could even pull it off if he wanted to. He did not possess the fingers that grew into fat sausages and cause the skin to squeeze the ring. There was no necessity it accompany him into the grave.

He did not mind being in his office at this hour in the morning. Was not the first time, would not be the last. He was waiting for the call. He eventually picked up the white porcelain demitasse cup that held his espresso. He smelt it. He sipped it. It was extra hot and excellent. He returned it to the matching white saucer. Of course it was good, it was Italian coffee! Thick in texture, dark, strong. Wonderful coffee, not like these prissy drinks from these fancy places they have today. His coffee was custom delivered from tried and true Italian merchants whose families had been involved in the trade for generations. He could not understand this new breed of young at all. The people's taste went from drinking weak filtered coffee to a craze-filled quest to throw the most ingredients they could find into paper coffee cups virtually overnight. In the meantime, they arced over the unmatched quality coffee his ancestors had loved and enjoyed and had been drinking for many years. The new breed of coffee connoisseurs went for the over-the-top outrageous *foo-foo* drinks, with their fat free milks, decaf or half-decaf drinks and extra shots of this or that - what was it, flavoring! Flavorings? And who the hell orders cappuccino after nine in the morning anyway?

No, he would only drink the best, real Italian coffee, made the way it was always made. He lifted his porcelain china cup, sipped and savored a truly great coffee. His thoughts shifted onto another subject. But first another sip. Ahhh. He was thinking about the guys who had his stuff. That joker who thinks he is something special, that aaaaahh...Mogul! "PEHRRR !!" He physically spat the word out. What an idiot! A West Coast punk. Little Sammy's organization and his boys did all the heavy lifting for this little operation. All that was required from him was to walk into an open vault. But he had to admit, if only to himself, Mogul had done it according to plan, without causing any commotion. He had accomplished his task – so far.

And so far no associates of his were bothered with questions from the local cops, or anybody else. That was good. He congratulated himself on how he had outsmarted cops for as long as he had enjoyed this coffee – hell, even longer! *Where was the phone call from his client?* He was here this morning to receive news after inquiries were made. It had taken a week. *Why the delay? Was this a good thing or a bad thing?*

He checked out the black satellite phone with sad puppy dog eyes and wondered how long before it rang. This time he would talk. He knew nothing of the technology of the communication system he was using or the attachments to modify the thing. His people had explained something about how the features of the satellite phone worked and how they were using the Low Earth Orbit (LEO) system. They had lost him after - "satellite phone".

His only question, "Does this thing work?"

He was assured it did.

There was also some crazy device hooked up to it, he didn't know what. All these things his people do to protect him, shelter him, give him the modern tools he needs, they do it because they are *his* people; loyal and to be trusted, but it is so complicated! The device that was attached to the Sat- phone would alter his voice, for protection against the U.S. Government. Against the system they told him about, that, ENSIGN, or ESCHELON or whatever it was called, if it hooked his conversation, he could easily deny it was him speaking. Prove it! His lawyers would have a field day with that one.

The Sat-phone rang. He picked it up.

Chapter Thirty-Four

Laguna Beach – California

December - Thursday – 7:22 a.m.

The hopeful prospects were for a bright and sunny morning. The forecast indicated it would reach a warm and pleasant seventy-three degrees. But that was foretold by somebody who gets to keep their job if they are right only fifty percent of the time. So who could tell? But considering all things, that was enough to get Kip thinking about getting into his pool and laying down a few laps. Another long night and Kip was dragging. He could feel the fatigue. These were not his college days anymore! These late, late nights were getting the better of him. After the pool workout he could catch some shut-eye, maybe a few hours; get refreshed and then do some serious work away from the distractions of the Bureau's office buzz. He had finally left the office a little after six that morning and traveled with a stream of cars southward, hoping to get home sooner rather than later.

Fifty-three minutes on he had arrived to an empty home. He came in through the garage entrance as usual and placed his car keys in the customary place. It was the third hook from the left at the mail center they had created, just beyond the mudroom as you entered the house this way. The house felt totally silent and still. He could, however, hear the small crash of tiny waves in a rhythmic thump as they landed on shore just beyond the windows. His cool pool water was waiting for him, so he entered his bedroom, stripped down and changed into a pair of shorts for swimming. He made time to drink a cool glass of water from the kitchen faucet and briefly gaze out the window facing the ocean. The vista never got old. The layout of the home was such that the kitchen was given a premium location for spectacular views. During the design phase for the home, they discussed what rooms were most utilized, and easily the kitchen was one of them. So the theory goes, enjoy the breathtaking scenery from the areas most utilized in the home. He finished his water in several gulps and then decided upon another. When his thirst was quenched he headed for the pool.

The well-landscaped backyard was a respite from the wind-blown and salt-sprayed western facing side of their property. The ocean front grounds were a deliberate attempt to recapture native beach plant species, complete with coastal dunes milk-vetch, the petite and low growing Menzies' wallflower; soft-leaved paintbrush and red sand verbena, covering blotches of the yellow blanket that was the sand dunes. The family worked hard at keeping out the likes of non-native and troublesome species such as ice plants, along with the pesky and invasive European beach grasses with their almost infallible rhizome tendrils that took no prisoners.

The backyard in contrast supported a grand old oak tree, purportedly one hundred and fifty years old. It was firmly rooted on the property when they purchased it, with its majestic trunk and broad branches. It acted as the anchor for everything else, and held a place of pride in the yard. The design allowed for fringed palms to be dotted about, an abundance of ferns that did their best to hide a meandering paved trail to and from the pool. Bolt upright straight and tall coconut palm trees, as well as colorful bushes that bloomed in sequence throughout the year and an assortment of flower beds had been planted with care and reason. Space was provided for a small field of grass. An area where the family could enjoy running around, play games, chase one another, hear the sounds of laughter and the crying, too, and for the most part, enjoy the great outdoors.

Kip reached out and touched the tiled wall at the end of the pool as he had been trained to do at so many swim meets from his youth. His lungs were burning and his tired shoulders and upper body were crying out in pain, but it sure felt good. He allowed himself a few seconds to catch his breath, resting shoulder deep in the water before raising him-self up, flexing his powerful upper arms while trails of lightly tinged salt water drained from his body. He used the soft-to-the-touch ultra-cotton towel that rested over the back of a nearby deck chair to dab himself dry, then hung it over his shoulders as he returned to the house to shower.

After the hot shower, he grabbed red shorts and a white long sleeved t-shirt. The shirt advertised lettering in blue down both sleeves of a well-known urban outfitter. Then it was back to the kitchen where he made a simple breakfast of two boiled eggs, strawberries, orange juice and three slices of wheat toast.

With a content stomach but still leaning on a heavy burden of disappointment over adding zero to the tally sheet of contributions towards the case, he resigned himself to address the current situation of sleep deprivation. So he darkened the bedroom sufficiently and pulled the bed covers down. Off came all his clothes down to underwear, and he fell onto the cool sheets of the comfortable bed. Too quickly for Kip, the bed sheets felt clingy; he kicked at them, feeling a sense of claustrophobia. Finally, he pushed them off altogether. It was a struggle to sleep with so much going on and many thoughts racing through his mind. He focused on his breathing, to slow it down, to keep it rhythmic. He fought through his fatigue and the problems associated with being over-tired, and he somehow managed to doze off into a fitful sleep.

He caught up on three hours of borrowed sleep. Somehow twenty minutes seemed more like the right number. Maybe attempting to sleep during the day was the problem; he had heard it was an adjustment one never got accustomed to - just ask graveyard shift workers. Or staying overnight in a bed that was not your own, it just did not feel right. They were hours you were never going to get back. Some aura or karma was missing. In his case, it was his wife. Sleep was always blissful with her nearby.

It was no use. He got up and made coffee and when it had brewed, sat with a cup at his desk and started going through events as he could best piece them together. Burglary takes place on one coast, while at the same time people are abducted on the other. *Why did they wait until Sunday to perform the robbery?* Considering the current situation, four days later, he had to admit their plan was working so far. Not much to go on and they could be just about anywhere by now. Time was against him.

He made a call to Ted Atherton who had just arrived back at the office. Ted brought him up to speed with the latest.

"They sent a team over from where they believe the van drove away as shown in the photo," Atherton told him.

"Anything?"

"Well, there is a three story public parking garage on the street just two short blocks away from the race route."

"And?"

"And, the preliminary analysis is not good. Nothing we can pin our hopes on. No cameras in or around the ramp, no one we can find who could tell us about the van or how long it had been there or where they had parked. Parking is free over the weekend, so no record they were there."

"OK, thanks, Ted." Kip signed off. Nothing major happening.

He mulled over cloudy thoughts a while longer then he used the bathroom. When he got back to his desk he felt a presence in the house. He began to search, methodically checking rooms. He approached one of his boy's bedrooms. It was Raef, his eldest. He grabbed the door handle and turned while at the same time moving swiftly into the room. He stopped suddenly. It was Raef and his friend from school, Jacob. Jacob was handling a python that was slithering through his hands.

Kip smiled, "Hi, boys. What do you have there?"

"It's my pet python Ralph," Jacob said with pride in his voice, but without looking up to meet Kip's gaze. He was more interested in the machinations of his pet. And so, too, was Raef.

Ralph looked at him, though, and warbled his forked tongue at him.

Raef finally looked over with a huge smile across his face. "Yeah, Dad, he's way cool. Can we get one?"

The plea was somewhat expected, particularly when a thirteen-year-olds friend has something new and exciting to share. Like every kid ever made, he wanted one, too.

"Well, let's talk about it later, OK?" Just like most parents ever made, he chose to deflect the question and delay his answer, at least until he had backup from Mette. What else does one do when confronted with a question like that? So he would wait for his son's excitement to drain, then they could discuss the possibilities of a dog, or a potbelly pig, or a hamster!

Still admiring his snake, Jacob nonchalantly said, "It's a Regius Python snake from Africa. I wish it had poison though."

The python was not large. Well, large enough, Kip thought. It had to be four inches in circumference and about four feet long! It was adorned with camouflaged skin and was constantly flicking its tongue out, searching for something. He knew enough about Pythons to understand that this was a smaller one. That was a bonus. He recalled how, when feeding on prey they would wrap around their victim and suffocate them to death, not crush, and then eat them whole. Right about now he was thinking the hamster was looking pretty good to take the pet prize.

Twenty minutes later all his children and Mette had returned to the house. Everybody was having a good day. Kip was keen on some fresh air so he suggested everyone join him in a beach walk. Before they exited the house he grabbed a bottle of water and a pear. They were off to have some fun.

Chapter Thirty-Five

A SLOW BOAT

He was leaning back relaxing on the poor excuse for a deck chair. Designer sunglasses were on over closed eyes, his shirt was off. The only piece of clothing he wore was a forest green pair of nylon shorts ending just below the knees. The green was interrupted by two equal stripes painted down both sides. A fresh cigarette lay resting between two fingers of his left hand. He had reclined on a chair with chipped plastic armrests that occasionally scratched his wrists when he wasn't paying attention, and his weight was supported by sagging and stretched vinyl strips that performed badly. He habitually and continuously flicked at the butt end of the cigarette; willfully removing whatever ash appeared from the lit end. Between drags on the cigarette he would blindly reach down and grab the neck of the beer bottle sitting on the floor and bring it to his lips for a swig. The sun's energy had increased from warm to hot in the last few days; he could feel it and welcomed it. Despite a constant breeze because of the moving ship, he could go shirtless. He had been relaxed for four days now. In fact, it was getting boring aboard this rust bucket. He opened his eyes and looked to his left at the living conditions. This was certainly not the way he was accustomed to traveling, but ...

It was an aging cargo freighter. Best guess, built in the fifties but not ruling out the sixties. It was rusted out ...everywhere. It was undoubtedly a single hull piece of junk. One minor bump to the hull and she may well go down, and take them with her. This could very well be its last voyage before chugging off to the scrap yard to be melted down for washing machine

shells. He would not miss his, for lack of a better word, "cabin."
He knew there were mice, more likely rats, in the darker corners
and recesses. He could hear them at night chomping and nibbling
away at some form of food - he hoped it wasn't his shoes. And
speaking of food, the food they dished up – it sucked. It sucked big
time. He was thankful for his American beer and cigarettes. He
justified living in these atrocious conditions by accepting he could
lose a few pounds anyway. Return nice and trim. Come back a new
man. That would be an added bonus he had not thought of. He
smiled to himself. Yes, the ladies would love it.

He continued to smile as he spotted most of the gang still
struggling to grow hair. He noticed the bristle on their chrome
domes and for some, on their faces, too. But what made him enjoy
the moment was the fact that without exception they were all
constantly scratching and rubbing their heads because of the itch.
If he didn't know any better, he would say they all had fleas. He
pulled himself up to sit upright on the lounge chair. He sank down
partially through the chair as about every third vinyl strip was
missing. *What a piece of crap!* The colors on the vinyl had long
ago faded and the chairs should have faded away, too. He held the
beer bottle once more and drained the dregs of the warm amber
liquid. Now empty, he spun the bottle around in a half-turn. He
grabbed it by the long neck, adjusted it a little in his grip. Droplets
of beer and foam trickled down and caught him on his leg at the
knee. He ignored the liquid and placed his cigarette between his
teeth. He stood up and threw the bottle end over end out over the
rail at the stern of the ship. He watched with satisfaction as the
bottle spun through air towards the open water while more foaming
droplets left the bottle. It finally made a quick entry into the
churning and white bubbling sea that trailed the boat.

Mogul set his forearms on the rail in front of him, pulled the cigarette out of his mouth and sent smoke through his nose. His hair was blowing in the wind, he was staring at the horizon; he was somewhere in a vast expanse of ocean and he was confident no one knew where he was. Yes, everything was going according to plan. He was having a good day.

Chapter Thirty-Six

Laguna Beach, California

December - Thursday - 3:43 p.m.

The kids were doing what they do best. Racing up and down the beach chasing each other, involved in some old-fashioned kid approved fun. Annika, making her decision to join in with the boy's seaside teasing, would then quickly change her mind and decide "it was not fair!" three against one; so she would race back to her mother's arms, half-screaming, half-laughing as her two brothers and Jacob were closing in, desperate to catch her. Things would settle down for a minute or two, and then the cycle would repeat itself. The afternoon sky canvassed an interesting scene. Predominantly blue but large tufts of white clouds meandered across it, shape-shifting into various forms. Someone in the group decided to start identifying them.

They picked out the roaring head of a lion, mouth agape; some teeth were identifiable as well as a flowing mane. From the neck down, his body melded with the rest of the cumulus cloud and he appeared to be carried along as if in a procession as the cloud drifted by.

A turtle, or was it tortoise? was spotted amongst the clouds. All four feet were jutting out of its shell. It was swimming through the liquid sky. The cloud sketched in many of the details from its head to a well-formed tiny snub of a tail.

Trek tried hard to convince everyone that an elephant was up there. He pointed to a shape in the cloud and could not believe no one could see it! But the cloud was moving and changing like a ghost in a strong breeze, and no one could confirm what his gift of imagination offered up. Appropriately, the last animal to be spotted was a shark, with its dorsal fin clearly showing. The shark's nose was pushing into the cloud ahead of it, suggesting it had found lunch.

The small group made their way back to the house. The sun was finishing up for the day, as usual; ready to travel beyond the horizon. Thirty minutes is all it would take. Kip decided on staying out a little longer and shooed everyone into the house so he could spend time alone on the beach. He needed to think.

He headed south along the shoreline and was now about two hundred yards away from the house. This spot was one of his haunts, a little patch of sand at the rise of a small dune heading away from the sea. He scaled its shallow height and was at the crest where a plateau, a viewing platform, if you will, awaited his arrival. He collapsed his legs and went into a minor free fall, bracing the buttocks for a soft landing. Kip then drew his knees towards his chest, making tracks in the sand with his heels, and submerged his feet into the sand. Spreading his toes apart allowed granules of yellow cake sand to fill in the cavities between each digit. He unscrewed the cap off the water bottle and sipped slowly. He debated over the choice to bring the pear with him, as he was now unsure about wanting to eat it. He replaced the cap on the water and set it down behind him, sheltering it from direct sunlight.

He reflected upon how he returned to this location often. Here, or a sea cliff nearby, just to sit and stare out at the horizon. A solitary figure on a beach, alone but not lonely. Here he shared this place with the body of the sea itself and the incoming rolling surf. Here, at the eastern edge of the Pacific Ocean, at the very edge of the continent. Beyond, a vast expanse of tangy tasting salt-water, that he never tired of gazing over. It was a peaceful place, serene and timeless. Whatever troubles happened on sea or land never altered its rhythm, it simply rolled on.

He watched now with idle interest as sandpipers went scurrying up and down the sand, timing their run with the crashing waves as the spent force of water slid in, paused a beat, then retreated out. Back and forth. In and out. Their stick-like legs carried their tiny bodies with amazing speed and they were able to dash just ahead of every incoming threat. They chased the wave out to sea again and then stuck their pointy beaks in the wet gurgling sand, hoping to gain some appetizing morsel. He looked over to see two men from the south end of the beach coming towards him with metal detectors. Both had one arm extended, clutching thin and round dull metal poles out ahead of them, pointing downwards. With headphones on, they raked the beach, performing slow methodical sweeps of the sand. Kip knew them as regulars; they came here often, and he knew their method. Working together, about five feet apart, the range of their arcs tipped the others inside sweep; that way they could cover the maximum ground effectively. Both men were elderly. Their clothes were almost ragged and well-worn, the cuffs of their khakis rolled up a notch or two. No shoes. *Why would they need them?*

For both men, long, mangy gray hair protruded beneath beige colored baseball caps, while matching three-day whisker stubbles thinly covered their weathered faces. They looked like brothers. Rumor had it they were brothers. But they were unruly and downright rude if bothered while working the beach, so nobody knew for sure. These were men with time on their hands. Their pace was slow and the time it took to sweep the beach each day was great. When you thought about what they could hope to find, particularly anything of value, well, the return on the investment was small. The metal detector, as the name suggests, detects metals. So when you think about it, when searching for money, what was the best you could hope to find? A quarter!

Time versus Reward.

Kip squinted quickly and shuffled his feet in the sand once more before his gaze moved away from the brothers Grimm and returned to the small waves, watching as they beached up on shore. The lip of every wave rising up, then cresting, then so suddenly pounding down in a constant grind on the beach, as if to say … *take that!* The incoming waves had an effect on him he could not explain. He watched the rhythmic cycle and he listened to the waves; each one sounded like small echoes of distant claps of thunder on a dark and stormy night, lulling him into contentment. He loved the ocean. He always had. Many saw the water's edge as an end point, a barrier, a border, or perhaps an aquatic boundary fencing you in; a final destination or the road's end, but he saw it as a vehicle to carry you off to faraway lands. His desire to be by or in the sea and explore its mysteries would always be there. Whether it was the excitement of diving down to access the entry into the hotel under the sea in Florida, or diving the coral reef walls off Costa Rica and Belize. All was a thrill. Or visiting the many other diving locales off the coast of Florida and down into Bahamian crystal waters, venturing to Hawaii to ride and swim with the giant sea turtles. These were all great adventures. He recalled experiencing magnificent diving in Palau, Bonaire, the Maldives and the Great Barrier Reef in Australia. These places needed to be revisited.

Kip finally pulled away from the hypnotic trance and tracked the sun's path. He squinted again towards its location. As was often the case, he monitored its late afternoon arc across the endless sky. It was settling now, just above the distant blue line that served as the boundary between night and day. A perfectly round lead ball glowing molten orange was melting slowly, pouring yellowish liquid into the waters before it would take the surprisingly quick plunge into the abyss. The sun was ready to dissolve away for another day.

How do you open a safe that can't be opened?

Kip needed water for his thirst. His right hand reached behind him in search of the bottle. He was tapping the dry sand back there with no luck. He did not want to take his eyes off the spectacular sight of the setting sun.

How do you bypass a time lock system?

Where was that bottle?

He was thirsty. He told him-self, *I could use a drink!* Huh. *Where had he heard that line recently? That's right ... Special Agent Gannich.*

He recalled the man's reasoning to sample happy hour so early in the morning. Then it happened. It all happened in less than a second, but like a dream it played out forever. Answers finally assembled one after the other into cohesive thoughts. He was trapped in a place somewhere on a dark and moonless night. Not knowing which way to go was debilitating; groping around, lost and drifting but then suddenly, runway lights switched on, an airstrip appeared out of nowhere and the mystic clues unscrambled and became instantly clear and recognizable.

The once ignored answers lined up like pretty tin soldiers all in a row, like a multitude of planes on final approach, one after another, patiently waiting their turn in an orderly fashion-ready to perform perfect three-point landings on the lit airstrip below now active in his brain. The answers came, mystery almost solved. He now recalled what the captain on the flight back to L.A. had said. He had heard those words announced countless times before on planes. He just never connected the dots. All the while he kept his eyes on the setting sun and blindly searching for the water. The bank vault, Sunday, Gannich, the pilot's words, the metal detectors, the setting sun. It repeated itself over and over and over again like the waves that rolled in from the sea. The bank vault, Sunday, Gannich, the pilot's words, the metal detectors, the setting sun, the little hints ready to land in consecutive order at "the aha moment airport." The tiny clues once a jumbled heap rolling around in his head, the ones tugging and pulling at the corners of his consciousness, now demanded to be recognized, finally having their day. The answers now racing through his head and repeating themselves over and over. All he needed to do was to accept them.

The words came out, spoken to no one. "That's it! That's how they did it! That's it!"

He jumped up, patted down the pockets in his shorts searching for his phone, but all he felt was the pear. He sprinted home. However, his mind was ahead of his body; slipping in the sand as he tried to gain traction he looked more like a stumbling amateur at his first track meet, failing to make it out of the starting blocks successfully. Clumps of sand shot out behind him as he raced along the beach. The western horizon was breaking down into afterglow, but he never noticed its captivating beauty. He covered the two hundred yards back to the house quickly and took the wooden steps to the top four at a time. He threw open the front door and froze! Ralph was in the foyer. Kip took half a second to readjust and carefully skirted around Ralph who was sitting there all coiled up and possibly, at least to Kip's way of thinking, anyway, ready to strike. Ralph's forked tongue poked in and out, not making friends with Kip at all.

"JACOB!" Kip shouted. "COME AND GET YOUR SNAKE!" He then went for the phone.

"Oh, cool! You found Ralph!" he heard from somewhere in the house.

Definitely no snake, he made a mental note of that one.

Kip retrieved his phone. He could have sent a text message but some news, he thought, you just have to deliver with the spoken word. He scrolled through the phone's list of numbers, found the one he needed and hit speed dial. He waited four rings, it was an eternity! Then it switched over to voice mail. He impatiently waited for the instructions he had heard a thousand times before telling him how to leave a message.

"…. after the tone." Beeeeeep!

"They're on a ship!"

Chapter Thirty-Seven

THE RIDDLE REVISITED

The thing is, with a global economy, a world has now been created where resources are competitively vied for because of greater worldwide demand. *Emerging Markets* create a shift in manufacturing locales with the never-ending quest to produce a cheaper product. Most legitimate and responsible corporations are stretched to the limits to find the right balance between quality and acceptable work trade practices for the employees in the host country, but above all – price! How much can we make it for? How much can we sell it for? How much profit?

Corporations continually search for these labor forces everywhere, for when it comes down to it, the fundamental goal of a company is to continue to produce their product, the one that, in their opinion, is better than that of their competitors, which in turn keeps the wheels of industry turning. The one certainty for having a job tomorrow. Part of the formula is now commonly achieved by producing it at a more cost-effective price far, far away. The balance for the corporation is to keep that gap between cost of goods to produce and value of goods to sell (the margin) as wide as possible. It's cheap, and we still manage to make great profits. By doing this, the rehashed motto is always, in the end, the corporation and the consumer win together. A win/win.

Alas, everything has its drawbacks and downsides. One pasted over consequence is the displaced and now disgruntled workers who were left behind, without a job. Poverty is always knocking at their door. They hold hollow comfort in knowing that the product that they proudly produced for three generations can now be purchased for thirty-two cents cheaper at the local store. And the quality, they point out, is also at least thirty-two cents less.

But time waits for no man, and progress is the cornerstone of civilizations, or even man himself. So, as went the industry of manufacturing the carriage and buggy into the annals of inevitable extinction due to the arrival of the automobile, so to do the professions of people whose comfortable earnings have been taken away due to relocation of factories they worked at their entire lives. Training is provided and new vocations in even newer industries are offered, holding out the possibility of sustainable employment and income for what they hope this time is a career that will see them through to retirement.

Another downside to consider is the lack of accountability and control. In the never-ending quest to produce it faster and make it cheaper mentality, either driven by the company's bottom line or today's share price on Wall Street, the risk is spread globally. The four corners of the world are brought into play and a company's ability to keep everything tight and ship- shape starts to look a little shaky. Holes in the protocol, either through different customs, regional traditions, and miscommunications because of the language barrier or colloquial slang starts to appear. The cracks open as the chain gets longer and somewhere along it, a link is weak. And it is an awfully long tangled chain to unravel and uncover and repair for what started out as a small problem. Has anyone ever heard of cover-ups?

So, for a smart person wanting to take what is yours, the last place they try is the one location where the security is the tightest. The strongest. Impenetrable. Corporate head office where all the secrets are kept safe under lock and key and surrounded by the latest security measures. And so that smart person looks elsewhere in the global chain. The weakest link. The path of least resistance.

The smart person has many options. It is just knowing where to look, who to prod. Is it just an amount of money that will dislodge what you want? Or will it require a little more applied pressure in just the right place?

Could be a supplier who, through threats of the corporation taking their business elsewhere, has had his margins whittled down so far that it is now so hard to turn a profit. Surely they could hand off snippets of corporate information – for the right price – of what they know.

Who would find out? After all, it is not like they have information about the entire product, just basic things like material costs, purchase price per unit, what makes up the components they themselves provide. If a supplier could hand off tidbits of information to, let us say, an interested party considering entering the market, that would in turn provide the opportunity for a second revenue stream to the supplier, because the new party would now buy from him, also; then that supplier in turn would become a valuable asset to an additional player. One who would gladly pay a little more to get into the game. And when this happens, two clients competing for limited resources, well, then who is going to pay that little bit extra to be ensured priority of supply?

Then who could blame the supplier? Who would know what he has done?

Besides, international espionage happens all the time – doesn't it?

Another endless source is the disgruntled employee or perhaps even more to the point, the disgruntled ex-employee. One carries a grudge ... because ... who knows why? There are too many reasons to offer just one explanation. Passed over one too many times for promotion? An office fling with a boss gone bad?

So is it revenge?

Maybe it is a lack of recognition. Julian, for example, works hard on solving an issue they have had with a code in the software program. He hands it off to his superior, who gladly marches it down the hall to the powers that be, and it is he who is congratulated for a job well done.

Current employees with a passion for hating their employer are dangerous, as they still have access to what they can get their hands on. If they are crafty enough, they can steal and pass on valuable information for as long as it takes to get caught.

Still, a slightly more dangerous character is the disgruntled, can't wait to get back at you, ex-employee. Who, for maybe the same reasons, packs up his computer bag one night, stuffed full of copied files and documents, downloads secure company information onto flash drives and quits by text message the next day. This person can now do complete damage at will because there is no need to sneak peeks over his shoulder while trying to look like a diligent employee anymore. All burdens have been lifted and he is free to start swinging the wrecking ball.

And then there is always the number one reason of all time. Money.

It may go something like this. You pay enough people a lot less than what they "think" they deserve, and after some time, the resentment builds and you have created your very own, extremely large cesspool of unhappiness and discontent. Not good. It is capped off with an over-confident, swaggering leader who dresses loud and drips with expensive everything as he paces through the faraway offices and production plants proclaiming self-importance. This "leader" flew in on the company's private jet. Funny how it is the "company's" jet, but he seems to be the only one that gets to fly in it. This guy certainly knows how to rub it in people's faces.

He boasts in the annual company prospectus, handed out to every employee, that the company has had yet another record year. Sales and profits were up and in light of this outstanding performance, the CEO, amongst other board members, have all been awarded huge cash and stock bonuses for their efforts, all granted by the board on which they all sit and were handpicked by the Chairman, whose relative is the current CEO.
The prospectus goes on to say that the board expresses concerns about rising material and labor costs. These issues would be addressed in the coming year to help reduce Wall Street's fears of price increases and reduced returns on their forecasts.

And as the employee reads this while on his twenty minute lunch break, after doing the math and deciding to go with the cheaper lunch meal today – again - he continually conjures up the color photo of the big, fat- faced, suntanned, (not from working too many hours under the hot sun) well- groomed smiling mug of the Chairman. It is pasted on the inside cover page, top left hand corner of the prospectus, for everyone to see. The guy who is making him work more hours for the lowest amount of pay he can find on the planet. On the planet! And while he is flying around in corporate jets, you shop at the least desirable but only affordable places you can find to help stretch the troubled family budget.

These people are the easiest to find. It is just as easy as picking the low hanging fruit. And so it was that they found the people who they were in search of. It was just that easy. They tracked down the disgruntled, the vengeful, the greedy, or those in need of just a little more. Those associated with Hausen-Tervo, the German-Finnish joint venture company. The maker of the world's first impregnable vault, utilizing their patented time lock system.

Chapter Thirty-Eight

The research was in.

The assessment concluded that there was no need to infiltrate the bank.

Compromise the technology. That was the key.

Locate the weak link.

There are ways. In today's world, systems are global. Resold through a series of distributors. Companies close to their customers receive profits from the markup on the merchandise. Simple capitalism.

But products today are also designed to fail. If not fail, at the very least require constant maintenance and upgrading. Thus you have created another industry, or perhaps for the wily distributor, another revenue stream. The anonymous world of service and warranty contracts.

Reno Cavil, born in Idaho, (go figure with a name like Reno) was overworked, underpaid and most of all undervalued. Or so he thought. He was a bitter man. At fifty-two, he was tall, thin, except for the paunch belly; no wife, not many prospects for a companion, and this made for a lonely life. Male pattern baldness left him with a horseshoe rim head of hair, hair that departed many years ago. Dull, depressing blue eyes sat atop a long thin nose that went with thin pale lips. An unkempt bushy grey-flecked beard added up to someone that wasn't much to look at. And he knew it too well.

He was followed and observed for several weeks. His routine was fixed and plotted. A few weeks later a casual conversation was struck up with a "new friend" at the bar he frequented after work each night. Nothing to go home to.

After several more "you here again?" coincidental chance meetings, a few rounds were bought for his new good friend Reno. The friend vacantly listened to Reno's armchair quarterback commentary on all of America's sports. A few more rounds were offered and eagerly accepted, and the topics moved closer to home for Reno. The more he drank, the deeper and darker the tirades became about how "if only he ran things .... things would run more efficiently, problems would get solved, he would get noticed."

And so after a couple of weeks of enduring his new best friend, and after more drinks, an idea was proffered. A new start-up company, from people with money to invest, wanted some technology, a particular technology that only Reno new how to master. This new company could, with Reno's help, of course, reverse engineer his current employer's design. Study its workings. Find its flaws, its faults, for instance, say - neutralize them. Improve on the system, and then introduce a new range of products far superior. If Reno was willing to help out, for a substantial fee, you understand, who knows, it could lead to something bigger? Perhaps head of R&D and the newly founded corporation?

And so through droopy eyelids and heady visions of greatness one night after a few too many, Reno agreed to acquire the information on the surveillance camera technology they required. Reno handed over the company secrets and they in turn handed him $15,000.00 for his troubles. Then Reno never saw his newfound friend again.

Using these tried and true methods they found what they went looking for and eventually chipped away at the bank's security measures. Just like ducks all lined up in a row, they knocked them down one by one.

Everybody has a price!

All tasks were completed except for the safe. It was an envelope of impregnability. But they were self-assured and knew they would solve that issue, too.

A vault door made of hardened stainless steel plates surrounding molded concrete panels, stainless steel high strength rods embedded in the walls, all encased in hardened concrete. Motion sensors to detect digging or tunneling.

The only way in was through the front door. Well …. if you insist.

Chapter Thirty-Nine

SOMEWHERE

Seamus O'Hanlon sat and waited. He knew his mission. It was simple enough. As he waited, he had time to spare, so his thoughts paged through the various episodes in his life to try and recapture and embellish, for better or worse, the craziness his mind could remember. But in the end, they always came back to the same thing.

As Irish as his name announces, he was born in Dublin into one those large families that crammed as many family members as they could into the council flats that lined the working class streets. As a boy, he was often in trouble, with a Dad who had no tolerance for the mischief he would get into. He was dealt his share of thrashings from his overworked and pushed-to-his- limits Dad. Whatever the reason, whether the school sent him home for fighting, or theft, cheating, or any other number of misdemeanor crimes that he would be involved in. To Seamus and others like him, school was boring and a waste of time. But he could spend hours behind the boy's toilets, smoking the end butts of thrown away cigarettes of the older boys and listen to Brian Quinn stories (most had to made up) of his eldest brother's fight for the cause. The IRA. He would tell of adventures of Farley's passion to join. And, once accepted by the boys up north, he started out with the menial work, roughing up some of the locals who were not "fully committed" and holding back on giving to the cause. Seamus would listen intently but at the same time had the ability to have one eye and ear cocked for Mrs. McKinney if she ever made it around the corner. Experience with her gave him sharp senses, and she was a worthy opponent. Brian told stories of his brother's petty thievery break and enters, small-time hold ups, and always two steps ahead of the law. Eventually Farley worked his way up to daring raids. Such as the time they targeted a British Army fuel truck for destruction – driver and all. What could send a better statement than to ignite a truck full of petrol that would be seen for miles around? That would send the Black and Tans running to go hide under a rock or two!

The infamous British Army in Northern Ireland was referred to by the Republicans as the Black and Tans. This name was promoted to make their connection known to the despised British recruits working for the Royal Irish Constabulary that were sent to Ireland in 1920. In 1920, Ireland was still held under the fading control of Britain. These British soldiers paraded around in a mishmash of thrown together uniforms due to shortages after World War I. Mostly, but not always, khaki pants, black belts, tan coats and a baggy black cap were a common sight. They say the name was coined because of their appearance being similar to that of hunting hounds known as "Black and Tans." The Black and Tans were notoriously cruel and metered out punishment indiscriminately to the innocent as well as the "presumed" guilty, and at will. The people of Ireland have never forgiven or forgotten them.

Brian continued with the infamous tale for the twentieth time, for unfortunately, this truly brilliant plan had run amuck. Some wanker ratted them out, and at the ambush site they found themselves surrounded by black hooded British SAS troops. One smart guy went for a handgun, and after he received a bullet between the eyes that blew a hole out the back of his head, the others saw the futility in a fight. All of them raised their hands and good brother Farley quickly shuffled off to Her Majesty's (spit to the ground thrown in for effect) Prison Maze, also known as "H blocks" near Lisburn, Northern Ireland, where he was sitting to that very day as a paramilitary prisoner.

Seamus did not care too much for Farley. Why, he didn't even know him. But the stories! The high adventure! It was the closest he would come in his country to real life cowboys and Indians.

Although Seamus could never bring himself to want to get involved with the IRA, there came a time in his life when his parents, in particular his father, told him of the choice he had to make. After the Garda had brought him home by the neck collar one night, another bungled small-time burglary, he was told in no uncertain terms, either the Navy, for his grandfather was a fisherman and for some strange reason this made good sense towards his Dad's choice, or the streets of Dublin, as he was no longer welcome in their home.

"Aye, aye, Captain," Seamus said with a grin, a lazy snap to attention and a mock salute. That got him a hard thump to the ear from a father who cared no more. And so Seamus was to become a seaman.

Scraping through at eighteen, Seamus was stationed aboard the LE-Aisling P23, an offshore patrol boat of the Irish Navy. Seamus took to the life of a sailor. But not at first. From the beginning it was extremely hard work and regimented. Being young and the new recruit, he was the butt of the crew's pranks. He felt sure, more than often than not, he would just slip away one night and never return. But to his credit, he stuck to it. He enjoyed the wide-open spaces the sea offered up, something he never felt in the claustrophobic streets of Dublin. And even though his ship never went outside of Irish territorial waters, he relished the sense of adventure that he could almost taste.

And slowly, eventually, for some unexplainable reason, he also took to the discipline. He needed the regularity that came with the work. It kept his mind focused and it gave him assurance knowing someone always had the answer for him. Not a lot of thinking required.

After two and a half years aboard the Aisling, there was an "incident." The LE-Aisling sailed upon a 330 ton fishing trawler from Spain, *Sonia*, illegally netting in Irish territorial waters. *Sonia* spotted the Aisling heading her way and with full speed made for the open sea. A pursuit ensued and *Sonia* refused the calls from Aisling to halt and be bordered. Multiple warning shots crossed the bow of *Sonia* in an effort to persuade her to cut her engines and be boarded. After five hours into the grueling chase LE-Aisling broke off and returned to base. It was later reported that *Sonia* went down in violent sea conditions and only thirteen crewmembers survived.

A full investigation was conducted, as the Spanish government was furious over the conduct of the Irish Naval vessel. However, no misconduct could be proven and the LE-Aisling and its crew were exonerated in the eyes of the Irish public. But a second line of enquiry was being run internally by the Irish Naval Services and they found that there was the strong possibility of misconduct by one Able Seaman O'Hanlon. He had disobeyed orders to fire over the wayward trawler and instead chose to fire deliberately and directly into her hull. This action may have precipitated the *Sonia* sinking in rough waters.

After the public noises quieted down, the Navy quietly sent Able Seaman O'Hanlon on his way.

It was an easy choice for him. He never went home. He never contacted his parents, never saw any friends. He walked down to the dockyards at Cork Harbour just near where the LE-Aisling was based, found an available freighter looking for an extra set of capable hands and sailed away.

He drifted around the oceans of the world for nine years. And in those nine years he saw his fair share of smuggling. At first he resisted. But it did not take long to see that the money was just too darn good to say no. He was involved in all sorts of contraband and he became deft at getting it in, under, over and around customs. He enjoyed the life and he had no intentions of settling down. Then he came to America.

Her name was Kyra. He was with the lads, at a salty, smoky bar one cold misty night somewhere near where the freighter had docked at the Port of San Francisco, California. She tended the bar. All night he engaged her in conversation with his beguiling Irish brogue. As he recalled later, he ran up quite a tab just so he could continue talking to her and then she informed him that she only charged him for half of what he ordered. The ship was in the country for three days. For the entirety of those three days he stayed with her at her place, by her side, mostly in her bed. And when it finally came down to it, he let the ship sail without him.

As her name suggested, she had Irish blood and her name was a perfect match for her dark hair, Celtic green eyes and pale skin. It was comforting to finally find someone, who although she had no clue half the time of what he was saying, let alone knew the intimate details of where he came from or what his boyhood surroundings looked like, she somehow understood him.

It took five weeks. But he wandered down to the docks each day and with a few of the right questions to the right people and a little money changing hands, with the complete understanding that everything was on the "qt."

"Not a word, right?" he would say with a smile and a wink and a strong calloused handshake. He eventually found people who were willing to hire an illegal. No questions asked, as long as he kept his head down and did what he was told. As he told Kyra, there would be times when he would be away for long stretches but to make no mistake, he would always come back. Seamus kept his word.

It started out innocently enough. The men he worked for ran contraband. And they were good at it, too. He would bring her home trinkets from his trips. One time it was some bottles of tequila but as she explained to him, "Seamus, I work in a bar! A bar that sells alcohol! I can get my own tequila!"

Sometimes it was jewelry. But as he gained trust and became one of the core crewmembers, the gifts became more lavish. At first it was marijuana. They had it often. Trying it was nothing new. The quality was good. Very good. Next came hashish. Then the coke. You are never aware of the "creep effect" when you are enjoying a good thing. One healthy dose of a drug, introduced a small portion of another. Several simple words always initiated the motivation. "Let's just try it. It'll be fun." The quality Seamus brought home was good. It was oh, so very good. He came through the door with a grade of product that was always beyond a comparable street level. In fact, it was too good. Over time, it turned them both into heavy users. More so Kyra than Seamus. Her body craved it. They had now moved on to heroin.

One cold and frosty February evening he walked into the house. He was cold to the bone from that particularly icy night. He had been gone for eight weeks. It was about two weeks too long for Kyra. She went crazy for the drug and she had quickly run out of the supply he had left for her. She cursed him for that. It was all she could think about. *Where to get it and how?* Over and over she cursed him. She was desperate and crazy and thirsted for more and so went in search of the drug somewhere, anywhere, but she had to have it.

Through somebody at the bar who knew another somebody she landed in a seedy patch of town. She bought all that she could afford. She raced home and started to shoot up. The drug had very little effect on her. She was used to better. So to take away the awful feelings, she took more. And then more still. Seamus found her lying on the couch. She was cold. She was rigid. He was probably several hours too late, but he had no idea how long it had been. At first he threw up everything he had and wretched more until his stomach ached from the pain and the involuntarily spasms of heaving. Then he held her lifeless body and cried with her until morning light.

He knew he couldn't stay. He was spent and he was suicidal. But one tiny piece of him told him to hold on. Run. Live another day. Even if it was just one more. Run. And so he ran.

Now, every day was just one more day to hang onto. And he never forgot Kyra. He eventually found Mogul and he made out to be a loyal lieutenant. He was a man who needed somebody's help, and a man who could not complain to anyone if he had a problem with the way things were. Just the way Mogul liked it.

So Seamus reminisced and mourned as he looked out into the never. He heard tiny splashes as the occasional ripple lapped up against his craft. Just wait. It would happen soon. He readjusted his black cap over his black hair and waited, just wait and as he did, he absent-mindedly ran his hand along the side of the craft and felt the embossed bold black letters. His fingers played over them and traced the outline of each and every one. They were all slick and smooth. His hand passed aimlessly over them, back and forth. Back and forth. To and fro. The alarm on his watch beeped, it was illuminated so he could verify the time. The twenty-four hours were up. Time to head back. He fired up the engine and adjusted his course with the onboard computer. As he drifted while performing the tasks, fumes wafted over him and he happily inhaled the familiar fetid gas. He shifted into gear and began his journey back the way he came.

Chapter Forty

SOMEWHERE STILL

O'Hanlon sped due east retracing his path back. It was pitch black but Seamus knew exactly where he was going. According to his compass and his GPS he was right on course. He had maintained a location exactly one mile due west of the line so as to not accidentally drift across it in the twenty-four hours he sat waiting. All was going according to plan until out of nowhere red and green lights blinked in the distance. Running lights!

Where the hell did that boat come from?

Although the oncoming vessel had no way of seeing him, as he had no lights switched on, he wanted to remain hidden. He instinctively pulled the boat ninety degrees and headed due south, never slowing down. He estimated he could do this safely for about two miles, sweeping around the unidentified craft, and then alter his course once more and proceed on his original track. The wind whipped his face and salt spray splashed him, served up from unseen crests and waves. He bounced along like a bobbing ball. *The plan will still work. No harm, no foul as they say.*

What Seamus failed to realize was that he elected the very spot where the line came into play. He was weaving ever so slightly back and forth over either side of the line.

Twenty-four hours earlier he was plopped in the ocean, he and his rubber runabout by the mother ship, which then sailed off to complete wide circles around his position before picking him up at the very same spot twenty-six hours later. His orange runabout was identified as the lifeboat that it was. In the unlikely event a boat came across his position, his story was that his crewmates were having some fun with him and would be back to rescue him sometime soon. To prove it, he could show them the rations, the water and radio equipment he had stowed onboard. If that was not convincing enough, he had his Glock nine millimeter tucked in the small of his back for any good Samaritan who got too close and asked too many questions. He was far outside any shipping lanes and the chances of being sighted were minimal.

With time on his hands, he cast a line over the side to take part in one of the oldest sea professions there was. Between fishing and his mind left to its wanderings, time passed, albeit slowly. He bobbed up and down on the ocean swell, but he did not even notice. This was his land.

There was a sharp trill of a sound and that instigated his tapping a key on his computer that revived it from sleep mode. He viewed the information that popped up on the screen. He grabbed another handheld computer device and carefully keyed in twenty-three strokes. Double-checked it was the correct twenty-three. The task completed, he fired up the engine and it roared into life; he gunned it. Due west, two miles. His lifeboat/runabout, with its manufacturer's name proudly displayed on the side, "Sunday," would get him there and back sometime after the next twenty-four hours. No worries.

Chapter Forty-One

It is far away, and it is a lonely place. It can be hot. It can be cold. It endures extreme tropical heat and the coldest of subzero temperatures. And everything in between.

The IDL is an imaginary line. It is an arbitrary spot on the global map that has been chosen to be what it is. Its number is for the most part 180. It is the place where naval officers can claim they now have the right to get a golden dragon tattoo once they cross it.

It is the 180th Meridian and together with its opposite, the Prime Meridian, that form a circle that divides the globe into the Eastern and Western Hemispheres.

The IDL is commonly known as the International Date Line.
It is far out at sea and somewhere near the midpoint of the wide and expansive Pacific Ocean. For the most part it lies at 180 degrees longitude and is primarily located on water.

It is the location where the international community recognizes the difference between one calendar day and another.

The entire global economy relies on this line being honored. Satellites tracking time require this distinction. A satellite that relays information from a transaction a customer makes at say, an ATM, or swipes their credit card, recognizes this date and time service. Global financial markets rely on the existence of this imaginary line to record large fund transactions across multiple time zones. All this worldly business tracked by satellites that must be precise in their ability to accurately record the times. This imaginary line in the middle of nowhere is vital to world trade. Every official and corporate body recognizes the significance of this line drawn in the water and carved out on maps. East of the line is Sunday and west is Monday and no one disputes it.

Chapter Forty-Two

Los Angeles, California – FBI Headquarters

December - Saturday – 8:03 a.m.

He finished a workout earlier in the day and it felt good. He thought, *Once I wrap up this report with John, I will spend the day with the boys. Maybe toss a football around at the park or throw those kayaks in the water,* like he promised himself he would. *And later, some quality time with Mette.*

   John and Kip once again found themselves in John's office in Los Angeles and this time they were enjoying their morning cup of coffee. Although it was Saturday, John still wore a perfectly tailored blue suit, white shirt, dark blue tie and black dress shoes. Kip was not quite up to the task. He wore black chinos, belted, an open neck collar light blue button-down shirt, and casual black shoes. Anita was good enough to come in that Saturday morning too, wearing black slacks, white blouse and a red silk scarf wrapped around her neck. A well-chosen accent piece that complimented her dark hair. She was there not only to put on a fresh pot of coffee, because as John well knew from the many years working with Anita, she had made it clear he was capable of making his own coffee; but she would also be writing the reports that needed to be detailed. Through scattered clouds and a low hanging haze, the morning light managed to break through enough to shine into the east-facing windows. This was their third meeting in less than thirty- eight hours. They had met at the same time yesterday to assess Kip's theory and they were here again today to explore and expand it some more.

John still required convincing and reassurances with this one, even though he had already endorsed it with the agency. In fact, all sixteen security services were now deploying based on this radical theory. John had returned Kip's call on Thursday evening after he was left with the cryptic phone message, and they met to discuss it soon after. John listened to Kip's ramblings, assumptions, theories and just plain guesswork, and then tried to poke holes in it.

It was a crazy notion, but it could work. Finally John was able to fathom the train of thought that was flying through Kip's head at streamlined bullet-like speed. It was bizarre, but what else did they have?

Just a little more than twenty-four hours earlier, Kip explained it like so, "I see it this way, John. Time is constant, it never changes. You can't stop it, slow it down or reverse it. Sure, we can alter it for an hour in the summer and enjoy more daylight at the end of the day, but that's about it. It always bothered me in the reports that I read how a time lock safe, tied to the Prime Meridian via satellite as it is, how it would open on the following Monday morning one minute late. Why would it open one minute late? It didn't make sense, but there is precedent for a reason here, John."

"What do you mean?" John asked, bewildered.

"An incident occurred out at sea some time ago, when no less than six F-22 Raptors, you know the ones, the stealth fighter jets? Well, these six jets crossed the IDL in formation but as they did so, for all six, multiple system malfunctions caused the onboard computers to crash. This included their communications that went offline. They had to physically take over flying the planes while trying to figure out what happened. Fortunately, the pilots were experienced and landed safely. The systems were diagnosed and tested and later rectified. But it explains how some basic computer codes in conjunction with the International Date Line could disrupt and alter computer software at the highest levels."

"I see what you're saying," John confessed.

"So, if it holds true that you cannot change time, then why did the safe open late? Or more importantly, what caused the change? It came to me in pieces. One of your agents in New York made a throwaway comment; he said, "*It's beer time somewhere!*" It didn't mean anything at the time, but it must have registered in my subconscious. I retained another tidbit when flying back from New York. The pilot unconventionally gave a speech about flying time, altitude, the weather in L.A. that we would expect and so on. But he also said something else. And if he had not mentioned it, I would not have given it a second thought as my watch automatically resets for the time zone wherever I find myself. But he announced, "*reset your watches back three hours as we were now entering Pacific Standard Time.*" You don't here that from pilots much anymore, there's not so much of a need as most people's devices are synched with the satellites above. I put two more pieces of the puzzle in place when I was on the beach watching the sun go down over the horizon on Thursday evening. First, a couple of guys with metal detectors were out there. You know how they sweep the sand and look for coins?" Kip gave a small demonstration of how it is done with both hands while remaining seated.

John nodded. He could picture the image in his mind easy enough. It was a fairly common sight to see.

Kip continued, "Well, it was the process of it I was thinking about as I watched them. They sweep, hit metal, and a signal is sent. They receive the signal. They locate the coins by a signal."

"O...K." John said slowly, still wanting to know how this all tied in. "Go on."

"Well, still not putting it all together yet, I sat there watching the disappearing sun and I just knew that while it was getting darker where I was, it was going to be a new day wherever the sun went. A new day, John. A new calendar day. Los Angeles's time zone sits almost at the very end of the global calendar day. I'm betting they found a way to override the system that held the daily code and sent a signal to somehow push, not time, but the *day* itself, forward. This would allow a whole day uninterrupted to work inside the vault. Which is why they pulled the caper off on a Sunday and not on the Friday! Friday makes more sense if you want more time and distance to escape from the bank."

"Well, I have to stop you there," interrupted John "they never got the code!"

"No, I think they did get the code, but not from the source we think it should have come from, I'll agree with you there. But maybe that was just a diversion. How hard did we really look at anyone else except Walker? There were two other guys in that room when the code was entered. And what about where the code is generated? That Hausen-Tervo company. Maybe someone there was involved. I think we need to go back and take a look at other possible suspects."

"OK, maybe," John sighed in submission. His coffee cup remained static in front of him on the desk while he gently rocked back and forth in his chair. "But what makes you so sure it's way out at sea in the middle of nowhere? It could have taken place in New York, or Europe or anywhere for that matter."

"No. Not when you reason it out. Firstly, I'm speculating that they gave themselves as much time as possible to pull this off. When you think about it, it could not have been New York, or even Europe.

"Why?"

"Because New York is only three hours ahead. By the means and methods they used, if they chose New York the bank vault would open for them at 5:00 a.m. on Monday morning. Somewhere in Europe would give them an extra what, five to eight hour window? We know from the film footage taken and the still shots from the photographers that at least some of them were in the race on Sunday morning carrying full bags of something. That puts the time line at nearly twenty-one or so hours earlier than Monday at 8:00 a.m."

"And …"

"And…" Kip complied with the prodding from John, who he knew wanted to have rock solid answers when he himself was questioned over and over again about this. "And secondly, they had to get the day back to Sunday so that the safe would not only relock, but would also reopen on Monday morning in L.A. So remember, they had the code only for Monday, as that was the only one available. If they were anywhere else besides the Date Line, they would have to carry their hand held device west to catch the time zone. That would require a plane, great coordination, and a lot of luck. What if something went wrong? No, it would be much simpler to just walk it back over the imaginary line from where they came that was right there in front of them and place them immediately into the next day."

"OK. But according to our Intel there are multiple locations the Line passes through land. Why not just do it there?"

"Yes, I thought about that too. Russia and Antarctica. Let's look at Russia. Now I don't think it was a Russian gang - they're making plenty of money from straight cyber-hacking. This is a step above and out of their comfort zone and for anyone else. I think Russia is too risky. Too many security forces and suspicious, prying eyes. It's more of gamble going there and getting caught; that's not consistent with the careful planning they've done with everything else. Antarctica is subject to too many adverse weather conditions. For example, if a storm came up it could abort their plan, maybe even the possibility of the signal not getting through. Also, the distance for communicating could present an unwanted challenge. I don't think they wanted to take that chance. I still believe strongly that the ocean was their best hope. It gave them privacy, and ease to get the code back and forth over the Line."

"Yes, I see your point Kip." John leaned forward to rest his forearms on his desk. "Now, one more time. Walk me through how having a code in the middle of the Pacific Ocean helps them with opening a bank vault in Los Angeles?"

"Well, here's how my theory goes. They somehow acquire the code, not sure how. The code for that specific day, Monday, as it changes every day, right? So the code is channeled to a colleague sitting in the middle of the ocean, somewhere awfully close to, but east of longitude 180 degrees, and it's still Sunday. This person enters the code into a handheld device that would override all access and authority for the bank. Let's say, for argument's sake, the last one to enter the code theoretically has control. Now they can effectively manipulate the time lock and that vault door in Los Angeles. Wherever the handheld device goes, so too goes the time lock system. The clock stays constant as Sunday but as this guy somewhat "walks" it west over the International Date Line – Pop! Instantly it's Monday and the time lock clock reads it this way. They wait until the job at the bank is done, and then this same guy heads back east, retracing his steps. As the code is only good for Monday, they head back over the Line and its Sunday again. There is no need to reset the code as the time lock clock reads the device as Sunday once more. Just like my watch resets. When they're done robbing the place, the guys close the vault door and the time lock waits for Monday morning 8:00 a.m., Pacific Standard Time to reopen."

"But still, if this were true, firstly, the Pacific Ocean, Kip? We have no idea where, and it's now six days later. They are long gone. Besides, the guy bobbing on waves in the middle of the ocean is not the same guy robbing the bank in Los Angeles."

"I understand that entirely, John, I really do, but it gives us a starting point, somewhere to begin looking. And now we have the Navy and Coast Guard stopping vessels, maybe we get lucky. Nothing has given us a break in the case yet except the possibility of an unidentified dark colored van being used as the getaway vehicle, possibly being driven by Santa Claus."
What we need to do now is -"

After a quick rattle on the door, one of John's agents burst into his office. With a worried expression on his face he blurted out, "Sir?"

John looked up, "What is it Ben?"

Ben stammered, "Sir, we have just received word that the Navy has detained a ship approximately four hundred nautical miles northwest of Hawaii. The vessel was deemed to be acting suspiciously."

John felt conflicted upon hearing the news. Any new event leading to a possible recovery of all the treasure including Yurushi and Hammerhead was good. But experience had his gut instinct literally feeling the early warning pangs of something close to bile. A knowingness that this news came tainted with dark consequences. He could read it on the agent's face, he had seen it before. He quickly surmised the situation. Detaining a ship, if not U.S. registered, and in international waters no less, was cutting it thin. It could quickly escalate into a worldwide incident.

The press in all their twenty- four-hour news service glory would devour this. A breach of a nation's sovereignty and all that. The big bad United States of America acting as the world bully once more. He could see the headlines, endlessly looping, the same breaking news announced every fifteen minutes, the same dialogue would crawl across the bottom of television screens constantly, then advise the public of updates as they happened. In the meantime they would repeat the same breaking news for forty-eight hours. The talking heads, pundits, retired this and that's, all cramming the airwaves. The endless hype, speculation, guesses, hunches and information from anonymous sources within the administration, taking shots at everyone concerned and prognosticating would-a, could-a, should-a scenarios. Telling the public sensationalized half-truths, and filling in the gaps of what they don't know with wild theories. The television news outlets would quickly conjure up a title for the incident.

How would it read? *"Standoff on the High Seas"* or some such similar awful tagline. Maybe some theme music had been pre-recorded waiting for such an occasion. Could be a slow beat from a snare drum, military style. The tempo would rise to indicate the intensity of the situation. The music would be the backdrop for a highly paid announcer who would then introduce the program host, who with any luck for the network, was reporting it all live from, if not the scene itself, somewhere that looked important close by.

John prayed for a U.S. ship to be caught up in this incident or worst-case scenario, some small friendly nation who would understand. He looked concerned as he said, "They were outside of our territorial waters - suspicious how?"

"Well, sir, the Navy called in the ship's registered name and found that it had left the Long Beach Port on Sunday. They spotted it coming from the southeast, heading in a west by northwest direction. But by plotting its chartered course and knowing its destination, given how much time had elapsed since setting off, it was nowhere near where it should have been. Also it was outside of all known shipping lanes."

"So what did the Navy do?"

"Sir, the Navy halted the ship and boarded it. After receiving unsatisfactory answers from the ship's captain, they began a full inspection. They uncovered a cargo container, sir, with an improper seal. They broke the seal, opened the container doors and found a single black van inside."

John jumped out of his chair. "That's great news!" He looked at Kip, smiled gave him a wink and repeated the words while looking directly at Kip, "That's great news." He turned back to the agent and asked, "And our would-be criminals, Ben?"

Ben took a moment, then replied, "Everybody on board was rounded up and checked sir. All were crewmembers, no question about it. After a thorough search of the ship by the Navy, there were no additional people found on board."

"Well, that's impossible. You have their getaway vehicle, and what about the contents of the safe?"

Ben was looking greyer by the moment with all this questioning of the messenger. "No sir, no men who potentially committed the crime were found, and no trace of the stolen items either."

"Well, any in any event, we are making progress. Thank you, Ben." At this point, John wasn't feeling too badly about the way things were shaping up. They were shutting this thing down. Let the press print that.

At this point Kip chimed in, as John had forgotten to pursue the line of questioning of whom exactly we had stopped in international waters.

"And so, Ben, who did you say the cargo ship belonged to?"

Ben hesitated with a longer pause this time. "Well, sir, we know none of the crew on board were involved in the robbery. They were all sequestered on their ship at the dock in Long Beach. All personnel are Chinese nationals."

John's mouth opened agape and his eyes involuntarily widened, astonished at what he was hearing. "Oh, no, you mean …."

Ben finished John's sentence for him, "The ship is registered in China, sir."

Chapter Forty-Three

December - Saturday – 3:39 p.m.

Where do people from Hawaii go for vacation? It was a question Kip had pondered more than once. He read somewhere, he could not remember where, that statistics showed the greatest percentage of people who live on the islands in the state of Hawaii visit Las Vegas.

Maybe so. Kip peeked out the plane's tiny cabin window locating how far they were from the approaching island of Oahu. The scene outside was spectacular as always. First thing that pops into one's mind on seeing it. Tropical. Or perhaps, paradise. He could just picture a big hitting advertising firm in full stride in their sales pitch promoting the islands:

"Now here's what we're going to do." The guy swept an arm in a huge arc in front of his captive audience. "There will be an ever present irresistibly colorful rainbow in the mountains, right behind Waikiki and Diamond Head as a symbolic backdrop for the beauty and serenity that is the Island of Oahu." He lowered his booming voice, moved in close, leaned in and went all confidential, "The details of how this is to be done have yet to be worked out, but we'll get there! Gigantic billboard like the HOLLYWOOD letters on the bluff above Los Angeles …. something like that."

He straightened and returned with the booming orator's voice once more, "People on the inbound flights will be ecstatic about arriving here on vacation seeing the "lifelike rainbow" that will greet them. People leaving will see it and pine for their next visit. The rainbow will ingrain itself in their hearts, and those folks from wet and damp Washington will cherish the loving memories of the paradise they found and the awesome times they had. We get them coming in and we get them going out, and they will have absolutely no trouble opening their wallets for their next visit when recalling such a wonderful image."

With a cheesy grin, the image consultant wiped his hands together indicating the show was over, job well done on his part. *Sign the contract here and here, and ... right there, folks. Press hard, three copies.* "So, wadaya think?"

After a brief pause the select committee of Hawaiian tourism bureaucrats, made up mainly of Hawaiian natives, all looked at one another, perplexed. The puzzled answer came back, "But Mr. Beasley, we already have that." The woman pointed out the window. "God gave it to us. Look!"

And Kip looked. Using the lush verdant tropical scenery and volcanic mountains behind Waikiki and Diamond Head as a backdrop, a God-given rainbow was arcing ever-present over the landscape. Right on cue.

A flight leaving just prior to 1:00 in the afternoon from L.A., with around five-and-a-half hours' flying time, will land Hawaii around 3:30 in the afternoon local time. Call it time travel. Kip turned to the matter at hand and stayed focused. He spot-checked Ted Atherton sitting next to him who was still deep into the brief. John had stuck them both on a plane, again. He wanted Ted and Kip to be close to the action, and he wanted constant monitoring and feedback. Events had shifted on the ground in ways he could not imagine. Saturday had started out well, but it soon turned ugly. And it went downhill from there. The media had got wind of the armed hold-up by the United States Navy in the middle of the Pacific Ocean. More than likely from a source from within the Chinese Embassy. Now the entire news media were all over it. TV crews shoved cameras into the face of anyone who looked remotely important. Microphones did much the same thing from bloodhound news reporters.

The White House had taken cover from a barrage of questions, including from the Chinese press and more importantly, the Chinese government. The Chinese Ambassador was desperately trying to seek a meeting with the President and if not him, then the Secretary of State and everyone down the line in order of importance. He told the press he was just trying to find someone to plead with to let their ship and crewmembers go. The Pentagon also felt the effects of the onslaught of questions, as did the State Department. It was mayhem in the nation's capital. The media were in a feeding frenzy, having a riotous field day and loving every minute of it.

Kip's phone call to Mette prior to leaving L.A. was not a pleasant one to make. The immediate banishment to distant lands never gets you the permission slip you are asking for. The person requesting wants the good will and blessings that they are seeking from the ones left behind. Particularly when it comes from last minute calls. And particularly ones that leave the person at the other end of the line alone to handle three children and all daily trappings. The response is never, *you want to solve the world's problem – tonight! Well, go right ahead, you are the one destined to do it. I always knew it could only be you that could make things right and I know there is no one else in the entire department who can handle the job. I would wish you luck, but you don't need it. Go get 'em, Tiger!*

Kip also hated to leave. It was partly the reason for his early, very early retirement. He enjoyed his life as a husband, and as a dad. He enjoyed all the trimmings of being a family man. He did not want his life to flash by in a blur. He did not want his family members to be a blur either. And at the pinnacle of his career that is all it was. Everything else came first. Catching one plane then stepping onto another. Always some crisis to contain. Always calling home in hurried rushes because someone was tap, tap, tapping their foot waiting for him to attend yet another meeting or some such thing. Telling your kids you love them over the phone is no substitute for leaning over them, watching them sleep, hearing the tiny breaths they take from their safe, warm beds, and gently kissing them goodnight. Sweet dreams.

But it hit him in a surefire way one day in some place far from home. He woke suddenly and sat bolt upright. He was panicked and in a half-baked sweat. Was it tainted food again? Someone looking through a window? Had someone desperately knocked on the door? Was it all a dream? Where was he again? He just couldn't remember. He searched around in the stifling blackness of the room he was sleeping in. He could hear the noise of the loud air conditioning unit. But as he tried to make things out, all he could recognize was that he was in a hotel room. But they all have the same familiar trappings. Which hotel room? The dark heavy curtains were drawn tightly closed. No light entered the room. He had only drunk one beer.

But in those few moments, between the restless sleep and being startled awake, in that semiconscious state, for the life of him he had no clue where he was. Which hotel, which city, which continent for that matter. It scared the hell out of him. After he calmed down eventually it all came back to him, where he was and why he was there. But then and there he decided to end it. He wanted to get off the perpetual merry-go-round. His decision was solidified soon after when he was in yet another hotel room, having trouble adjusting to the local time zone, yet again.

He was watching some old forgettable movie when he heard an unforgettable quote. Well, in his frame of mind at the time it was unforgettable. A women and a man were standing beside the bed of a frail elderly fellow who had just passed away. The two of them stared down at him for a moment before she spoke, "You want to know something, Pete? He was my father, but as a child growing up we rarely saw him. I have very few memories of him being around let alone playing with him. His work always came first. I never really knew him, and it's sad he died a lonely man."

Pete nodded in agreement, "You know the old saying, no one ever says on their deathbed, 'I wish I had spent more time at the office.'"

Kip really did not want to leave his family again, but this case hooked him. This crime intrigued him no end and a selfish part of him wanted to have a role in seeing it through. He was torn. Before he and Mette broke the connection, each one took it in turn to express to the other how much they were loved. Mette ended with, "Stay safe."

The reason for the hasty departure was due to recent events that had overtaken the situation on the ground. Along with all the diplomatic wrangling over this incident, the Chinese wanted to show some muscle as well. To add fuel to the already blazing fire, China announced that they had sent two 052C class Naval Destroyers to intercept the restrained cargo ship and to escort it safely back to China. They were steaming ahead at flank speed. They would join the cargo ship in around seventy-two hours. The

Chinese were becoming proficient working with Western media. Along with this announcement, they also released footage of the Luyang II class Destroyers. Was it actual footage of the ships making the voyage, or file footage? No one could verify. But pictures tell a thousand words, and this spoke volumes. A full-on frontal assault to confront the crisis; a pre-emptive strike response. The international crisis for which they squarely laid the blame entirely at the feet of the United States. Clearly, this was an unprovoked attack that required a firm response.

The Chinese representative to the United Nations was calling for an immediate resolution and for the United States to release the ship. The motion was gaining ground and China was garnering new friends of sympathy within the council.

In the meantime, The U.S. military internally confirmed Chinese estimates of seventy-two hours, give or take, before the Luyang II Destroyers reached ground zero.

The plane banked hard to its right. Ted shut down and closed his computer, slipped it into its travel bag and looked over at Kip.

"That's quite a theory you proposed."

"Well, there must be some truth in it. They found something on that cargo ship and here we are racing to Hawaii."

"That may be true, or just dumb luck. I guess we can gather more Intel when we get there and put more of the pieces in place."

"Sounds like a plan."

The plane was now trying hard to reach out and touch a solid surface. But it was not Honolulu International Airport that it was making for. Instead the plane would hit a runway that dissected the runways at Honolulu International and then taxi towards Hickam Air Force Base, which was juxtaposed to

Honolulu International Airport. Kip and Ted hitched, or more accurately, were assigned, a ride with military transportation.

Chapter Forty-Four

Warm tropical breezes blew against him. For someone like Kip who welcomed the heat like a duck to water, it was a comforting gift, and a far cry from his trip to New York. There, the thin icy winds in no way enveloped him in comforting arms, but rather pierced right through both body and soul. *Had it only been five short days since he was in New York?* After trotting down the stairs the men met their escort. A slender and fair- haired uniformed naval officer introduced himself while shaking hands.

"Gentlemen, I am Lieutenant Rainey, Admiral Pollard's aide. The Admiral is in meetings all afternoon and has asked me to keep you for a few hours. He will meet with you at Pearl Harbor later today."

And with that they strode from the black tarmac with painted white stripes to the awaiting car. They placed their collected baggage in the trunk and the lid was snapped shut. The sun glinted off the plastic covered red taillights as the Lieutenant swung the car around and away from Hickam. Pounding heat baked the rooftop of the car, but all three men sat comfortably cool inside with Kip and Ted stretching out on the leather seats in back.

The Lieutenant asked with eyes reflected in the rearview mirror, "Hungry?" Both men were. There was not much in the way of food on the transport plane. With the island's population of roughly sixteen percent claiming to be of Japanese descent, due to the migrant farm laborers of the nineteenth century, Kip offered up, "Yes, you know any good Japanese restaurants?"

"Sure, we have a few. I know a good one."

Although Hickam and Pearl Harbor were now known as one base, a matter of economic necessity, the combined JBPHH, that is to say, The Joint Base Pearl Harbor-Hickam, sat miles apart. Their plane had taxied over to a northern runway. Rainey turned onto a service road that passed a military…wait, was that a golf course on the right? Rainey confirmed this with, "Hickam Golf Course."

Enough said.

They exited the base and headed southeast on Kuntz Avenue and traveled past contrasting scenery. Neat rows of trees and well-maintained grass strips on the right hid military institutions, while the left grew into an industrialized landscape. Standing shoulder to shoulder were huge bleak one-story colorless warehouses. Blacktop carpeted everything else. An abundance of bus stops along the route had military personnel standing at many of them, basking in the heat, waiting for transportation.

They joined up with the N. Nimitz Highway, or Queen Liliuokalani Freeway - another way of saying it is HI-92. It all depended where you were on the stilted and divided multi-lane concrete deck. Pearl Harbor was one destination along this road and should take fifteen minutes to get there, but this detour to eat sent them in the opposite direction.

The rest of the journey was uneventful and the lieutenant did not attempt to engage in any more small talk. All the windows were up and the air conditioning was blasting away somewhere close to high, which seemed a little more than was necessary. For although the day was warm it was not the anticipated intense heat you immediately associate with Hawaii. After a few more turns, they snaked down the narrower Pahounui Drive and found parking on the street near their destination restaurant, eleven minutes after they left the base.

Standing on a cracked sidewalk under the tropical sun, Kip inhaled the intoxicating sweet scent from the mix of pungent fragrances in the air. Stepping off the aging concrete path that had a canopy of well-insulated power lines sagging ever closer overhead, Kip saw the panoramic view of aqua marine harbor waters; to his left, the sailing club and marina. They crossed the street and walked on into a new commercial development, harbor side.

Lieutenant Rainey explained. "This was once an industrialized zone that has been converted into commercial real estate. The city, along with a healthy number of business people, sees this as Waikiki's expansion plan. This very site was once a sand and gravel pit. That's all gone now and replaced by this."

The irony in removing the gravel pit facility for beautification and progress purposes was that the redemptive cycle had come full circle. Because by its very nature, the pit assisted in providing material for roads that spread the sometimes-ugly urban sprawl. It also supplied concrete for construction that built fast and cheap industrial complexes as well as strip malls that tired easily and became eyesores very quickly. The gravel pit had now been filled in and replaced with the very structures it was designed to create.

The path they walked upon was laid with what they were calling "brown bear" colored pavers in a herringbone pattern, tastefully designed with no obtrusive power lines overhead. The rich smell of tropical fragrances that wafted over them earlier had to have emanated from this location as the flora was everywhere you looked. Colors to captivate the eyes and smells to intoxicate the nose. For the non-horticulturist shoppers and tourists, the flowers and plants had plaques planted in front of them to aid in their identify. The plants included Birds of Paradise and patchworks of varying colored orchids weaved in amongst the arrangements of Sago and Areca fanned palms that lined both sides of the wide promenade. Heliconia in both red and pink were on display as well as Torch Ginger, Hibiscus, Lokelani Roses, and Oahu's state flower the Yellow Ilimas.

These tropical wonders were intermingled with Watermelon Obake Anthuriums, giant green-vined plants sprouting watermelon colored spathes. Tall rigid palm trees stood at attention and escorted you along the walkway until you came to the Banyan trees scattered amongst the restaurants. They provided cool shade for the diners who sat outdoors to enjoy the parade of yachts, boats and ships that sailed by. The Banyans had grown their noted aerial prop roots that dropped down from branches above to support the trees growth and stability. Decorative lights laced the prop roots to stunning affect for night dining.

The development hosted several opulent restaurants whose designs included an abundance of water-facing windows to take advantage of the views, together with outdoor dining. Reasons why they enormous rents were demanded and paid. A steeply pitched gable roof made of standing seam metal, factory finished in bright red and guaranteed not to fade, successfully contrasted with the emerald green water only a few steps away. They passed the steak house and seafood restaurant and entered *The Samurai's Table*. There was a healthy crowd still lingering at the outside tables. It was too good a day to throw away working or walking around souvenir stores. A petite young woman, fulfilling the role of the welcoming Japanese hostess, greeted them.

The restaurant was dark and cool and had ample welcoming ambiance. The décor was a true representation of exquisite Japanese living and dining. Mette would appreciate this place. The two men would forego the sake while on duty. Between jetlag and sake it would not have made for a very good impression on the Admiral they were to meet. Kip instead opted for water and Ted asked for sparkles in his water. Lieutenant Rainey declined the invitation to eat at 4:00 in the afternoon and instead headed outside to wander around. He left the two men sitting in their booth on wooden benches with blush red cushions, facing opposite each other, separated by a smoky black table. Kip watched him go and noticed that as soon as he was out the door, he placed a cigarette in his mouth and walked away, blue smoke drifting away in his wake.

When they could eat no more of the Miso soup or their selections on the sushi platter, the udon noodles, Tataki seared tuna and both shrimp and vegetable tempura, they turned to discussing matters of the case. The food was indeed excellent and met its very expensive price point, but it was time to move on. Sitting at in the far end of the dining room per their request offered privacy they could control and a clear view of the restaurant. Professional training had taught them these basic procedures.

The efficient waiter removed the check and platter off the table and when he was gone Ted asked, "So I've made some of my own assumptions about what's going on here...what's the rest of your theory, Kip?"

"Let's hear it then. You first," Kip challenged Ted.

With a sure smile Ted was delighted to offer the following scenario, "OK. The thieves rendezvoused with this Chinese cargo ship, which was commissioned to take the prize out of Los Angeles. They're now somewhere in the middle of the Pacific, southeast of Hawaii, far away from prying eyes. They retrieved their treasure and doubled back to the U.S. mainland. If not the U.S., then perhaps Mexico or another South American haven."

Kip used a follow-up question, "Why would they involve two ships and double up on their exposure? Why not stay with the ship they were on? What if the Chinese just ran with everything they were given and sailed directly back to China? There's no insurance policy there for the gangsters. That doesn't make sense."

"There's always an insurance policy with these guys. Maybe they were holding the Chinese gang's imported human slaves as collateral in San Francisco somewhere. Who knows? But after their meeting at sea, the crooks collect the bounty and now have the luxury of heading for any number of destinations based on where they are floating. They could make a runaround play getting into Mexico. They wouldn't dare risk crossing the Mexican border by land with what they had on them. Particularly now, with our Customs and Border Protection Agents on the lookout for weapons being smuggled into Mexico. Too much risk after what they had pulled off. No, they thought no one would be suspecting a ship coming into the country with imported goods carrying their stuff. Either that, or they're on a beach south of San Diego throwing back Coronas right about now."

Ted was satisfied with his answer and while reaching for some water said to Kip, "Your turn."

"Well, for me, they are still on a ship, charting a westward course."

"How so?"

"They took something out of that vault in which the Chinese were already complicit. For our friends the vault snatchers, boarding the Chinese cargo ship and taking back their goods was already in the plan - no accident. Now granted, the

Hammerhead plans were more than likely a lucky bonus, I don't know for sure. There seems to be too much planning that went into this, so trying to grab the file at the last minute doesn't add up. It had to be something else. It could have been the possible billions from the Hollywood crowd, but I don't think so. The Chinese have no need to go after the money. Maybe it was Yurushi, but that was an unplanned deposit into the bank as well. So if the Chinese were involved from the beginning, then included in the plan was the delivery of goods to the Chinese. A direct handover."

"Then why leave the cargo ship?"

"I can't answer that. But my reasoning tells me the perpetrators are still heading towards China, on board something else." Kip's face cracked a smile as he added, "We just have to find that something else."

"Huh." Ted changed the topic, "You know, John's getting hell for this robbery from everyone. But you know where the greatest pressure is coming from?"

"Ah, easy …The Pentagon." Kip answered defiantly then sipped some water.

But Ted just shook his head.

"The White House?"

Another head shake.

"The State Department?"

"Nope."

"The Bureau?"

Head shake.

"The ….. Oh, I don't know, which department is it?" Kip finally conceded.

"Actually, it's the guys running showbiz. No one can ramp up pressure like those guys. They want it all back, Kip. And they are persistent in letting John know it. Senators, Congressmen, other political officials, not to mention their own lawyers, ex-Bureau members, you name it, they are all over him and they ruthless about it, too."

"They have insurance to cover the loss. They have the bank to sue, right? I don't understand the problem here."

"Well, it's like this. They want their money back now. They don't like anyone taking what's theirs. Insurance and suing takes time. They want the money back now. There are films to make."

"Ok," was all Kip could muster.

There was a moment of silence and then Ted moved on to another topic. "So the objective that was discussed back at headquarters is still the way forward?"

"I can't see how it's changed. We will get a briefing from Admiral Pollard and hear his take on the situation, but our responsibility lies in retrieving all that was lost in the vault."

"Have you ever seen this diamond they're talking about?" Ted asked.

"No. No pictures exist. I just picked up on some sketchy rumors. With Mette involved in the arts in our community, it's been talked about in "what if" conversations. I thought it was folklore. You know, like the Loch Ness monster. It would be a sight to see if the rumors were true enough."

Mentioning Mette had Kip thinking how he never had the chance to make it home before leaving Los Angeles. The reason for not returning to grab essentials, and also to explain to Mette in person about his sudden departure, was due to the hastily assembled team meeting at the Bureau. It was also the reason for not getting on a plane until one 1:00 in the afternoon. Kip, Ted and

John were hastily mapping out a plan of attack, which is never a good thing. There were still multiple possibilities for what happened, but other agents would work those ideas while they stuck to this objective.

They knew from reports coming in that the Navy and Coast Guard were patrolling in a sweeping line from the Aleutian to Hawaiian Islands. Still more ships were on high alert for anything from the Hawaiian Islands all the way to the mainland of the United States. But all the same, the area was too massive to cover. Kip's theory, if proven correct, had the culprits skirting south of Hawaii and losing themselves through the myriad of South Pacific islands. It was a matter of knowing where to begin the search. The task was daunting and resources ultimately limited.

Almost fifty minutes after entering the restaurant, Lieutenant Rainey stopped back at their table and looked at his watch. "We should be heading back to base."

Both men agreed. They paid for their meal and left the restaurant.

The return journey had them brushing past the airport again and making their way to Pearl Harbor Station. Here, Lieutenant Rainey dropped them off at their quarters where they could regroup and shake off some of the lag they were beginning to feel. Both men showered and were ready to be escorted over to Admiral Pollard's offices one hour later. The clock now read 5:52 p.m.

Chapter Forty-Five

Pearl Harbor - Hawaii

December - Saturday – 5:58 p.m.

Pearl Harbor was a sprawling place and it took Lt. Rainey's driving at a slower pace due to traffic, a few minutes to reach their destination. They parked outside a nondescript low-rise building and entered an outer office, a welcoming area where another staff member was seated. He snapped his head in the direction of the incoming to see who of importance had arrived and then immediately went back to rapidly typing on his keyboard. His curiosity had been satisfied and as the men were not in high-ranking uniforms, he was curious no more. The lieutenant put an arm out sideways to motion the two men to halt. They would wait while he went forward into Admiral Pollard's inner office to make sure he was ready to receive them. Obviously he was available, as he sent the lieutenant out to fetch them. But this was protocol and everybody played their part. Kip and Ted stood patiently waiting in the "outer sanctum" for a few minutes longer. A large industrial three-bladed fan rotated above their heads at a modest speed. From experience, it was adjusted so as not to send all the papers on the desks scattering. The fan swayed slightly and teased both men's hair as the air *whooshed* around the room. The inner door opened and they were ushered inside.

Admiral Morgan Pollard was the no-nonsense Commander responsible for the United States Pacific Fleet. Abbreviated, it is USPACFLT, garrisoned at Pearl Harbor. His actions are held accountable by United States Pacific Command. They were abbreviated as CDRUSPACOM. They are also stationed on Oahu at a town not too distant named Salt Lake. They are in command of all forces inclusive of land, sea and air in the Pacific.

Pollard's office was certainly spacious if not a little outdated. Either there was no room in the budget for upkeeps, which seemed unlikely for an admiral; he, of course could "make room" for such things, or the man was all business and the intricacies of having a glitzy office meant little to him. Behind the man that stood at the desk hung huge windows. Almost floor to ceiling. This allowed Pollard sweeping views of the open parade grounds beyond and further beyond that, his second home, the sea. It was now after sunset; a soft orange haze had settled on the horizon, but it was already descending into a violet hue. Above the orange flare, the sky glowed red and a few stars eagerly awaited bursting onto the night sky far brighter than their current pale flickering.

Dressed in dark navy blue trousers, a white shirt and tie firmly knotted in place, Pollard was all business. Given the circumstances, who could blame him? He was bent over his desk writing something on a notepad. Like he just had a thought and needed to record it for future reference more so than just making a mental note of it. It struck Kip as odd in this day and age of computers that someone was still "writing" things down on paper. Someone as important as the admiral. Perhaps it was the lieutenant who had the unenviable task of transferring his thoughts to eternal posterity via the keyboard. He finished writing with some gusto, and with just a little too much dramatic flair for his audience. Then he plopped the pen down on the notepad and looked up at his guests.

"Gentlemen, I am Admiral Pollard, you have obviously met Lieutenant Rainey," he made a sweeping hand gesture over to his aide and even half-turned to look at him, "That will be all, lieutenant, thank you." With a quick salute he dismissed Rainey and turned back to the two men, "And you are …" his voice trailed off.

"Sir, I am Special Agent Ted Atherton with the FBI, Los Angeles headquarters, and this is Kip Keplar who is aiding in our investigation. My Director, Deputy Assistant John Brozski sends his regards and asked me to convey his appreciation for extending the courtesy of this meeting and providing the FBI the latest information on the situation."

"I have to say from the start that I have very little time for this interruption. As you know, my people are being threatened with what is coming close to an act of war." He eyed the two men intently as he continued, "Something I have been led to believe started within your Agency. So let's get on with it, shall we?"

No seats were offered. None were taken. Pollard could easily be your motion picture admiral. He was about five feet ten inches, but that could always be heightened in Hollywood with camera angles, hiring leading ladies that are inches shorter than him and so on. He was trim, but not wiry. There was muscle under his crisp uniform. Not bulk, just strength. He was weather tanned by the elements and you could sense you were in the presence of a hands-on leader. One who interacted with his fighting men, and rewarded them with the respect he demanded in return to run a disciplined organization. You could just picture him, when not working hard, playing hard. Water sports were most obviously his game. Wind surfing, kayaking, yachts maybe even kite boarding. Kip placed him in his early fifties. He could have been younger, but he would not be surprised if he found out he was older. A more youthful man would mean an impossibly fast track to admiralty. Early fifties seemed about right. He had piercing blue eyes and nut-brown hair. His hair, as one would imagine, was short but styled. He wore a broad gold band with an emerald colored gem ensconced in it on his left ring finger.

Ted began, "Sir, could you provide us with the very latest INTREP as you know it?"

The admiral glared directly at Ted with disdain in his eyes. "As I know it, Special Agent Atherton, the latest Intelligence Report has one of my lightly defended Littoral Class combat ships, The USS Gunnar, standing watch over a Chinese owned cargo vessel, while two heavily armed destroyers from the People's Republic of China continue to bear down on her."

The Littoral Class combat ships had replaced the Navy's aging frigates. They were lighter, quicker and more sophisticated, but also more vulnerable to attack from something like battle ready destroyers.

Pollard continued, "We have a vehicle cargo ship, the SS Rowan, complete with cranes, booms and hook arms on board all but ready to get underway and make for the cargo vessel. It will arrive at the scene in approximately twenty-eight hours if all goes well and the weather cooperates. We pray for calm seas as we have been ordered to extract the storage container with the vehicle inside from the ship. The Rowan is then, at full speed, to return to base. The USS Gunnar is positioned west of the cargo ship as a form of blockade should any threatening ships appear. I have been ordered, I say, *ordered*, not to send more of my fleet into harm's way as our government does not want escalate the tension of this situation any further, gentlemen. The Gunnar right now is a sitting duck if events don't go our way and she loiters too long. That is the situation as I know it!"

"You do understand what is at stake, sir?" Ted offered.

"Of course I know the damned stakes, son!!" The older man fumed, raising his voice. "I find it reprehensible that the Chinese continue to steal our secrets, our weapons systems, our technology and then cry foul and play the victim! The Global Hawk drone is a perfect example of what I'm talking about."

The admiral stepped from beyond his side of the desk and came around to join both men. He stared intently at them for several moments. By now, he had regained his composure. In a calmer voice he intoned, "You know, boys, the thing is, it's the timing. To have our latest technology fall into the wrong hands at this point in time is our misfortune. As you may know, the Chinese have developed a new weapons system themselves. It is a revolutionary missile that troubles our aircraft carriers. They call it the Dong Feng 21D. Dong Feng means East Wind. For us, it's classified as the DF-21D."

Kip asked, "Exactly what does it do, sir?"

The admiral relaxed a little more and with folded arms across his chest, leaned against his desk and said, "It could be a game changer for us. They are calling it the ballistic missile carrier-killer. They are land based launches and our intelligence indicates that the missiles can hit moving targets and strike with deadly accuracy with a range of up to a thousand miles. It can be equipped with nuclear or conventional warheads, so for the first time our carriers would be vulnerable from a payload delivered by this weapons system. We have nothing like it. This pushes our ships further out to sea and you know what that means, don't you?"

Before either had a chance to respond, the Admiral asked and answered his own question. "With the potential loss and advantage we had with the *Hammerhead* technology, coupled with the completed working model of the DF-21D, it could shift the balance of power as we now know it in the Pacific theater. There's the difficult part to chew on. We went from having the high ground of superior strength and technology to potentially losing it almost overnight."

He closed with the statement, " This places Taiwan in imminent risk."

There was silence in the room for a moment, but then Ted followed up with another question. He wanted to shift the focus. "Sir, what is our cover story for stopping the cargo ship?"

"Well, here the situation gets more twisted. China typically accepts scrap TV and computer monitors, hard drives and all types of peripheral equipment from us that we do not allow to be dumped on U.S. soil. Pollution, soil contamination, all those environmental reasons. Well, China has no problem burning this material at their trash sites for a price. We are claiming that we are recovering contaminated computer hardware that was incorrectly and improperly discarded. This particular container has radioactive elements from the place where it was removed. Our line is that we do not want to put the people of China at risk. So we will take it back. And you want to know what the funny part of this tale is?"

"Ah…, what's that sir?" Ted asked, almost raising his hand in asking the question. It was the admiral's strong persona that almost had him doing it.

"The Chinese are not refuting the argument. They know all too well why we stopped this ship and they're not saying otherwise, except to complain loudly that we had no right to halt and board a Chinese vessel, under any circumstances, let alone in international waters. If this isn't bad enough, more information just recently came in." The admiral went on, "The Chinese have just announced that they have launched the SSF into immediate war games. Up until now, there has been no mention of their South Sea fleet initiating any such war games. They have effectively indicated that wherever they go in the Pacific is a no go zone for ships from all other nations. We are naturally tracking their movements, and it's early, but it looks like they are fanning out. There are no war games here, they are up to something."

And Kip knew what it was.

This showdown with the Chinese destroyers was Pollard's battle to fight, and his own role in it was less than zero in shaping the outcome. He sensed Pollard could handle it. Besides, his mission…his battle, was clear. Retrieve what was stolen. With the two plays running simultaneously, both needed to be successful to win the war. He looked beyond Pollard and out the large windows into the darkening night sky. There was still a pinch of twilight left. The quarter moon sickle appeared distant in the sky; he had not noticed it there before. And he knew that beyond the horizon, he was to take up the hunt. He also knew he had no more time to lose. He returned his attention once again to Pollard.

Kip took a half step forward and made his bold request, "Admiral, this is your fight and we wish you luck. However, our mission takes us elsewhere. And to complete it, sir, we need ten of your best men."

Chapter Forty-Six

He was the key to the entire plan. Without him, nothing existed. Without him, nothing was set in motion. He provided the means, and at the same time, he was the buyer.

Chu Shing was ready for elevated status. As far as he was concerned it was a long overdue. Shing's life started out privileged enough. His father was slightly ahead of the other small time businesses. He knew when it was time to become a member of the Communist Party. That gained him preferential treatment, and he operated a number of manufacturing businesses that assisted in the Chinese Government's needs. And he did whatever else was needed. At the end of the Cultural Revolution he could see the light at the end of the tunnel that few others saw, and he set his sights on expansion. The Communist leaders needed people to run "their" autonomous enterprises. Chu Shing's father was one of those men elected to a position of importance. Trade blossomed internally and then expanded to neighboring countries such as Japan, North and South Korea, Mongolia and eventually to Hong Kong.

As a young teenager, his father had handed out to his fighting Communist "brothers" bowls of rice and vegetables as they passed his village on their march towards glory and victory in destroying and pushing out the Nationalists. His family had always been there to assist, but they always fell short of being able to pick up a weapon to serve the cause through direct combat. It was why the Communists had a leash on his family members in restricting their rise through the ranks of power. Chu's father was old and cantankerous now, and continued to run some minor parts of the business. For Chung, he saw it as giving him something to do and kept him out of the way.

Chu had his father's entrepreneurial skill set, but he also had the ability to take his father's businesses to another level. He was conniving, scheming and ruthless. By now, he certainly had the money. He could buy or bribe anyone or anything - but true power came through being an elite member of the upper echelons of the Communist Party. He knew that coming from the family he did, he could never attain it. Not at least by conventional means. Sure, he could serve them, and they welcomed that, but he could never be one of them. Not unless he could use his services to perform glorious deeds that no one else could. He searched for the unique, the prized and the impossible to offer up to the leaders of the Party. Something remarkable, something special, something worthy and unforgettable that would forever place them in his debt. What Chu wanted was a choice of options from them so he could so he could ultimately make the decision. The power would be in his hands. And he wanted a seat at the table so that others would serve him.

As China's economic achievements soared, so too, did Chu Shing's fortunes. His operations touched many fields. He was now exporting something to somewhere every day all over the world. In the beginning it was so easy. Demand for his cheap products exceeded his expectations and as China knew nothing else, to fulfill the outrageously low contract prices demanded by the Western companies. Officials had no problem looking the other way in regards to quality when the price to do so was well rewarded. There was always only going to be two ways. The price of labor and shortcuts. For Western companies it always boiled down to price, or how much cheaper? China's manufacturing

economy beginning in the 1990's was at a point where the
Japanese economy was forty years before. The products were
produced and sold on the premise of being "cheap." During
Japan's early forays into manufacturing, the jokes began and
people would scoff at items "made in Japan." But the irony was,
people still bought them. Japanese companies discovered what was
required to improve their product in order to sell more of that
product to willing open markets. And Japanese companies were
hungry to sell and prosper, and for their people to live a better life.
Thirty years on, after all those jokes about Japan's quality, nobody
makes those same stabs at their quality anymore. Instead, when
people ask for "top of the line products" they need to know that
they are made in Japan. Japan had arrived, and no one was
laughing anymore. Other nations were now mocked and ridiculed,
and that is where China found herself.

So, the Chinese young and green free enterprise machine
was stacked with much vulnerability that a clever person could
exploit. Chu was one of those, and he found a particular weakness.
He was a master at unscrupulously substituting inferior materials at
will. For the longest time no one was the wiser. As he well knew,
laws are created only after the dirty deeds are committed and
exposed. So, when a cost-cutting procedure was strangled to death
due to tougher policing laws, he would "volunteer" a fall guy
within one of his organizations. This poor soul would apologize
profusely for his wicked ways and the shame he had brought upon
his family's good name, before his head rested on the
executioner's block. All this to satisfy the Western world clients.
Chu would always find another way to discount his production
costs and naturally, ensure the "fee" was paid to satisfy the local
authorities; they would, as usual, allow the new process to continue

and with any luck, not get caught. He was able to do this time and time again and skate along without being personally incriminated. This allowed him to move on freely to yet another scheme.

He sat like a king on a throne looking down on his operations and his vassals who managed them, entrapping them into remaining complicit in his schemes. He imagined big picture ideas, schemes and scams, and others worked them. He also operated in partnerships. Well, partnerships at first. He would sniff out businesses that required cash, provide the funds, shake down the hard working owners, strip them of everything and then kick them to the curb. And if intimidating them did not work, he was not above eliminating them. It was all a part of his M.O. His methods were simple and he was good at it. His money was injected into so many ventures, including the supply of construction products such as roof shingles, siding products, sheetrock, plastics, stone, plumbing fixtures, electrical cables, steel, concrete, fiberglass; almost all were produced with built-in flaws to save money. He sold inferior automotive parts, honey and milk - the milk that caused the melamine scare - and he was forced out of that commodity. He escaped by throwing a couple of middle managers to the wolves and paying an extremely heavy ransom to avoid prosecution and jail.

Textiles were another trade of his, and even children's toys (some containing lead paint) were not tactics that were beneath him. Whatever made a buck or two, he was there. He owned real estate both in China and abroad. He owned a stable full of horses and went to Macau to watch them race. His energy was endless. His greed fed the unquenchable thirst for always wanting more.

His companies kept their costs low because he demanded it. Worker's rights were a concept largely saved for the Western world. His employees worked long hours, six and even seven days a week for dollars a day, and if you did not like it, literally thousands of people were available to take your place. It was the universal way of conducting business for emerging industrialized nations. People poured into the cities from rural areas looking for work, any work, and a paycheck. His managers knew that they had to cut costs, or they would be cut. And so they did. There were sweatshops producing children's clothing, produced by children for children. His manufacturing plants were selling goods to major U.S. retailers. A large proportion of these retailers gave lip service about wanting fair trade practices operating in the company's factories that they purchased from. It was not good PR back home if it leaked that they were complicit in assisting sweatshops.

However, the U.S. and European companies repeatedly made the same basic mistake when touring the facilities. They would give his companies notice and schedule appointments to see him and his operations. It gave him time to shuffle the deck, bring in fresh employees with new and clean uniforms to work in his production facilities. They even hired fraudulent managers. They would recruit Americans and Europeans who were living in China and keep them around for as long as it would take while clients were loitering in the factories. These young nobodies would be in the background but to visitors who noticed, it would give them a psychological comfort level knowing that people like themselves, young people who dressed well, would not be engaged in anything illicit. So it gave the impression that Shing's offices were dutifully connected to Western culture and customs. It was not unlike duping the Swiss inspectors who toured the German prisoner of war camps during World War II and reported back that almost everything in the camps were run according to the Geneva Convention.

Shing also had a hand in electronic components, computer chip manufacturing and several companies that specialized in cast molds. He produced items in steel, fiberglass and plastic and contracted work for producing microchips. These industries gave him entry into his latest crime. Shing was never satisfied. He was self-driven and always needed more. He felt rich but neglected. Overlooked by the people that mattered. He had to have what they had and an idea grew on how to get it.

It was certainly an exercise in time and patience. He had gathered up the grocery list of items and they began testing the equipment. They went to gas stations with stolen credit cards and stolen cars. A man in a black non-descript sweatshirt, with the hood pulled over his head, would slide a credit card at the pump. The card information was fake and would be easily detected once the information was sent by satellite feed to the credit cards main system for verification. Twice the gas pump computer readout would tell the user that the card was denied and the anonymous man with the card would hop in his car and drive away. After some tweaking, the cards were run again and the next eight attempts showed they could now beat the system undetected. The card was swiped, the information was sent by satellite feed, but they intercepted the signal. They could then control the response and approve use of the card. The obstacle of controlling the satellite signal was achieved. It was as though the transaction never happened.

Chapter Forty-Seven

Chu Shing. Naturally enough, had dark hair, dark eyes and at five feet six inches was considered short. So, too, was his temper. A constantly angry scowl on his face vouched for this. To summarize, he was just plain mean to the bone. The clinical diagnosis would have called it for what it was - sociopathic, bordering on psychopathic. Beyond these attributes, as some unfortunate people came to find out the hard way, there was yet a more intensely dark side to him. His neck bore a hideous growth that he deemed a curse, and deeply humiliating. It crawled up his neck like a sickening brownish slug. He was frightened beyond reason of needles, let alone surgery, so he could not consent to having it removed. Instead he covered it up.

On one occasion, while walking through one of his many textile plants and berating the sycophant managers, as was his custom about the slow productivity output, a young girl working at a sewing machine made two mistakes. Firstly, against all orders, she looked up. They were told to keep their heads down to show how hard they worked. But when she heard the voices of the approaching group she could not help herself. For the briefest of moments she made eye contact with Shing. The girl was far from plain; in fact she was strikingly beautiful. Shing had not successfully buttoned his shirt that morning and remained unaware of his error. The top button had popped open, exposing the growth. When he saw the girl, who was not more than fifteen or sixteen, he was caught by her beauty and reflexed a smile at a pretty face. She in turn brought her hand up to gently touch the side of her neck as if to say, *you have something there*, and pointed to the same spot on his neck. Like others before her, she had mistakenly pointed out his shame and embarrassment to everyone in the room. The instant she made the gesture Shing froze, as did the managers around him. They knew better than to mention his defect although all were aware of the button incident. Shing slapped a hand over his neck to cover up the embarrassment. He quickly rebuttoned his shirt and in the time it took to secure the button he felt the vile rage boil up inside. He had been humiliated beyond imagination, in front of all of those worthless nothings. It was reprehensible!

With blind rage and anger spun around, grabbed the girl by the hair and threw her to the ground. He began to beat and kick her mercilessly for several minutes. She was screaming in pain and fright and he was yelling at her in anger. Spittle flew from his mouth as he loudly cursed her incessantly. And no one stopped him. When the beating ended, he walked away and left her lying there. The underlings followed him out of the building without looking back at the crushed heap on the floor. Later, the girl badly bloodied, battered and bruised was unceremoniously hurled out a back door where the trash was thrown. She was close to death and needed serious medical attention but there was nobody around to help. She was one of the many who had come from the rural areas to the cities in search of work. She knew nobody and she was thousands of miles from home.

Chapter Forty-Eight

He tried in vain for years to join the elite circle. Oh, sure, they gladly pocketed his money and he was invited to certain events, but try as he might, he was always looked upon as the outsider. They treated him as such and he felt the shame. He needed to offer up something special in order to have them accept him as one of their own.

When alone, and in occasional quiet times, he would cast his mind back to happier days of his childhood. As a boy, an elderly wise man was sent to tutor him. In his own way, Chu Shing developed a fondness for this very old man. To Chu Shing, he knew everything, and he told the most wonderful stories of China past. He was the man who introduced him to the secrets of *Nei Qiang*. The old man attempted to impress upon him the importance of embracing the rare beauties in the world and the dangers of greed.

Most who took possession of the Diamond-Jade treasure often met with a tragic fate. But that warning missed its mark and through the intoxicating stories, a spell had been cast over Chu Shing and he was captivated by the wonder of the diamond. A seed was planted within him; deep cravings for this treasure haunted him ever after. He amassed his fortunes, but found his life empty. So he turned his sights on what he saw as a life's challenge. He began his search for *Nei Qiang*. The lust took hold of him. Possessed him. He convinced himself that it was a national treasure that belonged to him and also to the Chinese people, and if only he could reclaim it, it would be the prize that would catapult him to the place he deserved to be. He never stopped to consider that the whole thing was a fable and that the old man might have made the entire story up to keep him entertained, or the fact that Genghis Khan was a Mongol. In his mind, The Emperor operated out of China and took on many Chinese customs and ways and therefore, naturally, the gem belonged to China.

He began financing expensive operations to try and find it. He operated his quest in secrecy. He needed no partners for this quest. He sent teams to Japan. No luck there. He sent people throughout China in the event that it made its way back somehow. Nothing ever came of it.

His Chinese researchers were limited in their access to information from Japan. They could not penetrate the formidable wall of privacy the Royal Family had built and were unable to glean any information they might possibly have. Therefore they failed to pick up on the fact that the diamond had been transferred to the United States via Commodore Matthew Perry. This was not recorded by the Japanese. The Japanese did not care for the gift they were given and were glad to be rid of it. Therefore when Chu Shing's people came looking for it, the memory of *Nei Qiang* was long forgotten. So for all Chu Shing's people knew, it was still behind the fortified walls of the very private Japanese Royal family. Perhaps hidden in some obscure place somewhere within the palace.

At first he cursed his people for missing such vital research information. Out of the blue, he received information about a name he was tracking in communiqués from a Professor Bigelow back to the United States. A paid informant working for the MSS delivered the information to him personally. The MSS, being the Ministry of State Security (the Chinese equivalent of the CIA and NSA combined) operated the third largest Intelligence Organization in the world, behind the United States and Russia. The word *Yurushi* continued to pop up in open communications over the following days and China intercepted all of them. Shing knew *Yurushi* was Japan's blasphemous renaming of the prized *Nei Qiang*. His anger for his people's failure, their having no inkling as to the whereabouts of his *Nei Qiang* was tempered by the sheer luck of receiving this news. He offered his informant a generous bonus to find out where it was and where it was headed. He couldn't catch up with this Bigelow person, wherever he was, but they did track where it would go.

Was it luck or divine intervention that all these events were falling into place for Chu Shing? People with his state of mind always saw the world revolving around them, and as if to confirm this personal aggrandizement, he received the report that *Nei Qiang* had temporarily landed at American Trust in their Los Angeles branch.

American Trust? He knew this name. It was the very same place that his American contacts had asked about supplying technical support and hardware. They had come to him some time ago. They needed a compact handheld keypad device to receive a satellite feed. They knew he could discreetly provide it through his molding and machining businesses. That was easy. The harder request came for the supply of technology for the computer chip technology from another of his clients. Hausen-Tervo, who had subcontracted out the manufacture and production of their processors, computer chips, hard drives, memory boards - you name it - all of it manufactured in China. Chu Shing could lay his hands personally on some of the items, and through industry contacts he could buy what else he needed. China was rife with piracy. Copying and stealing intellectual property from the West was common practice, yet was often reined in by the government.

It was one of the hazards of dealing with Chinese companies. Ultimately, the industrialized world risked it because the bottom line trumped all, and where could you get a better deal today than in China? Shing knew the final item requested could be obtained but at great expense. They needed China's satellite technology.

Chu Shing had come to know his American connections through earlier trade dealings. It all began with a simple shipment of knock-off designer polo shirts to the United States. The goods were inspected and rejected at the dock by U.S. Customs due to incomplete paperwork. He would continue to have container loads of his products rejected for any number of reasons by both U.S. Customs and by customers alike. He had run into the world of rules and regulations and customer expectations trumping everything. The goods would be returned all at his expense. His apparel was rejected for all types of crazy reasons such as, incorrect labeling or labeling only in Chinese, threadbare quality, wrong colors, etcetera, etcetera, etcetera. But, always the entrepreneur, he adjusted. After all, it was costing him big dollars.

So he short-changed them in other ways. He sourced cheaper and more toxic chemicals to use in the dying process; cut labor costs by recruiting anonymous third party factories and paid them far less. Anything at all to keep the wheels of free enterprise churning back in China. But what to do with the rejected products? He had an idea. He made some calls and connected with people who would "help him out" and "take it off his hands" for a substantial discount, of course. He would lose money, but as long as he did not have to take it back it was at least more of a salvageable situation. Even at the prices offered it was more cost-effective to release them than shipping the cargo out to sea, only to have them bob on the waters until he could find another destination, or worse still, shipping the product back to China. So the merchandise was reloaded onto boats and sailed out of one U.S. port and over to another.

His new friends helped arrange, with the support of "friendly" Customs agents, the safe passage of the goods through the docks. Delivered to no-name warehouses and distributed to who knows where. Carried off by the likes of guys named Frankie and his pals. With the help of Little Sammy's people, Chu Shing's goods found a home in America. And so the connection was made with Little Sammy, although the two men had never spoken until this caper.

Chu Shing's timing could not have been better. He did not have all the details, but he knew the bank to be hit. He wondered about when? He had to make the call and find out. Could they do it when his diamond was in the vault? There wasn't much time.

Contact was made. Questions were asked like, *what was he after? How much would he pay?* It wouldn't be easy, but OK, they would grab the diamond. The price was eight hundred million. Little Sammy had a deal.

Little Sammy was earning extra money for being in the right place at the right time. Little Sammy would pass on the information to Tony and Mogul. It was vital they grab the diamond.

Chapter Forty-Nine

THE MILLION MAN SWIM

Someone once claimed that Mainland China could take back
Taiwan anytime they wanted to, and bring it back into the fold of
The People's Republic of China. And this will happen just as soon
as they can find one million soldiers strong enough to swim across
to the island and take it!

That jocular statement was made a long time ago when
China was still a back-water. Back when Japan was vying for the
prize of being the number one industrialized country in the world.
No one was paying any attention to what China was up to. It was a
time when everyone invested in learning Japanese – for business
purposes. Well, in thirty or so short years the times had changed
and that was no longer the case. Chinese languages were in and
teaching centers were popping up everywhere. Everyone invested
in learning Chinese languages – for business purposes. That old
joke was made way back when because at the time, one look at
China's diminutive Navy told them – no way. They couldn't even
defeat a decent size fishing fleet. But Mainland China wants
Taiwan, this is crystal clear, and has repeatedly made claims on it.
Always have. Always will. Always will until they own it. And the
statement, or joke, about the one million swimming soldiers had its
fair share of people chuckling at the remark back in the day, but
very few will laugh at it now.

China's presence as an emerging force is no longer ignored.
Its economy, the fastest growing of any on the planet, is
inextricably tied to its capacity to spend money on its military.
China's goal is to pare down its 2.3 million standard foot soldier

army into a 1.5 million man highly efficient fighting force and direct its attention and funding to technology, greatly enhancing its military advantage, as most modern industrialized countries do. It can be seen in its quest to launch interspace rockets, and its goal to land men on the moon. It is investing heavily in its own research and production of new fighter planes for the Air Force, tanks for the Army, and drastically increasing the size of its Navy. This would include the Dong Feng 21 series of rocket launches including satellite and carrier killers.

All indications of its burgeoning strength, power and importance in the region. And the acquisition of *Hammerhead*, a turnkey production model, operational and ready for action, meant they could do without having to spend the multiple billions it would take to create with their own design. It would be a compliment to their arsenal. They possessed the internal capabilities of arming and manufacturing it. As the military brass knew, if parts were not already manufactured in China, they were industrious enough now to replicate them in-house. Another by-product of obtaining *Hammerhead* was to get an intimate look-see at American technology, and better understand just how they stacked up against Chinese advances in weapons systems and designs.

The Communist Party had taken their time responding to Shing's request for payment in regards to obtaining U.S. submersible stealth technology. What Shing did not know was that the MSS were being very thorough. *Who was this person making these claims?* They scrutinized his background, his businesses, his associates, his social habits and haunts. They needed to know if he was genuinely a loyal Communist, or a spy working for the United States. If it were the latter, he would soon be a dead spy. While delving into his Communist commitments, MSS were also picking up frenzied communications, so called "cryptic messages" between the highest levels of U.S. government agencies. With their sophisticated spy network in place that had hacked away at U.S. intelligence for many years, they had long ago broken the foreigner's codes, and were now listening intently to it all and recording copious notes. Armed with this new information being shouted out from the U.S. about stolen plans for the Navy's latest technological advanced drone, MSS considered Shing's request more closely.

When a Chinese registered ship was detained by a United States naval vessel in international waters, the People's Republic of China took action. Get the plans for *Hammerhead* whatever it takes. We will pay.
Chu Shing had his green light. It had taken seven nerve-racking days, but there it was. His orders from the highest levels.

It was now his time to shine. Nothing could stop him. He would become one of the elite. He used his tongue to wet his dry lips; he could almost taste the power that was coming his way. Without any more hesitation, he made the call to the United States.

Chapter Fifty

East Coast

December - Sunday – 11:35 p.m.

Little Sammy was excited about making the call. New plan. Cut and run. Run as fast as you can. The prearranged meeting had an accelerated time frame with a new item added to the list. It was simply a matter of getting to the rendezvous point and handing over the booty as quickly as possible. Naturally, the exchange of "gifts" would take place after confirmation of the money transfer.

He savored the conversation he had the day before with Shing. He was ready to haggle. *Come now, my friend, this information is priceless! How can I possibly let it go for that much!* All the worst-case scenarios played out in his mind. Protest, complain, threaten to call the whole deal off, lay out in detail how much effort he had gone to in getting everything in place, and without a hitch! The tremendous amount of heat he would feel if suspicion fell on him for handing over U.S. military secrets to foreign nationals, and so on and so forth. But when Shing announced in plain language he would pay two billion (that's billions with a huge "B") dollars in U.S. funds at the time of the transaction, he had a haggle-free deal.

Little Sammy would receive more than twice as much money for handing over the keys to some type of submarine as he was getting for the queen of all jewels. He was pleased with himself when he negotiated a sum of eight hundred million for the diamond. He had little idea of its true value, not many did. But for the beholder, the object was worth all that and more; unbeknownst to Little Sammy, Shing would have gladly paid more.

Due to current events, a new time for the meeting was arranged. It would be the same place but two weeks earlier. No point in delaying the inevitable, and both parties were keen to seal the deal.

Little Sammy was enjoying a fine red wine. A fruity Chianti from the Tuscan region, Ruffino Riserva Ducale Oro, an excellent wine before the call and before his dinner consisting of wild boar ragu. *Aarhh ... his damn full bladder.* He had to use the bathroom, again! Too uncomfortable just to sit there and ignore it while talking on the satellite phone. He rose out of the chair with a pained expression on his face, his only annoyance of the evening.

Chapter Fifty-One

Pago Pago, American Samoa

December – Sunday - 5:35 p.m.

Without knowing it, around the same time as Little Sammy was making his call and six time zones earlier in the day, Kip was waiting for Ted Atherton to finish his phone call to confirm their next flight. They were at yet another airport, in another part of the world, in another time zone. They continued heading west and until they crossed the IDL, or International Date Line, they would continue to steal back time. For as it took five hours to fly from Hawaii to American Samoa, their watches only reset back several hours to adjust to the new time zone.

Kip looked over and saw that the two SEAL members, Byers and Rash, were in a huddled conversation. Maybe something along the lines of … *What? Has the Admiral lost it? What the hell are we doing with these two jokers?* Only two SEAL members because that was the limit Admiral Pollard would allow. Kip understood that when he asked for ten, or for that matter any amount, of Pollard's elite force, there would be pushback. No one in the admiral's position would just lie down and be subservient to the demands of a brash outsider. Kip knew if he asked for two, he would maybe get one. And one was not enough. They negotiated, of course, but the trump card was in Pollard's hand. As it turned out, Pollard was a junior serving under Admiral Alcott at an earlier time in his naval career and he respected and admired the calm man immensely. That was the ultimate reason why he allowed two of his finest to be assigned to the FBI.

It had been a week full of air travel.

Just like the old days.

This port of call, which would be brief, was to secure an aircraft to take them further west towards China, a few islands at a time. Besides scientific research stations in Antarctica, the strip of land they were landing at was the United States' southernmost outpost in the world. It is also one of only two territories controlled by the U.S. located in the southern hemisphere - the other being Jarvis Island. On the map, they were at latitude 14 degrees 20 south, longitude 170 degrees west, just south of the equator. West of here, they would know that they were for all intents and purposes, on their own, and in a new day. This was about as far west as you go before crossing the International Date Line. If someone decided not to make the return trip from west of here a complete twenty-four hours of his or her life would just vanish.

Kip, John and Ted had put together a hastily thought out plan, and it was still quite rough around the edges. John's problem was that he had agents everywhere trying to track down people who he was yet to identify. How do you do that? Kip's theory was one of many possibilities. He got something right about the ship, but where did the bandits go from there? The Hawaiian Islands as far as anyone knew. If they felt their plan was working, then why not lay low in style? It was far enough away from the heat around L.A. South of Hawaii, they could escape to Mexico, Colombia, Tahiti or one of the hundreds of other islands that made up the South Pacific islands. They may have gone to Vancouver, Canada as far as anyone knew. Anything was possible.

Ted, with his list of reservations about Kip's hypothesis, had now joined him in his line of thinking. Their goal was to make their best guess as to where a ship in the South Pacific might be. A guess that may uncover what they were looking for. Then, with the aid of the SEAL team, board the ship, overpower the crew and retrieve what was stolen before it all landed in enemy hands. John certainly could not be blamed for having doubts. It was not the way the FBI ran cases. Therefore, only two men from the FBI were assigned to the chase. Get out of the Navy what you can. It was *their* toy that was stolen.

So the score currently stood: Four men versus the Pacific Ocean.

What did Kip know about the Pacific Ocean, anyway? Mainly one thing. It was the body of water surpassed by none on the planet. The precise facts he did not know, or he may not have started out on such a crazy sea hunt. The Pacific Ocean swallows up almost half of the Earth's water surface or one-third of the Earth's total surface. Another way of saying it was 70 million square miles. It was BIG! And for the most part, it was empty. It lies off the West Coast of the United States and stretches to Asia. It touches both the Arctic and Antarctic. The Pacific Ocean has eight time zones running through it, as well as the Equator and the International Date Line. Try finding one ship in all of that! Finding one needle in a field of 10,000 haystacks in twenty-four hours would be an easier task to accomplish.

The supply lines were stretched thin, and they were now far from reliable resources. Low on equipment. Low on supplies. Low on backup. The United States did not consider the Territory of American Samoa as a vital place to base a large fleet, a massive Air Force base, or thousands of combat troops. This wasn't Guam. This was a sleepy part of the world. It is by no accident that they were near an equatorial area called The Doldrums, where seldom do the winds blow.

It was hot. Unbearably hot. The equatorial regions consist of two seasons, not four. There is a dry season and a wet season. South of the equator December brings the wet season. At the equatorial divide, the northern and southern hemispheric seasons are reversed. So, while winter in December can be mild and sometimes pleasantly warm in L.A. or snowing and ice cold in New England, it was blisteringly hot where Kip currently stood. Very hot, extremely humid, and with the enormous volumes of humidity also come the rains. The cool refreshing rains.

Chapter Fifty-Two

SOMEWHERE ELSE ENTIRELY

December – Wednesday - 7:18 p.m.

There was a breeze off the water. It created just enough wind to make the man on deck turn away to momentarily light his cigarette, using his body to shield the flame. The figure standing in the shadows saw his opportunity and he took it. He hopped over the rail and walked away.

It would be another five hours before he returned. Getting back on board that late was not a problem. Two hours after he was back on board, the ship's crew slipped the heavy ropes off the round wooden pier posts. The wooden posts, twelve inches in diameter and buried deep in the seabed below, swayed against the aging dock. The wooden posts, with rusted metal bands, one crowning the top, another ringing the bottom and one centered, were there so the aging wood was prevented from splitting due to absorption of seawater. The wooden posts were bleached of all color and now uniform in a dying grey tone.

Wooden posts that bobbed around in the water and gave one the impression that they were likely to topple over at any moment. But they never did. Throughout the years they functioned as designed, again and again. Tying up ships from, and releasing ships to the sea. The only witness to all this had scampered on top of one of the wooden posts. She took a quick peek over at the vessel, but beyond that paid no attention to it. She was here for more important reasons, and besides, the beast was too far away to harm her now. She looked around for something to eat. She was out of luck. Eventually, sitting there bathing in the deep heat, even at this time of night, something would be made available. She began to rub her antennae together several times to sense for danger. Nothing there. The baby cockroach stared but did not comprehend what it saw as the ship with no running lights on made for open water and sailed away.

Chapter Fifty-Three

SOMEWHERE ON THE WATER

December – Thursday - 7:14 a.m.

With a curt nod of his head, authorization was given and the other man in the room knew exactly what to do. He stepped over to the man sagging in the chair and struck him in the stomach. There was the sound of a dull thud and then the expected …

"Umpff!"

Another hit, this time more of a crack, then …

"Awwww!"

It sounded painful. Both men hoped it was.

The man giving the orders got a sudden itch inside his left ear. With his index finger he dug around in there then removed his finger and looked at it. He had extracted earwax. It was easy to see in the sterile but brightly lit room. Three naked bulbs shone powerfully from their sockets. After inspecting the small treasure for a moment, he attempted to flick it away, but it stuck to his finger. He tried a second time but got the same result. He had no time for this, so he rolled it against the pant leg of the guy in the chair. He bent down and got in the face of this guy in front of him. He was holding onto a cigarette and brought it up slowly to his lips and drew on it for some time. His eyes squinted, he held his breath for long moment, and then he blew the smoke out hard but slow into the other guy's face. The face grimaced then coughed a little, and his body shuddered some before he could turn his face away.

The guy in the chair had no chance of getting up, let alone escaping. His legs were duct taped to each front leg of the chair.

His hands were placed palms down on the armrests of the chair with his wrists duct taped as well. He wasn't going anywhere. The face was busted up. It was bloody and messy. The lips were split. The gums behind them were lacerated. Blood leached out from the mouth. One of the first things to break was the nose. Now only a small trickle of blood leaked out from the one remaining blood vessel that was able to pump blood, and gravity was hard at work getting the small red stream to his lips. The guy's left cheekbone was fractured, a deep and bloodied gash on the surface of the skin could attest to the abuse coming from someone's use of a leather-bound billy club.

Mogul stood back up to full height and dropped the cigarette butt on the ground. It continued to burn.

"I'm not going to ask again. What did you do? Who did you see?"

Bo, with his head still turned to the side, went to great pains not spit on Mogul, all the while his mind was thinking, *I don't want to make things worse for myself.* But he had to get the bile, spit and blood, and maybe some floating bits of teeth out, so he could talk. So he spat it all out before saying with some degree of pain, "I swear to God, Mogul, I didn't do anything. I didn't see anyone."

It was a feeble plea he had repeated again and again.

Mogul stepped back a little to avoid any splash or spray from the projectile coming out of Bo's mouth. He looked down at it then looked back up at him and repeated Bo's last line in a sarcastic and high-pitched voice, trying to imitate the voice of a girl.

"I didn't see anything. I didn't see anyone. So why did you leave? You were told not to leave the ship!"

Mogul wanted to grab some hair and yank it out in clumps. But Bo only had stubble waiting to grow back. That was infuriating to Mogul. So he leaned over again to be at eye level with Bo and instead grabbed him by the ears. He yanked down hard while at the same time twisting and turning them. "Huh! WHY? You little puke! Huh? WHY?"

Mogul was shouting now and continued repeating *why* over and over, and as he did so Bo joined in with his answer. Pleading, almost crying it, repeating his reply until the cacophony of words mixed into an unintelligible shouting match.

"I don't know, I don't know, I don't know …."

Bo then thought of something better to say, "I just needed to get off, alright, and get a beer. I'm not a boat guy."

At this Mogul let go of his ears and stepped back, stood at his full height once more and screamed, "YOU'RE NOT A BOAT GUY!! This isn't a damn cruise where you get to come and go as you please! I told you, no one was to get off the ship. PERIOD!"

And with that Mogul stepped forward once more and slapped him hard across his gashed right cheek. White-hot pain shot throughout Bo's body and he caught his breath as he winced. Mogul looked at the fresh blood now on his own hand. Mogul then stared down at him for a few seconds more, weighing his answer. *Was he lying?* He couldn't tell. He placed his still blood-smeared hand against Bo's forehead and pushed his head back forcefully in disgust. Bo's head snapped back with the motion. Then he slowly brought it forward and rested his chin on his chest, exhausted from the exchange. A smudged palm print remained on his forehead. At another time, Bo would have freaked out about his current ridiculous appearance, but looking hip and cool right now was the least of his worries.

Mogul walked several paces away and then angrily turned around. He pointed a finger at Bo, but Bo didn't see it. "If you screwed this up for me I'll kill you myself." He turned to Tony, eyes burning with hate. "Make him hurt."

Tony smiled. "Oh, yeah," was all he said.

Although Tony had very large meaty hands, hands that could surely take care of the job that he would enjoy doing, he was no fool. Why hurt his own hands inflicting the pain when the butt of a gun and the billy club can do it better? So that is what he continued to use. He stepped up to Bo and with pleasure let him have it. Within three more hits Bo had passed out, but the pain inflicted on him continued.

Mogul heard a few more blows connecting before exiting and then he headed for the deck. He leaned on the rail while running scenarios through his mind. It was early morning, but still it did not take long for a bead of sweat to appear on his forehead. It had to be another three or four minutes before Tony joined him. Tony was wiping his hands with a bloodied towel. They stood next to each other for a moment longer before Mogul asked, "What have you done with him?"

"The Irishman, what's his name – ahh, Scott. He, Ray and Ricky are dragging him back to his bunk. They will lock him in."

"Irishman's name is Seamus," Mogul said absent-mindedly.

More moments passed before Tony told him, "It's time to hand over the diamond."

Mogul shot him a look.

Tony shrugged. "Boss's orders."

With an enormous amount of reluctance Mogul pulled the diamond of wonder out of his pocket and turned away from the sea. He stared at it for a long, long time. He felt its smooth polished texture, rolling it over in his hand several times. He was amazed yet again at its dazzling clarity. He was no man of the arts, but this masterpiece was the ultimate. He was fascinated by it. The green from the jade dragon glowed and the pure diamond threw out a prism of colors in the early morning light. To him, it was mesmerizing. More than once he thought … *if there were not so much at stake*, he would be half-tempted to keep it for himself. But that was not the case. With one final admiring look, he threw it gently up in the air and then caught it again, squeezed it tightly in his hand until he white-knuckled. The he released his grip and handed it over to Tony. Tony took it and placed it in the velvet pouch that it came in.

Now Mogul had two problems to deal with. And for him, on what was supposed to be a flawless mission, that was two problems too many. Firstly, had Bo endangered their position by jumping ship and going ashore? He didn't know. And that bothered him.

Secondly, Little Sammy had broken communication silence and told him to cut and run.

Cut and Run.

What did he mean by this? He did not receive enough information to work with. Was this a good thing or a bad thing? They now had a rendezvous two weeks earlier than scheduled.

The original plan was perfect. Just perfect, he thought.

He didn't like this turn of events. He didn't like it one little bit. He began to get ghost pains where his small toes used to be. It sometimes happened when he got anxious.

If only he had received a transmission from Little Sammy twelve hours earlier, he would have bypassed the island stop and avoided a potential problem. The only reason for stopping at the port in Rokalufu was to pick up some prearranged supplies. They could have skipped it altogether had he known earlier, although leaving the cargo may have alerted someone if it went uncollected. He hated the plan being tampered with.

He turned to Tony, pointed to the diamond and said, "C'mon. Let's get this back downstairs and stored away."

Chapter Fifty-Four

Rokalufu – South Pacific

December - Thursday - 7:16 a.m.

Kip focused on the island through powerful binoculars. They were ten minutes from docking. Wikipedia told him this was a small island that held onto about fourteen hundred souls. This was the fourth day, (or was it technically their third day of searching?) since landing in American Samoa late Sunday afternoon. Monday for Kip and the team was literally gone. It did not exist. As they crossed into a new day, a day and time zone that were arbitrarily represented only by a dashed line on maps, that line being the International Date Line. Sunday night immediately became Monday night. So Monday for them was only a few hours long and with the following two days, that was all the time they had for searching the big blue, and it all ended in a bust. They continued to come up empty.

It is extremely difficult to find something when there were so few clues as to what to look for. Nothing out of the ordinary; no hints, no ripples in the water, so to speak. They visited dozens of tiny island communities and uninhabited bays and inlets as they headed on a west by northwest direction and came up with nothing. Kip was beginning to feel foolish for pushing this idea into reality. He knew Ted was growing frustrated with their results too.

They initiated their search northwest of the main Fijian Island group on the assumption that if it was a boat they were in pursuit of, it could be in this vicinity and heading west. Originally, a chartered plane carried them from one tiny island to another on the shortened days of Sunday and Monday. But the pilot had to return to American Samoa Wednesday morning, so a boat was found to continue the assignment. Progress was now slower and the thought of the thieves slipping away was maddening.

Low on equipment, low on supplies, low on backup.

Kip's dress code had changed from Saturday's arrival in Hawaii. Now dressed in FBI supplied navy blues, he was wearing a heavyweight cotton T-shirt. The banded short sleeves were now stretched tight around his biceps. The capitalized letters of FBI were emblazoned yellow on the back. He was given cargo pants, complete with many oversized pockets, zippers, buttons and Velcro. His attire was finished off with ankle high black leather combat boots. The entire outfit was totally inappropriate for the conditions.

From afar, the island they approached looked altogether idyllic. The tranquil ocean water shimmered specs of light off its turquoise surface, pristine and crystal clear. The sea below appeared to be endless. He could see white sands that would greet them and palm trees bending their trunks, suspended over the water. White sands and lush green jungles, with deep blue skies and crystal clear waters.

The picture postcard.

But Kip knew that these people, although while probably enjoying their island life, were not living the postcard dream. Many of them eked out a living on subsistence incomes, and life could be hard. The young left the island to search for a life elsewhere. Above him and stretching into the horizon, ultra-white billowy clouds funneled up to become cumulonimbus. The base of the clouds was flattened, as if sheared off precise and level, like a sharp blade and setsquare had been used. They formed from the uplift of hot thermal air meeting the cooler air above. Soon it was going to rain. And rain hard. You could sense it, smell it. You even welcomed it. It was hot, tropical and it was still early morning.

Shuttling over to the island there was no escaping the heat. The blistering rays of the sun strongly suggested burning of the skin. The sun had a bite. Even Kip's hair was hot and weighed heavy and uncomfortable on his head as the heat and steamy humidity felt so stifling. The moisture soaked hot air seemed to singe his nasal passages with every drawn breath, and deep intakes of air seared all the way to his lungs. The attacks not only came from the heat of the sun but from the dense water vapor that saturated the atmosphere. The suffering humidity weighed heavily on both body and soul. The combination of both had you feeling listless as the heat worked its way inside you and the humidity was ever present. Kip thought, *maybe this is where the expression, "make your blood boil"* came from. It could be you were actually cooking from the inside out. In this weather, it was hard to believe but wet clothes hanging on a line took forever to dry.

Kip summoned up an image of old style postage stamps, used before the advent of the self-adhesive backing. They could very easily, in this water-soaked environment, affix themselves to limp, damp envelopes. No licking required. He could not remember the last time he felt this uncomfortable under the sun. The fireball blazing sun. The sticky, steamy and thick muggy air that sapped your energy, made you feel languid and lethargic was tugging at your core. It was just plain hot.

Rash tied the boat off to a post on the pier while Kip stepped ashore onto the wooden dock. Ted used the wooden pier post to steady his balance as he leaped ashore. The two Navy men would wait by the boat. A silver gray cat with questioning green eyes lay on the dock. She was in a playful mood, but studied the strangers cautiously, her tail swinging lazily in the heated air behind her. Kip looked down and smiled at her, but he and Ted walked on by. The cat herself was busy. She bent her head down and returned to what was trapped between her paws. She was involved in a hunt, chase and capture game, which she knew was soon coming to an end. Besides, she was tiring of the game. She partially lifted her paw to reveal a small cockroach now in its death throes after many minutes of tormented play by the cat. The scene had repeated itself many times. Release the cockroach, let it briefly flee, pounce on it. Release the cockroach, let it briefly flee, pounce on it. For the cat, it was as good a way as any to pass the time. If only Kip knew that the bug now barely clinging to life had the answer to what he was looking for, and if it could speak the words, he may have lunged for it there and then. As it was, the baby cockroach would be good for no one any time soon.

The two men came off the dock and walked on blades of tough grass as they passed blooms of purple flowering bougainvillea and heard the humming rhythm of cicadas murmuring in the background. It was a steady relentless throb and when listened to long enough, it became the noise in your mind that you drifted off to sleep with. They entered a building, rather more like a hut, complete with a thatched roof that acted as the official Customs office. The meet and greet store for the island. Instantly Kip caught the strong odor of mold. It was a common trait in humid conditions such as these. No cool air from an air conditioning system greeted them. Instead several overhead fans were whoop, whoop, whooping at top speed but provided little in the way of comfortable relief from the heat. The hot air was pushed around in spiral patterns all over the room. At one end of the room standing behind a counter was a man contently reading a newspaper laid out in front of him.

The man was a local islander who looked unaffected by the sweltering heat. Even from where they stood he was tall at around six feet six or so, and possibly tipped the scales at two hundred and eighty pounds. His hair was short, black and tightly coiled. His skin was the color of coffee. He was wearing a traditional type of wrap-around sarong or sulu, around his waist, dyed a solid red color. It was decorated with white hibiscus flowers. Draped over the sarong he wore a purple polyester shirt sporting white and yellow flowers. It looked so comfortable and light to wear and suited the local well. The men approached and Kip placed his hands on the counter which had a slick film of damp grime layered on it. The large man was reading the comics. Eventually he looked up. With wide dark eyes and a large heavily jowled face, a soft gentle voice said, "Can I help you?"

"Yes," Kip said for the second time today. "We are with the United States Government and we are conducting an investigation."

There was nothing in the man's facial expression to indicate surprise. He had a carefree look and he just listened. Kip continued. "We would like to know if you have seen any suspicious activity by any crew members that may have passed through here recently."

It took a while, but the man finally said, "Suspicious? How do you mean?"

"Well, that's just it," Kip stated awkwardly, thinking *what a foolish line of questions to be asking*. "We don't know. We are tracking suspects and have reason to believe they may have passed this way?"

"Well then, what do they look like?"

"We don't know."

"What was the name of their ship, maybe I can look it up?"

"Ah… we don't know."

"Where were they going?"

"Well, we don't know that either."

The local man smiled and held out the palms of his hands turned up. He looked at both of them then said. "Gentlemen, if you do not know what you are looking for I do not know how I can help you find it." He returned to the comics.

Kip said, "Let me try again. We don't know who they are, but maybe someone did something while visiting your island and you took note of it. Maybe it placed a hint of suspicion in your mind?"

The local man looked up again, "It is true, when I occupy this desk I do so as our island's Port Authority and Customs Officer, but I'm sorry, I have neither seen nor heard anything." He returned to his comics once more and the conversation was over.

Dejected, Kip added, "Well, thanks for your time." He and Ted walked away from the desk to the other end of the building and huddled together in conference.

Ted ran a hand through his thinning hair and in doing so wiped away sweat from his brow. With a measure of exasperation he said, "I'm not sure how much longer we can do this, Kip. I mean, how many more islands are there to explore, hundreds? We don't even have faces to show them. Be honest, we're chasing ghosts here, right?"

"You may be right." Kip said. "I don't know what I was thinking. These guys could be anywhere. Maybe already in China!

Flew there by plane from somewhere. That also is as good a guess as any."

"That's right. We flew by plane for a while. Faster than a boat."

"I know, I know," Kip admitted with his head down, hands on his hips. He felt beaten. But he knew that the dogged determination inside his very being would never give up.

Just as the two men were talking, a man and woman led a teenager into the building. They were accompanied by a local police officer. Kip looked over briefly at them. The adults appeared to be the teenager's parents. The family was visibly upset, and the girl was crying and burying her face into her mother's shoulder. The mother was rubbing her back and comforting her. The four of them went over to the Port Authority and Customs Officer. The quiet man behind the counter received them, but reacted in much the same way he attended to Kip and Ted's and questioning.

Ted was trying to talk to Kip, "We should just cut our losses now and return to Hawaii - maybe we missed something there?"

"I don't know, Ted. We've come so far to just give up now. Besides, others are in Hawaii carrying out investigations."

Kip looked over at the people at the counter again who were having their own conversation.

"But we don't know what we're even looking for, Kip."

"Well, neither does anyone else. Here or in Hawaii."

"I just don't know." It was Ted's call. He was in charge of the operation. He clutched his chin with one hand and was giving serious thought as to whether they should abandon the search. As he did so, he looked towards the crowd at the counter. Kip followed his gaze. "I wonder what's going on over there?"

"Not sure." But Kip held his gaze a little longer in his curiosity. The girl was very emotional, raising her voice, stamping her foot and raising her arm and pointing a finger towards the direction of the sea.

Ted was saying something but Kip was not listening anymore. "As it is my call, I say we noti -"

Kip started walking away towards the counter and threw back over his shoulder, "I'm going over to see what the problem is."

"Kip, it's just a domestic dispute. For God's sake, don't get involved."

Ignoring him, Kip came over to the ring of people with the girl who was now physically shaking. "Excuse me for interrupting, I see you're upset. Maybe I can help?"

The police officer turned to Kip, annoyed at the interruption to the private conversation. "And who exactly are you, sir?"

"Sir, I am with the United States Federal Bureau of Investigation. We are pursuing suspects in a case we are investigating. But right now I see this young girl is terribly distressed. Can I ask why?"

For some reason the officer was extremely impressed and was now feeling very important; he was rubbing shoulders with fellow law enforcement officers, from no less than the FBI of America!

The girl's father answered for the family in a deep voice. "My daughter has suffered an injustice and we seek the person who did this to her."

At this the mother of the child held her tighter, and the teenager squeezed out more tears that went streaming down her young face.

Kip asked gently, "Sir, I'm very sorry to see your daughter in so much pain. But … why would you come here?"

"This is a delicate situation." The man looked at his little girl longingly, then back to Kip and went on, "My daughter has only just turned eighteen years old. She went to a restaurant to meet with friends to celebrate her birthday." He paused to gather his emotions, and then continued, "There was a man there. A white man."

Kip's heart skipped a beat and by now Ted had walked over to join them.

The girl unfurled herself from her mother's arms and now stood ready to tell the story in her own words.

"He looked so kind but sat all alone. He looked lonely. He had a beautiful smile." She even smiled at the memory of it. Then her face fell back to sorrow as she continued, "He was wearing a scarf around his head. He said he came from a ship, or a yacht." The girl was now fighting back tears as she told the story. "He said he had to wear the scarf because all his hair had fallen out due to chemotherapy to treat his cancer. I remember noticing even his eyebrows were hardly visible."

The girl paused to wipe away tears. Kip could sense something here. He urged the girl, "I'm so sorry for what has happened to you. This may be very important. Could you please continue?"

She nodded her head yes as her father then rubbed her back for comfort and support. Her mother rested her head on the girl's shoulder with tears in her eyes also. The girl was openly sobbing now. There was no need to fight the emotions anymore. "He said he was having some time to himself after all the sickness he had gone through. So he and some friends were cruising the South Pacific islands to celebrate his recovery. His 'remission' is what he called it. We talked for a very long time."

"What happened next?" Kip gently prodded. "Did he say where he was from?"

"He said he was Canadian."

"I see," said Kip.

The girl started her story once more. "My friends wanted to go and he said he would walk me home." She looked at Kip and Ted directly to emphasize a point she was about to make. "Our people are very open and trusting, this did not seem unusual here."

She then began crying uncontrollably. As her mother hugged her it was the police officer that finished the obvious conclusion.

"The girl was violated by this man and we are seeking his arrest."

The police officer turned back to the Port Authority and Customs officer. He asked him in his most officious voice, "Now, in the last twenty-four hours how many foreign ships have pulled into port?"

"There were two," he replied as he looked over to the young girl weeping and her parents who were consoling her.

"Can you describe them, and where did they go?"

The large Polynesian man turned back to them and said, "I don't know where they went."

"And why not? You have their documentation, correct?"

"One was a yacht cruiser, destination unknown. Perhaps Kiribati?"

"And the other?" demanded the police officer.

"Why, it was a tramp ship."

"Oh, no," was all the police officer could say.

Kip was not entirely sure so he had to ask, "What exactly is a tramp ship?"

Chapter Fifty-Five

December – Thursday - 11:32 p.m.

Aravinda Paranawahera believed he was watching intently. The captain had seen to it that Aravinda was in charge while he went down to get some sleep and as Aravinda was second in command of the tramp ship *Free Wheeling* it was the right call. Aravinda was to steer them on a direct heading to a small island off the northwest coast of Choiseul Island in the Solomon Islands chain. Choiseul Island itself was not large, but Taro Island measured only 1.5 square kilometers and that is where they needed to be. Taro Island had excellent reasons that qualified it as a good place to meet. It was small, with only a little over five hundred people populating the island; it was remote and it had an airstrip. The people they were meeting were arriving by plane. Most of this information was unknown to Aravinda, as he was only a crewmember and not included in all of the details of the operation. His only concern was getting there the quickest way he could.

      Aravinda had found a channel through the precarious reefs through which they now traveled. He couldn't understand it at first. The sound was not one he should be hearing. Then the slight shudders began to occur and he quickly realized the ship was in trouble because what he could hear was coming from the hull. It was the screeching and scraping of metal on coral. He was somehow running the ship aground on a reef. He sent the ship into full stop and made a course correction. But these metal giants do not stop on a dime and all the while the screeching and vibrating continued. Aravinda started to sweat and it was not because of the heat. With the help of the coral reef below it took another thirty or forty seconds for the ship to come to a complete halt. But by this time they were beached.

All hands except Bo came into view on the main deck.

Mogul sized up the situation quickly and without further hesitation pulled out his Smith and Wesson M&P 45 pistol that he was carrying in the waistband of his shorts and pumped three quick successive rounds into Aravinda's chest. Bang … Bang … Bang. Before dying Aravinda performed the dead man's jig. As the impact of the bullets hit him, his arms shot out, also from his own surprised reaction to being hit. His feet left the ground with every puncture to his body. Aravinda gave the impression that he was being handled by a master puppeteer, controlling his every move, pulling his arms out and lifting his feet slightly off the floor to perform a little death dance, before finally cutting his strings, symbolizing his life's blood was gone and he was dead. He was released to fold into a heap on the deck.

With the smoking gun in his hand and waving it around angrily, Mogul asked; "Anybody else want to piss me off?"

Dead silence.

He yelled … "WELL?"

When no one answered the question he continued. "I've had all the screw-ups I'm going to take." He pointed his gun at the body on the deck and screamed, "This is what you can expect if you fail to do your job!! You got that?"

There was more deafening silence from his crew.

"Now throw this piece of trash overboard and clean up the mess."

He looked at his watch to check the time. "We need to take care of the problem with the ship at first light."

And with that he walked off.

Chapter Fifty-Six

December – Friday - 5:45 a.m.

Mogul was beyond frustrated at the many events going wrong, and it started to worry him. His plan was unraveling. He had to get it back on track. He carefully planned this for over twelve months. Yes, it was true that Little Sammy had given him the idea and the tools, but the people that were recruited for the job were selected by him. The wonderful timing of doing the job during that stupid race was a great cover, and again his idea. And he was proven right! They got away with it, had they not? Little Sammy, through his contacts, had secured them passage on the Chinese freighter out of Long Beach – big deal. But he had to admit it was a safe bet, as who the hell was going to stop a Chinese cargo freighter?

His guy Seamus helped with the ship that would pick them up out at sea. It was brilliant. Hook up with this tramp ship in the middle of nowhere and sail around the Pacific Ocean for twelve months. Spend some lazy time on tropical islands here and there with no actual destination, there was no way anyone could find them. Hell, he wouldn't even know where they would be at any given time.

After twelve months, they would then steal themselves back to the west coast of the United States. They would leave the ship via a small craft and land on the coast of Portland.
Two days before going into action Little Sammy had contacted him and told him to grab some certain diamond in the heist. After four weeks at sea he was to meet at an island called Taro, one of the Solomon Islands, wherever the hell that was, and hand off the diamond to some Chinese guy. He had to look these islands up on

a Google search. This last minute change to the plans bothered him at first, but after Little Sammy told him his take for the drop off was another twenty-five million, he stopped complaining. As for this motley crew who he never really vetted, Seamus assured him that they were solid. He had worked with them all. The captain was easily persuaded to go along, for a good-sized fee, and his crew would follow.

Mogul thought it over again. Great cover. The ship was legit, an 1120 gross ton, 185-foot long freighter. The crew was a band of ruffians made up of five men from Sri Lanka, all deserters from the Navy who did not want to fight Tamil Tigers anymore, and seven men from the Philippines. One was living in the States, the others, acquaintances, were all ex-Navy with shady pasts that served the person with the most money. All trained fighting men if the need called for it. A total crew of fourteen, including the captain and Seamus. Now they were thirteen, after someone got sloppy.

He heard the rain in his cabin, just another obstacle he thought. He knew that soon the sun would be up over the horizon so he headed out to assemble everyone for the inspection.

After viewing the damage it was a relief to realize the situation was more positive than he feared. It seems they hit the very edge of the coral reef at possibly the absolute lowest ebb of the tide. They could see the scrapes along the hull. But they appeared to be superficial. Aravinda had panicked and turned the ship to avoid any more damage. By all tried and true methods, this was the correct action to take. But he had also brought the ship to a stop, which caused them to get caught on the reef's edge instead of plowing through it. Now they had to wait for high tide to lift them off it. The problem was that they would miss their rendezvous, so it was imperative they make contact with the people they were meeting.

Several attempts to use the Sat-phone failed. This weather was hampering communications. It was the system they chose. The low-orbit Sat-phone would encounter this problem because of its coverage due the location of the satellites in the sky. It was no use. Mogul peered out to the tiny island just to their south and decided they should try for a higher elevation and attempt to pick up a signal. They could also survey the area, scope for other ships and see just was beyond the islands' peaks. The top of the cliff would offer this vantage point. It was 8:21 a.m. when he took Tony, Ray and Seamus with him. Mogul noticed once they landed on the coral and headed towards the cay, the water level had risen significantly since their first journey out this morning. They may save this situation yet.

Chapter Fifty-Seven

December – Friday - 8:39 a.m.

Take the shot! Take the shot! It was all Kip could think about as he waited in the water. He caught a break in that the sea was churning gray from all the tumultuous rain. These conditions helped his cause. The dead body floating in the water that had snagged on the coral helped as well. The corpse was floating face down. Kip inspected the shirt and located three clean exit wounds through it, there was no blood; it was all washed away by seawater and the drenching rains from above. It was great camouflage. Only the top of his head would occasionally be exposed. From time to time he looked around for the odd hungry shark that may take an interest in rotting flesh. He was poised at the edge of the coral about ten feet away from the ship's drop ladder. When given the signal, he was ready to grab on and climb up swiftly.

Rain cascaded down in heavy sheets and warm, fat drops pelted the Navy SEAL from Texas. Grady Byers, as he lay as best he could on the uneven terrain, legs sprawled as he gripped his sniper rifle, held steady by the bipod, waited for the shot. He heard the pummel of water that was ricocheting off the bill of his cap that protected his entirely baldhead. The sound was similar to someone tapping his or her fingernails quickly on a wooden desk. The dark rain bands fell in waves. The rain would ease, then without warning and only after gathering its mighty power once more, would the clouds swell to full capacity, hold no more and burst open to repeat the cycle. This happened all morning. Like the professional soldier he was, Grady remained patient, his breathing was rhythmic and he knew the opportunity would present itself. He waited.

Upon hearing about what the tramp trade was, Kip and Ted devised a battlefield plan. Tramp ships roam the oceans with no particular destination. They operate on the spot market. This means they pull into ports, usually smaller ones, to pick up or drop off cargo. They go wherever the work takes them. So with no ship's manifest to guide them, there is no certainty to know in which direction they go. The cargo a tramp ship just loaded at your dock may not necessarily directly deliver it at their next port of call. Or even the one after that.

As there were two ships to track down, they split their forces. Ted would take Rash. They would charter a plane and head for the Kiribati group of islands. From there they could coordinate a search for the yacht. It was also closer to home to call up resources for help. Kip and Grady would take the boat and head in the direction they had been charting. Why not? They may have caught a break with this information. A man with a shaven head who was also missing his eyebrows. It would fit with covering the eyebrows with fake ones when wearing the Santa suits. No eyebrows may attract attention. Someone would remember. It also made sense to shave every hair off your body so as not to leave behind hair samples for DNA testing. The cancer patient story would make for great cover. Was he Canadian? Maybe, maybe not. Generally, people have a hard time telling the difference. In any event, it did not matter.

They blazed across the waters all night, full throttle. Kip piloted the boat for five hours, and then Grady took over so Kip could rest up. The sweltering heat never relented, although it was cooler on the water than on land. It was prior to dawn cracking open a new day that the rains started in. Usually, the thunderclouds come later in the day after a build-up of intense heat. But this storm started early and became static. There were no winds to move it along. And with the sultry moisture in the atmosphere, the storm could feed on itself. The bellies of the ominous black clouds continued to grow heavy. The system set itself up to regurgitate the water it had just spilled. The stalled clouds hung low over where Kip, Byers and the thieves all came together.

With the berating sound of the rain, the boat's motor was silenced as they moved around the atoll. But before they sailed past the eastern side of the tiny island's cliff faces, Grady killed the engine and brought them to a drifting halt, ensuring they were not exposed to anything beyond. Just ahead lay a flattened area of the atoll where a small beach was formed. He wanted to know if there was something of interest past the spit. They drifted a moment more before Grady dropped anchor and then jumped overboard into shallow water. The outgoing tide had drained the tiny bay of most of its water. He walked over coral in a diagonal direction, careful not to expose himself to anything that was ahead of him.

When he arrived at the beach he crawled over coarse coral and shells to take a peek. Dull morning light was just breaking and visibility was poor due to the dark clouds and heavy rain.

There was good news, and there was bad news. The good news, Grady reported to Kip that he found himself staring at the back of a ship that appeared to have run aground. The description fit with what they were looking for. Black-hulled with a white-edged gunwale. Liberian registered flag of convenience. Oh, yes, two other items. *Free Wheeling* was written in obvious white letters across the stern of the ship under the flag, and there was a body floating in the water below.

The bad news, the secure satellite phone, and all other communication devices, could not penetrate the layers of thick cloud cover to send a signal. They were on their own.

The two men hatched yet another plan. They discovered after surveying the area that there were in fact two islands, or more precisely, an atoll. Both islands were small and uninhabited, separated by a ribbon of water about eight feet across. The islands were almost identical, created by volcanic activity millions of years in the past. All that was left were remnants of the southern end of the crater's edge. Both now formed an incomplete semi-circle, practically mirror images of one another. Both islands had giant walls of jagged rocks and cliff faces climbing steeply, reaching over eight hundred feet into the air. They were covered in palm trees, wild native brush and tall ferns. The only difference appeared to be that the island that Kip and Grady now commanded had a small beachhead. The contour of this continued to swing around in an arc like a right arm being flexed.

The bay swung away from the stranded ship. Deposits of coral and sand accumulated here over time and in front of the islands a reef had formed. The reef gave way to a narrow channel that the ship *Free Wheeling* had attempted to sail through.

Kip and Grady surmised the problem with the ship. It had tried to go through a narrow channel and missed the mark. That channel, which on any given sun-filled day, would be clear blue water, was now a roiling and churning deep, angry grey due to the weather. Perfect for their plan.

Added to their fortune was the fact that there was no wind or lightning. The lack of wind meant the storm would not be pushed onwards, and one of Grady's concerns was diminished as no significant winds meant he had less to calculate when he needed to fire his shot. The lack of lightning meant Kip's journey in the water would not come with fear of an electrical shock. Just sharks. Some background thunder, however, would have been nice to hide any noises he may happen to make, or the shot Grady would take. Well, you can't have everything.

Grady made his way up the side of the cliffs, doing so while trying to stay hidden from view of eyes on the ship. He could do it. No sweat. He wanted to reach an elevation somewhere in line with the main deck of the ship. The beach's position presented a poor angle. In the meantime, Kip would use a CCUBA while diving out to the ship and doing so undetected. This unit and mask came from Grady's kit. It was a Closed Circuit Underwater Breathing Apparatus, or a re-breather. He would use the channel as a guide. Helped by the dull gray color of the sea, visibility would be extremely limited not only to him, but also more importantly to anyone looking over the side of *Free Wheeling*. Aiding his concealment would be the steady rains pounding the water's surface and then bubbling up like effervescence from a freshly opened bottle of soda. This would in turn hide any air bubbles that may possibly escape to the surface from his equipment. Kip also packed Grady's Sig Sauer modified P226 complete with SEAL alterations. Stainless steel and CNC milled internal mechanisms, stainless steel slide and a hardened anodized aluminum alloy one-piece casing, black finish. If left the metallic silver color, it would create unnecessary risks. A lighter color is too easy to spot, it catches the eye; the sun could reflect off it, giving away the carrier's position. The gun used a suppressor but he could not secure it in the holster with it on so he carried it separately. Grady gave him six 10-round 9 mm magazines. One already loaded, the others stuffed in pockets. His other tool was two-way pagers set on vibrate, concealed in an airtight bag, but fastened close to his leg.

Grady told Kip that during his recon he watched how six men climbed down a drop ladder at the stern of the ship shortly after dawn's light. The men were walking on the coral in ankle-deep water, sloshing around and looking at the hull for some time. They studied the hull as if they were interested in buying the ship. All that was left was to do was kick it. Some angry hand gestures were waved; it seemed blame was being metered out and received. About twenty minutes later they all climbed back on board. That move by the men came too quickly for Kip and Grady to act. They waited for their next break.

Some two hours later Kip and Grady watched four men climb down the drop ladder again and proceed to walk across the coral over to the furthest island. Kip lay on the beach; Grady had already made his way up the cliff face and was camouflaged in position. Two men carried rifles, one carried what looked to be an oversized black phone – almost certainly a Sat-phone; the other guy carried nothing. Possibly the leader. They could see the water and tide were returning, already up to their calves, higher than before. The high tide was coming in fast. Four men were taken out of play. They had their chance. They would have to deal with whoever was left. Kip slithered away from his position on the beach back to the boat so he could make preparations to swim over to the ship.

Chapter Fifty-Eight

December – Friday – 8:41 a.m.

Grady studied the man in his scope for about ten minutes. If a better opportunity did not present itself soon he would fire. The problem was the man was in the bridge. The man was almost always facing away from him, towards the bow of the ship. Occasionally he turned around to, more often than not, look through binoculars to survey the horizon. He had no clue Grady was there. Grady confirmed he was the captain. He wore a weary black-peaked cap and a rumpled and faded black polo shirt. High consoles hid anything else. Grady picked up on the man's rifle resting against a wall on a counter top nearby. The trouble was the glass. He had no idea of its density. How thick or tempered? More than likely not bulletproof, but it was too hard to tell at this range. He had a distance of seven hundred and thirty-two yards to cover. Although it was raining, he wanted as little noise as possible, and for the bullet not to be deflected.

The man lit a cigarette and then stepped out onto the landing with a protective canopy overhead to smoke it. Grady could see ragged black and gray stubble on the man's face from several days of growth. He stood there looking north, directly out to sea and giving a Grady a side-on target. Grady got comfortable with his Mk 14 EBR sniper rifle. A 7.62mm NATO round loaded in the chamber. Through his scope he had aimed at the man's torso, or more specifically, his lungs. The torso was a large target and he waited until the man exhaled to take him down. He was assisted by the man's smoking. When the target brought the cigarette to his lips in his right hand, with the ominous dark clouds beyond him, it gave Grady the separation between foreground and background he needed.

The man pulled on the cigarette and brought nicotine and smoke deep into his lungs; the end of the cigarette glowed orange. Grady paused half a beat then fired. By the time the target had exhaled most of the blue smoke the bullet ripped through him, punctured the lower portion of his right lung leaving a gaping hole. It sliced through the upper half of his left lung and blew a hole through his left bicep leaving the body stone dead as the bullet continued on into open water. Grady's trajectory was from a slightly lower point than that of the target who was about five feet above him. So as the bullet traveled it climbed, therefore the entry and exit wounds were angled points in the body. Grady wanted the man to be exhaling when hit so he could not catch another breath with which to scream, once shot through the lungs.

The man instinctively fell sideways and forward, hit the rail, then continued to fall sideways and toppled onto his back.

Kip's pager, set to vibrate, hummed to life. He hesitated. One long hum of lasting three seconds meant *get the hell out of there!* Grady would cover him as best as he could from up on the ridge, the plan had failed. But two vibrating hums spaced with a three-second interval meant he had a green light, head aboard. He felt the second vibration and immediately climbed out of the water. He held onto the sharp, jagged coral. He scored several small cuts to his hands in doing so. It could not be avoided. He was fully clothed, including shoes, which he needed to get over the coral. He quickly discarded the diving gear and mask and scurried up the ladder, both as fast and cautiously as he could go, knowing Grady was tracking his movements. He made it to the top, climbed over the gunwale and made his way along the deck to the bridge, whereupon he found the sprawled-out body of a man in a black polo shirt, dark blue denim jeans and boat shoes. The peaked cap was lying off the distance. Blood was oozing out of the wound. There was no need for Kip to check for a pulse.

Kip turned in the direction of Grady and gave the "OK" signal that divers use. That told Grady to get over there and provide backup – quickly. This line of work was not Kip's area of expertise and he had not performed anything like this for some time. He was physically fit and capable, but he lacked the practical experience from lack of use. He was rusty. *What was he doing here?*

He grabbed the body under the shoulders and dragged it back into the bridge. He could do nothing about the trail of blood. He unholstered the SIG and removed the suppressor from his pocket; then he threaded it onto the end of the barrel. He stood there momentarily to regroup and catch his breath. His adrenaline was pumping, but would it still be there by the time Grady arrived. He sure hoped so.

Kip positioned himself between the door leading to the deck and a small slither of solid wall. He never heard the footsteps because of the rain, but he saw a shadow cast due to the overhead light that was on under the covered deck outside. The light shone because of the heavy weather. Then a man called out "Captain …. Are you OK?"

The voice was accented, Americanized English. East Asian? Maybe Korean or Filipino was his guess.

He saw the shadow hesitate, and then it came running towards his position. He tracked the shadow and timed his move as the footsteps drew near. Kip pivoted on one foot and swung a roundhouse kick into the oncoming body. He caught the man in the larynx; the man stumbled back and began to fall backwards. Kip moved quickly and before the man could thump to the ground Kip slowed his fall then produced the pistol and put it to the man's temple. He was Asian all right, more than likely from the Philippines, and he was scared. His dark eyes were bulging out of their sockets and he was holding his throat giving the indication that he couldn't breathe. Kip had the advantage.

"I know you speak English." He looked into his eyes for a hint of recognition. "I also know some of the answers to questions I'm going to ask you." Kip pressed the tip of the gun a little harder into the man's head. "All the answers you give me better be the truth. OK?"

The guy nodded his head.

Kip looked up to verify no one was approaching then back down at his captive. There was a pool of water amassing at his feet because he was soaked. He asked his questions in rapid succession so the guy had no time to think about his answers and whether or not he should decide to alter the truth.

"How many men left the ship to go the island?"

"Four."

"How many crew on board?"

He hesitated for a second as if counting, before saying in a choking whisper, "Thirteen, no wait, twelve ...uhmm, no, it's eleven! Eleven are alive including me." He looked over at the captain dead on the floor. "Twelve including the captain." He motioned with his eyes.

Kip pushed the tip of the gun hard against the man's temple, "Which is it ...Thirteen, twelve or eleven?"

"It's eleven! Don't kill me! You're making me nervous with the gun at my head. We had a total of nineteen on board, four left to go to the island this morning, the dead captain over there and one man," he hesitated and took a painful gulp "…. died last night. That's eleven crew onboard still alive."

Kip thought about the body floating in the water. So far so good he thought.

"How many non-crew members still on board?"

He coughed a little, still trying to catch a breath. He was hesitating again, but he was not counting, Kip was sure of it.

He said the next words slowly, "Don't lie."

"Two, but one is badly hurt."

"What was your last port-of-call?"

"Rokalufu."

"Where are you headed?"

"Somewhere in the Solomon's."

"Why?"

"I think we are meeting someone, but I don't know for sure, they don't tell me everything."

Kip checked the doorway again and tried to listen hard through the roaring downpour for footsteps. Nothing.

"Where are the others that are still on board?"

"Down in the mess. We were all told to wait there until the others got back."

Good, thought Kip.

"Then why are you here?"

"I was *releeving* the captain."

The man's Americanized English was good, but there were words he would always have trouble with. "Relieving" was one of them.

"Why were you running in here, did you hear something earlier?"

Kip was concerned the crew heard Grady's gunshot.

"Huh … no. I saw blood on the deck, there outside. I thought my captain was hurt. I was running here to see for myself."

OK, good.

"Where is everything that was taken from the bank?"

The guy did not say anything.

Kip looked into his eyes. He gave him a cold hard stare with his deep blue eyes, a killer's stare that he reserved only for times like this. "I don't have time for games. First I blow out your knees; then we get serious. Where is it?"

The man was in no mood for more pain. "Downstairs. I can show you."

"OK. First we keep your friends safe."

The guy with the damaged larynx did not understand what he meant. Kip started to help him up, but looked once again in the doorway and saw Grady standing there leveling his rifle at the other guy, a puddle of water at his feet also. Judging by the pool of water at his feet, he had been standing there for some time.

Kip smiled, "You're good. I didn't hear a thing."

"The way it's meant to be," Grady said unapologetically. "We best move quickly, I had to expose the boat to the guys on the island. I spotted them high up the ridgeline, but you can be sure they're making their way back down real quick. I'll go and hold them off for a spell."

"OK. He is going to lead me to the goods. I'll take care of the others; they're in the mess. Then we meet up again at the stern. Ten minutes?"

"Affirmative." Grady made a sweeping motion with his rifle for the captured man to move along. While looking down the black hole of the barrel, the guy did as the motion requested him to do.

Chapter Fifty-Nine

December – Friday – 8:52 a.m.

The good news for Mogul was that the climb of almost eight hundred torturous feet in the air, on a miserable day like this, was the right decision. They picked up a signal to contact Little Sammy. The meeting was delayed twelve hours due to their mishap. Mogul had just ended the call when the bad news escaped from Seamus's lips.

"What de hell is thart?"

From around the point of the northeast end of the atoll a boat chugged along at top speed, heading directly towards their cargo ship. They all turned to look but no one needed binoculars to spot it.

Mogul looked from the approaching boat back to the ship and noticed no action on deck indicating anyone was trying to do anything about the intruding vessel.

"Quick!" he yelled over the buckets of rain, "Back to the ship."

Chapter Sixty

December – Friday – 8:56 a.m.

Kip's first thought was, *how do I keep twelve guys plus this one here he was dragging around, on ice?* Kip and his prisoner were headed for the ship's mess with the Sig pressed hard into the guy's back, just to let him know he had limited options. They snaked beyond a corner and the guy halted and raised a pointed finger towards the door of the mess. Kip in turn motioned to remain absolutely quiet and still. The prisoner nodded. Before departing with Grady, Kip asked for his handcuffs.

Originally, Kip's idea was to cuff his captive once he was finished with him, but keeping an eye on him seemed like a better idea. He now studied the door at the end of the hallway and a plan began to take shape. He inched along the corridor a short distance towards the door and noticed some peculiarities about the door's design that would benefit him. He turned to the man at the other end of the corridor and motioned for him to walk towards him – slowly. The man reached Kip and was gestured with hand and gun to sink to the floor and lay down. Generally a cooperative guy, he did as he was told. Kip held a finger to his lips indicating no noise, and waved his gun at him to ensure he received the message. The man nodded.

Kip stayed out of range of a swinging foot or leg grab, but in a good position to prevent an attempted escape back down the corridor and around the first corner to perceived safety. He would have time to fire off a muffled shot if need be. Kip was satisfied the other guy knew it, too. Kip slowly and steadily crept along towards the mess door, open cuffs in one hand, gun in the other. As carefully as he possibly could, he eased one loop of the cuffs around an adjacent three-inch metal plumbing pipe and secured the cuff around it. He checked for the guy in the corridor; still there, he hadn't moved, his head was buried in the floor. Good. He extended the other link of the cuffs as far as it could reach, securing it to the wheel handle on the door and locked it into place as well. He returned to the guy on the floor and tapped him on the shoulder with the barrel of the gun, indicating for him to get up. They both backed up towards the other end of the corridor and left quietly. Kip asked and received information on a certain cabin.

Kip growled at the guy, he had no time for games, "Is this it?"

"Yes."

"You know your penalty for lying, right?"

Nodding his head and acquiescing, "Yes. Yes, I know. This is the one. It is the cabin of the one they call Tony. He holds onto everything. No one is allowed in. This is it."

Kip checked the door. Locked.

He reached into his pocket and pulled out a set of keys. He had gone through the dead captain's pockets and found them.

"Would one of these keys work?"

"Maybe."

The guy was very uncomfortable giving up all this information. He kept looking around to see if anyone was listening in. That would be very bad for him. But with a gun pointed at him all the time and excruciating pain still in his throat, a source of the constant reminder of consequences, he felt he had limited choices. He saw his captain dead. He did not know it was not Kip who fired the fatal shot. He had no idea what Kip's reputation was except for the threats he made against him.

He pointed, "Try that one."

It looked like all the others. Brass colored, no particular significance.

Kip looked at him as to say *why this one?*

"I think it's the master key for all cabins. Captain has access to all rooms."

Kip slipped it in the lock and turned. He heard the bolt slide back.

He looked over at the guy. He did not know what his chances of survival were after he left, with the help he was providing, but he did manage to say to him, "Well done."

Kip entered the room, found the light switch and the room lit up. In the small room without a porthole, he spotted four very large red sacks. He moved across to them and looked inside one of them. It had bundles of U.S. cash. He had no time to go through all of them. All four were coming with him.

He turned back to the guy standing in the doorway just watching and holding his throat. "I'm tying you up."

After securing the guy with ripped bed sheets, he started hauling the sacks out of there two at a time. They were too large and heavy to do it any other way.

On his second trip to the stern of the boat Kip spotted an orange runabout. It was called *Sunday*. A curious name he thought. But he thought of something else, too. They would have a jump on the marooned ship, but the lifeboat with the huge outboard motor could cause trouble. He dropped the sacks and climbed up to where it hung hoisted and entered the small-enclosed cabin. He raced over to the console, and placed his hand underneath. Clutching wires he ripped and pulled. After repeating this several times, he was convinced enough damage was done to disable the craft and so give them the time needed to put distance between them and anyone on this ship.

While Kip was busying himself hauling Santa's sacks around and destroying property, Grady had taken position on the main deck and waited. He spotted all four making their way down the cliff and through the vegetation at a pace that was as fast as they could go, considering the terrain and wet conditions. They were at the bottom and breaking for the reef when he fired off his first volley of warning shots. The men immediately retreated to the safety of the trees. They returned fire but nothing came close to hitting him.

There was silence for about two minutes before he caught the movement in the trees, so he decided to mess with them some more. He fired several more rounds in their direction and ducked down as he waited for the return fire that came immediately. He altered his firing pattern and position another three times before melting away to join Kip.

Grady found Kip climbing back up the drop ladder to retrieve the last two sacks to carry away.

"Hurry, we don't have much time," Grady urged.

With a nod Kip acknowledged the request.

Both men grabbed a sack and made their way down to the boat below.

The water was rising fast now and was up to their waists. The atoll was located in a particular area on the planet that experienced extreme tidal shifts. The tide was returning and would ultimately replenish an amazing nine feet of water. This would eventually assist in lifting *Free Wheeling* up and off the reef and allow her to sail away.

Kip was in the lead and hoisted his red sack over the deck rail and thumped it into the bow of their boat. With the tide rushing in it twisted the little launch around and toyed with it. The anchor was not holding her steady. Only the nose of the boat was accessible. Kip jumped on board and rearranged the sacks to make room that allowed the last one to be shoved on. Grady approached the boat with his weapon slung over his shoulder. He hoisted the sack up and was reaching to hand it to Kip when he felt a painful pinch in his upper right side. It caught him off-guard and he dropped the sack.

Kip yelled out, "No!" as he watched the sack hit the water, fill with water, and then gurgle towards the bottom. *Did it have Hammerhead's information in it, or Yurushi?*

Then he looked up at Grady, who was assessing his own situation.

In an instant Grady knew he was finished and also knew he would be a burden. His time was over. While stretching up with the sack, he had exposed a vulnerable part of his body above his Kevlar vest body armor that protected his chest. The bullet found the weakness, at his armpit, and it went through the side of his body. The wound was significant, ripping and tearing through his carotid artery. His final act was to unsling his rifle and throw it to Kip who instinctively caught it, and without another word, Grady fell into the water. He followed the sack down to the bottom and only a tiny patch of blood temporarily marked the spot of the watery grave into which he had plunged.

In a mere matter of seconds Kip repeated the word just spoken, "No!" as he stared helplessly at Grady's deed. He had no time to mourn as another bullet splintered the wooden rail dangerously close to his head; he was forced to duck. With flying hot metal whistling all around him trying to pick him off, he remained low and raised anchor. In a crouch behind the low gunwale he made his way to the wheelhouse. Glass rained down on him from bullets spraying the cabin. He hit the ignition switch and the motor bubbled to life in the water. No miraculous no starting at first as they play it out in the movies. He slammed the throttle into gear and the boat motioned forward. He used the ship as cover and headed west out of the channel and into the safety of open water.

He wiped rainwater, sea salt and sweat from his face. For now, there were to be no tears for a lost sailor. He was primed with adrenaline and escaping was the priority. He had to stay focused. Later he would reflect on these events, and some form of grief would emanate from that. This loss of a brave talented man - *Kip did not even know if he was married ... children? Not to mention parents and other relatives,* for whom few would ever know the full account of just how his acts of heroism had helped so much.

Kip sped away with his head down and absolutely no idea where he was headed.

Chapter Sixty-One

As Kip was wrestling the stolen belongings off the ship and towards his boat, the men on the island were held hostage to its shores. After the third round of gunfire pounded into the trees, rocks and ground, Mogul was lying on his stomach protecting his very being. He was dumbfounded as to why no one on board was doing anything to end the shots being fired. There were more than ten men on that damned boat! He grabbed Ray and they made for the eight-foot wide body of water separating the two islands. It was surprisingly deep, but they managed to cross over into the protection of the trees on the other side. No gunfire followed them. He wanted to get a clear view of that boat that he knew bobbed next to his ship. He could not see it from his original position. Moving one hundred and fifty feet eastward gave he and Ray the option he was looking for.

After the crack of rifle fire in his ear and seeing the results, Mogul pulled his eyes away from the binoculars, the ones he had wrenched away from Seamus, and turned to Ray.

"Good shot, you nailed him."

Without peeling his eyes away from his rifles scope Ray said, "Actually, I was aiming for the other guy, the one in the boat."

"Oh," was all Mogul could say. He was surprised at Ray's miss.

"But don't worry, I'll get him, too," and he released another round and took the recoil in his shoulder.

But that was all Ray would chalk up. The two other men on the small atoll, under Ray's cover fire, progressed slowly through the rising tide and made their way to the ship. Eventually, Mogul and Ray did the same. There was no sign of life on board the ship but they would search for the others soon enough.

To everyone's surprise, Mogul was calm, not raging out of control or striking out at someone, or everyone, for that matter. His two missing small toes did begin to their tingle thing, though. The four men were on the top deck drenched to the bone, watching a tiny speck on the horizon getting smaller and smaller. Mogul watched for the longest time, without saying a word as the boat slowly disappeared into the low hanging, wet grey clouds.

There goes the swan leaving the sewer, he thought to himself. Finally he said to no one in particular, "If he's still alive, bring me Bo."

Chapter Sixty-Two

Owaraha Island – Solomon Islands

December – Friday – 10:23 a.m.

Kip spied the white underbelly of a plane that was set against the background of the bright blue sky. It fell low over his head and was obviously preparing to land. The airstrip was close to the coastal edge of the island. He made his way towards its position.

He had traveled more than two hours west before spotting this place. His GPS helped with its location, but its proximity helped with his fuel reserves. Once again the sun was shining; the sky was a patchwork of white cotton balls, but the ferocious weather was now far behind. He had exited from beneath the precipitous rains and black clouds an hour ago. The sun was back and beat down with its bite once more. The place he escaped from, with all its darkness and death, seemed deliberately staged, exclusively designed for the drama that unfolded within its confines. Set up in that cocoon-like arena, the outside world was kept at bay by nature's forces.

But now, with the sun burning and the humidity once again overwhelmingly thick in the air, he had to ask himself, *was I really only two hours distant from it?* It could have easily taken place a lifetime away, or in a powerful dream.

Kip ran his boat aground on the white sandy strip of beach that was at the end of the placid aqua-colored water. He had no other options. The instant he placed a foot on shore he was attacked by thousands of tiny black gnats, or something similar; they were determined to eat his flesh off. He swatted at them and batted them away as he battled through the tropical foliage and made his way towards the airstrip. Twenty yards into the dense jungle he spotted a place to temporarily hide the three remaining sacks. He was not sure if someone here would be asking questions and it was hard to explain the bounty. In this heavily shaded location, a fallen tree thick with moss lay over a large sunken depression. The tree acted as a bridge over the small ravine, but more importantly for him, it was a marker. Kip could easily place the sacks in this nest in the ground; cover them up with leaves, debris and branches. Leaving them on the boat was not an option.

He realized for the first time he had yet to look inside the bags. He needed to be certain that what he had retrieved were the things he was chasing down and more importantly, the one that sank to the bottom of the sea did not contain *Yurushi*. That was a brave thought on his part, as his primary mission was to retrieve or destroy *Hammerhead*. And still, he felt now was not the right time to positively identify the contents. His murderous pursuers were back there somewhere and they would be closing in. He was sure of it. He raced back for the bags. With the difficulty of carrying the heavy red sacks, two trips were necessary. The first expedition was more difficult - waddling along with one huge heavy sack over his shoulder and the other held out front. On his last trip back to the boat, he secured the Sat-phone. He already had his weapon, and brought both along. Once he completed his task of burying the sacks, he moved forward.

He had landed on Owaraha Island, formerly known as Santa Ana Island. It is nine miles east of the southeastern tip of its larger neighbor, Makira Island, which was itself formerly known as San Cristobal. Owaraha was another of the small islands that dotted the Pacific Ocean. Both islands formed part of a cluster inclusive of the Solomon Islands chain. Any thoughts of the Solomon Islands usually associate it with its World War II connection of Guadalcanal. Known as the naval battle of Guadalcanal, and the Guadalcanal campaign, in 1942-43 it was a pivotal turning point in the war against the Japan. Kip pushed through the final low-hanging branches, scrub brush and spider webs to arrive at the perimeter of a landing field. He saw a plane parked in the distance and several men lumbering around it and unloading supplies. He made his way over there.

Kip walked on the sandy soil; to one side was an expanse of patched concrete served as the island's only airstrip. The far end of the runway strip headed out to sea. On the other side and in the direction he was heading, a small grouping of one-story metal buildings stood in the heat of the day. The one plane being unloaded was the only customer. There were three men working on the cargo shipment, two were clearly locals. Both these men wore white shorts, one with a canary yellow t-shirt, the other, a lime green. Both shirt colors were eye candy for pilots, and helpful for wearing around prop engines. Catching the eye of a pilot helps prevent accidents. Neither man wore shoes or looked like they needed them. The other man in all likelihood was the pilot. He molded to a pilot's profile. Kip approached this man from behind, who was on his haunches unstrapping buckles on a cargo pallet.

Kip asked, "Excuse me, is this your plane?"

Without turning around, getting up, or stopping what he was doing, the man grunted, "Yeah, who wants to know?"

Kip walked around to face the man directly so each could see the other more clearly. He thrust out his right hand to make formal introductions. "Hi, my name is Kip. I wonder if we could talk?"

Still squatting, the other man turned his head slightly towards Kip and shaded his eyes to get a better look at the person asking questions. Then he began rising to his full height and as he did so, made his reply. He didn't shake the extended hand.

"Dunno. What for?"

But before Kip could answer, the man was rotating his head around in all directions, and then quickly followed up with another question, "And where the bloody hell did you come from?"

"Well," Kip said, and made with a slight chuckle while putting his hands on his hips, simultaneously casting his head down and shaking it, "These are good questions I can answer if we could just talk over there. In private?"

He jabbed a thumb behind him to a patch of open field. It was no different than anything else around, but far enough away to be out of earshot of the others.

The man was curious, but cautious. This request came from way, way out of left field. He looked over to the other men who were on the strip with him. They shrugged, he shrugged in return, and then turned back to Kip.

"OK, mate."

Kip smiled, "Good." And he walked away.

Kip found his patch of dirt then turned and studied the man coming towards him. Both men were close to even in height and about as broad in the shoulders. He was trim and owned a full head of light brown curls, the hair bleached blond at the tips of the ringlets. This was evidently because of his time in the sun. His skin was a hard brown, well earned by working outdoors. As he approached, Kip spied the crow's feet tracks at the corners of his hazel eyes. If met under different and less suspicious circumstances, Kip could imagine those eyes dancing with good humor. The man wore khaki cargo shorts and a white, long sleeve lightweight shirt, with the sleeves folded over several times to the elbows. Sunglasses were looped on a cord and presently hung down like a chain on his chest. A pair of dusty, desert-colored boots worn over pale gray, heavy woolen socks that lapped over the ankle-high boots. He wore these over muscular tanned legs with bulging calves.

The pilot was yet in private conversation range before he said, "So, what's this all about? As you can see, I'm busy with my shipment." He jutted a thumb back over his shoulder towards the plane.

Kip followed his thumb and said, "Yes, I can see that. Listen; let me start at the beginning. Firstly, as I said before, I'm Kip, Kip Keplar. I'm an American."

"Yeah, I can tell." the other man interrupted.

"Sure. And you must be … I'm going with Australian. Not a Kiwi, right?" Kip knew the man would be even more abrasive if he had chosen the wrong nationality. Both Aussies and New Zealanders were sensitive about this topic, and how all too often people from North America got it wrong.

"Yeah, that's right. The name's Tucker. Go on." The man folded his arms across his chest, but then brought a hand up to his chin and rubbed at his whiskers as he listened to what this guy had to say.

"Tucker. Is that a first name or last name?"

Tucker didn't reply.

"Anyway, my boat is almost out of fuel, I just beached on the shore not far away, and I need a ride."

The other man just stood there and kept rubbing his chin. He just stood there saying nothing.

"Anyway, I would like to commandeer your plane."

"Why?" Tucker asked in an, *I'm not surprised, this should be a good answer*, dry sarcastic tone.

"Because I need to get to American Samoa."

"Why?" More sternly this time.

"I actually can't discuss the details of that with you, but I can assure you, you would be well compensated for your assistance."

"I see," Tucker said. He stood there a moment longer.

"So you'll do it?" Kip asked with high expectations.

Tucker dropped his hand from his chin and both arms moved to his side. "Not interested." Then he turned and walked away.

Kip started to protest, "What do you mean you -"

Tucker swiveled back around with fire in his eyes and a voice to match. "So, who the hell do you think you are? You show up out of nowhere and start demanding," he gestured with air quotations to emphasize the word *demanding*, "to be taken to … where was it? … American Samoa? Yeah, right mate. Pull the other leg - it plays *Jingle Bells*! Listen, I have a plane, *my* plane, which is for my job, which is going nowhere near American Samoa! Do you have any idea how far away that is? Get yourself another taxi driver. There should be another plane along … maybe tomorrow."

He turned away once more while shaking his head, mumbling something about "unbelievable" before having another thought. He stopped, turned and added, "If you don't like that idea, get yourself over to Kirakira Airport on Makira, you might have better luck there."

As he walked towards his plane once more he called out, "And no, I won't take you!"

Kip was mad with himself. He handled that poorly; this being his only possible ticket out of here, and away from the pursuers he knew were coming. He involuntarily looked towards the trees. He could imagine them bursting through there, guns blazing, no one would survive the onslaught. He tried again; he needed to convince this guy.

He yelled at Tucker's back, no time to worry about who heard what now. "I'm with the FBI. This is a matter of national security."

Tucker stopped dead in his tracks. He slowly turned on his heels. He allowed a grin to cross his mouth. "You know what, mate? You bloody Yanks amaze me. Somebody farts near an electrical box and you guys run around with guns drawn screaming, *National Security! National Security*!"

As he said the words "national security," he bent his knees and raised his arms. With palms facing Kip he shook his hands in a trembling motion. He spoke in a mocking, terrified tone and satirized the words … *National Security*.

Kip ignored the theatrics and solemnly told him, "I'm one hundred percent serious when I tell you this."

Tucker stood straight once more, "Yeah, well it's not *my* national security."

"Ever serve your country, Tucker?"

"What's it to ya?"

"So … Tucker? Is that your first or last name?" Kip held out a hand as if asking for help.

"It's…mind your own bloody business, that's what it is."

"OK, O.K. I'm not looking to make an enemy out of you. Can you give me a minute?" Kip asked. He held his phone up and starting punching numbers on the keypad.

"Take all the time you need, mate. I'm refueling and heading out of here soon enough."

Again Tucker walked away and Kip watched him go. Every now and then this Tucker guy was jerking his hands in the air as he spoke angrily to, well… no one and everyone. Kip heard only parts of a conversation one man was conducting entirely for himself. It was hard to track; he talked too fast for Kip, with an accent, using slang. His retreating back made it more difficult for Kip to make out as he saying all kinds of things.

"Bloody Yanks ….. these blokes think they own the.. damn chauffeur ……people need these supplies ….

And so it went as he drifted over to the two men who had stopped what they were doing and were looking at him quizzically.

Tucker shouted, "Go on, back to work. I need to get out of here." He never looked back.

Kip heard a voice on the other end of the call half a world away. "It's with great urgency that I speak with Ken Maylon."

Kip waited for a reply.

"Yes, you can tell him it's Kip Keplar and this is a matter of," he looked over at Tucker as he spoke the next words, "National Security."

Kip waited.

"Yes, OK, I'll hold."

Chapter Sixty-Three

Owaraha Island – Solomon Islands

December – Friday – 11:05 a.m.

Kip walked over to Tucker once more, and once more he spoke to his back. "Listen, Tucker, I'm sorry. We started off on the wrong foot. I should not have been so abrupt when I spoke to -"

"You got that right."

"But I have a very good reason why I need your help and I hope you can give me another chance to explain."

"Tell someone who cares," he said without looking at Kip and continued to stay busy with his business.

At that moment Kip's phone rang and he pushed a button to answer it.

In a voice loud enough for Tucker to hear, Kip spoke into the phone.

"Hello. Yes, it is. Yes, I believe he is here with me, I'll put him on."

Kip extended the phone to Tucker and said, "Ahh …. Excuse me, Tucker, but it's for you."

With a puzzled expression on his face, Tucker turned around and said, "What?"

"The phone call. It's for you."

"What sort of game are you playing?"

"No game. They want to speak with you."

"Who did you call, my Mummy?"

Kip kept the phone held out between them and gestured for him to take it.

Tucker paused for a moment more, then swiped the phone out of Kip's hand and put it up to the side of his face; annoyed this joker wouldn't leave him alone.

"Yes! What!" he said abruptly and with a gnarly tone into the receiver.

"Yes, this is Tucker Parrish." He shot Kip a nasty stare that squinted his eyes and curled the ends of his mouth. "But how do you know who -"
He stopped midsentence and asked a different question. "Who's this?"

The response from the other end of the line altered Tucker's behavior. He literally stiffened, stood taller and chose his words more carefully.

"Yes Sir."

"Yes Sir. Ahh, that's correct, Sir, served twelve years in the RAAF. Wing Commander, 0 5. Yes Sir."

He pronounced it R … double A … F. It was the acronym for Royal Australian Air Force

"Yes Sir, I will Sir."

"Yes Sir."

"Yes Sir."

"No I'll make sure it happens, Sir."

"Goodbye Sir."

He ended the call and held the phone away from him but just stared at it. In a low guttural mumble that Kip got the gist of, Tucker said, "That was the Deputy Prime Minister of Australia."

He was half-talking to himself and half to Kip. "I have to get you out of here. He told me to … offer all available assistance."

Then he followed that statement up with ... well, with words that seemed to get caught in the back of his throat. He hesitated, aghast at what he was about to say, "Said it was a matter of ... national security."

Tucker quickly cocked his head towards Kip and said, "Just who the hell are you, anyway?"

Kip smiled, trying not to resemble the Cheshire cat so as not to aggravate his pilot. "I'm your passenger."

Tucker finally sighed and handed back the phone. "Well, mate, I suppose I'm all yours. Orders."

"Good," Kip said, satisfied things were now going his way. "We need to get to American Samoa as soon as possible."

This time Tucker smiled. The same smile as Kip, and shook his head slowly. "Nu-ahh. Not going to American Samoa."

Kip was puzzled. "Then where are we going?"

"We're going to Australia." Kip heard the word pronounced as oStraylya. The "o" was spoken quickly, and almost not said at all.

Kip was confused and dismayed. "But that's in the wrong direction. We can't go that way!"

Tucker walked past him, and as he did clapped a hand on Kip's shoulder. "oStrayla's more than one island."

Kip thought about this. The map in his mind brought up another island. *Tasmania?* That's worse. It's even further away.

Kip was about to call out his protest when, as if reading his thoughts, Tucker yelled back, "It's not Tasmania, either."

Kip was out of ideas and stood there clueless.

Tucker was lengthening the distance between them, but Kip was sure he heard him say, "We're going to Norfolk."

Chapter Sixty-Four

Owaraha Island

December – Friday - 12:17 p.m.

The tarmac was strewn with supplies, equipment and airplane fixtures not necessary for the trip. As Tucker explained to Kip, the journey to Norfolk Island was at the outermost limits of his plane's range. They needed to top up with fuel and reduce their weight to have any chance of reaching it in one leap. No stops. Deputy Prime Minister's orders. Tucker was the proud owner of a DHC-6 Twin Otter- Series 400 aircraft. A 20 passenger STOL. STOL was the abbreviation for short takeoff and landing. It was a utility aircraft perfect for the jobs he performed. It had a cruising speed of 150 knots and a range of 970 nautical miles, or 1050 miles. It had two powerful Pratt and Whitney PT6A turboprop engines. If all went well, this machine of the sky should get them there.

Kip was offered fruit from inside one of the buildings at the airport. He gladly took the food. He bit into a banana and downed a bottle of water. He also grabbed an ice-cold Coke taken from an ice-packed cooler. Always refreshing in weather like this. Tucker told them to put it on Kip's bill, as well as the fuel. He told Kip he would be paying for it later. It had taken an hour to fuel up and jettison all items inside the plane not needed for the trip. Tucker was playing it safe, so he even removed some seating and left it on the ground. He warned the fellas at the airport that he knew how many seats were there, and he would be back for them, adding that he held them responsible for their safekeeping. The two men just shrugged.

While Tucker was preparing the plane, Kip went back and retrieved the sacks from the nest. He also went back to the boat to retrieve Grady's kit and weapons, including the rifle. He loaded everything into the plane.

Kip and Tucker buckled themselves in. While seated, Kip worked on another banana and he still had two apples, a mango and another banana to go. He was hungry. It had been some time since his last meal.

Tucker reached down and grabbed an extra pair of aviator sunglasses that were tucked away in a side compartment. He reached over to Kip and nudged him. He motioned Kip to take the blue/black-tinted shades.

"Here. Put these on. They'll help."

"Thanks." Kip slid them on, pushing them on between the headphones and his scalp until they rested behind his ears. The arms of the glasses were a little loose and a little too wide, no doubt from years of use and of putting them on and taking them off; thus they were now relegated to be a spare pair. But they would do.

Tucker opened his windowed and yelled, "Clear!"

Tucker activated switches and started up the twin prop beauty. He turned to Kip and yelled over the noise, "You better hope we don't run into a head wind, or you'll be swimmin' to Norfolk."

The two men left standing by the plane moved aside and Tucker swung the tail around in a quick movement. He taxied the plane out to the runway and faced the majestic sea. He caught a slight headwind for takeoff. He throttled up and they rolled down the runway. The Otter was up in the air in no time, as the STOL suggests. They cleared the island heading northwest and not long after, Tucker banked to the left and came around until he had a compass reading of south.

"Never get tired of the view," he half-yelled into the microphone of his headset. The rumble of the engines was still loud with headphones on.

Kip turned to him and Tucker nodded towards the blue and green speckle colored water.

"Yes, it's great," he said. But his thoughts had already lingered elsewhere.

The two grounds men were leaning over, going through the goodies left behind on the field when one suddenly felt an object pressed hard to the back of his head. The other man saw the barrel of a gun reach his companion's head and turned to see what was going on. As he did, he caught the butt of a rifle squarely on the jaw that sent him sprawling to the ground.

The man with the gun to his head saw his colleague fall and heard the question, "Now, where exactly is that plane headed?"

Chapter Sixty-Five

The plane was in the air for twenty minutes lofting over small air pockets and pushing further south. Kip had finished eating his meal of fruit and gulping down the dark sweet liquid that had warmed since first grabbing it. The salivating expectation of enjoying it ice cold had been replaced with some sour disappointment because he waited too long to drink it. Coke does not taste the same when warm, and so he was a little short of embracing total satisfaction. And he was still very hungry and a little sticky. He was sticky because he ate the mango without the aid of utensils. Just ripping and tearing at the skin with his teeth, peeling back the outer layer to get at the tangy flesh inside made the mess. Juice dribbled down his chin and over his fingers, stinging the cuts he sustained while grabbing onto the coral, and then it continued to spill onto his shirt and pants. It was not a pretty performance of etiquette.

Then halfway through finishing his meal, Tucker, with a smirk plastered on his face offered up a penknife. Kip, with the fruit up close to his mouth, was trying to manage this delicious yet messy mango. He shot Tucker a look that could kill. Kip was not impressed by his attempt at humor.

"Go on, take it. It will make it easier, " Tucker said with the smirk still shining on his face.

"No, thanks," Kip said. "I prefer to eat my mangoes like a three year old."

"I've got some serviettes here, too. You might want to wipe your face," Tucker said, ready to break out laughing.

"Maybe later," Kip retorted.

"So," Tucker began over the mic, although the din of the engines seemed to be dissipating by mere monotony; the beat of the engine was still consistent and ever present. "So how exactly did you find out who I was?"

"Oh, easy. I made contact with the Director of the CIA. I gave him the serial number on your plane together with the only name you gave me. I imagine he in turn contacted his counterparts from your country and they were able to track down your registration information and who you are."

"Nice," Tucker said sarcastically.

"So, I believe, they reached your Deputy Prime Minster and emphasized the importance of my leaving the island?"

Tucker ignored the question with its innuendo of implying how he had been trumped.

"So, what's in the bags?"

"Sorry, I am not at liberty to discuss that with you."

"Yeah, no, I didn't think you'd give up that info, but I thought I'd give it a shot at asking anyway."

Kip gave a little smile and decided to change the subject himself.

"I take it you were in the Australian Air Force?"

"Yeah, served in the R double A F for twelve years."

Kip knew this to mean the RAAF. The Royal Australian Air Force.

Then Tucker continued the thread of the conversation. Like he was almost glad to have someone to talk to. "After leaving the Air Force, I took flying jobs. First commercial airlines, but that life wasn't for me. Too constricting. I joined the Flying Doctors Service and became a bush pilot and I enjoyed doing that for a while."

"Is that the service where you fly all over the outback taking medical personnel to people in remote places?" Kip queried.

"Yeah, that's right. Anyway, a friend asked if I wanted to join his team in flying medical supplies, food and sometimes people to remote islands in the South Pacific. Sounded like a good gig, so I went out on a limb, bought the plane. Now I'm a puddle jumper and the work suits me just fine."

"That's an interesting name on your plane. How did you come up with it?"

"Two things actually. The first being Qantas."

"How so?"

"Well, flying in these remote areas, I wanted a plane that would keep me safe. Call it superstition but I called her Pal Joey. I named her after Qantas because they are the only international airline never to have crashed."

"Really?"

"Yeah, no - not a crash in her entire long flying history."

Kip listened to a voice that was higher-pitched than those of his compatriots. He noticed that about Australians tone in general. He also caught onto the response given with negative answers. They say, *Yes,* or more precisely Y*eah,* then *No.* What they are doing is acknowledging the question, as in *Yeah,* your right, but the answer is then immediately followed up with the negative answer *No,* and then the explanation behind it. At first it sounds a little confusing.

Tucker continued, "Yeah so, you know that movie *Rainman?*"

"Yes."

"Well, Qantas is talked about in that movie, like how they have never crashed and the one guy wants to only fly with them.

Anyway, after that movie came out, Qantas was the only airline to show that movie on their planes!"

"I see. Great publicity for them. Not a ringing endorsement for everyone else."

"Exactly. And Qantas has the symbol of the Flying Kangaroo on the tail of their planes. I took the baby kangaroo, the Joey, and used him as mine. You know, like if the image of the kangaroo helps them, maybe it will keep me flying."

"And how's that working out for you?"

"So far so good."

"And the second reason?"

"Oh, yeah." Tucker smiled to himself and Kip could see him reminiscing over something. "Meaghan."

Kip asked. "What's that? Megan?"

"Huh?" Tucker came out of his trance. "What Megan? No, not Megan. Meaghan." He pronounced it Mee-gan.

"She was a beaut. She had long silky black hair that fell down her back, it shone almost blue. She had a fringe-cut, almost in her eyes it was. You know, in that exotic way?"

"A what cut?" Kip interrupted.

Tucker looked over at him, "You know, a fringe!"

Kip shrugged his shoulders. He had no idea what a fringe, or fringe- cut was.

Tucker shaped two fingers into a pair of scissors, charades-style and proceeded to open and close them while moving his fingers along his forehead. "A fringe-cut!"

"Oh, oh. You mean bangs," Kip blurted out, half-laughing at the caveman-like communication between two men who were supposed to be speaking the same language.

"Yeah. A fringe." Tucker was exasperated at the exchange. As if to say, *My story, my plane, my words, mate – keep up.*

"Yeah, well, anyway, just below her fringe-cut, she had the most dazzling blue eyes I've ever seen. They were warm and when she spoke to you, it was like it was only to you and there was no one else in the room, or on the planet for that matter. She had your full attention. It was all perfect with her smile and her pouting lips." Tucker lingered on the memory. And somewhere there, Kip's mind brought into play images of the woman who had that same effect on him.

"So, how does this relate to the name?" Kip finally asked, bringing them both back to reality.

"It was when I was working with a commercial airline. We had landed in Sydney and I was stepping out of the terminal to catch a cab. It was pouring rain. The cabs were scarce. She stood at the curb with a newspaper over her head, also looking for a ride to a downtown hotel. I noticed her immediately. I mean, it was hard not to. She was beautiful. I managed to snag one and she had such a forlorn look on her face; her newspaper was starting to sag with the weight of the water. So naturally, I offered her a ride."

Kip nodded in agreement.

"We talked and got to know a little about each other. She was in show business. She asked me to come along and see her in a musical play she was performing in at a theater in Sydney. Not really my cup of tea, but I went; she had that way about her, you know. So I went one night, sat smack bang in the middle of the theater, the lights went down and I was in a different time and place. Meaghan had the lead role. And then she came to this song I'll never forget. It was *Bewitched, Bothered and Bewildered.* The American musical was called *Pal Joey.* The song was great. Her rendition left me legs all wobbly. It was as good as any I've heard, and I've now heard plenty, I can tell you."

"So where is this girl of yours now?"

He was regretful in explaining. "Well, you know how it is. We dated for about a year or so. She was off touring, I was here and there with my travel, and then I took up the gig with the Flying Doctors. Our schedules kept us apart a lot. Eventually, we just drifted away from each other. But I thank her a lot for the time we had together, and for giving me the name."

Tucker turned to look at Kip as he spoke into the mic over the noise. "You know what, mate? You can't always be where you want to be."

Kip nodded in agreement.

Tucker asked Kip with a wry smile, "So, you expecting a posse when you get to Norfolk?"

"I'm sure your Government is putting all appropriate security measures in place."

"How much of a posse do you expect?"

"I don't know, given the importance of my mission, say ten to twelve security personnel, perhaps."

Tucker chuckled. "Let me tell you a little story about oStraylyan security measures. A few years back when we weren't on so friendly terms with our northern neighbors Indonesia, friction was building between the two countries something bad, and their politicians and military were doing some serious sabre rattling. So our people had some concerns. And so the Prime Minster at the time goes on TV and announces measures to appease the public. He said, *My fellow Australians, let me assure you that your government is doing everything in its power to protect this country and its citizens from external threats. We take the recent threats seriously. I stand here tonight to inform you of our commitment in sending the Coast Guard to further protect the thousands of miles of our nation's northern coastline from foreign invasion. And I go even further to add that, if the threat from the north intensifies, or if further assistance is required and called for, there will be no hesitation from this government in sending another bloke to up there to help out the one we just sent!*

"Are you serious?" Kip asked in amazement.

"Nah. But it's not far from the truth. You know, when you sent troops to Iraq and Afghanistan, we did, too. And in proportion to our population of twenty or so million, we sent an adequate force of a couple of thousand in ratio to your one hundred-fifty thousand soldiers. But your population is over three hundred million people. All I'm saying is, you're not in Kansas anymore, Dorothy. This isn't the U.S. where you send in overwhelming forces. We do things in moderation."

Kip looked away and out over the thousands of shadow islands resting on the sea below, the illusion created by the sun and the clouds. *That can't be right* he thought. *This is too important.*

By now he was also experiencing a lag. His eyelids were heavy. He had raced backwards in time over multiple time zones, then leaped forward losing out on twenty-four hours. His body clock was all out of whack. As he started to drift away, the engines now white noise in the background for him, he remembered Tucker had said something during their conversation and it stuck, and he took that with him into peaceful serenity.

"Wakie, wakie. Helloooo? … Kip! …Wake up!"

Kip came out of his slumber a little slow and a little confused. He found Tucker shaking his arm.

"OK, OK. What's up?"

"I told you this place was at my outer limits. We're going to have to put down in the water."

Kip was still fighting off the grogginess. He peered through the shaded lenses of the borrowed sunglasses. "What? What are you talking about?"

"We're out of fuel. I went to reserves some time ago. I radioed ahead to let them know. We'll come down in Duncombe Bay, not far from the Island."

Kip looked out to find the sun trying to escape in the west, but the day still had some life left in her. About another hour or so, he thought. He saw the Island of Norfolk ahead.

Tucker tipped the plane from side to side a few times in an attempt to extract the last traces of jet fuel fumes from his plane. About a minute later the left engine quit. Seconds after that, the right followed suit. They were gliding now.

"Strap in tight," was all Tucker said as he concentrated on the water landing.

Tucker put himself in the best landing position possible and the plane angled down, leveled out and touched the water. They had luck. The water was calm at that time of day in the bay, they were not fighting ocean wave chop. If they had, without the aid of the engines, the plane may have tipped. Instead it carved through the water for a perfect landing. Kip appreciated the DHC-6 Twin Otter's dual function as a floatplane as well. With the aid of the pontoon undercarriage, the plane stayed buoyant in the water. No harm, no foul.

"That tug heading our way is coming to tow us in," Tucker said while pointing. He added, "You'll be paying for that, too."

"Yep, add it to the invoice," Kip said.

"Already done," Tucker replied.

Kip remembered something. He grabbed his Sat-phone with secure communications. While they waited to be towed in, he said to Tucker, "I need to make a call."

Chapter Sixty-Six

Norfolk Island - Australia

December – Friday – 6:30 p.m.

Norfolk Island is beautiful. It was given the distinct honor of the only place Captain James Cook, who discovered it among his many discoveries, called *paradise*. Discovered by Cook in 1774, it came under British sovereignty and was twice established as a penal colony. The first attempt in 1788 was abandoned in 1804. It was deemed too difficult and remote to colonize. It lay untouched until 1825 when a second penal colony was attempted, precisely because of its remoteness. But after several years word reached the concerned, that conditions for the convicts were beyond harsh and possibly the most inhumane of all that the British ruled. The second penal settlement was closed in 1855.

      In 1856 descendants of the mutineers from the *HMS Bounty* searched for and found the island. This flock of people traveled the ocean from Pitcairn Island where Fletcher Christian and his crew had settled with Tahitian natives after confiscating the *HMS Bounty* in 1789. Pitcairn Island's population swelled to unsustainable levels, so with the British Government's blessing, volunteers decided to leave the island for a new home. With the clear understanding they were to be a separate colony from that of mainland New South Wales, it came to pass that they should enjoy Australian protection, but answered to no one but themselves administratively. The Pitcairn Islanders utilized the buildings built by convict hands, and to this day their descendants play the largest role in the fabric of Norfolk Island life.

Norfolk Island's other distinguishing feature is the Norfolk pine tree. Originally sought after as ideal for English ship masts, they later proved ineffective for this purpose and the venture was abandoned. Norfolk Island holds the distinction as the easternmost occupied territory Australia possesses, and she stands alone and far out to sea.

Kip and Tucker were met at the jetty in Duncombe Bay by Kathleen Tanner. Kathleen was in her late twenties, five and a half feet tall, and still bore her youthful looks. With light brown hair pulled together in a ponytail, she looked eager to please. She wore an official olive green colored Park Ranger uniform complete with sun hat, sunglasses and hiking boots.

"Hi fellas!" she said joyfully while waving. "Welcome to Norfolk Island. I'm Kathleen Tanner. Call me Kate."

"Well ... kiss me, Kate," Tucker proclaimed.

"Huh, funny," Kate said. "Never heard that one before," her retort dripped with sarcasm as she laughed off the flirtation. "Now, which one of you is the American?"

Kip raised his hand and Tucker also pointed to him. Kip walked over to her, casually wiped his hand on his pants, and then extended it for a handshake. "Pleased to meet you. I'm Kip Keplar."

She warmly took his hand and smiled as she said, "Very nice to meet you, too." Her voice was high-pitched but sweet. "I'm to take you to where you will be staying tonight. Alright?"

Kip nodded in agreement and returned the smile. "That sounds great."

The three of them walked to her car. Kip awkwardly carried two sacks and Tucker brought along the third slung over his shoulder, together with Kip's kit bag. Kip was careful to conceal the rifle inside the elongated bag. The car was a station wagon, local manufacturer, associated with GM. It was the Holden VE Commodore wagon, plain white. Kip loaded up the vehicle. They lowered the back seats to in order to shove it all in.

Kip stood face to face with Tucker and as they were shaking hands said, "Tucker, thanks for volunteering to give me that ride. I really appreciate it."

Tucker shook his hand firmly and said with a smile, "Don't thank me until after you've seen my bill. And when you pay it, I'll be thanking you."

Kip smiled and nodded. He moved towards the passenger car door, opened it and sat down. A split second later, he gasped a little moan, a moan someone makes when they realize their stupidity. His head lay back on the headrest in surrender, "Oh, no."

Tucker motioned for Kate to throw him the car keys and he crouched down beside Kip's open window, dangling the key ring from a finger. "If you're going to drive, you'll need these."

Driving in Australia means keeping to the left side of the road. Kip knew this, but it had been a very long and foggy day, and force of habit had him naturally jumping in the right side as a passenger. But now the steering wheel was his to contend with. He climbed out, snatched the keys from Tucker and made his way around to the other side, giving Kate a sheepish grin, along with the keys.

As they drove away he heard Tucker yell out, "Good luck, Yank!"

Kip stuck an arm out his window and signaled to him with a goodbye wave.

Driving on the "wrong" side of the road, they made their way up a gently curving hill and within minutes reached the top. They turned left onto a graveled driveway that disappeared around and through a forested section of native pines. After a hundred yards they broke into a clearing and drove towards a remarkable old building. It was an impressive single story creation; its building blocks were sandstone. It was in the classic homestead style of Australian architecture, with a porch seven feet wide decorating the perimeter of the building. The green tiled roof sloped down and covered both the house and porch, and finished with a bull nose that wrapped around the outer edge. It then hung down and partially protected the porch and its occupants from the sun. Kip eyed two wide brick chimneys jutting out the roof.

The car's tires crunched over gravel before Kate slid it into an adjoining garage. She killed the engine and made her way to the trunk, pulling the luggage out while Kip came out of the garage to admire the structure.

"It was built by convicts," she informed him. "1832."

"Impressive," Kip said. "Nice porch." He turned and looked around at what Kate was up to, struggling with a red sack. He strode over to her, "Here - let me get those, they're very heavy."

"Oh, thanks. You're right about that. We call it a verandah," she stated.

"What's that?" Kip responded as he started to gather in the big bags full of goodies that Santa could only dream of delivering.

"We call a porch a verandah." Kate clarified.

"Oh. Good to know."

Kip hauled his temporary possessions into the homestead, making it in several trips. They entered a large area that was the main receiving room for any public visitors. Kate moved along and led him to a locked door at the far end. Stenciled in red on the door yelled the words "NO ADMITTANCE."

She used her key to open the curiously heavy door, and they entered a strangely narrow storage room that ran the length of the large room beyond the walls. This storage room contained wooden shelving systems, placed against the walls opposite each other. They also ran the entire length of the storage room walls. Piled on the shelves were books on nature and wildlife, Norfolk Island and administrative procedures; boxes of files, office stationary needs, equipment and accessories were also there. Further along there were glass cases containing species of plants and preserved furry land animals, birds, spiders, and snakes. More items occupied space further down, but Kip could not see them because the room was dimly lit with yellow light. It did however, have a fresh outdoor aroma to it. Kate led the way and halfway down the room, a small gap between the wooden shelves revealed another door in the far wall.

Again, another heavy looking locked door required security access. This time entry was authorized by a wall mounted keypad, skillfully hidden behind a very large glass case of live and dangerous looking spiders. The spiders were busy scurrying around looking for ways to escape, smacking up against the glass. Kate slid the glass case away and entered the code. The door unlatched itself and they entered a darkened place. They took a few more steps down the corridor and on their left, an open door revealed an enormous cavernous room. Although dimly lit here, too, Kip could clearly identify sophisticated communication equipment all aglow. He looked at her enquiringly.

"Didn't you know? We're a listening station for the Australian government. We monitor communications in our region."

Kip shook his head slowly, he did not know.

Kate went on, "From time to time we also act as a safe house. Like tonight."

Kip noticed no windows or exterior doors, even though the outside of the building clearly showed framed windows and doors in the sandstone structure in this part of the building. He only saw solid walls. He rapped on the door behind him. Yep, solid and secure too.

"The communications room is the most secure room in the entire building once I close and lock this security door. You can rest assured about leaving your belongings in there." She proffered the room for his cargo. He accepted.

"This way, I'll show you to your room."

They moved across the corridor and down a small hallway to another locked door, which she opened.

"This is David's sleeping quarters. But as he's not here, you can have it for the night."

"David?"

"I work with David. But he is on holidays back on the mainland. Visiting family. He won't be back for another week."

They returned to the main room. Kip collected his belongings and took them to the communications room to stow away. Once again, he had to make several trips.

When finished, he called out to Kate, "I'll be out in a minute."

"Righty-O," was the reply.

Kip closed and locked the door. He surveyed the room. It was large, but the surface areas were occupied by equipment, some of it humming away at that very moment. So he sat on the floor to open and examine the contents of the sacks. This was the first safe opportunity to do so. He still had no clue what was in what bag, and perhaps had already lost what he came looking for, possibly resting at the bottom of the ocean. He carefully examined the exterior of the closest sack. It was made of a smooth but flexible substance, a thick rubberized material with a nylon outer coating. No trace fibers would be left by these at the scene. He loosened the drawstrings. Opening up the throat, he placed his hand inside and began extracting objects.

Huh, he thought, *no cash in this one.* A great assortment of bejeweled trinkets, dazzling baubles, collections of both exquisite and gaudy jewelry and ornamentations lay out before him. It seems people's taste covers a wide range. He instinctively knew the contents were worth millions.

After he emptied out bag number one, he worked on the second. This one had the Hollywood bearer bonds in it. He fanned out wads of thick paper notes. He had no idea of the value here, and no interest in counting it. He found them and that was good enough. He put these aside as well.

He was hoping *third time's a charm* as he checked out bag number three. The first item he pulled out was encased in a velvet pouch. With his probing hand he reached into the pouch and felt something cold. He clenched it and withdrew it. He opened his fingers to reveal an object of stunning beauty. It was *Yurushi*. No question. It defied description and lived up to its mystique. Even in the low light inside the room it twinkled and gleamed. Few could deny its allure. Minutes passed before he was able to break the trance and place it safely back in the pouch.

After several innocuous items were inspected, Kip removed a case, about the size of a backgammon board. It was black, unobtrusive, but on the side was written three letters – D.O.D.

He had it. A quick check of the contents, as someone had already gone to the trouble of breaking it open, and he confirmed he possessed what he traveled halfway around the world for. This was what he had risked his life for, and still another had made the ultimate sacrifice. He made a tally of the drives, twenty-five as there should be. He closed it and placed all the contents back in their respective bags. Once he was finished, he left the room and locked the door to go join Kate.

He returned to the great room and searched for Kate. Many windows here lit the room with golden afternoon light from the late afternoon summer sun. He stood between two desks holding laptop computers. They guarded the entrance to the NO ADMITTANCE door he had just come through. A number of glass displays filled the center of the spacious room. Images of wildlife, flora, fauna and pictures decorated the walls. Tourist brochures were racked and slotted in a stand near the entrance. The wall where he was standing ran to a corner. Here a small room began; inside the room was a tiny kitchen. Through the entrance to the kitchen Kip saw Kate moving back and forth, busy with something. He made his way over to her.

"Kathleen?" he queried.

"Just making some tea. Would you like a cup?"

Tea? "Ahh, no thanks. I'll take some water, though."

"Fair enough." She went to the refrigerator and pulled out a cold bottle of water.

"Thank you. So how exactly does this work?"

"Hmm," she said, slightly distracted. "ASIO's operation you mean?

Kip nodded.

"Well, officially, to the general public, it's the Ranger Station."

"Ranger Station?"

"For the National Park next door." She pointed towards the trees.

He tracked the direction of her pointed finger. "Oh … so do you get many tourists through here?"

"Actually, not really. There is a smaller Ranger station at the entrance to the park, and that is where most of the public and their enquiries end up. This place has more limited access, but David and I wear the appropriate attire just in case someone strays our way. We do, however, get some visitors. It makes for legitimate cover. The park is a National Park, owned and operated by the Federal government, as are we. Any administrative paperwork for the park actually takes place back on the mainland." She said all this with a pleasant smile, a twinkle in her eye, and a delightfully pleasant voice, speaking as if they were talking about any ordinary 9 to 5 office job.

"Oh, I see. You're operating in plain sight."

"Yeah, that's right," she said with a smile and a little nod in agreement.

"OK, and unofficially ASIO utilizes it for its own intelligence purposes?"

Kate finished making and then pouring herself steaming hot tea while she answered. "Yes, you see, this facility is the property of the Australian Federal government and operated by ASIO. I don't think I'm telling you anything I shouldn't be, as you are with the CIA."

Well, as Kip knew, that was not entirely true, but it worked for now. It was, however, a good thing for him that he knew that ASIO is the Australian Security Intelligence Organization. He could keep up with the narrative Kate was feeding him. ASIO was as close as Australia came to having something similar to the CIA. He recalled working joint ventures with them on a couple of occasions. But in the present, apparently Ken Maylon's call opened doors and ensured a safe zone inside a trusted ally's secure borders.

"My boss, David," she spoke the words ending with an upward inflection, "anyway, we work well together. He takes on the role as Park Superintendent, and I'm his assistant. Nobody knows otherwise."

"And what exactly do you do out here?"

"People see this place as a preservation building, or government institution, so we carry on unnoticed. Some official cars come and go as part of the parks ongoing duties. Nothing too high profile of course, nothing to attract attention; but it helps with the cover story. But most that stop by here on official business do so for other reasons."

Kip gave her a coy smile and said. "And what would that be?"

"Well, I can't go into details, you understand, let's just say we have big ears, and we are a bit of a busybody. We do need to know what's going on in our part of the world, so we act as a listening post, a collector of gossip, you might say."

As an after-thought she added with a dour expression, "We've had a lot of trouble with Fiji, East Timor and the Solomon Islands in the last twenty years or so. It's nice to know what's going on in your own neighborhood, wouldn't you say?"

Kip drank some water while nodding in agreement. He could see how people were fooled by this woman's persona. He would never have guessed her role in such doings. That old rule about books and covers sure had significance.

Kate went on with her summary; she seemed pleased to be playing tour guide and have someone to share her secret story with. "This place was used by the Australian coastal watchers in World War II. They were doing the same thing. Picking up on Japanese movements and communications and reporting back to the government. Operated out of this very building. We've been doing the same thing ever since."

Kip looked out the window; he was keen to stretch his legs after the long flight. "I'll take a look outside, if that's OK?"

"Yeah, no - of course it is. Go right ahead."

Kip slipped through the door facing the sea. He walked about twenty paces and turned to face his newest temporary place of residence. In the late afternoon sun the sandstone building shone supreme gold. The windows were inset and the walls appeared to be at least two feet thick. Kip turned again to face the sea so he could enjoy the scenery around him. He was standing in an open grassy area that stretched unabated towards the sea, another fifty feet or so. As his eyes swept over the vista he surveyed the land; both this side to the north, and also to the west was open green plains. Turning slowly, anticlockwise in motion, he looked south above the homestead and saw the treetops. To his left, the trees were unbroken there too, heading to the cliff's edge and the water below. He mapped out that the south and east sides corralled the building with a heavily wooded forest.

Satisfied with the view, he made tracks towards the water. Sounds of crashing waves could be heard in the distance as he strolled to land's end. High above the ocean on the sea cliff he was greeted by a gentle onshore breeze. The evening light was setting in and although it was later in the day, he knew the searing heat and humidity he had experienced in the last … *what five, or wait … was it six, or maybe four days?* had vanished. He was too tired to do the math, what with the, add a day here, take away several hours there - he didn't know. Anyway, it was now a comfortable and pleasant seventy-five degrees.

There was activity of bird life out at sea and on the rocks far below. The drop of two hundred feet from the craggy cliff edge displayed a menagerie of feathered wildlife. With the late afternoon sun glinting off whitecaps out at sea, Kip transfixed on an image beyond the birds that flew in and out of his immediate periphery. He focused on an image in the vast sea beyond his physical view. He went to the place in the middle of nowhere of the wide blue ocean and remembered with solace his fallen companion left behind. It was tragic that a good man, simply and honorably doing duty for his country, would be unable to go home. He was yet another man, an anonymous man to many, whom Kip could never forget. His thoughts drifted further still across the deep blue landscape to home. Mette and the children. He could not help it, he smiled. He smiled at the thought of her and their children, too. Just one short week ago he was looking out over the same body of water in the opposite direction from where he now stood.

Then he frowned. To think how just one bullet would not have allowed him to make it back to see them. Tomorrow he would be on his way home. The smile returned. For now, though, he was regrettably still on his mission, so contacting the family with the obligatory *I'm OK ...be home soon*, would not be forthcoming.

He wandered west on the open grasslands then stopped to check out the old convict building from a different angle. It was certainly built to stand the test of time, and he was sure being convict-built, there were many stories this old gal could tell. Lots of heartache, sweat, tears and literally blood went into erecting such a fine monument. The west end of the building was clearly an addition, a newer version of the old. He looked more closely at the windows, which were backed by heavy curtains so seeing inside was not possible. He knew now that these were false window frames that excluded eyes or entry. Solid brick walls met anyone who got past the curtains. Neat trick. They were there for decorative purposes only. He walked west again and saw that the coast weaved in and out and finally headed south. Not too far away, a gaping bay opened up and would swallow up anyone who was careless enough to miss it.

Kip had seen enough of the west and now headed east to help stretch those tired legs. He walked past the building and over to the islands other natural wonder, the straight and tall Norfolk pines. They were clustered together and formed the very edge of the forest that Kate had described. They stood their ground no more than thirty yards away from his residence. He placed a hand on one of the trees trunks; felt its coarse texture while also smelling its fragrant pine. A twig tumbled down from above and landed at his feet. Kip looked at the twig then at something else that caught his eye. It was convex shaped, clear plastic, not unlike the bottom of a plastic soda bottle, buried upside down in the ground. He swept his right boot over it and studied it for a few seconds more. Then he was interrupted by a sound. He snapped his head to the right and peered down the road. A white van was coming towards him. He broke from the tree and moved towards the homestead.

He entered and Kate looked up. "Oh, I'm glad your back. They're here."

Kip smiled, "Who's here?" he queried.

"Your protection detail. They landed fifteen minutes ago, when you were outside."

Kate, with car keys in hand, walked towards the front entrance door and said to Kip, "Now they're here, I'm off to get everyone dinner. Be back soon. See ya." She turned before making it through the door and added in an offhanded sort of way, "You must be important!"

"Why is that?" Kip asked.

"Well," she said, "they sent four men to protect you."

Chapter Sixty-Seven

Norfolk Island - Australia

December – Friday – 7:22 p.m.

The light of day was fading on this summer afternoon when the four men stepped into the building. The first man through the door spotted Kip, gave a friendly nod and said, "You must be Mr. Keplar from the United States?"

"You can call me Kip."

"Agent Nathan Lamb, good to meet ya."

Three other men pushed past the two getting acquainted at the entrance and dumped their gear in the main room. Lamb pointed to the other members of his team. "This here is Nguyen, Contaros and Sieco."

The three men, in turn, between pulling on zippers, extracting equipment and weaponry and other similar tasks, each gave Kip a perfunctory nod.

"Right," Agent Lamb said to the men. "I need two of you," He pointed to Sieco and Nguyen, "Ross and Lee, sweep the perimeter of the property, report anything suspicious."

"Yes, sir," Lee spoke for both of them. They shouldered their weapons, picked up flashlights and left.

Lamb had Contaros set up the radio communication equipment so contact could be made with base. Three minutes later he called in to confirm their arrival and safe and secure possession of their "package."

Twenty-five minutes later Kate was back, armed with dinner. She placed the bags down on a large table near the small kitchen. "Fish and chips all right?" she asked the crowd of men as she was handing over the wrapped packets of food.

Aw, yeah ... tah, dear ... thanks, love ... and other expressions of the men's gratitude came flowing Kate's way.

She placed cans of soda on the table as well and told the men, "Well, I'm off now, you won't be needing me anymore. I'm staying down in Kingston for the night in a hotel." She looked at Kip. "Hope you enjoy your stay with us, bye." She extended her hand.

"Thanks for everything, Kate," Kip said. "I appreciate everything you and your country have done to help me." He shook her hand and then pulled her in close for a hug.

"Oh, it's quite all right," she said with a genuine smile that he could not see.

After Kate was gone, the men tucked into their butcher-paper wrapped food. The Australian men tore open the top of the wrap and stuck their fingers deep inside to extract pieces of fresh fish dipped in batter, or to nab a steaming hot chip. Kip mimicked the local custom.

When in Rome!

He struggled, scalding his fingers while attempting to pull out three incredibly tasty chips before giving up on the local tradition and unrolling the encased food. The art of eating that way was too painful for the tips of his coral-cut fingers. The steam rising from the food, not to mention the salt scattered over it, prevented him from enjoying his meal.

He sipped his soda and said, "Mmm ... good food. So, where did you guys come from?"

Agent Lamb spoke for his men. "We shipped out of Brisbane. We're part of the Tactical Response Group. Told us we were needed out here for protection services."

Lamb spoke friendly enough, but he had short quick answers.

"Well, I appreciate you coming, thank you," Kip said.

"Yeah. No worries. Oh, and your people will be here at 0600. Coming in from Hawaii. Was told to tell you that," Lamb said.

Kip acknowledged the information but was still feeling weary, so he told the guys he was going to catch some shut-eye.

Within ten minutes, exhausted, Kip was fast asleep on David's pillow.

Chapter Sixty-Eight

Norfolk Island - Australia

December - Saturday – 1:03 a.m.

They came at night. They always come at night. Mogul and his crew crawled into position and hid amongst the tall pine trees, careful not to give away their element of surprise. Mogul had brought everyone with him. Everyone. No exceptions. Mogul gave himself a brief moment to recall how they got there while everyone readied themselves for the oncoming assault.

Mogul watched as the boat sped away in the rain. Once the steel cuffs were removed from the mess door, Bo was dragged topside. Mogul put him to work to track the sacks' locations. Three of the four sacks' trackers beeped to life. Mogul had faith in his men who performed the heist, but he was no fool. Each sack had an embedded tracking chip, sewn into the lining between the inner and outer casings. This was his insurance, and it was a wise decision. There is honor amongst thieves – to a point. Mogul knew he would not be with them on the initial break-in and theft, so he needed a little edge, just in case things did not go according to plan or the men decided to get stupid and greedy.

The chips had a range of one hundred square miles, so tracking them to Owaraha Island was easy. Finding them here on Norfolk needed additional assistance. Seamus took command of the ship as the newly appointed captain, as ordered by Mogul. No one objected, and they left the former captain to bob around the ocean as fish food.

Once the ship broke free of the reef with the aid of the rising tide, tracking the thief to Owaraha Island was not a problem. They anchored in deep water near the island. The men drove the duly repaired *Sunday* to shore. But they were minutes too late from taking pleasure in killing the man who stole what was theirs and from retrieving the bounty.

Their distress call earlier in the day alerted the meeting party to their plight, and four hours later his Chinese clients arrived on Owaraha. They did not come alone. Another planeload of men bearing gifts also arrived. After the workmen at the airfield offered up more than shrugs, with a little persuasion from Mogul's men, they had given up the destination of the plane, an island many miles from anywhere. Mogul formulated his plan.

With the aid and cooperation of the men who arrived on one of the planes, he knew the outcome was secure.

Passengers on the second plane were Military and Intelligence Officers. Men from China. They supplied Mogul with all the necessary equipment and information he needed for the raid. The information was first-rate intelligence. It was the location where his stolen goods would be. Australia's secret safe house was not so secret. Chinese intelligence knew exactly where it was, and more importantly knew the main function of the secondary Ranger station. China, with a growing sphere of influence in the world, also wanted to know what was going on in its own backyard, and where the other players on the chessboard had placed their pieces. This vital fact would later be corroborated when China's MSS intercepted *Pal Joey's* radio transmission calling a *mayday* while landing in Duncombe Bay at Norfolk Island. Position confirmed.

So, Mogul now had a fix on a location and was armed to the teeth with a cache of weaponry. The armaments supplied by the

Chinese were American military. The irony of the Chinese supplying weapons made in the USA was lost on everyone concerned. The Chinese were no dummies, though; they were discreet and made a point that they would have no direct involvement. No clear trail leading back to their role in this operation. No blowback. The transportation and pilots, also provided by China, played a secondary role. Mogul was ready for some payback. His trained men were ready to go. They arrived by the same means as Kip and Tucker – seaplane.

With his eyes adjusting to the surroundings, clad in black and equipped with the latest communication technology for talking with his people, he quietly moved his men into position. Mogul was annoyed at the appearance of a half-moon that peeked out from behind the scattered clouds. And he was dismayed at the voluminous quantity of stars that seemed to pop out of the sky here. He did not remember there being so many! Or so bright! He staked his position out at the edge of the trees - a mere thirty yards of open ground before bursting through the doors and killing everyone. That was OK. There was, however, one problem to overcome. Even with all China's know-how, supplies, information and intelligence reports, there was no head count for how many were in the building. *How many men with guns were waiting for them beyond those doors?*

As someone's luck would have it, Mogul's group, all seventeen of them, arrived at the 1:00 a.m. shift change. His men counted off four men in the main room. *How many more in the back rooms?* Ultimately, it had no bearing. They were going in.

That is the thing about guards, or sitting ducks; the terms are interchangeable. Guards are great when there is no imminent threat. They impress the old and young alike. Civilians feel safe or scared by them. With no one attacking, they appear to be invulnerable. But take away all the niceties, and add the element of surprise, the ultimate advantage is to the men intent on wanting to kill them, and a guard presents one's self as an easy target. The other thing, bursting into places under synchronized timing did not happen on the quarter hour. He was not going to wait for 1:15 a.m., or 1:30 a.m. If anything, trained guards become even more alert at these times, men who are ruled by rules and regulations. No, it was better to pick a synchronized time like 1:07 and thirty-two seconds. Surprise was on their side.

Just then, Mogul was receiving headset traffic from his men. Through the night vision scope on his rifle, one reported that he was trained in on a guard in the house. Target was visible through a window on east side of building. He had him in his sights. *Could he fire?* Another call came in. Another target was standing still at the south entrance door. He had just walked out, flashlight in hand, but he stopped to adjust something around his waist. *Could he take him out?*

No time to think through the strategy. His first thought, *take the opportunities that are presented to you.*

"Fire! Fire!" he called into the mouthpiece.

The shots rang out and the man inside the building fell away. The man standing at the door received two headshots. He fell backwards through the partially opened door. It only took a second for him to hit the floor, but his own blood splatter and brain matter got there first. As he fell, he pushed on the door and it widened further. The door that he had sworn to guard and protect was now vulnerable.

Chapter Sixty-Nine

Norfolk Island – Australia

December – Saturday – 1:03 a.m.

Kip opened his eyes into blackness. It was deeply silent. The time lag had him wide-awake. It would take days to untangle and readjust his internal time clock. He rolled out of bed and carefully felt his way towards the door. He needed water. That salty meal had made him thirsty. He navigated the hallway and passed through one security door and was caught between the threshold of the storage room and the great room when the gunfire started. Instinctively he dove to the ground. Several rapid shots. He looked to his right and saw a body propelled through the front door that hit the floor with a thud. After the initial shots, bullets flew in every direction throughout the building. He jumped off the floor and in a crouch, made it over to the dead man. It was Contaros. His feet lay beyond the entrance and his body was holding the front door open. Kip grabbed the body and dragged it inside, then slammed the door closed.

Lamb was already at a window returning fire, spraying the dark, so too, was Nguyen. Kip was pulling off the Kevlar vest of Contaros when Lamb yelled at him, "GET THE HELL OUT! WE'LL HOLD THEM!"

Kip nodded. He had to get away. He raced through the *NO ADMITTANCE* door and was gone. Forty seconds later he was back reporting to Lamb that there was no other exit. All doors and windows were bricked solid. He was literally up against a brick wall.

A safe house.

Kip recalled what Kathleen Tanner had said. *Everyone thinks we are what we say we are. No one suspects a thing.*

Lamb had extinguished all lights to reduce the prospects of easy targets. But everyone gathered here tonight knew Night Vision Equipment would solve that problem.

Kip recalled something from earlier today. He moved over to Lamb who was drawing too much gunfire.

"I have an idea," Kip told him.

Lamb nodded and continued to fire his weapon. "I'm listening."

"Maintain steady aim at the trees to the east, on my mark you will have identifiable targets. Fire at them."

"What the hell are you doing?"

Kip ignored the question. He yelled over to Nguyen who was protecting the south and east corners of the building. "Get ready!"

Nguyen nodded then fired another few rounds out the window and into the unknown.

Kip dropped to his stomach and slithered over to a panel of switches on the east wall. Chips of sandstone flew in all directions, glass shattered all around him as display cases blew apart and wood splintered. Bullets bit into all surfaces or ricocheted to embed into other objects. Kip used a flashlight he had removed from Contaros to direct the light at the wall as he searched for a switch. They were all labeled, *what was it called again? ... it started with a "V"*. He found it. He raised the sniper rifle he had retrieved when he tried to escape through the back rooms. He readied himself and yelled out, "THREE, TWO, ONE NOW!"

Bright light flooded the outside of the building. Light flashed over the homestead and its verandah, the surrounding grounds instantly exchanged night for day. Powerful beams bleached the Norfolk pine trees white from in-ground lights buried at their trunks thirty yards from the homestead. All at once Mogul's men were taken by surprise, and stole a natural pause. The battleground conditions had changed instantly and Mogul's men were exposed. All those wearing NVG's and utilizing them with great effect seconds ago, now lifted them above their eyes or turned their heads away from the illumination that temporarily blinded them. Men who were sheltered by the darkness were now apparent to the enemy and three died quickly from precision headshots.

Like dear caught in a headlight, four men froze when the lights came on. They were crawling along the open plain on the north side of the homestead; just twenty short feet away from entry, but caught in no-man's land. Lamb, who momentarily switched from hunted to hunter, sprayed them with bullets as they hopelessly attempted to make it back to the safety of the trees. Three more men sunk to the ground never to rise again. Tony, who was in the group, desperately ran, then tripped and crawled to safety, shrugging off two blunt rounds intended for the middle of his back, defended by the Kevlar vest. However, he kept the bullet that speared his calf muscle into a bloody mess.

The reprieve from ferocious volleys of gunfire only lasted seconds, but for the guys defending the homestead, they welcomed the slight leveling of the playing field. For the next two minutes, half of Mogul's reduced squad was busy taking aim and extinguishing the lights that made them easy targets. Lamb raced over to the radio, and during a small lull in the firing, he contacted his controller. He spoke with surprising calmness as he apprised him of the situation.

"This is Ranger One, we are engaged in a gun battle and receiving heavy fire. Our position has been compromised. We are two men down. I say again, we are two men down."

"Roger that. And the package?" came the matter of fact response.

"Still intact."

"Need for local forces as backup?"

Lamb knew the five men and one female local constabulary was no match for whatever was out there and the weapons these people carried. He paused before saying, "Negative. The opposition numbers are too strong and heavily armed. They would be cut to pieces. Unable to advise how long we can hold on. Do what you have to. Over."

"Roger that. Good luck."

Lamb returned to the fight, checked his ammo, and continued repelling the intruders. He had no time to reflect on the actions and death of Contaros who had paused at the door too long because his utility belt caught on the doorknob. Nor did he think about Sieco, who on commencing his shift went to the kitchen and began filling the kettle with water to make tea while standing in front of a window. Both men were sloppy. They paid the ultimate price. His anger was reserved for the fact that this was assigned as a protection detail. In these circumstances, not all the equipment he now needed had been brought along as it would have been on an assault mission. Less weaponry, no damn helmets. All the men were wearing soft shell baseball caps.

"Damn it," he muttered and continued firing.

Chapter Seventy

Brisbane – Australia

December - Friday – 10:36 p.m.

It was Saturday morning on Norfolk Island, but Friday on mainland Australia had yet to expire. Norfolk Island was two-and-a-half hours ahead of where the man, standing in the command room somewhere in Brisbane, was contemplating a difficult decision.

Two-and-a-half hours, because the state of Queensland, and therefore its capital Brisbane, does not observe Day Light Savings time or DLS. However, it is invoked in the summer months in the other east coast states of New South Wales, Victoria and the island of Tasmania, sharing the same time zone. Norfolk Island is constitutionally tied to the New South Wales government, and so DLS applies to the Island. Without DLS, the standard time difference is one-and-a-half hours. Therefore, legally, on the clock, Brisbane remains two-and-a-half hours away. It was 10:36 p.m. on Friday in Brisbane where Jace Williams stood thinking.

After receiving the distress call he knew he was, for all intents and purposes, inconveniently a long way away. Jace Williams cradled the receiver and a decision was required, one he did not want to make. His men were in trouble and he was too far off to reach out and offer reasonable assistance.

His thoughts fell back to a television broadcast he watched years before. President forty-one, George Herbert Walker Bush of the United States of America was delivering a speech to the American people. He was announcing his decision to send into harm's way, a U.S. led coalition of soldiers to dislodge Saddam Hussein from Kuwait. His speech categorically called for overwhelming strength in numbers to do the job right. President Bush wanted an unquestionable victory. Jace tried to recall his words, *what was the expression he used, something like, ahh yes ... "Our brave men and women will not be asked to fight this conflict with one hand tied behind their back."*

Overwhelming force.

Jace had the authority to make the decision. His orders were clear. He had no choice.

Protect or destroy.

Agent Lamb understood those same orders. They got it wrong once already. Jace did not hesitate one second longer. He picked up the phone and was immediately patched through to his counterpart in the RAAF.

"Scramble four jets."

The on-duty pilots waiting in their flight suits heard the high-pitched tone of the siren. *Another drill?* They zipped up, stepped into boots, grabbed helmets, and ran to their awaiting aircraft. The RAAF flew F/A-18A Hornets. They were a few years away from receiving the Joint Strike Force, F-35 Lightning II. Anytime, now - guaranteed! The operational launch of the F-35 had been delayed more times than anyone cared to count. However, the Hornets were sleek fighters, trusted and formidable fighter jets, more than capable of holding their own.

The pilots buckled in and the first two jets lifted off four minutes after notification. Captain Petr Stevens and his wingman Flight Lieutenant Glenn Anthony were airborne and heading east out to sea as was the protocol. The two follow-up jets were forty-five seconds in arrears. The procedure for heading directly out to sea was predicated on the theory that any incoming threat detected early enough to deploy fighter jets would approach from over the water. Therefore, the Number 3 Squadron, based at the RAAF Air Base at Williamstown, some one hundred-and-twenty miles north of Sydney, would intercept whatever came over the horizon.

The jets stayed low as they raced over the water. Their sudden entry into civilian air space could cause dire consequences. Captain Stevens tore open the package giving him the code he needed to proceed with any future orders. If you were prepared to attack, shoot and destroy a target unquestioningly, you needed absolute proof the orders you received were genuine. He requested verification and received it.

"Mission?" he asked.

"Norfolk Island. This is not a drill," was the distant reply.

"Please confirm."

"I say again, Norfolk Island. This is not a drill. Proceed at maximum speed. You will receive further instructions en route."

"Affirmative," was his response.

"Caesar. Set coordinates for Norfolk Island. Maximum speed. This is not a drill, I say again, this is not a drill."

"Affirmative," came his response.

Norfolk Island lay almost due east of their takeoff position, so minor course corrections were all that was required. The estimated flight time to Norfolk Island from their current position was forty-seven minutes. The aircraft's wings were hydraulically drawn in to allow for maximum speed. They hit the afterburners and accelerated to supersonic. The jets skimmed over the dark waters some two hundred feet below. Cargo ships and fishing trawlers would have witnessed a highly unusual sight to see these two birds of war, screaming over the Pacific Ocean with blue flames pouring out of their twin engine exhaust nozzles licking the air behind them.

At the predetermined destination, the jets adjusted from flying horizontally low across the water to angling into a climb, setting their aircraft at a sixty-degree vertical pitch, to reach their optimum cruising altitude of 50,000 feet. This was airspace reserved for them exclusively, as it was for military aircraft only; 10,000 feet above the maximum flying altitude of civilian aircraft. The thinning atmosphere aided in a number of ways. It allowed them to arrive earlier. Maximum speed was Mach 1.8 or 1,190 miles per hour. Up here in the heavens, there was less drag on the aircraft, allowing them to conserve fuel as they burned it up fast. The jets cut a path forever upward and were in an area of space that few traveled.

The F/A-18A Hornets were not modern fighting jets. These in particular had seen twenty years of service, but were still ranked as some of the best fighting craft in the world. Over the years, their interiors had been continually updated. Through the newly configured onboard computer system, Stevens received his target coordinates. He studied the information through his visor for a long time. He could hear his breathing into the oxygen mask. He understood his mission. It was land based and on Australian soil. A call came in from his wingman.

"Sir, are these coordinates correct?"

"Roger that, Caesar, they have been twice confirmed."

"But Captain, it's a land based target on Norfolk Island."

"That's affirmative."

"Why?"

"Caesar, the authority and channels this came through have been verified. Don't ask why. Just follow your orders. Is that clear?"

"Yes Sir. Target coordinates confirmed," was the response of a man trained to follow orders.

Stevens had his doubts, too. But for different reasons. His problem was tactical. The static position of the selected target concerned him. The Air Force jets placed on high alert were designed to intercept fast incoming assaults from the air. For this he was prepared. If it was seaborne, the Navy would intercede, therefore careful thought, not to mention their exercises and training, focused on preventing that type of attack. To this end, the jets were pre-armed with ordinates that were overwhelmingly air-to-air missiles. The Hornet had one 20-millimeter M61 Vulcan nose mounted cannon, and stacked with AMRAAM, Sparrow and Sidewinder air-to-air and long-range missiles. Heat seeking. He carried just one AGM-65 Maverick air-to-surface missile. He knew both he and Caesar had one shot to get it right. The one- shot precision would be like that of a cowboy on horseback at full gallop, taking aim with a six shooter - one bullet in the chamber, trying to hit a tin can off a fence one hundred feet away. He hoped he had the ability. He would know in thirty-eight minutes.

Chapter Seventy-One

Norfolk Island - Australia

December – Saturday – 1:34 p.m.

The shooting match continued for some time and it was slowly grinding down to a stalemate. Bullets still somehow found glass to shatter and everyone kept down low or behind cover. The opposing teams had staked out their positions and became virtually impossible to dislodge or take out. Mogul's men were tactically smart enough to fire several rounds before relocating to another position amongst the trees, so as not to be picked off from incoming rounds. Kip and the men inside did not have this luxury. They had to stay put and try to hold their positions in a wide arc. Moving around would cause gaps in the defenses. All the while bullets whistled through the complex, and many times all three came close to being hit.

Kip, after firing off a volley of bullets, replaced his magazine and looked in Lamb's direction. Lamb sensed the eye contact and looked his way.

Kip yelled out, "Backup?"

Lamb yelled back, "Fighter jets. On their way. About twenty-five minutes."

"What are our chances?"

Lamb only responded with a shake of his head. Then shots interrupted the conversation and he was back to repelling the onslaught.

Kip shot a glance over at Nguyen who was holding his own then looked back to Lamb, who had since made his way over to the north wall to check on any more ground-crawling attacks. Kip kept on firing.

Mogul's men were becoming uneasy. They wanted nothing more than to charge the building, but who would be first across the thirty yards of open ground, the no man's land, while trained men with guns inside were shooting? Meanwhile, Ray, who was positioned on the south side tree line, stopped firing.

He had an idea.

He motioned for two men to help lift him up the pine tree; he needed help to grab even the lowest branches. They muscled Ray up on the far side of the tree so as not to get shot. Ray heaved and pulled and climbed over several more limbs before settling on a satisfactory position. He hid behind the branches and they gave him great cover as he searched for a target. He found one. The shot was not a kill shot, but it would do. He removed his NVG's to look through the scope. The low overhang from the roof meant his angle had no sighting for a headshot if anyone was standing. He knew they were wearing vests, so body shots were last resorts. But this was it. Below the overhang and through one of the deeply indented south side windows an object was moving slowly along the far north wall. He aimed for the leg.

Lamb was up against the north wall and keeping the wolves at bay, but was low on ammo. With his back hard up against the wall to minimize the shots that were coming from the east woods, he called over to Nguyen, "Need more amm ......Arrgghhhh!!"

Both Kip and Nguyen snapped their heads in Lamb's direction as his distressed voice shouted out. There was nothing they could do.

The first bullet ripped into his leg, splintering his shin. He managed to stay up, but yelled out at the impact and the pain. With clenched teeth to stifle the pain, he instinctively bent over to clutch the hole in his leg, but in doing so he gave Ray the shot he was looking for. Ray fired off three more rounds. The first bullet tore away part of his left ear. Lamb had no time to react to the dirty deed, or wince at this secondary pain. The second shot burst through the back of his skull, spiraled through his brain and smashed through the back of his teeth. The bullet was eventually stopped by the Kevlar jacket protecting his chest. The third bullet was high and chipped the wall. Lamb slumped down the wall. With legs sprawled out in front of him, he appeared to be resting peacefully with his chin touching his jacket, but that was not the case.

Kip did not catch the whole act being played out by Lamb. Instead, he searched the trees in time to see the muzzle flash from the final bullet Ray had peeled off. Kip aimed and fired. He caught sight of the man falling from the tree.

The men at the base of the tree helped Ray up off the pine needle matted ground.

"You all right?" one of them asked.

Ray held his right hand up for inspection but it was hard to see in the dark beneath the shadows of the trees, even with the moon and bright stars.

Ray lifted his bloodied right hand and in a surprised voice said, "They got me in the hand. My thumb's all shot up. Look."

Ray was bewildered at his injury, as if to say, *why are they shooting at me?* His thumb was sliced through to the bone and was dangling. Blood was pouring from the wound. He could feel the warm liquid running over his hand. He asked one of the men for something to wrap it in and he stayed behind the tree just staring at his misfortune.

Kip shuffled back to check on the arrival of the jets. He did not even bother to identify himself, the accent was enough.

"We are down to two men! Where are those jets?"

"Hold them for fifteen minutes," said the voice on the line.

Easier said than done, thought Kip. *And then what happens*? was his second thought.

Recover or destroy.

He knew what the, *then what happens,* was.

He went back to the wall and did the only thing he could do.

Less than ten minutes left, and Nguyen thought he had clipped another assailant. He told Kip so. It may have been poor timing on his part to lose focus or a coordinated attack against him, but Nguyen was caught in a triangulation of crossfire. They hit him in the torso and face with too many red-hot bullets. They caught him through the cheek and behind his ear to knock him to the ground and end his life. Now it was down to Kip.

He went back to the phone. "How long?"

"Less than nine minutes. Hold on."

Kip dropped the phone and returned to firing his weapon. *What could he do? What could he do? How could he hold them off?* There was no way he could defend the entire place on his own. Once they realized there was just one left inside they would rush him. *Welcome to the Alamo,* he thought. Then he remembered. Not the Alamo but another battlefield. A different kind of tactical ploy.

The Battle of the Bulge. World War Two. He had studied it during a tactics class in Quantico. The Americans were surrounded, outnumbered and outgunned while holding the small town of Bastogne. The Germans wanted them to surrender, but they would never surrender. The Americans had one plan. Send every available body to the point of attack and make it appear as though there were many more troops holding the town than there actually were. He would take this idea and modify it slightly. He would run from wall to wall and throw at them inordinate amounts of firepower so as to give the appearance of many more inside than just one man left standing.

Kip removed the bullet stopping jackets of the fallen and stuffed them tightly into four of the windows. It was difficult to do while trying to maintain the appearance of being many. He then leaned all the rifles and weapons with all the ammunition he could find against the walls at various locations near windows facing his assailants.

He worked quickly, but time as many know, is relative. It can go slow. It can go incredibly fast. Those who visit a casino will notice no indication of time once inside. No windows to track day or night. No clocks on the walls, no guides for your own internal clock that could say, *maybe it's time for a break or time to go home.* No interruptions, no distractions. Just focus on the task at hand, which was usually, slide money over the table for the casino to keep, despite what most people claim when asked. And after the unexplained loss of time at the table or slot machine, it's always the same statement, *time sure flies while I'm here.*

Or consider the other end of the spectrum. While performing mundane, boring, or repetitive tasks, or for someone in pain, its excruciating waiting for it to end. These people

constantly monitor and check the clock more times than they want
to, only to be frustrated at how slow time is moving.

Time is constant, yet sometimes it can be painfully relative.
At that moment, at that point in time, Kip was aching for time to
move along. He had to keep busy, or stall, for another eight
minutes or so and it felt as if time had stood still. He was fit, he
was in great physical shape, but usually he was not literally
running for his life. He was pumped up on adrenaline and
maintaining a crazy pace up and down the east and south walls and
monitoring the north wall too. He raced like a fiend, shooting a few
rounds from each weapon before moving on. Keeping the pattern
random. If he had time to pick out a target he tried to line
something up, but mainly it was suppression fire. Keep the wolves
at bay. Keep their heads low. Prevent them from storming the
place. He knew he had no chance if that happened. So he fired and
raced, and fired some more. It felt like hours. If only he had time to
check, he would have seen that only three minutes had passed.

Four minutes into his desperate plan to stay alive he was hit
by a bullet. He was diving past one of the small rectangular slots
that framed the windows when a bullet clipped the heel of his shoe,
tearing it clean off. He was now lopsided in his movements, but it
did not slow him down. The second hit was closer. He landed at a
window and came up firing. As he did so he was hit in the Kevlar
jacket, which knocked him backwards. His chest pounded with the
force, but he was OK. The bullet was a ricochet off the deep inset
sandstone wall housing the window. Its velocity was weakened by
the bounce off the wall, and the delivery of death slowed just
enough to help him survive. If he had raised his head a hair later it
was a headshot. The game would have been over. But he recovered

quickly, and checked his watch. Less than four minutes left. *Would he make it?* He returned fire and kept on moving.

Chapter Seventy-Two

SOMEWHERE OVER THE PACIFIC

December – Saturday – 1:56 a.m.

The jets came screaming in from the west. They had dropped from high out of the night sky and the lead pilot, Stevens, used gloved hands to guide his jet into a position resembling a bomb run. His darkened visor reflected the luminous green computer readings that surrounded him in the otherwise pitch-black cockpit. The jets maneuvered and angled, but maintained an approach from the west.

The INTEL for the topography made it the ideal choice. Without question. A clear uninterrupted view all the way to the target. The south and east sides were shrouded with trees. They would lose little time making these course corrections, and they moved dead on target. Some buffeting from crosswinds, but that was readily accounted for and with no incoming flak to distract their run, all looked good. Time to target, three minutes thirty seconds. Stevens could picture the pilots in the planes forty-five seconds behind, almost in sync, running down the preparation list to ready, then arm, and then engage the target. All systems were go. It was time to focus in on the tin can sitting on that fence.

Chapter Seventy-Three

Norfolk Island, Australia

December – Saturday – 1:57 a.m.

In the end, the Allies won the Battle of the Bulge. Helped out by the smaller battles waged by the likes of the brave men at Bastogne. The American soldiers at Bastogne had won, too. Their tactics had prevailed. Their willingness to fight against insurmountable odds won them the day. Don't ever quit.

Kip was using this motto to guide him through the final minutes of his life.

The American soldiers at Bastogne had halted the German advance because they had outsmarted the German commanders. The Germans had the numbers, weaponry and momentum. What they did not have were the smarts. The Germans went about the business of fighting a conventional war. Their training told them that the Americans had set up a perimeter around Bastogne, and the soldiers would hold the line wherever they were. They did not. The Germans did not want to risk losing too many men on this small insignificant town, so they would attack with small units at different points around the town and try to pinpoint a weakness. They did not find one. In fact, the Americans found theirs. By only sending one unit at a time to fight, the American soldiers were allowed to shuffle their forces around and send everyone to the place where the German attack was perpetrated. Each time the German offensive was repelled, that German unit would stand down, and a different unit at a different location attempted another assault. Never together, and never a full on coordinated attack.

They would have broken through. But the American soldiers continually rallied to the location being invaded and repelled every attempt they encountered. The Germans had no idea what they were up against. If only they knew. Outsmarted by on the ground battlefield tactics.

Kip's plan appeared to be paying off. There was no rush of troops to take him out. He had maintained the bravado he wanted to achieve. But it took its toll on him. He was a fit man and had excellent conditioning, but he felt his stamina draining away. He was having trouble maintaining this pace. Bullets continued to rain down upon him, rounds whistled and zinged and wailed by him, but no significant charge had appeared. He glanced at his watch. It was getting close to two minutes before the inevitable. But he had a new problem. He was all but out of ammunition. He had to make contact with the outside world one final time.

He reached for the receiver, grabbed and said, "Where are they??"

Williams said, "There's a way out."

Confused, Kip asked. "What do you mean … a way out?" He had to talk fast. He had to get back to the windows. The whole time he kept an eye out for moving shadows.

Williams could not explain the entire situation to him. There was just not enough time. He could not tell him that Kathleen Tanner had been trying desperately to reach his office in an attempt to provide him with vital information. She had heard the gunfire, as did half the town. He could not explain to Kip, that unbeknownst to his office, and not indicated on the blueprints he was given of the homestead, that something was missing. He had no idea. Williams could not explain to Kip that the addition of the west wing, built at the commencement of WWII, was designed for the purpose it was used for to this very day. He could not enlighten Kip on the reasons why the Australian government had deliberately used this facility as a listening station of the south pacific, stemming from legitimate fears of Japan's expansionist policies. He believed the American already knew this.

But there was something the American did not know, what even Williams had not known, as it was never recorded in any of the files he reviewed. This was either a grave oversight, or possibly, because during those troubled times when the facility had been built, the credible danger of it falling into enemy hands, made the architects decide to leave it off any and all records. Only Kathleen Tanner knew because she lived there. She knew about the tunnel. Australian soldiers had dug the tunnel as a last ditch escape plan should the island be invaded and anyone attacked the homestead. Collect what you can and clear out. That was the rudimentary plan. Williams had no time to explain any of this to Kip. He needed to help save his life, so he needed to talk about just the facts. But while he pondered about all he did not say, he also offered nothing to say.

Kip broke his train of thought and demanded, "I NEED TO KNOW NOW! WHAT IS IT?"

Williams said, "A tunnel. A tunnel to get you out of the building. The planes will be hitting their target in around two minutes."

"Where?"

"Main bedroom. Aaahh … David's bedroom, to be precise. Hatch is directly under the bed. Keplar, I'm terribly sor-"

Kip had dropped the phone at the word "bed" but could hear the pleading from the swinging and banging phone as he raced away. Kip had no more bullets for the rifles. He was all out.

He had even used five of the magazine clips for the Sig Sauer handgun he carried. He had one clip left. He had to work fast. Two minutes to find a tunnel and go to … who knew where? The irony. Ten minutes ago he wanted nothing more than for time to speed up and end all this. Coming down to the final two minutes of his life he wanted time to slow down. The clip was loaded. It was simple enough. He would fire all but five rounds then get the hell out. Kip removed the suppressor; this time he wanted noise. He stood beside the window and sprayed the night with five shots of small arms fire. The sound it made, the effect it had, everything about this last burst of gunfire said, *this is all I got*. But there was nothing more he could do. He raced away from the window, head down, and as shrapnel and shards of glass and bullet fragments chased him all the way back beyond the *NO ADMITTANCE* sign.

Kip went into the communications room and grabbed at what was the priority. He balked for half a second before deciding to risk it all to bring along *Yurushi*. He knew exactly where it was and grabbed for it as well. He ran for the door and then stopped. He almost had himself spinning around and taking with him the highly liquid bearer bonds, the thick bundles of paper that he could clumsily tuck under his arm together with a gun, a flashlight, a gem and a small black case, that could be returned to the people of Hollywood. They would not be pleased if it was left behind, no matter what the circumstances.

"To hell with Hollywood," he said out loud to no one, and went across the hall into David's bedroom.

He took hold of the edge of the bed and flung it far away from the wall it was set against. He used his flashlight to see a floor rug and slid it away with one foot. He saw the handle and yanked on it. He could see nothing. A dark hole. He stuck his beam of light down there to gauge the drop and then with less than two minutes to go, he went in after it.

Chapter Seventy-Four

Norfolk Island - Australia

December – Saturday – 1:57 a.m.

While Kip was receiving the news from Brisbane, Mogul was speaking to his men through their headsets. Seamus and Bo did not need the aid of ear-buds; they were standing nearby. Mogul now regretted the decision to take the first two shots to eliminate the guards. That part of the plan had worked well, but he lost the element of surprise and the momentum. He cursed himself for it.

They did not gain entry into the premises, as he wanted. After the first failed attempt to slip in by the men crawling along the ground, he ordered men to swing wide and storm the building from the west. They returned, informing Mogul of windows and doors with brick walls behind the curtains. They were fake! Now he knew there were only two viable entry points into the house. The doors to the north and south.

Mogul did a quick tally in his head - seven of his men were dead, six sailors and Ricky; four more were wounded. But he knew no wound was life threatening. They would go on. The deaths were OK, too; fewer hands out when it came time to split the money. He would have killed that dirt bag who gave away everything on the boat earlier, too, had he not needed all the warm bodies he could get for this mission. No worries - Mogul noticed him lying amongst the corpses. No need to waste a bullet on him. He also knew there were casualties sustained inside the house. He had to break through; the Chinese pilots would not wait forever.

He spoke through the microphone to his men. "I need you in that house. Now! Attack the south door. I will give an additional one million dollars to the first man inside."

It was a generous gesture, but he was banking on whoever went through the door first would not survive the hail of bullets he was sure they would receive and therefore, no payment due.

"I'll go." Seamus stepped forward and volunteered his services. Death did not scare him anymore.

Mogul just nodded at him as if to say, *good man.*

Just then more gunfire from inside the house started up and they recognized it as coming from a handgun. Mogul instinctively ducked, even though he was protected by the trunk of a tree, as he was for most of the fighting. The shots from a single handgun could only mean they were running out of ammo. His men returned fire. Everyone outside waited another twenty seconds before there was a collective sense of no more shots being fired.

"Get in there!" Mogul yelled into the microphone. Seamus led the way; the men took off running and fired furiously as they headed across the thirty yards of open space towards the south door. As Bo was leaving to join the charge, Mogul called after him.

"Hey, Bo!"

Bo stopped and turned around. He was responding with a, "'Sup Mo-" But it was to be his last syllable spoken as Mogul shot him directly in his still badly bruised and swollen face. Partly because of his incompetence for getting them into this fiasco in the first place, and partly because someone had to pay the one million dollars he was giving away. It was beginning to look like a possibility he would have to pay.

"That's 'Sup.'"

Mogul ran past the body on the ground to catch up with his men and to secure his possessions.

Chapter Seventy-Five

Norfolk Island, Australia

December – Saturday – 1:58 a.m.

In a crouched stance, Kip shone the beam of light through the cloud of dust he stirred up when he landed in the pit. He could just make out the direction to go. The tunnel had a foul, dry old dirt smell. Nothing was undisturbed for years. He rose to sprint down the tunnel that went on for who knows how long. But he didn't go. Instead, he collapsed on one knee and reached up to feel for the shooting pain above his left eye. There was blood. He ran his light over the roof of the tunnel and held it on a splintered support beam; there were sharpened wood edges jutting out above him. He stood again, slowly this time, and realized that the tunnel was less than six feet high. Made some sense, but he would like to have known that earlier. It was built by men in a hurry; most of them less than six feet tall. It was adequate for them.

Kip was running out of time. He launched himself down the tunnel with a limp from one lopsided heel and running in a three-quarter crouch. Blood was now pumping from his wound, blurring his vision. During his entire journey down the tunnel he blindly attempted to wipe the blood away, but it kept coming.

How long did he have left?

It felt like a one hundred-and-twenty yard dash. Kip came to the end and waved the light in all directions. He spotted rusted u-shaped rods sticking out of the concrete block end wall. A rudimentary ladder hung in wait. He climbed up the shaft, but at the top a wooden lid trapped him. He hit it with the butt of the flashlight to gauge its potential to move. Not a hollow sound. He placed his left shoulder tight up against it and heaved, pushed and grunted, and then heaved some more with everything he had. He tried it a second time, and then a third. The lid did not budge. *How much time did he have before the gangsters caught up with him or the bombs from the jets would hit? Move*!

"C'mon!" *Move*!

The lid and earth above lay together, coexisting for decades. Mother Nature was doing her best to fight back against a personal assault. Over the years, above the wooden plate, she had sewn the ground together, melded it and the plate as one; keeping it in place by tangling stems and roots all around the foreign object, holding onto her claim. The men who laid the wooden slab sealed it in place by means of a rubber flange. The flange had since dried out and was brittle. Its original purpose was now rendered ineffective and replaced by roots. The lid that Kip pushed against was actually the bottom of the escape hatch, originally set four inches below the dirt and grass placed on top of it. But over the course of time, shifting earth, more dirt and grass added itself. He tried again; he gave it everything he had. Strength rushed to where he needed it from every inch of his body, every fiber of his being. Muscles tightened, his entire body stiffened and energy was compacted for the purpose at hand. He pushed hard from the balls of his feet, pressed against the metal rung of the ladder, his calf muscles bursting against the strain.

The countless long seconds felt like an eternity, *he wasn't going to lose now, not this way, not being so close!* And then ….

Chapter Seventy-Six

Norfolk Island, Australia

December – Saturday – 1:58 a.m.

Mogul followed his men into the homestead. The great room was shattered and strewn with debris and dead bodies. Mogul did a quick body count. He was expecting to find a cache of corpses. What the hell, only four! Then he scanned the room for the large red sacks.

Nothing.

He followed the sound of a voice calling him to the rooms in the west end of the building. Standing in a corridor he saw two of his men in the first room on the left. The throat of one sack was sitting on the floor, wide open. One of his men was waving reams of paper at him.

"Found it," the guy said.

Mogul moved to his right and towards the light. He wanted those still alive and responsible for this fiasco to pay. Pay big time.

Where were they?

Five men stood around the entrance to a tunnel playing light beams over the hole. They looked at Mogul as he approached.

Mogul peeked down the tunnel's shaft entrance and chuckled.

"Huh. What d'ya know, a tunnel." He looked to his men. "Well, Seamus …. get down there! Find them all, and kill them. Hurry. We need to leave."

Five bodies dropped, one after the other down the hole, guns at the ready. Mogul called over to the guys in the other room,

"Let me know when you have the diamond. We don't leave without it."

Funny, Mogul's two phantom toes began to throb. He wasn't anxious; things were working out for the best. Then Mogul went down the rabbit hole.

Chapter Seventy-Seven

Norfolk Island, Australia

December – Saturday – 1:59 a.m.

Kip stood on metal rungs in the shaft of the escape hatch, trying to
work his way out, but the thing just wouldn't budge. His ankles
and feet lay exposed in the voluminous tunnel. Pieces of dirt and
chips of concrete spat at his legs and then he heard the cannon roar
of gunfire. He glanced down and saw a weak beam of light hitting
the end of the tunnel. *They were here!* He raised his feet up and
was now hunched up in the safety of the shaft, away from the
flying bullets trying to find him. He needed to get out, just one
more
p…u…s…h ….

    Something shifted. The lid gave quarter … just a little. He
pushed again, straining, pushing upwards, hard. *C'mon!* It rose
grudgingly, and then a little more before sinking back down. He
tried again, veins in his neck bulging, ready to burst - the lid was
rising again. Eventually the resistance had to succumb to the
powerful upward thrusts Kip applied, and the entire thing sucked at
air and gasped its way upward. Out of the ground it flew like a
giant plug being pulled, or in this case, pushed. Mother Nature
finally ceded her grip. With dirt and grass flying everywhere, the
lid tumbled over and rested yards away from the hole. Kip
followed it out, gulping at the night air.

    He sprung to his feet but was disorientated. *Which way was
which?* He was on the sea-bluff, that much he knew from his recon
earlier in the day. He also knew that the cliff's edge cut in deep to

the west of the homestead. *How close was he?* He could hear crashing waves on the rocks nearby. For all he knew, he could take three short steps and plunge over the edge.

The moon and the stars were there, but playing hide-and-seek behind thickening clouds. When the moon and stars were out, it was bright, but when they were gone, it was very dark indeed. At this moment, neither stars nor moon were helping gauge the distance to danger.

He had no choice. He dropped down on one knee near the tunnel exit and pointed the handgun at it. If he saw a head pop up he would blow it away. He would waste all five shells and then run towards the sound of the waves. With the back of his hand he wiped the blood away that was oozing into his eye. He cursed himself for lapsing in professional training by not retrieving the NVG's so he could use them now.

Chapter Seventy-Eight

Norfolk Island, Australia

December – Saturday – 1:59 a.m.

Five sets of boots created more dust than they cared to. Flashlights crisscrossed like moonbeams as they oriented with the surroundings. A light finally found its way and directed everyone's attention to the tunnel leading away into the distance. Taking no chances, two men stepped forward with their automatic weapons and fired dozens of rounds down the gaping black hole.

They heard the bullets ping off walls and bite into dirt. They knew there was an end to the tunnel not too far away. All five ran down there, thrillingly shooting from the hip as they did so to clear the path.

Mogul followed slowly behind. He loved the sound of gunfire and hoped it was tearing the flesh off some deserving piece of crap. He loved the sound of gunfire, but … *what was that other sound he could now hear?*

That whistling sound outside the building. A sound far away.

It sounded like …

Chapter Seventy-Nine

Norfolk Island, Australia

December – Saturday - 1:59 a.m.

Intense white-hot and fluorescent orange light flashed and murderous sounds of thunder exploded before his eyes. Kip threw himself to the ground, covering his head. It was not just one explosion but two successive powerful blasts one after the other. The missiles came from behind Kip and hit the homestead in a spectacular fireworks display. The place was – obliterated. Everything inside – vaporized.

The piles of stone and burning debris propelled into the Norfolk pines at the eastern perimeter. Trees were badly damaged, others toppled altogether, and still others caught on fire. The house itself left nothing standing except remnants from one of the chimney- stacks. But the destruction was far from over.

The flames from the explosion reached out, searching for more. It found the tunnel. A wave of scorching fire raced along it and enveloped all six men within and kept searching. The wicked petroleum-induced heat reached the end and banked ninety degrees off the concrete wall, and then leapt up to touch the night sky. The fireball rocketed into the air in a raging orange spire that seemed to cry out a bloodcurdling scream as it peaked one hundred-and-fifty feet in the air. Kip felt hair singeing and steam iron-like heat painfully pressing at his clothes. He stayed low to the ground and prayed it was enough. The heated funnel exhausted itself, and fell away and back from where it came. Kip rolled onto his back, clutching a gun in one hand and a precious diamond in the other while looking through one unencumbered eye at a thousand other diamonds winking in the night sky. The gem itself, although Kip never noticed, shimmered brilliantly for a moment, the enchanting color of jade green.

Over the sound of a crackling forest fire and the not too distant ocean waves crashing to shore, Kip heard the familiar noise of loud plane engines roaring to life. The motor buzz increased in volumes as they lifted off, escaping out of the water. The engines quieted as they flew far away.

Chapter Eighty

Los Angles, California

December – Saturday – 4:00 p.m.

Kip could not help himself. Every so often, he touched the bandage on his left brow. The doctor called it a borderline decision whether to stitch it or not. Kip chose to let the wound close naturally. The scar would be his souvenir from the adventure. He took another sip of coffee. It tasted great. He needed it to stay awake. Kip was yet again somewhere else. He had stepped back in time to be in a place, in a time zone, to be more precise, which was almost a full day behind the island time he had left.

He was extracted from Norfolk Island in a bustled hurry, by a contingent of twenty heavily armed U.S. Marines and a C-130J Super Hercules transport plane which was parked next to four RAAF fighter jets on the civilian regional tarmac. They departed Norfolk Island on Saturday morning at 0700. Kip traveled back over the dateline and arrived in Los Angles just after 1:00 a.m. Saturday morning. He landed before he had departed.

John Brozski walked into his office and touched Kip on the shoulder with a manila file as he walked by. He sat in his chair facing Kip, cinched the chair forward to reach the phone, picked up the handset, pressed a button and then handed the phone over to Kip.

John said, "It's for you."

Kip gave him an inquisitive look then said, "Hello, this is Kip Keplar."

"Mr. Keplar, Jessica Eggins from the Smithsonian Institute."

The voice was quiet, yet strong. He remembered it well.

"Yes, hello again," Kip said.

"Mr. Keplar, on behalf of The Smithsonian Institute and somewhat presumptuously, the State Department, your country … and I, want to thank you. To you and the all those people who sacrificed their lives to recover this National Treasure."

"Thank you." It was all he could say.

"I'm so sorry I have to make this brief, but believe me when I say we will see to it that honors will be bestowed upon you for your actions."

"Not necessary, really. But thank you, anyway."

"Well, Mr. Keplar I will be in touch, in the meantime if there is anything I can do for you?"

"Well, now that you mention it, there is."

There was a slight hesitation.

"Yes? Name it."

"What does it mean?"

"What does what mean, Mr. Keplar?"

"What does *Yurushi* mean? And for that matter, the Chinese word for it."

"Oh. The Chinese word, *Nei Qiang*, can best be translated as "strength within." I'm sure it was Genghis Khan's way of saying; *you are worthy opponents who found the "strength within" to repel the greatest ruler of all.* A gift and compliment from one who regarded himself as having the "strength within" to hold such a vast empire together."

"I see," said Kip, "and *Yurushi*?"

"It means 'forgiveness,' Mr. Keplar. Have a nice evening."

With that, the call ended.

Kip reached over and handed the phone to John, who replaced it in its cradle.

John opened the file he held in his hand. "It seems as if we are on the hook for some damage to Australian property."

"Ah, yes," Kip said.

"The building that was blown up was on the National Heritage List?"

"Ah …yes it was," Kip nodded.

John continued. "I see more costs here for a civilian plane ride from The Solomon Islands. Seems expensive. And it says here the Australians sent four jet fighters to Norfolk from the mainland? That seems a bit excessive?" He looked over at Kip with a slight smile on his face. He continued, "Well, at least they are only charging us for weapons being fired from two aircraft. But we are paying for all of the jet fuel of four jets. It also says here we are incurring the costs for extinguishing a bush fire from the trees catching fire, and the replacement cost of the said trees."

John closed the folder then placed it on the desk. He looked over at Kip with sincerity. "You performed with bravery under harrowing circumstances. I am sorry for the losses that occurred due to this mission."

Kip just nodded, but chose to say nothing. He changed the subject as the limelight was uncomfortable. "So tell me exactly why I was taken to Norfolk Island?"

"Well, we did request the assistance of the Australian government. Their position, understandably, was if you were to be in their protective custody, they could only guarantee maximum safety if held on Australian soil. They chose the closest island they could to the rescue party coming to get you. Also, it was secluded and away from prying eyes. Their protocol was sound judgment, everyone agrees, and we were lucky to have their assistance. We also share in their grief for this wanton waste of life due to a tragic and regrettable incident."

"Yes, I agree," Kip said solemnly.

John continued, "This incident also exposed another foreign government's involvement in the plot to breach a country's sovereign territory. Chinese fingerprints are all over this, and the Australian government, with our backing, has already pursued this egregious act, discreetly, through the proper channels. No one wants to add any more fuel to this fire. But we are seeing results."

"How so?"

"China has recalled its fleet in the South China Sea and beyond. A relaxing of international tensions has begun."

Kip nodded again. This was good news.

Onto another topic.

"So, what about my question to you?"

John gave a little smile. "It's just like you said. The pieces are coming together."

Kip drank some more of the coffee. "Do tell. So he opened up huh?"

"Brought him in for some more pertinent questioning and he cracked like an egg. You could sense the stress he was under. But how did you know?"

"It bothered me from the beginning that everything was too perfect and that there had to be an inside connection. There had to be. But where? Then, someone on my journeys said to me, *you can't always be where you want to be.* That struck a chord. Here was my problem with the scenario presented. How did they know to call Walker exactly ten minutes before he was scheduled to change the code and know with absolute certainty that he would be sitting at his desk? They gave themselves a window of ten minutes. What if he wasn't there? What if he was at the water cooler, in a meeting, in someone's office talking, in the bathroom, on another call, decided not to take that particular call, out sick for the day, on vacation or a hundred other reasons why he was not sitting right there at that very moment? They were risking one huge operation, with everything in place, on the premise that he was going to be sitting in his office waiting for that call."

John leaned back in his chair and opened the file. "You called it right. We did not dig deep enough on this guy. It turns out his father's name is Walker, but his Mother's maiden name was … ahh, let me see here, yes, Nicolosi. He grew up amongst gangs. Never in one himself, he was a straight A student. He wanted a better life. But his father was an alcoholic, left the family when Walker was fourteen. He wanted to go to college, but they were poor and his mother did not have the money. Enter the loan sharks. They were there to help. Which they did. Paid for his entire education. No money was ever paid back. They tracked his career through banking and waited for the quid-pro-quo. He told us he went to them and said, as he was making good money he wanted to pay back the debt, but they wouldn't let him. Didn't take a dime. They wanted payback in other ways. They waited for their opportunity. They came to him two years ago and said they were working on something that he could help them out with. Then, this new security system for the vault turns up and he is assigned to manage it. For the last three months he has been told to, without exception, be at his desk on a Friday afternoon ten minutes prior to entering the code and expect a call."

Kip asked, "So was his wife in on it too?"

"No. And we believe him. They kept him in the dark about most of it. They knew that his phone calls were recorded for business purposes. They wanted the kidnapping and his surprise at the kidnapping to be genuine. More convincing that way. We have had our experts listen to the recordings and they all agree - he displays stress, anxiety and genuine concern for his wife. He had no idea what they were up to."

"Who are *they*?" Kip asked.

"Good question. He won't say. After we cracked him a lawyer arrived very quickly to haul him away. He is willing to indict himself, but no one else. But we will pursue it."

John went on. "Something else of interest, too. Guess how they got the code?"

"A recording device?" Kip gestured.

A little surprised, John asked, "How did you know that?"

"Well, it struck me as odd when I went to see him at the hospital. At the time he was under stress and duress from everything he and his wife had been through, I understood that. But I asked for his phone number to contact him. He seemed to have trouble recalling the number with all the distractions going on. I surmised that if he could not recall a number he should know by memory under some stress, I found it highly unlikely he could notate a twenty-three digit alphanumeric code after seeing it briefly, just once, when he was under a great deal more pressure. It had to be some sort of recording device.

"Any guesses?" asked John.

"I don't recall him wearing glasses; it could have been embedded in the frame. So I don't know; a cufflink?"

"No, he wore a necktie pin. It was there."

"Huh. Technology is incredible these days. The necktie pin was a camera?"

"Yes. They knew he would immediately become a suspect so they made it look like he could not go through with the request to provide the code. But the entire time he was in there, he was transmitting the code via a visual link to someone on the outside. They saw it, recorded it and knew with absolute certainty that they had the right numbers. It was brilliant."

"So where is he now if the lawyer got a hold of him?" Kip asked.

"He was released on bail, but wearing an ankle monitor. We know where he is at all times."

Just then John's desk phone rang. He picked it up, held up a finger to Kip to wait through this call, then he identified himself and after that just listened. He ended with a, "Thank you for letting me know."

John replaced the phone in its cradle. He sat back and looked at Kip.

"That was the New York office. Two hours ago Cam Walker was clearing out his office of personal items. Persons unknown grabbed him there. The GPS tracking system monitoring his device led police and investigators to the center of the courtyard atrium of his building, but they couldn't locate him."

John paused.

"Have they since found him?" Kip asked.

"Eventually, yes, he was found." John said. "The GPS had pinpointed the exact location alright, they just didn't look up. He was thrown from the forty-seventh floor and landed on the roof of the glass atrium five stories above the courtyard. No one heard him hitting the glass because of the noise of the waterfall. No one could see him because of artificial puffy clouds and decorations of mist high up in the atrium that hid the body."

Chapter Eighty-One

East Coast

December – Saturday – 4:00 p.m.

With the plans in ruins and the heist gone bust, there was nothing left but to destroy all the evidence. Nothing that had not been done before. It was a business. Procedures were in place. All around Little Sammy his people were busying themselves with removing items and information and placing them in boxes. Items such as the satellite phone would join everything from the drugs used on the Walker woman to the skeleton masks, to the vehicle used in the kidnapping. Everything associated with the venture would be shipped off somewhere to be incinerated.

The imported, then stolen clothes the men wore were not a problem. Burn those too although no receipts for these would ever be found. The van was dismantled, crushed and sent for recycling. Even the room that was used to hold the woman had already been painted and refurbished. No trace left behind. No loose ends like Cam Walker. No blowback. Little Sammy was a smart player and he would chalk it up to experience. You lose some, you hope to win more. His people were already offering up other schemes to keep their little enterprise bustling along for years to come. Little Sammy had already moved on.

Chapter Eighty-Two

Shanghai, China

December – Saturday – 5:00 p.m.

Chu Shing was not so lucky after all. In a small way the Chinese had failed. After backing Chu Shing to go after the design for *Hammerhead*, they had partially shown their hand and failed. Albeit in the world of secrecy, but still it was an embarrassment. Someone had to be held accountable. Someone had to pay.

The Chinese authorities moved quickly. A hasty trial was convened after his arrest that morning. A summary judgment had been handed down by a tribunal four hours later and the sentence was carried out. He was convicted of espionage against the State.

Stealing military information of satellite technology.

Punishable by death.

He was executed one hour later and the body was incinerated. His entire fortune was seized by the Party and his name would be forgotten. It was not the ending Chu Shing was looking for.

Chapter Eighty-Three

Laguna Beach – California

December – Friday - 10:47 p.m.

The rain tapped gently on the windowpane as he checked on his children. Raef and Trek each had turned their lights out an hour ago. Annika had drifted off to sleep sometime earlier. He stood over her for several minutes and enjoyed watching her sleep. Eventually, he bent down and softly kissed her forehead and quietly left the room.

Now it was just Kip and Mette. They were in their bedroom and alone together, for the first time in a long time. She raised her hand and cautiously touched the wound above his head that should have received stitches, in her opinion. His war wound. Then she lifted her hand and kissed it tenderly. They held each other close; he felt the tingles. In recent times he had doubts of this ever happening again. But he made it, and now had to deal with the monsters in the closet. Watching men die is never easy. Or if it is, those people should seek counseling. He would compartmentalize those recent memories in a place in his mind. A place he wanted to keep small, but was already fatter than he would like it to be.

He returned to the moment with his wife as they collapsed together on their bed, entwined within each other. Their mouths connected; it felt as it should. Hers was warm, soft, and supple. It always was. She felt good to him. He felt her silky smooth leg rub against his. He hoped he felt good to her. Mette had her eyes closed and was lost in that moment. Kip was not ready to go there just yet. He wanted to look at his wife a little longer. He missed his wife. He missed his family. This chapter in his life came very close to not happening. He continued to pour over every inch of her beautiful face. He did not want to let go – forever. Slowly, and by giving in whole-heartedly, he was immeasurably happy to embrace the moment, enjoy his wife, his children and everything life had to offer. Now he had another chance to live.

You can never fully appreciate the joys of life until you are faced with the inevitable alternative, and in doing so many times over makes it evermore a just cause to celebrate. No, he would not take for granted what he had. And he had the rest of his life to look forward to it. With a smile on his entire face, he submitted to the moment, to the pleasure of it all. It was his time, it was his wife. And so, he knew what he must do. To just let it all happen.

Slowly.

Sensually.

And the best way he knew how to do that was to simply close his eyes.

About the Author

Matt is just another mystery waiting to be solved. But to help unravel him are a wonderful wife and two great children.

Stay in touch with the author via:
Facebook: www.facebook.com/MattBaak
Twitter: http://twitter.com/#!/Matt Baak @MattBaak
If you liked *No Time To Lose*, please post a review at Amazon and let your friends know about the book.

www.ingramcontent.com/pod-product-compliance
Lightning Source LLC
Chambersburg PA
CBHW060144260626
47160CB00001B/108